THOMAS FORD MEMORIAL LIBRARY

3 1308 00367 6624

JUL - - 2019

W9-BSE-194

THOMAS FORD MEMORIAL LIBRARY
800 CHESTNUT
WESTERN SPRINGS, IL 60558

SOMEONE TO HONOR

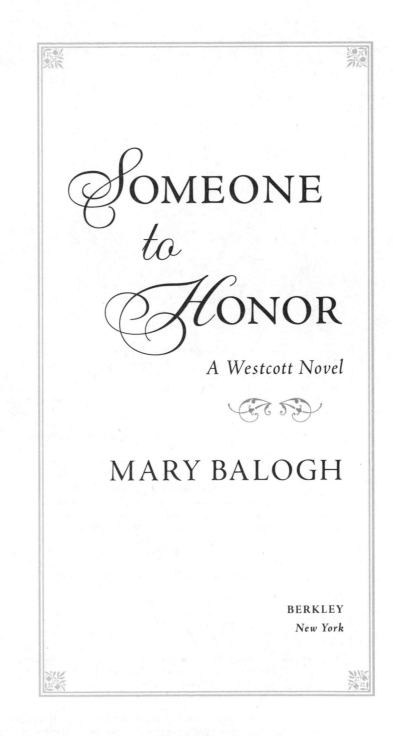

SOMEONE to HONOR

A Westcott Novel

MARY BALOGH

BERKLEY
New York

BERKLEY
An Imprint of Penguin Random House LLC
1745 Broadway, New York, NY 10019

Copyright © 2019 by Mary Balogh
Penguin Random House supports copyright. Copyright fuels creativity, encourages diverse
voices, promotes free speech, and creates a vibrant culture. Thank you for buying an authorized
edition of this book and for complying with copyright laws by not reproducing, scanning, or
distributing any part of it in any form without permission. You are supporting writers and
allowing Penguin Random House to continue to publish books for every reader.

BERKLEY and the BERKLEY & B colophon are registered trademarks of
Penguin Random House LLC.

Library of Congress Cataloging-in-Publication Data

Names: Balogh, Mary, author.
Title: Someone to honor : a Westcott novel / Mary Balogh.
Description: First Edition. | New York : Jove, 2019. | Series: Westcott series
Identifiers: LCCN 2019010137 | ISBN 9780593098103 (hardcover) |
ISBN 9781984802385 (ebook)
Subjects: | GSAFD: Romance fiction.
Classification: LCC PR6052.A465 S6583 2019 | DDC 823/.914--dc23
LC record available at https://lccn.loc.gov/2019010137

First Edition: July 2019

Printed in the United States of America
3 5 7 9 10 8 6 4 2

Jacket photographs: woman by Miguel Sobreira/Arcangel Images; park by Bildagentur Zoonar
GmbH/Shutterstock; park bench by Darryl Brooks/Shutterstock
Jacket design by Katie Anderson
Book design by Kristin del Rosario

This is a work of fiction. Names, characters, places, and incidents either are the product of the
author's imagination or are used fictitiously, and any resemblance to actual persons, living or
dead, business establishments, events, or locales is entirely coincidental.

SOMEONE TO HONOR

The Westcott Family

(Characters from the family tree who appear in *Someone to Honor* are shown in bold print.)

Stephen Westcott m. Eleanor Coke
Earl of Riverdale (1704–1759)
(1698–1761)

Andrew Westcott m. Bertha Ames
(1726–1796) (1736–1807)

David Westcott m. **Althea Radley**
(1756–1806) (b. 1762)

George Westcott m. **Eugenia Madson**
Earl of Riverdale (b. 1742)
(1724–1790)

Humphrey Westcott **Louise Westcott** m. John Archer
Earl of Riverdale (b. 1770) Duke of Netherby
(1762–1811) (1755–1809)

m. Ava Cobham
(1760–1790)

Mildred m. **Thomas Wayne**
Westcott Baron Molenor
(b. 1773) (b. 1769)

Boris **Peter** **Ivan**
Wayne **Wayne** **Wayne**
(b. 1796) (b. 1798) (b. 1799)

Jessica
Archer
(b. 1795)

Matilda
Westcott
(b. 1761)

m. Alice Snow
(1768–1789)

Viola Kingsley
(b. 1772)

m. **Marcel Lamarr**
Marquess of Dorchester
(b. 1770)

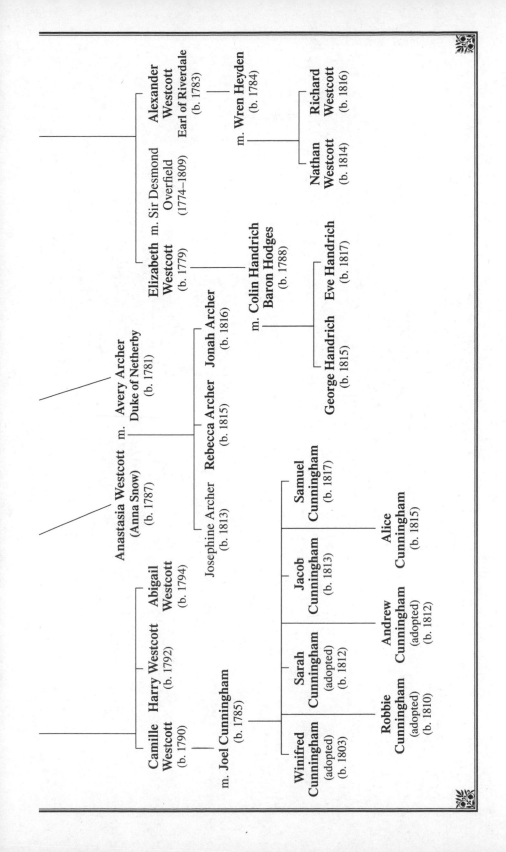

One

H ome at last!
Well, back in England, at least. Twenty months had passed
since his last brief, disastrous stay here, after the Battle of Waterloo,
in 1815. Now he was back.

But as Lieutenant Colonel Gilbert Bennington, Gil to his friends
and acquaintances, disembarked from the packet in Dover after making the night crossing from Calais, he felt only weariness, irritation,
and a heavy foreboding that coming home was not going to bring
happily-ever-after with it.

He grimaced at the sight of an elegant traveling carriage, ducal
crests emblazoned upon its doors, standing on the dock, for it was
obviously awaiting him. Or, more specifically, Avery Archer, Duke of
Netherby, one of his three traveling companions. Gil would have far
preferred to hire a chaise for the journey ahead, but he might have
guessed that nothing but opulent splendor would do for His Grace on
his own native soil. And it had to be admitted, grudgingly, that this
conveyance would be far better than a hired chaise for one of their
other companions, Harry. Harry was looking gray with exhaustion.

Gil had not intended to have three companions for the journey.

He had recently spent a year on the island of St. Helena as part of the garrison that guarded Napoleon Bonaparte during his second exile. When he had returned, on a ship bound for France rather than England for the simple reason that it was the first outward-bound vessel after his term of duty was over, he had gone to Paris. There he had discovered, quite by chance, that his old friend and comrade Major Harry Westcott, who he thought had died at Waterloo, was convalescing at a facility for military officers. Gil had last seen him after the battle, when his injuries had seemed mortal. But against all odds Harry had survived—barely. And after more than a year and a half he was itching to go home, though his physicians advised strongly against the strenuous journey. He was still not fully recovered.

Gil had offered to escort him, and Harry had jumped at the opportunity. He had invited Gil to stay with him for a while once they were back home, and Gil had accepted. He wanted to be in England. He *needed* to be there. But he was reluctant to go all the way to his own home. There were things that must be done first.

But then, at the last possible moment, two of Harry's kinsmen had arrived in Paris with the purpose of conveying him home themselves. And although Harry himself was a mere illegitimate member of his family, his kinsmen were powerful men. Aristocrats. They were Avery Archer, who had once been Harry's guardian—before the illegitimacy was discovered—and was now his brother-in-law; and Alexander Westcott, Earl of Riverdale, head of the family and holder of the title that had once been Harry's—also before the discovery of the illegitimacy.

It was a bit of a complicated family, Gil understood. Harry had never spoken much about it.

They had traveled together, the four of them, though Gil had tried to bow out. He did *not* feel comfortable in aristocratic company. Despite his senior military rank, he was in reality a nobody from nowhere and as illegitimate as Harry. A gutter rat, if one chose to call a spade a spade. But Harry had begged him not to change his mind, so Gil had come. His friend would need him after his relatives had conveyed him home and returned to their own families.

"Ah," the Duke of Netherby said now, looking at his carriage through the quizzing glass he raised to his eye. "A sight for sore eyes. How much did you wager, Harry, that my carriage would not be here?"

"Absolutely nothing, if you will recall," Harry said. "It would be more than the life of your coachman is worth, or his livelihood any-way, to be late."

"Quite so," His Grace said with a sigh. "Let us go find a nearby inn and enjoy a good English breakfast. I daresay there will be a meaty bone somewhere on the premises too."

The meaty bone would be for Gil's dog, a great lump of a canine of indeterminate breed that had followed him from Waterloo to England to St. Helena, to France, and now back to England. She stood panting at Gil's side, happy, he believed, to have her paws on firm soil again. Within moments she was inside the Duke of Netherby's carriage with the rest of them, draped over Gil's feet like a large sheepskin rug and half over Riverdale's boots too.

The carriage transported them the short distance to what Gil did not doubt was the best inn in Dover, where three of them ate a hearty breakfast and Harry nibbled without enthusiasm upon a piece of toast. His Grace then called for pen, ink, and paper and wrote a brief note to inform his duchess of their safe return to England and of the change in their planned destination. His relatives had intended to take Harry to London, where other relatives awaited him, including his mother, the Marchioness of Dorchester, and one of his sisters. But Harry had insisted upon going to Hinsford Manor in Hampshire, where he had grown up. He wanted the quiet of the countryside, he had explained to Gil. More to the point, he wanted to avoid being fussed over, and fussed over he would be if he went to London.

Having arranged for the note to be sent, His Grace joined the other three in his carriage and it proceeded northward without further delay. It was certainly a comfortable carriage, Gil conceded. It also attracted the gawking attention of everyone it passed.

Harry, on the seat opposite, next to Riverdale, was even paler than usual, if that was possible, and thin almost to the point of emaciation. His good looks and ever-cheerful, energetic charm had deserted him. He was twenty-six years old, eight years younger than Gil. Apparently for the six months following Waterloo the army physicians had been in daily expectation of his dying. He had been taken to Paris after the first month—why not back to England none of the military authorities seemed to know. Even after the six months he was being assailed by one infection and fever after another, only to have to face a painful, life-threatening surgery five months ago to remove an embedded bullet, which his surgeons judged had shifted closer to his heart. Having it removed would very possibly kill him, they had warned. Not doing so certainly would. He had survived the excruciatingly painful ordeal, but the renewed infections and fevers had almost killed him anyway.

Gil hoped the ordeal of their trip would not accomplish what all the fevers and infections had been unable to do. He hoped Harry would survive the journey, which Gil had encouraged and arranged.

"You must be happy to be back in England, Harry," Riverdale said. "Though it is unfortunate you are being treated to a typical English welcome." He gestured toward the window. Heavy clouds hung low over a landscape that was being buffeted by a west wind and assaulted by a slanting rain.

"It is indeed a good feeling," Harry said, gazing out upon the scene. "But I have been thinking and wondering. I suppose it is altogether possible I will be descended upon not just by rain in the next week or so. Do you think there is any chance the family will come visiting since I am not going to London to visit them?"

"I would certainly not wager against it," Alexander said. "They have all been eagerly awaiting your arrival in London. I doubt your choosing to go to Hinsford instead will deter them. It is not terribly far from London, after all."

"The devil!" Harry muttered, closing his eyes and setting his head back against the plush cushions.

"I suppose," Riverdale added, "you have chosen to go straight to Hinsford at least partly in order to avoid the commotion awaiting you in town."

"Yes, at least partly," Harry admitted—and then laughed unexpectedly without opening his eyes. "I ought to have known better. And if I *had* known better, I would have felt obliged to warn you, Gil. There is possibly no other family on earth that rallies around its members as the Westcotts do—and that includes those who are married to Archers and Cunninghams and Handriches and Lamarrs and . . . Did I miss anyone? Once a Westcott, always a Westcott, it seems. Even if one is a bastard."

"You know that is a word we never use within the family, Harry," Riverdale said. "Think of your sisters when you use it, if you please, even if not of yourself."

Gil, without showing any outer sign, was wishing like hell that Harry *had* thought to warn him that his fond family was likely to descend upon him en masse even though Hinsford was some distance from London. Most of them would be gathered in London now for the spring session of parliament and the social whirl of the Season. He might have guessed, of course, when these two men turned up unexpectedly in Paris as emissaries of the family. But it had not occurred to him even then that the rest of them would actually journey into the country to see Harry when he arrived home.

After all, no family had ever rallied around him, either on his mother's side—they had turned her out, never to relent, after she conceived him—or on his father's. The most his father had ever done for him was purchase his ensign's commission in a foot regiment after word had reached him of the death of Gil's mother. Gil had been at that time a sergeant with a British regiment in India. Later he had purchased a lieutenancy for his son too, but Gil had written to him on that occasion, and not to thank him—why should he thank a father who had ignored his very existence for more than twenty years, only to swoop down seemingly from nowhere with a gift his son had neither wanted nor asked for? Gil had written to inform the man that he need supply no further patronage and that it would be refused if it was offered. By that time Gil had been wishing heartily that he were still a sergeant. He had been happier with his own kind.

He and Harry had fought together in the Peninsula and at Toulouse and Waterloo. They had been friends from the start, perhaps because they had one thing in common apart from their regiment and military experiences: They were both bastards—yes, it was always as well to call a spade a spade—in a gentleman's army. In the officer ranks of the army, that was. Hard work and prowess, talent and dedication to one's men and mission, counted for far less in the officers' tents and messes than did birth and fortune. Oh, Gil and Harry had never been ostracized outright, it was true, but they had always been made in subtle and sometimes not-so-subtle ways to feel that they were outsiders. That they did not quite belong. That they were a bit of an embarrassment. Occasionally more than a bit.

He gazed out the window on his side of the carriage at the gloomy countryside, though it was only the heavy clouds and rain that caused the gloom. It was *England*, and he felt a rush of affection for his native land even if there were not very many happy memories associated with it.

He had a home of his own here, Rose Cottage in Gloucestershire, purchased during the Indian years when he had acquired what had seemed to him—it still seemed—a fabulous fortune in prizes. He had invested what remained of it after the purchase, engaging the services of an agent in London he had been persuaded to trust, happily as it had turned out. He could have lived like a gentleman from that moment on if he had chosen to leave the army. He had not done so, however. Nor had he done so anytime since. The army was all he had known since he left home at the age of fourteen in a recruiting sergeant's untender care, and on the whole it had been good to him. The life had suited him.

He *had* gone home after the Battle of Toulouse in 1814, though, taking his pregnant wife with him. He had taken her to Rose Cottage—a great deal larger actually than a cottage despite its name. And all his own. His anchor to this world. The place where he would send down roots. The place where he would raise his family. Home. The dream of happiness had become even more of a reality when Katy was born—Katherine Mary Bennington. Ah, that achingly happy day following hours of pain for Caroline and anxiety for him. That dark-haired baby. That warm little bundle of squawking humanity.

His daughter.

It was a brief interval in his life almost too painful to look back upon. Therefore, he rarely did. But some memories went deeper than conscious thought. They were *there* always, like a leaden weight, or like an open wound that would not quite kill him but would never heal either.

Happily-ever-after had begun to slip away when Caroline, her confinement over, had become more restless than usual and peevish about the inferior size of the house and the dullness of the village on the edge of which it stood, and the insipid nature of their social life there. It had slipped further a little more than three months after Katy's birth when Gil had been recalled to his regiment following Napoleon Bonaparte's escape from his first exile, on the island of Elba, and his return to France to gather another vast army about him.

Caroline had wanted to go too, leaving the baby with her mother. He had refused. Following the drum was no life for a lady, though Caroline had done it for a few months before he married her when her mother brought her to the Peninsula after she had finished her lady's schooling. And a baby needed her mother and a home and her father's financial support and the promise of his return as soon as he was able. A baby actually needed *both* parents, but life could not always be ideal.

He had tried to make it as secure and comfortable as was possible under the circumstances.

By the time he had hurried home after Waterloo, alarmed by increasingly mutinous letters from his unhappy wife, she was gone. So was their daughter. And her nurse. But no one—not their servants, not any of their neighbors—knew just where they had gone or when they were likely to return. He had not seen either one of them since, though he did know that Katy was in Essex, living with her grandparents, General Sir Edward and Lady Pascoe, to whom, unbeknown to him, she had been taken before Waterloo, soon after his own departure for Belgium. Lady Pascoe had refused to let him see her, however, when he had gone to her home, frantic for news. Caroline, he had discovered later, had gone off to a house party at the invitation of old friends and from there to another party and another. Gil could neither pursue his quest to retrieve his daughter nor go in search of his errant wife before he was abruptly and unexpectedly posted to St. Helena. Doubtless thanks to General Pascoe.

Katy was still with her grandparents. Caroline was dead. Word of her demise had reached him on St. Helena.

Now, more than a year later, the situation had become more fraught. General Pascoe was back at home, and he and his wife were determined to keep custody of Katy. They had acquired a lawyer who intended to see that the whole matter was wrapped up right and tight—and legally—in their favor. They had two angry, threatening letters he had written from St. Helena to use against him in addition to Lady Pascoe's account of the frantic, demanding visits he had made to the general's home and the lies Caroline had told when she took their daughter to her mother. He would be made to appear to be a violent, uncontrolled man and an unfit father.

Gil's first instinct upon leaving St. Helena had been to return as soon as he could to England, where he would rage at his in-laws until they relinquished his daughter into his care and he could take her back home where she belonged. A cooler wisdom had prevailed, however, and he had hired a lawyer of his own, a man recommended by his agent as the best of his kind in London. And Grimes—of the law firm Grimes, Hanson, and Digby—had insisted in the lawyerly letter he had written his client after the contract was signed that Lieutenant Colonel Bennington leave the matter of the custody of his daughter entirely in his hands and do absolutely nothing himself.

Doing nothing was the hardest thing Gil had ever had to do in his life. For a lawyer, even this one—*the best of his kind in London*—might not be enough. The general had considerable power and influence. So did Lady Pascoe. She was the sister of a baron who held a prominent position in the government. Both had been vehemently opposed to their daughter's marrying the bastard son of a blacksmith's daughter, even if he *was* an officer of high rank. They would undoubtedly have withheld their consent had Caroline not already been increasing. That fact had drawn their tight-lipped consent, but it had done nothing to endear him to them. It was also a fact that had deeply shamed him. After becoming a commissioned officer, he had tried hard to behave like a gentleman even if he could never be one.

Gil's offer to accompany Harry home and his agreement to remain with him for a while had been made at least partly for selfish reasons, then. It would take him back to England, not far distant from London, where he would be able to consult his agent more easily and the lawyer who did not really want to be consulted or pressed. Being back in England would give him a sense of purpose, of not simply doing nothing. But the offer had also been made out of genuine friendship and concern, for his friend could not travel alone or *be* alone despite what he might think. Yet he would not go to London, where his mother was living during the spring months.

The arrival of Netherby and Riverdale in Paris had seemed like a relatively minor annoyance at the time. Both had treated Gil with quiet respect, but he had assumed that they would return to their families and parliamentary duties in London as soon as they possibly could after conveying Harry home. Now it appeared he had assumed wrongly. It seemed very likely indeed that the whole of the Westcott family would descend upon Hinsford within days of their arrival and stay for who knew how long. How many of them were there, for God's sake?

It was a daunting prospect and one that might well force him into a change of plans. Indeed, he would surely have changed them at Dover if this conversation had been held over breakfast. But now he was stuck, at least temporarily. He did not have a carriage of his own or even a horse with which to leave Hinsford.

"He is asleep," the Earl of Riverdale said from the seat opposite, his voice little more than a murmur. "He is far weaker than I expected him to be after almost two years."

"He will recover," Netherby said, equally quietly. "If he has been too stubborn to die thus far, he is not going to do it now."

"What is your opinion, Lieutenant Colonel?" Riverdale asked.

"It is my belief," Gil said, gazing at his friend, whose chin had sunk to his chest, "that if Bonaparte were to escape again today and gather another army to lead against the allies, Major Harry Westcott would be volunteering to lead the first charge."

"Not you?" the Duke of Netherby asked. "It has been whispered, Bennington, that you once led a forlorn hope and were promoted from captain to major as a result."

Gil frowned. He never felt comfortable discussing his war exploits. There were thousands of men, many of them dead, just as brave as he. "I had men at my back who would not have allowed me to retreat even if I had wished to do so," he said. "It was not the accomplishment of a single individual, but one of a large group. Most military actions are that way even if only one man is singled out afterward for commendations and honors. Harry was one of the best. If there was ever danger for his men to face, he was there to lead them into it. He looks weak now, but he has a ferocious spirit. It may be lying dormant, but it is not dead, I assure you. He will recover fully."

"Or die in the attempt," the duke said.

Gil looked across into his eyes, keen beneath the sleepy lids, and was surprised by the flash of humor from a man who was an apparently bored aristocrat from his blond, expertly styled hair to his fashionable and immaculately tailored clothes, from his well-manicured, beringed hands to the tips of his supple, highly polished boots. A bit of a dangerous man too, Gil suspected.

Two

Anna, Duchess of Netherby, received her husband, Avery's, note on the same day it was sent from Dover. She went immediately with Jessica, Avery's half sister, to share the news with Harry's immediate family. One of them was Viola, Harry's mother, whose marriage to his father, the late Earl of Riverdale, had been declared invalid when it had been discovered after his death that he had had a secret first wife still living when he married her. Viola was now married to the Marquess of Dorchester. Her younger daughter, Abigail, Harry's sister, lived with them. Like Harry, Abigail was now officially illegitimate. Anna was able to inform both ladies that the travelers were back in England but on their way to Hinsford instead of London. She was delighted to be able to assure them also that Harry was bearing up well under the ordeal.

Jessica danced Abigail in a full circle, observing as she did so that it was probably far beneath her twenty-three-year-old dignity to react thus to the news that Harry was home—and it was a good thing her mother was not there to see her. Or Avery with his quizzing glass, she added with a theatrical shudder and a laugh. Anna and Jessica left half an hour later to take the news to Wren, Countess of Riverdale, Alexander's wife.

Jessica's mother, meanwhile—Louise, Dowager Duchess of Netherby, a former Westcott, sister of Humphrey, the late earl—took the news first to her mother, Eugenia, and elder sister, Matilda, and then to her younger, married sister, Mildred, and her husband, Thomas.

Abigail wrote to her sister, Camille Cunningham, who lived with her husband and children in Bath, and Alexander's wife, Wren, wrote to her mother-in-law, Althea, and her sister-in-law Elizabeth. They were both in the country at Roxingley Park, where Elizabeth, Lady Hodges, was recovering from a recent confinement with her second child, a daughter this time.

Before evening drew on, everyone in the family knew, or was about to know, the glad tidings that Harry was home in England at long last.

Now, just twenty-four hours later, Abigail was seated in the Marquess of Dorchester's traveling carriage beside her stepsister, Estelle. Her mother had married the marquess, Marcel Lamarr, nearly four years ago, and his children, the twins Estelle and Bertrand, had quickly become Abigail's friends. Marcel—she called her mother's husband by his given name, at his request—was now seated beside her mother and opposite Abigail herself in the carriage. Bertrand was riding a little way ahead. Conversation was not brisk inside the carriage. Yesterday's glad relief had given way inevitably to today's anxiety. Had Harry been strong enough for the journey despite what Avery had written in his note to Anna? Why was he still so weak even after all this time? Would their coming to see him help or hinder his recovery? But how could they stay away? And how could Avery and Alexander be expected to leave him all alone, with just servants to care for him?

Abigail was aware that Marcel was squeezing her mother's hand reassuringly from time to time. Estelle seemed to sense that chatter would not be welcome and quietly watched the scenery pass by through the window. Abigail, grateful for her stepsister's tact, did likewise. At least Harry was home and safe from ever again having to face the dangers of war.

It was almost two years since Waterloo. *Two years.* But he was still alive, even after that ghastly surgery. And back home. It was concerning that he had chosen to return to Hinsford Manor rather than London, where he would have had access to any number of physicians. But Abigail could understand why he was going to Hinsford. It was home. It was where they had grown up. They had been happy there—no clouds in their sky, no looming storms on their horizon. No premonition of the life-changing catastrophe that lay ahead for all of them— the discovery that they were illegitimate because their father had already been married to someone else when he wed their mother.

It was still home, even in these post-catastrophe years. And Harry had chosen to go there. Probably, Abigail thought, grimacing slightly, because he wanted peace and quiet while every part of him healed— body, mind, and spirit. Poor Harry. He probably did not suspect what was about to descend upon him. Or perhaps he did. For the Westcotts did nothing as well as they *rallied.* If there was a whisper of trouble for any one of them or any anticipation of something to be celebrated, the family gathered to support and plan.

If Harry had forgotten that fact—though how could he?—then he was in for a severe shock. For of course the family had arrived in force last evening at Marcel's London home. But it had not been enough simply to rejoice over Harry's return and the imminent arrival back in London of Avery and Alexander. Oh no, indeed. Harry must be seen in person and welcomed home and fussed over and worried about and planned for.

The aunts had spent all of half an hour with their heads together, trying to think of a suitable nurse to hire, preferably male, or perhaps one male and one female, but in any case someone who would be prepared to live for an indefinite time at Hinsford, worrying Harry back to full, robust health. They had not used the word *worrying,* of course.

If there had been an ounce of sense among the lot of them, Abigail

thought now, it would surely have occurred to someone that the best
way they could welcome Harry home and ensure that he recover fully
was to write him letters and stay far away from him, at least until he
indicated that he was ready for visitors. His mother and Abigail and
Camille were perhaps exceptions, though maybe not even them. Perhaps Harry wanted to be entirely alone.

"Not much farther now," her mother said from the seat opposite,
smiling at her. "Sometimes a journey seems endless, does it not? I
hope Mrs. Sullivan has hired extra help, as I instructed her to do."

Mrs. Sullivan had been the housekeeper at Hinsford as far back as
Abigail could remember.

"I am sure she has, Viola," Marcel said, squeezing her hand again.
"I daresay she is as eager to welcome Harry home and smother him
with loving care as you are."

"*Smother,*" she said with a frown. "I hope none of us will do that.
Though it will be hard not to, I suppose. At least he is not quite alone.
Avery told Anna in his letter that he and Alexander would remain at
Hinsford until Harry is properly settled in. And I cannot quite imag-
ine either of them *smothering* anyone with love."

The whole family—with the exception of Elizabeth and her husband, Colin, and Elizabeth's mother, Althea—was on its way to
Hinsford or preparing to be, and Mama had sent off an urgent letter
to warn Mrs. Sullivan.

Poor Harry.

But Abigail longed to see him. And she longed . . . oh, she too
longed to be back home. At Hinsford. She and her mother had lived
there for a while after Camille's marriage and before Mama married
Marcel and the two of them had moved to Redcliffe. Abigail had not
been unhappy during the past three and a half years at Redcliffe.
But . . . well, it had never felt quite like home, for which she was
entirely to blame. She had certainly been made to feel welcome there.

And then suddenly she *was* home. The carriage was turning onto
the drive leading to Hinsford Manor.

"Here we are," her mother said, leaning forward in her seat and gazing eagerly through the window, as though she expected to see Harry bounding down the drive to meet them. "Oh, I hope the journey all the way from Paris was not too much for him. I ought to have gone there myself. I ought not to have listened to everyone. He ought to have had his mother with him during such an ordeal."

"He would have hated it," Marcel said firmly. "It would have been humiliating for him to have his mama hovering over him every yard of the journey."

She looked at him in exasperation. "Sometimes, Marcel," she said sharply, "I hate you. Especially when you are right and I am wrong."

He grinned at her.

Abigail, traveling with her back to the horses, turned to look behind her toward the house. They had been spotted. She could see Alexander and Avery out on the terrace, and a tall, thin, frail-looking man at the top of the steps just outside the front door, his hand on the rail.

"Oh, dear God," her mother said. "Harry."

And then there was all the flurry of their arrival and descent from the carriage. There were hugs and handshakes and inquiries and the barking of a dog from the direction of the stables and the sound of an axe chopping wood—and Harry remaining at the top of the steps, looking down at them, neither smiling nor frowning. Abigail wondered foolishly whether she would have recognized him if she had passed him on a crowded street in London.

She was the first up the steps to touch his arm—she was afraid to hug him—and gaze earnestly into his face.

"Harry," she said. "Welcome home."

"Abby," he said, a smile hovering on his lips before she gave way to their mother, who showed none of Abigail's hesitation to gather him into her arms and burst into tears.

Suddenly Abigail found that she could not stay to watch. Neither could she step past her brother to go inside the house, where they would all follow within minutes, the turmoil and bright cheer of their arrival continuing. She needed some air before she fainted. She made her way back down to the terrace, waved away Marcel, who was looking at her in some concern, and turned in the direction of the stables.

She just needed to walk for a minute or two to clear her head, she told herself as she hurried along, and give herself the courage to look at Harry again without dissolving into tears as her mother had just done, or—worse—fainting. The carriage had pulled away to the carriage house at the far side of the stables. The dog she had heard earlier was over there somewhere too, objecting loudly to its arrival or perhaps welcoming it. The sound of the axe grew louder.

And then she saw the man—groom or gardener—who was using it. He was beside the stable block, tackling a large pile of logs, which he was reducing to wedges of firewood on a chopping block. There was a sizable pile of wood, neatly stacked, beside him. But it was not the wood that caught her shocked attention and stopped her in her tracks.

It was the man.

He was naked above the waist. Below the waist his breeches, more like a second skin than a garment, hugged narrow hips and long, powerfully muscled legs. Leather boots, old and scuffed, looked as though they must have been molded to his calves. Muscles rippled in his arms and shoulders and along his back as he wielded the axe. His dark hair curled damply at the nape of his neck.

Abigail swallowed and would have moved on, unseen yet horribly embarrassed, if a huge shaggy monster of a creature, which she did not immediately identify as a dog, had not suddenly erupted from behind the stables and come dashing straight for her, barking ferociously. She did not scream. But she did remain anchored to the spot as she raised her arms protectively before her face and whimpered or wailed or pleaded for mercy—truth to tell, when she looked back later, she could not recall exactly what sounds she had made, if any. Something humiliatingly abject, no doubt. But just as she expected the animal to leap for her throat, a deep voice issued a command.

"Beauty, sit!"

Beauty sat so abruptly that Abigail dropped her arms in surprise. She could see now that the animal was indeed a dog, a huge lump of a creature with a shaggy grayish white coat that hung over even its eyes and mouth, almost obscuring them. Its front legs were long, its rump wide and somewhat lopsided. It sat with mostly erect ears, one of which flopped over at the tip; a lolling, panting pink tongue; and a tail that thumped the ground. Abigail dared not move, lest the order to sit be forgotten in the dog's eagerness to attack.

"She will not harm you," the man said, reading her thoughts or perhaps the stiffness of her body. "She looks upon every stranger as a potential new friend."

Abigail switched her attention from the dog to the man without moving her head. He had straightened and turned to face her, revealing himself as tall and powerfully built, the muscles of his chest and abdomen, which she could see almost to his navel, well defined. His eyes were as dark as his hair, one lock of which hung over his forehead. His features were angular and harsh, his expression forbidding. Both his face and his body were badly scarred. Indeed, a scar slashed across one cheek, down over his chin, and along part of his neck before proceeding across the whole width of his shoulder. He bore himself in a very upright manner. His large hands were clasped about the handle of the axe, which he held at an angle across his body. He was glistening with sweat.

He looked like a fearfully dangerous man. Primitive. Magnificent. He was all raw masculinity. Abigail felt herself shudder inwardly.

He looked boldly back at her, his eyes moving over her quite frankly, as she supposed hers had moved over him. And terror gave place to embarrassment—had she really wailed or whimpered and thrown up her arms to protect her face? And had he noticed? But how could he not have? Was he laughing inwardly at her? Or worse, feeling a sneering contempt at her terror of an apparently friendly dog? Embarrassment turned to indignation—at his near nakedness and at his boldness.

"Were you given permission to remove your coat and shirt?" she asked him. Too late she heard the primness in her voice.

He cocked one eyebrow.

"You are in full view of anyone who walks even a few steps from the house," she said. "It is quite unseemly. Perhaps you have not been informed that Major Westcott has visitors and is expecting more. Including ladies. I shall report you to him and see to it that he has a word with your supervisor."

Belatedly it occurred to her that she ought to have had that word with Harry without actually scolding the man himself. She did not usually take it upon herself to berate servants. But she was feeling ruffled and hot cheeked, and he was still standing there looking steadily at her.

"Beauty," he said, "heel."

The dog, without having moved from the spot where it had sat when commanded to do so, had nevertheless begun trying, without success, to stretch its neck far enough to lick her hand. It rose immediately, loped with ungainly gait toward the man, its tail wagging, its ears flopping, and stood close beside him, rubbing itself against the side of his leg. He removed one hand from the axe handle in order to fondle its head and scratch it behind one ear while the dog gazed up at him with a silly look of worshipful bliss on its face. All the while the man did not remove his eyes from Abigail.

Insolent man, she thought, and just stopped herself from saying so aloud. He must be a new addition to the staff. He had not been employed there when she left with her mother. Perhaps he was a soldier discharged from his duties after the wars came to an end two years ago. His scars would certainly bear out that theory. And he looked savage. She could almost imagine him hacking and carving his way through enemy lines with that axe, the bloodlust high in him. It was a thought she did not wish to pursue.

"Beauty?" she said, looking down at the dog.

"Irony," the man said.

She was surprised he even knew the meaning of the word. But an uglier, less suitably named dog she had never beheld.

She turned without another word and made her way back to the house. At least the incident had taken her mind off the shock she had felt at first seeing Harry. For a brief moment in the carriage she had wondered who that frail old man at the top of the steps was.

From the direction of the stables the sound of the axe being wielded resumed.

GIL HAD ALWAYS FOUND CHOPPING WOOD TO BE AN ENJOYABLE form of exercise. He had never considered it a chore. It was also a productive way to work off frustrations and irritations and downright anger. The stack of chopped wood and the pile of kindling grew in direct proportion to the shrinking of the pile of logs. The axe felt nicely balanced in his hands, and it had a good, fine edge on it—one he had put there himself earlier over the horrified protests of Harry's head groom. The man had been even more flustered when he had realized that Lieutenant Colonel Bennington intended to chop the wood piled at one side of the stable block.

So, Harry's prediction that his family would descend upon him here had proved to be accurate. Gil had both heard and seen the elegant traveling carriage that had arrived ten minutes or so ago. He assumed that woman was a family member. He also assumed she had not come alone. And she had said that more relatives were on the way. It was not a comfortable prospect. It had been bad enough to discover yesterday that Hinsford Manor was a grander place than he had expected. It had been worse to realize this morning that Netherby and Riverdale were in no hurry to rush back to their own families in London. But now this.

That woman.

She was all delicate feminine beauty and vaporish terror before an ungainly softie of a dog like Beauty. No creature of the canine world had ever been further from ferocity than the one now stretched out beside him a safe distance from the flashing blade, napping because for the moment there was no play afoot and no chance of a good fur ruffling or ear scratching.

She—the woman, that was—had been terror personified for a few moments, cringing and whining and begging for mercy. And then she had looked at him as though she had never seen a half-naked man before—as perhaps she had not—and had become all stiff, aristocratic hauteur. She had mistaken him for a servant. She had asked if he had been given permission to remove his shirt and had warned him that she would report him to Harry. But if she had thought he was a servant, what the devil had she been doing giving him a good looking over before informing him that it was unseemly for him to appear thus before her?

She would probably have fainted dead away if he had taken so much as one step toward her.

Which member of Harry's family was she? He did not know much about them, except that Harry had briefly been the Earl of Riverdale, head of the Westcott family, and that they had all stuck by him and his mother and sisters after the discovery was made that the old earl's marriage to the mother was bigamous. The story had made Gil quite happy that he had never had any family at all.

Was the haughty, wilting beauty one of the sisters? Gil felt nothing but irritation and contempt for her, whoever she was. Though he was perhaps being a bit unfair. Actually, there was no *perhaps* about it. She had had no way of knowing what a softie Beauty was, after all, and the dog's size could be intimidating to strangers. And perhaps she really had not seen a man without his shirt before. Many ladies, as he knew from experience, were brought up in near seclusion, with very little exposure to the realities of the world. He could not for the life of him understand the reasoning behind it, but there it was.

He should perhaps have disabused the woman of her assumption that he was a servant. At the very least he ought to have laid down the axe and pulled on his shirt and made himself look marginally decent. Was it sheer perversity that he had done neither?

He did not like women.

The fact did not excuse him from boorishness.

It also made him seem peevish.

What he would like to do right now, Gil thought, lowering the axe and leaning on the handle, was borrow one of the horses from the stables and ride off somewhere, never to return. But he could not do that, could he? Where would he go? Anyway, he had just sent a letter to his lawyer to inform him where he could be found for the next while. Besides, Harry needed him here. His family presumably would not stay long, and he had been quite firm in his resolve not to go to his mother in London, where he would soon find himself smothered by love—Harry's own words—and in the care of yet more physicians.

Gil put the blame for his friend's deplorable condition squarely upon his physicians and surgeons in Paris. Their idea of treating a man who had lain in a near coma for six months, horribly wounded, and who had needed surgery not long after that was to feed him soft, tasteless foods forever after and keep him in bed or confined to a deep chair in an airless room with curtains drawn tight across the windows. Their idea to fight the fevers he still suffered was to bleed him. And their plan to rebuild his strength was to limit his exercise to the daily walk to the dining room to eat his jellies and watery mashed potatoes and soups so thin they might as well have been dishwater. Their theory appeared to be that any exertion on his part would use energy that needed to be stored until he was full enough of it again to resume normal life. Most of them spoke of that day in the way they might have spoken of the pot of gold at the end of the rainbow. As something that was an impossibility, in other words.

The doctors were idiots, the pack of them. Gil resumed his self-appointed task and chopped through one particularly hard, thick log as though it were butter. He turned one portion of it on edge to reduce it to smaller pieces. He had rescued Harry from all that when he had agreed to bring his friend home. Home here to Hinsford, not to London. Now, having done so, Gil must stay, overseeing his friend's recovery until Harry did not need him any longer. He could wait out the visiting family. After a few days, or a week at the longest, they would surely grow bored with cooing and clucking over their invalid and return to their balls and routs in London before the Season was over.

And *that woman* would go with them. It could not be soon enough for him.

His axe made short work of the segment of log and he lifted another to take its place on the block.

Several minutes later he straightened in order to stretch his back and roll his shoulders. He wondered if Harry would insist upon introducing him to his newly arrived family members and expect him to dine with them. But of course he would. Gil was, after all, *Lieutenant Colonel* Bennington, a gentleman's title even if he was not a gentleman.

It was time, he decided, to go indoors, preferably through a side door, and wash up. He cleaned the axe and hung it in its usual place in the tackle room before gathering up his shirt and coat while Beauty wagged her tail and looked hopeful.

Beauty had her way.

Before Gil had taken one step in the direction of the house, his ears picked up the sound of another carriage approaching along the drive. He cursed aloud, pulled on his shirt and coat in a manner that would have given any self-respecting valet a fit of the vapors, and took his dog for a walk.

Three

Abigail was sitting in the drawing room, her stepsister Estelle on one side of her, her cousin Jessica on the other. Abigail and Jessica had grown up as the closest of friends. Although it had always been likely that Abigail would make her come-out first, as she was one year older than her cousin, they had nevertheless dreamed of doing it together and taking the *ton* by storm. They had dreamed of making brilliant love matches and bringing up their children in close proximity to each other and living happily ever after, forever in love with their spouses and forever closer than sisters with each other. Those girlish dreams had come crashing to an end prematurely, of course, when it had become obvious that Abigail could not expect a come-out Season at all. Ever. For the haute *ton* did not admit to its ranks the bastard offspring of even the highest ranking of its members.

Jessica, lovely, charming, and brilliantly eligible though she was as the daughter and sister of dukes of Netherby, was still unwed at the age of twenty-three. She went dutifully to London each spring with her mother, Abigail's aunt Louise, but claimed to derive no real joy from all the glittering social events of the Season. She had a large court of faithful admirers long after most young ladies would have been considered firmly on the shelf. But she treated them all with careless indifference.

Abigail sometimes thought it was as though she felt guilty that the doors of the *ton* were wide open to her while they were shut to her cousin. And that in turn made *Abigail* feel guilty, for she did not want anyone to shoulder her burdens. Any suffering that arose from the sudden shift in her status six years ago was hers alone to bear and hers alone to deal with in her own way and her own time. She had never looked to others for either pity or reassurance—not even to her mother or her sister or brother. She had cultivated an outer dignity of manner in the vain hope of being left to find her own way forward.

This spring had been especially difficult. For her mother and Marcel had finally persuaded his daughter, Estelle, at the age of twenty-one, to make her come-out in London during the Season. The fact that Bertrand, Estelle's twin, had just moved there after completing his studies at Oxford had no doubt affected her decision. Abigail put up no fight about going along with them too. It would have been mean-spirited to insist upon remaining alone at Redcliffe.

The Westcott family had, of course, welcomed her with renewed hope and all sorts of schemes and plans to gain entrée for her at a number of respectable parties and routs and even balls. There was scarcely a one of them without a title. They all had considerable influence. So did Marcel, Marquess of Dorchester, who was adamant in his willingness to use it on behalf of his stepdaughter.

It had been endearing and horrible and exhausting. For Abigail had neither the wish nor the intention of slipping in through the back door where she was not welcome at the front. She did not want to be restored, slightly tarnished, to the world of the *ton*. She did not want a respectable husband who would be prepared to overlook the tarnish in return for a hefty dowry and a connection to the influential Westcotts.

It would be lovely, Abigail thought now as she looked about the drawing room, in which those who had already arrived were gathering before dinner, to be able to escape. Not to have to return to London to resist again all the family's efforts to force her into enjoying herself. It also seemed a disloyal thought. For she was dearly loved, and love was not to be scorned. She did *not* scorn it. But she just wished they *understood*. Or that *someone* did.

As Jessica and Estelle chatted and laughed over some minor scandal that had erupted during a ball they had both attended last week, Abigail thought again of the plan of escape that had leapt to her mind yesterday. It seemed even more realistic today, for Harry was surely not fit enough to be here alone, even with a houseful of servants to cater to his needs. When everyone returned to London, as everyone must, including her mother, who would need to be there for Estelle's sake, Harry would need company and nurturing. Not necessarily professional care, as her aunts had advocated last evening. For his wounds were all healed, and he suffered from no definite illness. He just needed space and time and peace and . . . company.

He was sitting beside the fire now, a rug drawn over his knees, though he had not put it there himself. Mama had. Abigail had fully expected that he would push it away impatiently. He had not done so, though he had looked a trifle irritated and had grimaced slightly as his eyes caught Abigail's across the room. It was an expression she recognized from the old Harry. *Mama is fussing again*, it seemed to say to her, *but I cannot hurt her feelings by complaining*.

No, he did not need doctors and nurses. Neither did he need to be coddled. He needed someone who would always be here with him without being intrusive. He needed someone who would encourage him to walk and talk and take some air and exercise even if it was only a drive around the park in the gig, but someone who would also leave him alone at times. He needed someone to reminisce with and laugh with—and even someone to laugh *at* him when necessary. He needed someone who would give him the chance to restore his soul.

And oh dear me, she needed all those things too.

She needed to be with someone who was not forever looking at her with loving concern. Someone who was not constantly trying to plan a better life for her without knowing what she would consider *better*. Someone who would not be hurt because she could not seem to respond to his well-meaning efforts. Someone to laugh at *her* occasionally. Someone to talk and reminisce with her and not fuss over her. Someone who would respect her silences and her gravity. Someone who would make her laugh.

Someone to understand.

But all this was not primarily about her. Indeed, she was in danger of falling into self-pity. This was about Harry, at whom even now she could scarcely bear to look. There was something almost . . . *gray* about him, as though death, cheated for almost two years since Waterloo, still hovered hopefully over him. But he was *not* ill, only not well. There was a difference.

She would stay with him when everyone else returned to London. That was what had leapt into her mind yesterday. She would persuade him that she really wanted to stay, that there was no element of martyrdom in her decision. This was home, after all, the place she had longed to be ever since her mother's marriage, kind as Marcel had always been to her and affectionate as Estelle and Bertrand had been from the start. Hinsford was comfort and security.

It was where she needed to be, for the present anyway. And Harry's return here had made it possible.

"Dinner is served, sir," the butler announced from the doorway.

"Oh good," Bertrand said, getting immediately to his feet and rubbing his hands together. "I am starved." Then he smiled ruefully down at Anna and Alexander, with whom he had been conversing, and grimaced across the room at his father. "I do beg your pardon. That was not the best-mannered response, was it?"

"I like the enthusiasm of youth," Aunt Louise, Jessica's mother, said with a laugh. "You may lead me into the dining room, young man, and tell me what you plan to do with your life now that your studies have been completed."

"Would you like a tray brought in here, Harry?" Mama suggested. "I will have one brought for myself too if you wish."

"I dashed well would not," Harry said with a flash of his old spirit. "I will eat in the dining room with everyone else. But where is Gil?"

Gil? Abigail stared at him blankly as she got to her feet with her cousin and her stepsister.

"A pair of hefty servants were carrying pails of steaming water into his room an hour ago," Alexander said, offering his arm to Wren, his countess.

"Who is Gil?" Estelle asked.

Harry did not answer directly. "Well, there you are," he said, addressing a man who was hovering outside the door the butler had left open. "Just in time for dinner. Come inside and be introduced."

He was a large man, tall, straight backed, broad shouldered, dark haired, dressed neatly though without ostentation in black-and-white evening clothes. For a few moments he remained in shadow, but then he stepped into the room. He had a lean, forbidding countenance, dark eyes, and a scar slashing across cheek and chin.

He was *not*, apparently, a servant.

"My longtime comrade and friend, Lieutenant Colonel Gil Bennington," Harry said by way of introduction. "My mother, the Marchioness of Dorchester, Gil, and her husband. My aunt, the Dowager Duchess of Netherby. My half sister, Anna, Duchess of Netherby. You already know Avery. Wren, Countess of Riverdale. You already know Alexander. My cousin Lady Jessica Archer, Aunt Louise's daughter. My stepbrother and stepsister, Bertrand and Estelle Lamarr. And my sister Abigail."

Lieutenant Colonel Bennington's eyes had rested upon each in turn as he acknowledged the introduction with a slight nod of the head. They rested eventually upon Abigail, looking quite unsurprised. He gave her the same nod. Nothing else. No raised eyebrow. No smirk. No hostile glare.

Abigail would have sunk through the carpet and the floor and

stayed there if she could. He was a *lieutenant colonel*. He outranked
Harry. He was a longtime comrade and friend. And . . . *what* had she
said to him?

Were you given permission to remove your coat and shirt?

Oh, she could die of mortification.

"There will be a written test later this evening after dinner," Anna
said, smiling as she walked toward him and took his arm. "By then we
will have been able to tell you also about the children in the nursery—
mine and Wren's—and about those family members who will be coming tomorrow or the next day."

He looked sternly down at Anna while the rest of them laughed
and moved toward the door. "Does spelling count?" he asked.

"He looks deliciously ferocious," Jessica murmured as soon as he
had left the room.

"He does," Estelle agreed, laughing softly.

No, Abigail told herself, she would *not* sink into the floor even if a
hole were to open obligingly at her feet right at this moment. *Or* die of
mortification. He had had no *business* chopping wood beside the stables
if he was a guest of Harry's. A *lieutenant colonel,* no less. He had had even
less business stripping to the waist for anyone to see who strayed even a
short distance from the house. And he must have known perfectly well
about Harry's guests and that some of them had already arrived. He had
looked her over quite deliberately from head to foot, as no true gentleman
ought to do. Any other gentleman would immediately have dived for his
shirt and apologized profusely and explained who he was. He would
have been intent upon saving her from further embarrassment.

It had been quite deliberate, that insolent behavior of his. He had
meant to embarrass her and cause her humiliation when she realized
her mistake.

Well, she was not going to be embarrassed. Or humiliated.

"There is nothing the least bit attractive about him," she said,
though she was careful to keep her voice low. "He looks like a barbar-
ian. And he is ugly."

She was being petty. And untruthful.

Jessica laughed. "But deliciously barbaric, you must confess, Abby," she said.

"And deliciously ugly," Estelle added.

"I am hungry," Abigail informed them as they laughed with delight at their own wit.

He had, of course, been ridiculously unfair earlier, Gil admitted to himself later in the evening. It was never sensible to make a sweeping statement about half the world's population—perhaps more than half since the male portion of it was more often than not intent upon killing itself off during endless wars.

He did not dislike all women.

He never had. He had generally liked the camp followers, the crowds of women—wives, widows, cooks, washerwomen, whores, and others—who had tailed the armies about in droves wherever they went, many of them loud, coarse, slatternly, cheerful, cursing, generous with their favors, courageous, lusty, undemanding, and tough. It was the *ladies* he had disliked, the wives and daughters of officers who had insisted upon bringing their families to war. They were almost invariably haughty and demanding. Often they were helpless and clinging and inclined to the vapors and expected every man to dash to their assistance, bowing and scraping and generally debasing himself as he did so. Almost to a woman they had despised those colleagues of their husbands and fathers who were of lower rank or—far worse—not true gentlemen at all.

He had despised the lot of them heartily in return.

Except one . . .

Except Caroline, Lord help him.

Even with ladies, however, it was unfair to generalize. There had been a few among them whom he had respected, even liked.

He liked most of the ladies here at Hinsford, grudgingly, it was true, since their very presence dismayed him on his own account and worried him on Harry's. A crowd of visitors was exactly what Harry did not need. It was why he had decided to come home to the country rather than go to London. But these people were at least amiable.

He sat between the Duchess of Netherby and Lady Jessica Archer at dinner, and they both conversed intelligently with him. The duchess was Harry's half sister. She explained to Gil how she had grown up at an orphanage in Bath, unaware of her true identity. She had been twenty-five and teaching at the orphanage school when she was summoned to London to learn that she was in fact the legitimate daughter of the recently deceased Earl of Riverdale.

"A Cinderella story," Gil said.

"In many ways yes," she agreed. "But Cinderella was unhappy with her life before she met Prince Charming. She lived with a wicked stepmother and wicked stepsisters and was given grueling chores she did not enjoy. I was well cared for at the orphanage and had good friends there, including the one who later married my half sister Camille. I enjoyed teaching. I actually liked my Spartan little room and my few possessions, which were very precious to me. I was not entirely delighted to learn the truth about myself."

"You would go back, then, if you could?" he asked.

"Oh, by no means. I did marry Prince Charming, after all." She laughed and her eyes twinkled, and Gil liked her.

"You spent time with the garrison on St. Helena, Lieutenant Colonel?" Lady Jessica Archer asked him. "What is Napoleon Bonaparte *like*? We tend to think of him as an evil, black-hearted villain, but I suppose the truth is far more nuanced. I expect he is a fascinating though dangerous man."

She was a dark-haired, bright-eyed beauty, the duchess's sister-in-law, and Gil wondered why she was not yet married. Was marriage not the goal of all young ladies as soon as they left the schoolroom at the age of seventeen or so? She must be several years past that age.

"I saw him a number of times, of course," he told her. "But I did not know him or ever speak to him. I felt sorry for him actually. If he had been made to face a firing squad, I would have approved. If he had been shut up for life in a fortress, I would have thought it a just fate. As it was, he was exiled to that island and housed in what many people seem to believe is a luxury he does not deserve. But in reality it is a house in ill repair. It is damp and unhealthy, and nothing has been done to make it more habitable. It seems to me that he is being treated not with justice but with deliberate contempt."

"And contempt for such a man is not justice?" she asked. It seemed to be a genuine question, not a snide comment. Her knife and fork were suspended above her plate while she gave him her full attention.

"No," he said. "I believe contempt says more about the person giving it than the one receiving. It demeans what ought to be righteous punishment."

It occurred to him that this was probably not at all the sort of thing he should be talking about with a young lady of the *ton*—a duke's sister. And it occurred to him as altogether likely that he was being treated with such warm courtesy only because it was assumed that as an officer he must also be a gentleman. But he could hardly be expected to stand up and announce himself to be the bastard son of a blacksmith's daughter and a man he had never met or even heard from until he was grown up and a sergeant in India.

After they had adjourned to the drawing room, the Marchioness of Dorchester, Harry's mother, sat on the arm of her son's chair and set a hand on his shoulder when he would have risen to give her his place.

"Lieutenant Colonel Bennington," she said, beckoning him closer. "I understand from Harry that you spent a considerable amount of time with him in Paris every day after your return from St. Helena. That was extremely kind of you. And he tells me you had already made arrangements for his journey home before Avery and Alexander arrived."

"He wished to come, ma'am," he explained, "against the advice of his physicians."

"It was poor advice, then?" she asked him, glancing down at her son with obvious concern and rubbing her hand reassuringly over his shoulder.

"I believed it was," he told her. "With the best intentions in the world, they were nevertheless coddling him in the direction of the grave. He might have arrived there before I returned to France if he had not been too stubborn to die."

"Oh." She looked a bit shocked.

"One knows oneself to be an invalid," Harry said, "when people talk about one as though one were not present to speak for oneself. I do not believe my case was nearly as dire as Gil describes it, Mama, but I will be forever grateful to him for taking my part and making the arrangements and coming home with me, even after Avery and Alexander arrived and he might easily have bowed out of the commitment he had made."

"I will be forever grateful too, Lieutenant Colonel," the marchioness said, smiling at him. "Thank you."

He inclined his head stiffly, uncomfortable with her gratitude. His reason for coming here had been at least partly selfish.

"We all will be," the Countess of Riverdale added. She had come to stand beside Gil, a tall, beautiful woman if one disregarded the unfortunately large purple marks down one side of her face. He had thought at first they were burns, but her features were not distorted. They must be a birthmark, then, and had doubtless caused her endless anguish through the years. Yet she seemed unselfconscious about her appearance. The marred side of her face was closer to him than the unblemished side.

"Harry, we all had to come here, you know, just to assure ourselves with our own eyes that you are indeed home safe at last and on the mend. Your grandmother and Aunt Matilda will no doubt be here tomorrow as well as your aunt Mildred and uncle Thomas. But you need not fear that any of us will stay long. You came home for peace and quiet, did you not?"

"Well—" Harry began.

"No gentleman could possibly answer that question without perjuring himself, Wren," her husband, the earl, said, and she laughed.

"And I would not be surprised," Harry's mother said, "if Camille comes from Bath in the next day or two. Abby wrote to her. She has not seen Harry since the Christmas Marcel and I were married. More than three years ago."

"I am sorry, Gil," Harry said, chuckling.

He had not done much chuckling or laughing or even smiling in the past few months. Although he still looked pale and exhausted, perhaps this invasion by his family was really not going to be so bad for him after all. At least it assured him that he was dearly loved.

Bleakness assailed Gil for a moment, but he shook it off. He could not miss what he had never had. Never. Not during his growing years—his mother had probably been too borne down by the necessity of feeding and clothing them to have energy to spare for any open affection. And not during his brief marriage. What Caroline had felt for him had never been love. The more fool he for believing it was—for grasping at the notion that it was. Besides, none of this was about him.

Yes, he liked these ladies. The Dowager Duchess of Netherby engaged him in conversation for a while after he had seated himself and she had brought him a cup of tea. Later Bertrand, Viscount Watley, the young son of the Marquess of Dorchester, had some questions for him about the wars in India, and the young man's sister, Lady Estelle Lamarr, came to sit with them and listened with apparent interest. He could not decide which was the elder of the siblings until the brother made reference in passing to his twin and the question was answered.

Only Miss Abigail Westcott kept her distance throughout the evening. As far as he knew she did not once glance at him. He probably would have known if she had, as he glanced a number of times at her. She looked ill-humored. He did not once see her smile. No, *ill-humored* was a spiteful description of her expression, which was . . . expressionless. Carefully so, perhaps, as though she cultivated an inner privacy. She focused her attention mainly upon her brother, though she kept her distance from him and made no attempt to speak with him. Perhaps she resented him for coming home and taking her away from the gaiety of the London Season for a week or two. Or perhaps he, Gil, was being spiteful again. It was impossible to interpret an expression that was not there or the thoughts and feelings behind it. It seemed that he wished to justify the dislike he had taken in her.

Not that he had any reason whatsoever to dislike her. He was the one who had chosen not to correct her misunderstanding of the situation outside earlier. He had enjoyed her discomfiture and the anticipation of her embarrassment when she realized her mistake. Perhaps he owed her an apology. But he did not want to apologize. For she represented all that had always most irritated him about the ladies who had crossed his path down the years. The entitlement. The assumption of superiority and power—*I shall report you to him and see to it that he has a word with your supervisor.* And the prudishness—*You are in full view of anyone who walks even a few steps from the house. It is quite unseemly.* And she had said that *after* she had helped herself to a good eyeful of him.

Yet she was Harry's sister. That meant she was as much a bastard as he was—a baldly spiteful thought.

She was undeniably lovely. She was no girl, a fact that perhaps enhanced her beauty, for hers was a woman's loveliness. She had a slender but curvy figure, finely carved features with a perfect complexion, large blue eyes, and fair, not quite blond hair, prettily, though not fussily, styled in curls at the back of her head and wavy tendrils over her ears. The upswept hair emphasized the graceful arch of her neck. She was dressed plainly but elegantly in blue, a color that suited her.

She was beautiful, yes. But she looked cold and unappealing. Somehow unknowable behind that expressionless expression. Perhaps that, rather than the stain upon her birth, was the reason she was still unmarried. Perhaps other men found themselves as little attracted to her as he.

Yet for someone who was not attracted, he nevertheless could not seem to stop himself from glancing repeatedly at her and noticing every slight movement and gesture she made. She had elegant hands, which rested quietly in her lap, her fingers interlaced.

The feeling grew on him that he might indeed owe her an apology. Half-naked men, especially hot, sweaty, badly scarred ones hefting axes, were not a decent sight for a lady's eyes. He was gentleman enough to know that. And Beauty, big softie though she was, had come galloping from behind the stables, barking her head off. Miss Westcott could be forgiven for not having recognized her friendly intent. Or perhaps she just disliked dogs.

His own sense of guilt irritated him and made him like her the less—and feel yet more irritated and guilty. And even as he was thinking it, she looked back at him at last while Lady Jessica was saying something to her, and he realized that he was probably frowning or even scowling. He was sometimes accused of doing both when he was merely deep in thought. She continued to regard him, her eyes steady, even after she realized *he* was gazing back at her. He was the first to look away.

They would all leave soon, the Countess of Riverdale had assured Harry earlier, even though there were more of them still to come, some from London, and possibly one, Harry's other sister, from Bath. The countess had been aware that Harry would prefer to be alone and perhaps needed to be. They were probably all aware of it. He could wait them out, Gil thought. He would leave Harry to their mercies while they were here and find some private occupation for himself, especially if today's fine weather held. Beauty would be delighted by the opportunity for more walks. She had not had a great deal of freedom in Paris, and had had even less during the journey here. Now she was largely confined to his room while the visitors remained.

Afterward, when they had all left, he would take care of Harry. Not with lap robes and potions and soft, sympathetic words, but with windows flung wide and outdoor walks, even rides later on, and hearty meals. Not that he intended to overdo the encouragement to the point of bullying. Harry needed peace and quiet and independence as much as he needed exercise and nourishment. But Gil would not sit idly by and watch Harry languish and expect good health and strength to return as though by magic.

Just as he could not expect his own life to sort itself out unless or until he did something about it rather than hide here in the country, using Harry as an excuse while the wheels of the law creaked around in almost imperceptible rotation. Perhaps he needed to change his lawyer. The man had so far been unsuccessful in persuading Gil's in-laws even to accept support money for Katy, let alone consider visitation rights. Yet he wanted vastly more than just those two things. He wanted his daughter back. He wanted to take her home to Rose Cottage. He wanted to *love* her, God damn it.

And damn his lawyer's eyes for ordering him to *do nothing*, just the very thing Gil found near impossible to do. He had always been a man of action. Perhaps he needed to go to London to confront Grimes in person. And do what? Grab the man by the scruff of the neck, raise his fist, and turn the air blue with language?

No. Remaining here, where he would at least be welcome and needed for a while, was still his best option. It was *not* an excuse, though it felt like one. It was a reason. He would not let Harry down. Nor would he let his daughter down by blundering around like a fool, making it more certain by the day that he would never see her again.

Perhaps a quiet stay in the country would somehow soothe his soul and make him a better father when the time came.

When. Not *if. When.*

But when was *when*, for the love of God?

A stay in the country might also drive him quietly insane.

Four

The next morning before putting her plan into action Abigail checked that everyone was occupied.

Her mother and Aunt Louise were having their morning coffee with Mrs. Sullivan in the housekeeper's room. Mama still hoped to persuade Harry to return to London with her and Marcel, but in the meanwhile she was making sure that everything was properly organized to function as a bachelor household if she should fail, as she seemed to know at heart she would. Anna and Wren were upstairs in the nursery with most of their children. Avery had gone out to the stables with Josephine, at age four his eldest, when she had begged to see the horses. Marcel and Bertrand had gone with them. Alexander was in the music room with three-year-old Nathan, the elder of his two sons, who was banging on the keys of the pianoforte as though to prove to the world that he was no infant prodigy. Jessica and Estelle were in the morning room, writing letters.

Only Lieutenant Colonel Bennington was unaccounted for. He had not said anything at the breakfast table about his plans for the morning.

Abigail thought he might be with Harry, who had gone into the library after breakfast at Mama's suggestion in order to read—and probably to have a nap too, Mama had added after he went. That was why everyone else had found something else to do for a while. The playing of the pianoforte might not be the best lullaby, of course, but the music room was quite far removed from the library. Abigail turned the doorknob slowly, careful not to make a noise. If the lieutenant colonel was there or if Harry was asleep, she would withdraw— without being seen, she hoped.

She found Harry was alone, however, a book open on his lap, though he was not reading it. He was not asleep either. He was gazing through the window beside him. He turned his head as Abigail stepped inside and closed the door behind her.

"I am not as bad as I look, you know, Abby," he said when she hesitated and stayed where she was. "I am still me here inside myself, and the outer me will change for the better too now that I am home. I am done with being bled every time I have a suggestion of a fever and of being fed gruel and kept in semidarkness and wheeled about in a bath chair."

He had detected her reluctance to come close to him or even look at him, then, had he?

"Come and sit down," he said. "Ring for coffee, if you will. I shall have a cup with you. I have not been allowed to have any, you know."

"Why not?" she asked as she pulled on the bell rope.

"It is too strong for me," he said. "It might stimulate me and have me leaping about the room from chair to table to floor and swinging from the chandeliers. And that would not be good for my general well-being." He grinned at her.

"Are we all a great burden to you, being here?" she asked as she perched on the edge of the chair opposite his. "And more of us still to come?"

"Not really," he said after giving it some thought. "I must confess that I was a bit dismayed when Avery and Alexander confirmed me in my fear that everyone would probably come. And I still hope nobody stays longer than a few days. But it is good to know that people care, Abby. That one's own family cares. For a time six years ago I expected that no one would. I am sure you and Camille feared it too. But they do care. Even Grandmama is coming, I understand, though she is surely in her middle seventies by now."

"Sometimes caring relatives can be a burden," she said.

"Have they been a burden to you?" he asked.

But she was prevented from answering by the arrival of a maid with the coffee tray. Abigail poured them a cup each and took Harry his along with a raisin muffin on a plate. She sat back down with her own cup.

"You cannot imagine," he said, "what it feels like to be able to sit here, Abby, in a spacious room in a familiar home. To sleep in my own old bed upstairs. To look out a window—any window—and see sky and grass and trees and flowers. To be in England. And at home. I will be fine now. You need not worry or be afraid to look at me lest I take my final shuddering breath even as you watch." He ate half the muffin before setting his plate aside.

Abigail pondered trying to coax him to eat the other half but said nothing.

"I *can* imagine," she said. "Maybe not as acutely as you. But this *is* home, and I have been homesick for it since Mama married Marcel and we moved to Redcliffe. May I remain here, Harry, when everyone else leaves? I can make myself useful by running the household, though Mrs. Sullivan is perfectly capable of doing it on her own, I know. I can offer you some sort of companionship, though I would not press my company on you when you would prefer to be alone. I like being alone too. And I think my presence here might reassure Mama, who dreads the thought of leaving you alone when you have not yet recovered your full health."

"Abby," he said, "you do not have to trot out a dozen or more arguments to persuade me to allow you to stay. Hinsford is your home as much as it is mine. Literally, of course, it is Anna's. She inherited it from our father along with everything else that was not entailed. Oh, I know she is always hoping to persuade me to accept it from her as a gift and has already made arrangements to leave it to me and my descendants in her will, but it is not mine yet for all that. If you wish to live here, you must do so. Were you afraid I might say no?"

"Yes," she admitted.

"Goose," he commented, sounding for the moment like the old Harry. "I had forgotten how strong coffee is." He grimaced and set down his cup, only half empty.

Abigail got to her feet and returned their cups and the plate to the tray. "I daresay you want to rest for a while," she said. "I will not keep you talking."

"A nap in the morning," he said, "and probably another in the afternoon. Just like an old man. But not for long. I am not ready to be old yet. Who is playing the pianoforte, by the way? One of the infants? I can remember doing that when I was small but rebelling mightily a few years later when Mama forced me to have some lessons."

"It is Nathan," she said. "Alexander is with him." She turned to look back at him when her hand was on the doorknob. "Harry, I am so, *so* glad you are home at last." And the tears sprang even before she could turn her head away.

"Goose," he said again as she let herself out of the library.

Harry napping in the morning and probably again in the afternoon. Just six years ago he had been a vividly good-looking, carefree, energetic young man, slightly on the wild side, very often exasperating to her and Camille because they thought he did not take his responsibilities seriously enough. It seemed like something from another era or another lifetime. He had been the wealthy, fashionable, enormously popular young Earl of Riverdale in those days. Would he ever return to being that person? Without the title and the enormous wealth, of course.

But he was twenty-six now, no longer a boy or even a very young man. He was not an old man either.

She ought to join Jessica and Estelle in the morning room, she thought as she stood hesitating outside the library door. She had letters of her own to write, most notably to Marcel's elderly aunt, who lived in the dower house at Redcliffe. Abigail was fond of her, and had promised to write frequently from London. It was more than a week since she had last done so. She was not in a letter-writing mood this morning, however, and did not want to face the chatter of her cousin and stepsister. She might do something as silly as bursting into tears.

She went out for a walk instead, not bothering to stop to fetch a bonnet or pelisse. The air was fresh but not uncomfortably chilly. There was no discernible wind. And there was no need for formality within the confines of the estate's park. She considered the summer house to the east of the main building as a destination, but set out the opposite way instead, across the lawn toward the trees and the small lake beyond. As she walked, she waved to Josephine, who called out to her excitedly from high on the back of Bertrand's horse, where she sat cradled within the safety of Avery's arms and thighs. Marcel and Bertrand were standing in the large gateway into the stable yard, watching. Who would have expected Avery, Duke of Netherby—elegant, bored aristocrat, who nevertheless exuded power, even danger, through every pore—to turn into a doting papa?

Abigail was soon deep among the trees, her favorite place in the park. She always felt perfectly a part of nature when she walked here, every sense alive. There were tree trunks and leaves to look at as well as the sky scored across by waving branches. There were rough bark and smooth leaves with their ribbed undersides to touch and the distinctive smells of the woods to inhale. There was the wonderful sound of silence except when the wind was sighing through the boughs or rustling through the leaves. She stopped walking for a moment and set her hand against the trunk of an ancient oak. She could almost feel the life in it, old and steadfast and wise—a foolish conceit, perhaps. But she felt the balm of peace seep into her soul.

Harry had said she could stay. She would not have to return to London, where everyone was constantly trying to persuade her to join in some carefully selected entertainments of the Season. And where she had to face the constant disappointment and reproach in Jessica's eyes when she refused. She could stay here instead and perhaps at last—oh, *at last*—find some definite purpose for her life, which had changed so drastically when she was eighteen that she still had not fully recovered her balance.

She tipped back her head and looked up through the branches of the great tree to the sky above. She breathed in peace and freedom, even happiness.

GIL HAD CONSIDERED COAXING HARRY INTO TAKING A SHORT WALK outside after breakfast, but his mother had settled him in the library instead with a fire and a book and a blanket and the point was not worth contesting. There would be time enough after everyone left to supervise a more purposeful convalescence, and he did not believe Harry would resist. For the present, however, it really was good for him to be in the company of his family for a few days.

Gil fetched Beauty and went for a walk. It was a lovely cool, bright morning, and he drank in the sights and sounds and smells of the English countryside with all his senses on full alert. He put the dog on a long leash when they passed beyond the confines of the park. One never knew when one might encounter other people or animals who might be startled, even frightened, by her size and enthusiasm, as Miss Westcott had been yesterday.

Damn it, he owed that woman an apology.

He definitely did.

The walk was sometimes a brisk one as Beauty strained on the leash, eager to break into a run. At other times it was excruciatingly slow, as when she insisted upon sniffing every tree in a neat row along the edge of one field. She had to stop again to bark ferociously at a flock of sheep grazing peacefully in a meadow. The sheep favored her with a steady look through the bars of the stile, found themselves unimpressed, and returned to their grazing. She barked a greeting at a farmer and his lad who passed them in a loaded wagon and touched their hats to Gil.

And he felt a sudden yearning for his own home. For Rose Cottage. His own space on this earth. There was and always had been so little that was his own. And so few people. He had an unbidden memory of taking his daughter, all wrapped up warm in a blanket in his arms, to look at the rose arbor on the west side of the house. There had been no roses to see—it was too early in the year. But there they were, the plants in beds and climbing over trellises, and the promise of their blooming had excited him. The warm bundle in his arms had excited him too. He had been filled with a contentment he had never known before—or since. And life, even with the growing difficulties of his marriage, had seemed very, very good.

"Time to go back, Beaut," he said, turning abruptly, the joy suddenly fled from the morning. He had no idea how long he had been out, but from the position of the sun he guessed it must be close to noon.

Beauty turned obligingly, stopped with ears erect—except for the one tip, which could never straighten up—to contemplate a distant rabbit, which was cheekily looking right back instead of fleeing. But the dog must have decided that even without the leash she would have no chance of catching it or even scaring it badly. She trotted cheerfully homeward. Gil removed the leash after they had passed through a side gate into the park. The dog bounded joyfully forward and dashed once completely around the lake while Gil waited for her.

And it struck him that *Beauty* belonged to him. She had actually chosen him. And he was glad. There was nothing inferior about a dog's love. Perhaps it was even superior to human love. It was total and unconditional.

They set out through the woods in the direction of the lawn and the stables and the house. Beauty ambled along, investigating whatever took her fancy. Then abruptly she stopped, raised her head and cocked her ears, and trotted straight ahead, a dog with a set purpose. The trot almost immediately became a gallop and Gil increased his pace. He hoped it was just another rabbit.

It was not.

"Sit, Beauty," a slightly querulous voice said without any conviction that it was going to be obeyed. And apparently it was not.

By the time Gil was close enough to see what was happening, Beauty had Miss Westcott backed against the trunk of a large old oak. The dog was in the process of setting her big front paws on the woman's shoulders while wiggling her broad rump inelegantly and waving her tail in ecstatic greeting. Miss Westcott turned her head with a muffled shriek as the dog proceeded to lick her face.

Good God! Did he not have her trained *not* to jump up on people?

"Beauty, down. Sit." Gil was the speaker this time, and Beauty obeyed both commands instantly. But the damage had been done, damn it all. Thank God at least for the tree behind the woman. She would have been bowled over had it not been there. Why had the stupid dog decided to take a fancy to this particular female? Only an excessive fancy would cause her to forget her training.

"She prances about most people but does not actually touch them," he said. "She jumps up only on people to whom she has taken a liking."

"That is enormously flattering," Miss Westcott said, her cheeks flushed, her eyes flashing as she rubbed the thin sleeve of her dress over her ear. "I am honored."

Gil strode forward, drawing a clean handkerchief out of his pocket to hand her. She took it almost vengefully and scrubbed the dog's saliva from her neck and ear and one cheek while he stood watching. She looked delicate and lovely in her muslin dress, her fair hair styled more simply than it had been last evening. But she also seemed very angry and very hostile—both of which emotions appeared to be directed at him rather than at his dog.

"I owe you an apology, Miss Westcott," he said.

She scrunched the handkerchief into a ball in one fist and looked him over before handing it back to him. He supposed he appeared as intimidating as his dog, with his dark-complexioned face and almost black hair and eyes and ugly facial scar. Not to mention his size. It was not fear he saw in her eyes, though. It was . . . disdain?

"No real harm has been done," she said curtly. "At least the tree trunk stopped me from falling over."

"I mean for not immediately identifying myself yesterday," he said, "or pulling my shirt back on. For causing you some humiliation last evening when you realized your mistake."

Her nostrils flared. "I was not humiliated," she said.

"My apology stands," he told her, and watched the color deepen in her cheeks.

"I was not the one who lied by omission," she said.

Which was exactly what he was apologizing for, of course. Well, he had done what he could. If she chose to bear a grudge, that was her business.

Beauty was sitting exactly where she had landed after removing her forepaws from Miss Westcott's shoulders. She was very erect, panting, head high, trying to look intelligent.

He nodded curtly. "Beauty," he said, "heel." The dog scrambled to her feet and came to his side, looking up at him eagerly for further instructions. He gestured ahead and took a few steps away from the woman.

"What breed is that dog, anyway?" she asked, sounding more irritated than curious.

He stopped and turned back to her. She was still leaning against the tree trunk, her hands on the bark on either side of her, her head turned his way. "I had no idea when I found her as a puppy," he told her, "and I have no idea now. I suspect there has been crossbreeding down so many generations that if one looked hard enough one would find traces in her of every dog breed there ever was and even a few there never were."

"Except pug," she said.

He looked at his dog and back at her. "I would not rule out even that," he said. "What she resembles most these days is a vastly overweight greyhound wearing someone's ratty old cast-off fur coat or else an unshorn sheep on stilts. But either one would be an oversimplification. Ultimately she is herself." Just the way he liked her.

Miss Westcott was gazing steadily at him, and for a moment there was a flash of something in her eyes—some sparkle, some warmth—and he almost expected her to laugh. She did not do so, however.

"Where did you find her?" she asked.

"On the battlefield at Waterloo after the fighting was over," he said. "I suspect she belonged on one of the farms, but no one came to claim her. She looked hungry but not starving. For some reason that I have never understood, she attached herself to me and refused to go away even when I shooed her and cursed her. Then I made the mistake of feeding her some stale scraps I had in my pack. One word of advice, Miss Westcott. If you ever want *not* to adopt a stray dog, do not on any account feed it."

Actually he did not believe the dog's advent into his life to be inexplicable. But he could not share his theory with anyone else without being pronounced raving mad. It seemed to him that some fate with a bizarre sense of humor or compassion had sent him Beauty at almost the exact moment the real beauty of his life was being taken from him back in England—still unknown to him at the time.

"So she found you rather than the other way around," Miss Westcott said almost as though she had read his thoughts.

"Meaning that I am her man more than she is my dog?" he said. "It sounds pathetic, does it not? But no one else wanted her. Even as a puppy she was a scrawny thing with no promise of better looks to come. I have suffered ridicule over this dog."

She continued to gaze at him, her expression inscrutable. He made to turn away again.

"Apology accepted," she said curtly.

He raised one eyebrow.

"I *was* humiliated," she admitted. "I felt foolish and was very angry."

"Yes," he said. "I know."

They stood looking at each other for a few moments. She rubbed her hands lightly over the bark on either side of her, and he looked down at them. Slender fingered. Caressing. There was something unconsciously erotic about the movement. She must have realized it or at least felt uncomfortable at his scrutiny. She curled her hands into fists in a closed, defensive gesture.

He turned decisively away then to stride off through the trees in the direction of the house. But something made him stop and look back.

"Are you on your way to the house?" he asked.

For a moment he thought she was going to say no and willed her to do so. Damn his impulsivity. Then she shrugged her shoulders slightly, pushed herself away from the tree with her hands, and stepped toward him.

"Yes, I suppose I am," she said.

Beauty wagged her tail.

ABIGAIL WAS AWARE THAT SHE HAD NO REASON TO DISLIKE HIM any longer. He had apologized for yesterday. And directly after the Battle of Waterloo he had taken pity on an ugly, half-starved puppy. He had some sense of humor—*what she resembles most these days is a vastly overweight greyhound wearing someone's ratty old cast-off fur coat or else an unshorn sheep on stilts.*

Perversely she wished he had not apologized, that he had not explained how he found his dog, that he did not have any sense of humor at all. Something about him gave her the shivers. Oh, she was not afraid of him despite his size, those well-remembered muscles beneath his coat and shirt, and his morose, scarred face. She did not fear he would do her physical harm. She just . . . It was the way he looked at her. Those very dark eyes of his seemed to see all of her, including her hands spread over the tree on either side of her just now, and left her feeling uncomfortable and breathless and . . . exposed.

Yet here she was walking along beside him and his dog, on the way back to the house when she had been intending to go to the lake. But there had been no point in continuing with that plan. Her peace had been shattered.

He was very tall. The top of her head must reach no higher than his chin. And he had a long stride. She was aware of him shortening it to accommodate her shorter one and almost felt his irritation.

That was unfair. How could one *almost feel* what someone else was feeling but not saying? He was not saying anything. Neither was she. He exuded masculinity. But whatever did she mean by that? Well, what she meant was that he made her feel hot and bothered and self-conscious and tongue-tied and she did not like any of it.

She did not like him.

Her only comfort was that he would soon be gone. He had accompanied Harry home, which was undeniably kind of him, though it had been unnecessary in light of the fact that Avery and Alexander had gone to Paris for that express purpose. Having arrived here, he had stayed a few days. That was kind of him too, for if he had rushed away he might have left Harry fearing that it had been a nuisance to come all the way to Hinsford with a semi-invalid.

But surely he would go soon now. He must feel the awkwardness of being the only nonfamily member here—and there were more to come. Did he not have a home and family of his own to go to? He must surely be eager to be on his way. He had been away from England for at least a year and a bit, had he not, first on St. Helena and then in Paris? She almost asked him when he planned to leave, but the question seemed impertinent.

She said nothing. So did he.

They walked on in silence. When he did speak, it was to his dog.

"Beauty," he said, "stay close to heel."

Abigail immediately saw the reason. They were drawing clear of the trees to find that the lawn was rather crowded. Anna and Wren had come outside with the children. Rebecca, Anna's two-year-old, was trying to catch up with Wren's three-year-old Nathan, who was presumably pretending to be a kite or perhaps a bird as he ran in a wide circle, his outstretched arms dipping from one side to the other. Nathan's brother, Richard, one year old, was toddling in a straight line toward the stables, where his father was in conversation with Avery and Marcel. Avery was holding Jonah, the baby. Little Josephine was at his side.

Josephine was the first to spot them. She came dashing toward Abigail, jabbering excitedly about her ride on Cousin Bertrand's horse.

Oh, family was a wonderful thing, Abigail thought, blinking away unexpected tears. She had taken hers so much for granted during her growing years—until she thought she had lost it forever. Her father's side of it, that was. The Westcott side.

"I saw you," she told Josephine. "You were up before Papa. You have a splendid seat."

But Josephine had spotted Beauty and stopped in her tracks when she was still several feet away. Nathan's human kite was headed their way too before he dropped his arms to his sides and froze, also staring at the dog. Rebecca came after him, shrieking with mingled excitement and fright.

"Doggie," she said, pointing.

Abigail was suddenly terrified for them. But Beauty stood quietly at the lieutenant colonel's side, panting and waving her tail in greeting—just as though she had never in her life even dreamed of dashing at a human and pinning her to a tree with giant paws on her shoulders and doggie breath in her face and tongue licking her ear and neck.

The children stood in a row a short distance away, gazing in fascination and trepidation at the dog. Beauty woofed.

"Does he bite?" Nathan asked.

Lieutenant Colonel Bennington went down on one knee and set a hand on the dog's back.

"She does not," he said. "She likes children. She likes to shake hands with them. She likes them to pat her head and rub her back. Come." He beckoned to Josephine, who shrank back for a moment before stepping gingerly forward and setting a small hand in his large one.

And Abigail watched incredulously as he showed Josephine how to let the dog sniff the back of her hand before turning it over and letting the dog lick her palm. She giggled as the dog lifted a paw and the lieutenant colonel suggested that she shake it. She moved closer then in order to pat Beauty's head and run her hand down the dog's neck and along her back.

"Let me," Nathan cried, jumping up and down on the spot. "Let me."

The getting-acquainted ritual was repeated, the man speaking quietly and unhurriedly, the child laughing and finally flinging his arms about the dog's neck and giggling outright when Beauty licked his ear.

Rebecca was sucking her thumb and holding her distance.

"Come," Lieutenant Colonel Bennington said, beckoning with his fingers and lifting the child to sit on his knee when she took a few steps closer. Beauty dipped her head for Rebecca to pat.

"Doggie," she said before turning her head and fixing her gaze on the lieutenant colonel's facial scar.

"What is her name?" Wren asked. She had come across the lawn with Anna.

"Beauty," he said, and Josephine laughed gleefully.

"She is not beautiful," she protested.

"Maybe not," he told her. "But she is beauty."

And Abigail had the strange feeling that he meant *beauty* with a small *b*, rather than just the dog's name.

Rebecca sat quietly on his knee until the other men drew close. Then she held up her arms to Avery, and he took her after handing the baby to Anna.

Nathan and Josephine were on either side of the dog, smoothing her sides.

"I think it must be almost time for luncheon," Abigail said to no one in particular, and she continued on her way to the house.

For some reason she felt horribly discomposed.

Because she had at first refused to accept his apology?

Because he ought to have made it much sooner?

Because he was good with children?

Because he was a *man* and . . . ?

Well, that made no sense whatsoever.

She went in search of Jessica and Estelle in the morning room.

Five

Several times during the course of the following week Gil wondered if he ought after all to have taken himself off as soon as Harry's family started to gather to celebrate his homecoming and fuss and plan for his future. Or if he should do it even after they came. He was keenly aware that he did not belong here with them. None of them knew who he was, apart from his name and military rank. To say they would be horrified if they *did* know would surely have been to understate the case quite severely.

Harry's grandmother, the Dowager Countess of Riverdale, arrived on the second day with her unmarried daughter, Lady Matilda Westcott, and another daughter, Lady Molenor, who was accompanied by her husband. The three ladies, along with the Dowager Duchess of Netherby and Harry's mother, spent a good deal of time after that either worrying over Harry or endlessly discussing what ought to be done about his future care after they left.

The men for their part seemed just as intent upon protecting Harry from being overfussed and often surrounded him, talking determinedly upon topics that had nothing to do with health or nurses or attendant physicians.

The younger people enjoyed one another's company and occasionally, when they had the chance, gathered about Harry. They chattered about everything that had happened in their lives since they last saw him. They even managed to coax a few stories out of him about the time he had been away.

The children played, for the most part either upstairs in the nursery or out on the grass, though young Richard, suddenly discovered to be missing one morning, was found inexplicably on Harry's lap in the library. Both of them were sound asleep.

And then on the third day two more carriages arrived, from Bath this time. The family had been half expecting Harry's elder sister, Mrs. Cunningham. But they had not expected that her husband and all their children would accompany her or that they would bring with them Mrs. Kingsley, Harry's maternal grandmother.

All the children meant thirteen-year-old Winifred, a plain-faced, serious-minded girl who was as straight as a rod, not yet having begun to bud into womanhood; seven-year-old Robbie, a glowering child who seemed as though he fully expected everyone to look upon him with hostility; four-year-old Sarah, a blond, pretty, sunny-natured little girl; four-year-old Andrew, who Gil soon realized was deaf and mute; three-year-old Jacob; two-year-old Alice; and baby Samuel. It took Gil a while to sort them all out and identify which of them were adopted—Winifred, Robbie, Sarah, and Andrew—and which had been born to the Cunninghams.

Mrs. Cunningham was a handsome, generously—even lusciously—proportioned lady. She appeared dressed for comfort rather than elegance and seemed quite undisturbed by the demands of her large brood. She explained after they had been borne off to the nursery to greet their cousins why they had all come.

"I had to bring Sam," she explained, "for obvious reasons. He is four months old. Then Andrew was in a panic when it was made clear to him that I was going to be gone for a while, so I decided to bring him too. But that necessitated bringing Winifred, because she is the one who invented the system of signs we use to communicate with him and she is still sometimes needed to remind us which sign means what. Then Robbie had a tantrum about being left behind because no one cared about him and Sarah wept over him and looked reproach-fully at me. One never wants to be the object of Sarah's reproachful looks or one invariably ends up in tears. So—Robbie and Sarah were coming. And then Jacob asked if Papa could go too so that he would not be sad before realizing that that would mean *he* would be left at home without a parent in sight. Alice thereupon climbed onto Joel's lap and hid her face against his waistcoat as though she thought he was being cruelly abandoned. Then everyone except Sam switched camps and decided to stay home with poor, sad Papa, who then pro-ceeded to annoy everyone, me included, by laughing at us all and re-fusing to stop. And . . . well, to add an abrupt ending to a ridiculously long story, here we all are, every last one of us. And since we had to bring two carriages and a nurse if we were to retain our sanity, we persuaded Grandmama to come with us, though she does not like to go too far from home these days."

She tucked a fallen lock of hair behind one ear, accepted a cup of tea from her mother, and looked critically at her brother, whom she had caught up in a long, silent hug upon her arrival.

"You need to put on some weight, Harry," she said.

She was, Gil concluded, as different from her sister as it was pos-sible to be. Miss Westcott had been cool and dignified during that week—cool toward him, anyway. He did not know what she was like with her family when he was not present, and he stayed out of the way as much as he possibly could. She did not entirely ignore him or be-have in any way toward him that would draw attention to herself, but he sensed anyway that she did not like him, apology given and ac-cepted notwithstanding.

For a few moments out in the woods he had felt something like an attraction to her—or perhaps it was only a momentary lust at the sight of her stroking hands—but she was not an attractive lady. Beautiful, yes. Attractive, no. Yet he found himself watching her far more than he did her cousin or her stepsister, both of whom were lovely and far more lively and approachable than she.

A few times, then, he thought about leaving, even if only temporarily until Harry was alone again. If he ever *was* alone, that was, and the ladies of his family did not have their way and hire an army of medical-type persons to take up residence here. But even if that happened, Harry would need the companionship of a friend. His family made it very clear that they would not stay longer than a week. He could remain in the background that long.

Besides, he soon had another reason to stay at least as long as the Bath contingent remained. Robbie, the mutinous boy, who had apparently suffered neglect and abuse at a home before landing at the orphanage from which the Cunninghams had adopted him, discovered Beauty on the morning after his arrival. He scarcely left her side afterward, even when she was in Gil's room. The dog, sensing the boy's need, let him cuddle and curled about him, making herself look more ungainly than ever, and licked whatever exposed part of him she could find.

And Harry needed Gil even though he had all his family. He made that clear when Gil accompanied him up to his room one night after he had rejected offers from various aunts.

"Don't leave here, Gil," he begged, supporting himself up the stairs with one hand on the banister while Gil kept his hands clasped at his back. "You are not thinking of leaving, are you? I am touched beyond words that everyone has come long distances to see me. And I love them all dearly. But after they are gone, it is going to be wonderfully peaceful here. Like heaven. And you need some peace too before moving on."

Harry knew some of Gil's story, though not all. He knew that Gil had been widowed while he was stationed on St. Helena and that his daughter was living with her grandparents. But he thought she was there only until Gil decided what he was going to do about his military career.

"It is not my needs that are important," Gil told him.

"No, don't say that," Harry protested. "If it is only *my* needs that are keeping you here, then I will feel a burden and might as well let my mother and the aunts find a nurse or three or ten for me. I have been firm with them about employing a valet. I can just imagine the sort of paragon they would choose. I would be forever hiding from him. I intend to choose for myself. Indeed, I already have someone in mind. But I need—No. I would *like* a friend here with me too. Stay because you want to, Gil. Or because you need to. Or not at all."

"I will stay," Gil promised. "Until I have sorted some things out, anyway. Or until you tire of my companionship."

"That will be a good long while," Harry said. "But I am growing impatient, Gil. I want my body back and my strength and energy. And . . . my life. I am not planning to sit around all day every day by the fire, a blanket over my knees, a book perched on top of it. I do not even *enjoy* reading, for the love of God."

Gil chuckled and watched his friend step into his room and shut the door firmly behind him. It was half past eight, a time at which the old Harry would probably have been only beginning to think about going out for the evening.

THE DEBATE ABOUT WHAT WAS TO BE DONE WITH HARRY WENT ON all week among the aunts and grandmothers, who could not bear the thought of leaving him to the ministrations of no one but servants. The men had generally avoided the discussion, as had the younger women, both of which groups recognized that Harry was weak of body but not feeble of mind. He had come to Hinsford for a reason, most probably to avoid the very sort of fuss that was being made over him anyway.

"Being alone here is precisely what will suit him best, much as we may abhor the thought," Camille told the younger ladies when she was upstairs in the nursery with them on a drizzly morning while the men were in the library with Harry, and the aunts and grandmothers were huddled in the drawing room. "Mrs. Sullivan is perfectly capable of seeing to all except his most personal needs, and he says he is going to hire a valet to see to those. Poor Harry. It is perfectly clear that he has been bothered by enough physicians and nurses to last him a lifetime or two." She turned her attention suddenly to her young daughter. "No, Alice. Be kind. Rebecca merely wants to look at your doll. There is no need to shove her away."

"I wish he would come to London when we return there," Jessica said after Anna had put an end to the squabble by giving Rebecca her own doll and suggesting that both little girls rock their babies to sleep. "It would be lovely for him to be there and lovely for all of us to have him so close. But I know he will not agree to that."

"Avery says he will let us all fuss and worry and plan and cajole and weep and wring our hands," Anna said, "and then wave us all cheerfully on our way while he heaves a huge sigh of relief."

"I am quite sure Avery is right," Wren said, laughing. "It is Alexander's opinion too. Are you ready for a nap, sweetheart?" She lifted a yawning Richard onto her lap and he snuggled against her.

Abigail drew a slow breath and released it. She had been afraid of saying anything about her plan too soon lest it be disapproved of and cause even more discussions and arguments and a concerted effort to get her to change her mind.

"I am going to stay here," she announced.

Everyone turned to look at her in some surprise.

"Stay?" Camille said. "Here at Hinsford, do you mean, Abby? After the rest of us go home?"

"Yes," Abigail said. "I have asked Harry if he minds, and he does not."

"But looking after him on your own will be a huge responsibility, Abigail," Wren said.

"He does not need looking after," Abigail said. "He is not an invalid. He is just very weak after two years of injuries and surgery and fever. He needs time and space and quiet in which to rebuild his strength and recover his spirits, and I am confident he will do that better without people here to agitate him, however well-meaning they are. He is not going to be content to be a semi-invalid all his life. I will be here simply as a companion when he needs one. And I will be able to run the house and lighten the load for Mrs. Sullivan."

"Abby." Jessica had been sitting on the window seat with Winifred while the girl told a story in such a way that Andrew could enjoy it too, though he could not hear. But she got to her feet now, frowning, and crossed the room toward her cousin. "I might have expected it. You never had *any* intention of rejoining society or of attending any balls or parties, did you? Even when you agreed to come to London this year for Estelle's come-out. You have clung stubbornly instead to your *stupid* fear that you will be spurned because of the stain upon your birth. *Everyone* has told you that is nonsense. Avery has and Mama and Alexander and the Marquess of Dorchester and . . . oh, *everyone*."

The other ladies looked at her, concerned by her sudden outburst of emotion. Even a few of the children paused in their play. Richard rubbed one knuckle over the eye that was not pressed against Wren and snuggled closer.

"Jessica," Anna said soothingly, laying a hand upon her sister-in-law's arm. But Jessica jerked it away.

"It makes no *sense*," she said. "It is stubborn nonsense."

"I am sorry, Jess," Abigail said. "I have explained to you time and again that I will never try to cobble together the tattered remnants of my old life. You have chosen to believe that eventually I must change my mind. It has been *six years*, Jess. It is the difference between eighteen years old and twenty-four. I am a different person than I was all that time ago. I am sorry. I know you have been hurt too. But I cannot— Well, I cannot heal your pain. Only you can do that."

The anger went from Jessica as quickly as it had come. "I am finally to believe you, then, am I?" she asked, though it was not really a question she expected to be answered.

"I will be staying here when everyone else leaves," Abigail said. "It is what I want to do, Jess. It is not because Harry needs me. He does not, though his coming here has made it possible for me to come home too. And it is not because I fear that at any moment I will be driven out of London over the scandal of my birth. I do not care to be in London or to be part of polite society. I need to live my own life on my own terms, and for the next while at least that is going to be done here."

Jessica nodded unhappily and turned to watch Nathan and Jacob, who were building a precarious tower of wooden bricks.

"Oh, Abby," Camille said with a sigh before smiling at Andrew, who had come to sit on her lap, story time being over. "I thought at the beginning that you would be the easy one. You were so sweet and placid and accepting when we went to live with Grandmama Kingsley in Bath while I hid and raged. But you were not the easy one after all, were you? You pushed everything inside and have not even begun to recover."

"Oh no, Cam," Abigail protested, grimacing and then laughing. "I will *not* be made into a figure of tragedy. I am not staying here to lick my ever-open wounds and live out my life in unhappy seclusion and self-pitying misery. I am *coming home*. Because I want to be here to live my life. Because it is where I think I can be happiest. For now at least."

No one understood. But how could they? She was on a journey she could not explain in words even to herself. She did not know what the next step would be and had no idea what the final destination was or even if there would be one. She knew only that she must take one step forward at a time and that she must do it herself, even when that made her family unhappy. For they all seemed to believe that if she could only find a place in society and a kind husband who would disregard the blot upon her birth, all would be well in her life. Once upon a time it had been her sole aim to make her come-out, find an eligible husband, and live happily ever after. But no longer. That dream belonged to another lifetime. She did not even feel nostalgic about it.

"Abigail," Anna said, getting to her feet, "will you come walking outside with me? I see that the rain has stopped." She did not extend the invitation to anyone else.

Six years ago Abigail and Camille had resented Anna because she had suddenly appeared in their midst, their father's only legitimate child. She'd come straight from her orphanage in Bath, where she'd grown up unacknowledged by him. She arrived the sole inheritor of their father's vast fortune and unentailed properties, which meant they and their mother and brother were stripped of everything that had made up the fabric of their lives, their titles included. Their very identities, it had seemed. Even at the time, of course, they had realized that Anna was undeserving of their resentment. She had suffered terribly too, though her suffering had been done *before* the big discovery, whereas theirs had just begun. She had grown up as an orphan, knowing nothing of her father and his family or of her dead mother and her mother's parents, who would have been only too happy to raise her and shower her with love if they had not been told she was dead.

Their resentment had faded over time for lack of fuel. Anna had never stopped reaching out to her half siblings. She had steadfastly refused to take offense at their rejection—though truth to tell that very saintliness in her nature had at first added to their irritation since it had exposed their own pettiness for what it was.

"A bit of fresh air would be very welcome," Abigail said, and went to fetch a bonnet and pelisse and stouter shoes before meeting her half sister downstairs in the hall. How typical it was of Anna to have sensed that she had needed an excuse to escape from the nursery after her big announcement.

They strolled along the cobbled terrace rather than venture onto the wet grass. The air still held some dampness, though it had stopped drizzling for the moment. Anna linked an arm through Abigail's.

"You must stop me," she said, "if what I am about to say is offensive to you. I will just come out and say it. I want you to have your quarter of our father's fortune. It has always been yours, set aside for you and your descendants after I am gone if you will not take it before. But if you are to live here alone, though Harry will be here too, of course, you really ought to have an independence, Abigail. And it is yours anyway. Please say yes."

Anna stopped and glanced apprehensively at her half sister when she did not immediately reply.

"I find it very distasteful," she added, "to talk about money. But it would be absurd for me to go home and then write you a letter. Abigail, you are my *sister*."

From the start Anna had seen the injustice of their father's will, made years before his death while he was still married to Anna's mother, before his bigamous marriage to Abigail's. He had never made another. It had seemingly never occurred to him to provide for the three children who knew nothing of their illegitimacy. Perhaps he had assumed the truth would never come to light. Perhaps he had forgotten all about that will, gathering dust in the offices of a lawyer in Bath. According to that will everything that was not entailed was to go to his wife and their daughter.

Anna had wanted to do what had seemed to her the only fair and just thing and divide the fortune into four parts, one for each of their father's offspring. In addition, she had made arrangements, even before she could be asked to do so, for Abigail's mother to recover the dowry that had been given on her marriage and all the interest it would have accumulated in the more than twenty years since.

Her half siblings had all spurned her offer as though she were somehow insulting them by making it. They had refused to take even a penny of the money. How ridiculous and ugly they had been, Abigail thought now, when they had chosen to be offended rather than grateful. But they had been so dreadfully, terribly hurt. Was that a valid excuse? Probably not, but when one was hurt to the core of one's being one could not always think in terms of fairness.

"It is legally your money, Anna," Abigail said.

"Yes, of course," Anna said, making a dismissive gesture with her free hand, "though I do believe the three of you might have made a convincing case against me had you chosen to pursue the matter in the courts. *If* it had been necessary to do so, that is, and if you had believed you were entitled to your share. It was nothing short of wicked of our father to deceive you and Aunt Viola all those years and then to leave you unprovided for. I am very glad I never knew him, Abigail. His will was an abomination and should not be binding upon us, regardless of what the law says. *Morally* his fortune belongs to the four of us, and the sooner you accept your portion, the happier I will be."

"Even if Camille and Harry never accept theirs?" Abigail said, frowning.

Anna started walking again, though they were almost at the end of the terrace. "Camille approached me in Bath before she married Joel," she said. "She told me she would accept her portion, not because she needed or even wanted the money, but because she did want to make peace with me and make more of an effort to accept me as her sister. I know that was an extremely difficult thing for her to do. I was a stranger who came into her life at the most stressful moment imaginable. But she has done what she was determined to do. She has given me a gift every bit as precious as the one I was able to give her. More so, since I gave her only what was rightfully hers."

"Oh," Abigail said, mortified and touched. "I did not know."

"No," Anna said. "We both decided to say nothing. We did not want to put undue pressure upon either you or Harry. Avery had a word with Harry yesterday. Not about his share of the fortune. That will have to wait until a more opportune time. Rather he persuaded Harry to accept the benefits of this house if he will not yet agree to a legal transfer of ownership. From now on he will receive the rents from the tenant farms and the income from the home farm. He saw the hole in the argument Avery made, of course, and insisted that if he was going to accept the income, then he must also handle all the expenses of the house and estate. But it is a profitable property. He will be able to lead a comfortable life here even if he merely maintains it as it is and does nothing to develop it—and even if he never will take his share of the fortune."

They had stopped walking again, having run out of terrace. Abigail bit her upper lip as she fought tears. "I have been wondering," she admitted, "how I can justify living here on Harry's bounty when he has very little himself except his officer's pay. I am not even sure he is still receiving all of that. At the same time I did not know how in all conscience I could continue to accept the very generous allowance Marcel has made me since he married my mother."

"Then wonder no longer," Anna said, squeezing her arm and turning back in the direction of the house. "Harry will have more than just his officer's pay, and you . . . Accept what is yours by right, Abigail. Please. We are equally our father's daughters."

Abigail released her arm, fumbled for her handkerchief, dabbed at her eyes, and blew her nose. Then she caught Anna up in a wordless hug.

"And may I say," Anna said after they had both sniffled a bit more, "that I admire your decision to do what you want to do with your life instead of giving in to what the family has been urging you to do for at least the last five years." They continued walking more briskly back to the house as a light drizzle began to fall again. "Trying to fit into society in order to find a husband is clearly not what you want to do, and I do not for a moment believe it is cowardice or the fear of rejection that holds you back. You will find your way eventually, or perhaps this *is* your way and you have already found it. Either way, I believe in you, Abigail. I really do."

"Were you by any chance a teacher once upon a time?" Abigail asked, and they both laughed, because indeed Anna had been a teacher at the orphanage. Together they hurried up the steps and into the house to get out of the rain. "I had better go and find Mama and the grandmamas and aunts and let them know that I will be staying here with Harry when they all leave. Perhaps then they will stop fretting over him so much."

"I would not count on it," Anna warned. "It is more likely they will merely add you to the to-be-fretted-over list."

They both laughed again.

"Oh, Anna," Abigail said as they turned to go their separate ways inside the house. She hesitated a moment. "My brother and sister call me Abby. You are my sister."

"Thank you, Abby."

And from this moment on, Abigail thought as she hurried away, that must be how she thought of Anna. Just as Camille had been doing apparently for the past five years. She must not just think kindly of her.

Anna was her *sister*.

Six

The Westcott family and Mrs. Kingsley left Hinsford a week to the day after the arrival of the Bath contingent. They seemed happy to have assured themselves that Harry was indeed home safe and no longer hovering at death's door. They were less happy at having failed to persuade him either to return to London with them or to allow them to send a nurse and even a physician to see to his future care. Harry—as the Duke of Netherby had predicted—had listened politely to all the suggestions made by his mother, his aunts, and his grandmothers, but had remained firm in his determination to stay at Hinsford without any resident medical care. He reminded them all that there was a perfectly decent doctor in the village even if he was probably seventy or so.

It was good to see his friend so firmly asserting himself, Gil thought. He had never really done it in Paris, quite unlike the old Harry.

Now everyone was leaving.

After breakfast on the appointed morning, all was bustle in the hall, out on the terrace, and on the staircase while various persons dashed up and down in pursuit of forgotten or might-have-been-forgotten items. Carriages were lined up outside while horses stomped and snorted or stood patiently awaiting further orders. Some of the men helped the coachmen and servants from the house sort out the luggage and load it onto its rightful vehicle. The women hugged Harry and the sometimes reluctant children and one another. Children darted everywhere, usually to places they were not supposed to be.

Gil helped load the carriages, though he kept an eye on Beauty too. She was always gentle with children, and she knew these particular children well by now. But almost all of them found it necessary to dash at her to give her hugs, and she was noticeably agitated, perhaps sensing that they were all leaving. The little Cunningham boy hugged the dog and would not let go even when his mother called him to the carriage. It was obvious to Gil that he was sobbing quietly into Beauty's neck.

"Remember what we talked about last night, Robbie?" his father said, coming closer and rubbing a light hand over the boy's shoulder.

"You will forget," the boy said sullenly, scrubbing the back of one hand across his eyes and nose before Gil handed him a handkerchief.

"No, I made you a promise," Joel Cunningham told him. "Have you ever known me to break one?"

The boy frowned up at him, sniffed, and shook his head. "I really, truly can have a dog all of my own?" he asked.

"And of your own choosing too," his father said. "We will set about finding one after we get home. You may take your time about it until you see just the one that belongs with you."

"Promise?" the boy said.

"I promise," Cunningham said gravely, squeezing his shoulder. "Give the handkerchief back to Lieutenant Colonel Bennington now. It is time to leave."

Robbie hugged Beauty one more time and subjected himself to a face licking. The back of his hand dealt with the resulting moisture and he dashed away to the carriage while Cunningham smiled ruefully at Gil and shook his hand.

"Thank you for sharing your dog," he said, "and even allowing

Robbie into your room. I think perhaps we have found an answer for him at last."

As Gil turned his attention to a large trunk of the dowager countess's that needed hoisting aboard her conveyance, he saw the boy seated inside his father's carriage. He was lifting his arm to set about the shoulders of his deaf brother, who must have been aware of his distress and had snuggled up against him.

What would it have been like, he wondered, to have grown up as part of a family? But before any of the old, pointless bleakness could intrude he shook it off and repositioned the trunk so that there was room beside it for Lady Matilda's smaller portmanteau.

Another quarter of an hour passed before everyone was finally aboard one or other of the carriages and coachmen were slamming doors and climbing to their perches. Horses snorted with impatience to be moving. Gil stepped back to stand beside Harry, who had come outside a few minutes ago.

And something struck him.

Miss Abigail Westcott was standing on Harry's other side. She was not hurrying toward any of the carriages. Neither was she dressed for travel. Her flimsy muslin dress was fluttering about her legs. She wore no bonnet. Beauty was seated beside her, looking silly with bliss because she was lightly scratching the dog's head.

What the devil?

"You are not leaving, Miss Westcott?" he asked.

"Oh no," she said. "I am staying."

What in thunder . . . ? *For how long?*

She partially answered his unspoken question before the first carriage rolled into motion and the others followed it down the drive.

"Harry's coming home has made it possible for me to come home too," she said.

When there was still half the social Season to be enjoyed in London? And a stepsister and stepbrother and cousins and other relatives to enjoy it with? And nothing but a country home and a sleepy country neighborhood and an ailing brother for entertainment here?

Harry and his sister stood waving until the last of the carriages disappeared from sight.

"They are a good lot, Abby," Harry said. "We are very fortunate to be a part of such a family."

"The only bad egg in the lot of them," she said, "was our father. How could he have been so very different?"

"There is one consolation," he said. "If he had not married Mama, bigamously or otherwise, we would never have been born. And I do not believe I would have liked that one little bit. Would you?"

She laughed, an attractive little gurgle of merriment Gil had not heard from her before. "I suppose I would not have been in a position either to like or to dislike it," she said. "I would not have been. There would have been no I. Or you. It is hard to imagine total nothingness, is it not? But ought you to be standing out here this long?"

"If you intend to fuss me, Abby," he grumbled, "I'll send you back to London on the next stage." But there was no real irritation in his voice.

Again that gurgle of laughter. "Very well, then," she said, linking an arm through her brother's. "Let us take a walk along the terrace. Could the day possibly be more perfect?"

"It could not," he agreed, "simply because I am living and breathing in it. It is also a lovely day."

"Lieutenant Colonel Bennington," she said politely, "would you care to join us?"

The perfect hostess. A woman at home with her brother. Making their guest into a stranger by the very courtesy of her invitation. Good God, why had someone not *told* him? Why had Harry not mentioned it? *Oh, by the way, my sister is remaining here indefinitely to ruin our peace.*

He fell into step beside them as they made a slow progress along the terrace. Gil remembered how Harry always used to stride everywhere, eager and full of energy, impatient to get where he was going.

"Lieutenant Colonel," Miss Westcott said, "you must be eager to go home yourself."

Ah. She was wondering when he intended to leave, was she? And hinting that perhaps it ought to be soon?

It was surprising the question had not come up more than it had during the past week. Harry's grandmother from Bath had asked him one day at luncheon if he was one of the Somersetshire Benningtons, but when he had said no, he was not, and had not immediately gone on to explain which Benningtons he *was* one of, she had not pursued the matter. Neither had anyone else. Perhaps there had been something in his voice that had deterred further questioning.

None of them had discovered that he was not a gentleman, even less of a one than Harry, in fact. Far less. At least Harry had been brought up as a gentleman in the aristocratic home of an earl and his apparent countess. He had been educated and groomed as his father's successor. Gil had been brought up in what had been little more than a hovel by a mother who was the unmarried daughter of a blacksmith. He could read and write and figure only because his mother had insisted that he attend the village school, which he had hated with a passion despite the long-suffering patience of the vicar who had taught it.

"He will be staying for a while," Harry said before Gil could respond to the question himself. "For a good long while, I hope. I do *not* need a nurse. I have had plenty of those and physicians and surgeons too for the past two years, and look where they have got me. Oh, they kept me alive. I give them their due and all my gratitude on that. But they also kept me only barely alive. No daylight allowed, no fresh air, almost no solid food, no exercise—and enough blood taken from me when I had the fever to give life to an army of empty bodies. There will be no more nurses. A good friend and comrade will do very nicely instead. And a sister, of course."

Gil watched Beauty wander along down by the trees, sniffing the trunks where they met the ground.

Three wounded souls. That was what they were. Though where that thought had come from he did not know.

But was Harry's *soul* as well as his body wounded by what had happened to him in battle, and in London six years ago when he was stripped of his title and fortune and everything for which he had been raised? He had never talked about it beyond the bare facts. There had been no more cheerful officer in their regiment than Major Harry Westcott.

And had Miss Westcott's soul been wounded by those same events? It was perhaps significant that she was still unmarried several years later and apparently not even looking for a husband in the great marriage mart that was the London Season.

Was *he* wounded? By . . . life? By what Caroline had done to him? But was it fair to blame her or anyone else for the state of his soul? And where the devil were these thoughts coming from anyway?

Life was a challenge. One big challenge forever splintering into smaller ones, just like a felled tree trunk under the axe. And if one got wounded, one licked the wound, applied a bandage if it would not stop bleeding, and kept reducing that trunk to logs and sticks of firewood and kindling—until the next one came crashing down and one had to start all over again.

"Provided that sister does not fuss you," Miss Westcott was saying in response to her brother's words, that thread of humor still in her voice. "But we are running out of terrace, Harry, and will need to turn back."

"You cannot know how good this air feels to me," he said, drawing in a deep, audible breath of it before turning, "and the sunlight and the smell of grass—and horse. And to have my legs under me. I am coming out again later. Perhaps we will have a picnic on the grass. How will that be for a grand adventure?"

"I am not sure I will be able to stand the excitement," Gil told him.

"I shall arrange it with Mrs. Sullivan," Miss Westcott said. "And how I like the idea of doing that—of being mistress of my own home."

Damn it, Gil thought, he did not like the sound of it at all. He had looked forward to being part of a bachelor establishment for a while. He had looked forward to Harry's family leaving. Most of all he had looked forward to *her* leaving. But why so? She had done nothing to antagonize him since that first day—which had been mostly his fault. Why, then, had he wanted her gone more than any of them?

Because he was attracted to her?

He wanted *no* entanglements with women. With women of her class, anyway. Her illegitimacy took nothing away from the fact that she was a lady, a member of a powerful aristocratic family, which guarded its own. She was also Harry's sister.

He turned his head impatiently and whistled for Beauty. She came loping across the lawn toward them, tongue lolling, ears flopping, rear end jiggling, tail waving.

A dog's love at least was eternal and unconditional.

And uncomplicated.

ABIGAIL HAD BEEN DISMAYED TO DISCOVER THAT LIEUTENANT Colonel Bennington intended to stay indefinitely at Hinsford. She felt cheated of the privacy and sense of home and peace she had so craved. She would surely not have stayed herself if Harry had thought of *telling* her.

Anyone but him, she had thought.

But why?

He was not the brute she had taken him for on that first day. Besides, he had apologized for his behavior on that occasion, and she had accepted the apology. Was she still bearing a grudge? It would be unreasonable and wrong if she were. He had done nothing to offend her since then, or anyone else in the family. Quite the contrary, in fact. He had kept away from them for long spells each day and never joined any group or conversation when he was present unless he was drawn in by someone else. And he was undeniably good with children, a fact that had taken her completely by surprise since it seemed to contradict his severe, sometimes almost morose looks and demeanor. He had apparently even allowed Robbie, that troubled little boy whom even three years of love and patience from Camille and Joel had still not quite soothed, to spend hours in his room with Beauty.

And of course he was Harry's friend. Her brother, she guessed, needed male company more than he needed that of a mere sister. She ought to be happy the lieutenant colonel had decided to stay for a while.

She was not, though. She was not happy at all about it.

But why?

She asked herself that question as she directed one of the male servants in the placement of the chair he had carried out onto the lawn for Harry. And then she sent him back for two more so that her brother would not feel that he was being treated like an invalid while she and his friend sat on a blanket on the grass. Or perhaps she sent for extra chairs because she did not want such proximity between herself and the lieutenant colonel.

Oh, this was ridiculous. Why was she so resentful? She ought to be enjoying the chance to play hostess for a guest.

Was it because she was horribly aware of him as a man?

Horribly?

And *was* she?

He was not even handsome. She did not believe he ever had been, even before he acquired that scar on his face. His hair and eyes were too dark, his features too harsh and angular, his complexion too sun darkened, his habitual expression too stern. And he was too big. Every time she glanced at him she remembered what he looked like without his shirt, his breeches riding low on his hips, the huge axe held diagonally across his body—which had been glistening with sweat. It was uncivilized. It was barbaric. It—

She sounded like a prude. She probably *was* a prude.

But that realization did not endear him to her either, though he was not the one who had called her that.

He made her feel uncomfortable. What an inadequate word—*uncomfortable*. But she could not think of a better one. She wanted to be able to think of him merely as Harry's friend. And she wanted to see him every time she looked at him or thought of him as *having his clothes on*. She wanted to obliterate that ghastly memory of raw masculinity.

Oh come, Abigail, she chided herself, *it was not ghastly*.

She had never encountered masculinity before. Men, yes. Handsome men, yes. Attractive men, yes. Masculinity, no. Not *raw* masculinity, anyway. Not naked chests and . . . Oh dash it all, she really *was* a prude.

She watched him now approaching slowly across the lawn with Harry. She did approve of the way he never tried to assist her brother physically, though he must often be tempted to do so just as several members of her family had been, especially the females. Nothing could be more designed to irritate Harry. Lieutenant Colonel Bennington kept his hands clasped at his back whenever he walked with Harry, though he stayed close enough to offer assistance should it become necessary. He bore himself very erect, a military man in every line of his body. She wondered if his men had feared him—or adored him. Or perhaps a bit of both.

Harry stopped and looked at the chairs and then at the single blanket spread on the grass. The picnic hamper had been set across one corner of it.

"Expecting a few elderly ladies with rheumatic knees, are you, Abby?" he asked with a nod of the head to the chairs.

She smiled ruefully. "I suppose you are offended by them. The chairs, I mean."

He grinned at her. "At least you were tactful enough to have three brought out," he said. "I suppose you fear that if I get down on the ground I will not be able to get up again. If you should prove correct, please do not summon any servants. I will crawl back to the house on my hands and knees and you may say *I told you so* to your heart's content."

With that, he lowered himself to the blanket and moved to one side of it. It was good to see Harry recovering his sense of humor, Abigail thought as the lieutenant colonel gestured to the blanket beside Harry.

"Miss Westcott?" he said.

"Oh no," she said, "I shall serve the food before I sit."

She went and knelt beside the hamper and set about filling three plates with chicken and ham and bread rolls lavishly buttered, and with cheese and pickles and hard-boiled eggs out of their shells. There were currant cakes and small custard tarts and three brightly polished apples at the bottom too under a folded towel, she could see, but she left those for later. Propped against one corner of the hamper was a carefully wrapped large, meaty bone for Beauty, who was sitting beside the blanket, waiting with panting impatience.

The lieutenant colonel came down on one knee beside Abigail and poured the wine. He had large, strong hands, Abigail noticed—they would have to be, of course, for him to wield an axe the way he did and probably other weapons too. There was a faint scar across all four knuckles of one hand.

"How long have you been a military man?" she asked him.

He seemed to be doing the mental calculation. "Twenty years," he said.

So long? "How old were you?" she asked.

"Not quite fifteen," he said. "I lied about my age. I was impatient for adventure, and a recruiting sergeant came along and offered me just that. I took it, along with the king's shilling."

"A recruiting sergeant?" She paused to look at him in considerable astonishment, Harry's plate held in her hand. "You joined as a private soldier?"

"I did," he said, taking the plate from her hand and passing it to Harry after adding a linen napkin. He picked up his own plate with a word of thanks and moved across the blanket to leave room for her. He had balanced the glasses on a flat tray he had found against one inner side of the hamper.

To hide her surprise, Abigail turned aside to unwrap the bone, which had a great deal of meat still attached to it, and set it on the grass beside the dog. Beauty scrambled to her feet with a woof, sniffed it, and attacked it.

Returning her gaze to her companions, she decided it would be far too intimate to squeeze in beside the lieutenant colonel. But Harry had not left enough room on his other side. She took her plate and sat on one of the chairs.

"A touch of the rheumatics," she said with a smile when Harry glanced up at her.

Lieutenant Colonel Bennington had been a private soldier. Not an officer from the start. His family had been too poor, then, to purchase a commission for him? Or . . . There was another explanation, especially as he had been signed up by a recruiting sergeant. Perhaps he was not a gentleman. But if he was not, how on earth had he made the jump through the ranks to become an officer? She had heard that only a deed of extraordinary valor made that possible. She did not ask, and he did not volunteer any further information. Instead he was listening to Harry, who was declaring how wonderful it was to be alone at last, just the three of them.

"It seems horribly disloyal to say so aloud," he said, "when they all made a great effort to come here just for my sake and were so touchingly glad to see me back home. But . . . Dash it, Abby, I had forgotten just how delicious our cook's fried chicken is."

"She made it especially for you," she told him. "She remembers every one of your favorite foods and just how you always liked them prepared. She has been sending a steady stream of servants to the farm and the village to gather all the ingredients she is going to need. She is quite determined to fatten you up."

"She is likely to succeed too," he said. "I am rediscovering my appetite."

But as her brother expressed his pleasure, Abigail was distracted by the thought that during the past week Lieutenant Colonel Bennington had revealed almost nothing about himself though he had been in conversation a number of times with various members of her family. She knew his name and his military rank. She knew he had spent a year with the garrison on St. Helena, guarding Napoleon Bonaparte. Now she knew he had been recruited at the age of fourteen by a recruiting sergeant. And that was all. Oh, and he spoke like a gentleman and behaved like one—except when he was chopping wood, half naked beside the stables.

"I am a bit surprised actually, Abby," Harry said, "that none of our neighbors have called even though we have both been here for more than a week. Do people forget so soon? Or do they see us differently than they used to do? Are we pariahs?"

"I assure you we are not," Abigail said. "When Mama and I came back here to live, we were treated as we always had been. Most people even continued to address Mama as *my lady*. The neighbors were kind and attentive, and our friends were still our friends. Perhaps—"

"I believe I can throw some light upon the matter," Lieutenant Colonel Bennington said. "Your neighbors judged that having all your family here has been enough excitement for you to contend with, Harry, much as they are eager to pay their respects to you and see for themselves that you are recovering your health. I daresay they will come flocking now that everyone has left."

Abigail looked at him in some curiosity, but Harry merely chuckled. "And is this a guess on your part, Gil?" he asked. "Or have you been out meeting the locals during your absences from the house?"

"Not all of them," his friend told him. "But you inevitably meet a number of people of all classes when you spend an hour or so of each day at a village tavern. And *they* meet *you* without any reluctance or reticence. Seeing a stranger is a rare enough event, I gather, that they will soon find ways to worm out of him his life history, his political views, and his reason for being in their neighborhood."

"I believe you." Harry laughed again. "Sometime when you go, Gil, perhaps I will come with you. But it is good to know that everyone has not taken a disgust of me just because I lost my title and fortune six years ago."

"Vicars tend to grow animated and garrulous too when a stranger is discovered reading plaques on the walls inside their church on a weekday with no service scheduled," the lieutenant colonel continued. "They tend to take his presence as a good reason to deliver a lengthy history of the church. And then, if that stranger is lucky—I was—he gets invited into the vicarage for an excellent luncheon with the man and his wife. And he is regaled as he eats with tales of all the mischief Mr. Harry and, to a lesser degree, his sisters used to get up to when they were children here. The vicar even shed a tear as he described the consternation there was in the village when word reached here that they were like to lose Mr. Harry after Waterloo. He declares he will be the first to call upon you the very day after your good family leaves."

"The Reverend Jenkins has been here forever," Abigail said. "His sermons are as dry as dust, but I always liked going to his church services anyway just to bask in the glow of his saintliness. I am sorry I missed last Sunday, as we all did."

"I tell you what, though, Gil," Harry said. "One reproachful twinkle from those eyes of his was a far more powerful deterrent to mischief than all the wrath of our mother or any of our servants."

"Indeed it was," Abigail agreed. "Do you remember the time, Harry, when we sneaked over the wall into the vicarage garden to steal apples from the tree there only to discover that the vicar himself was standing at the back door watching us? And he smiled at us and told us to enjoy them? Camille burst into tears and I set my apples on the ground and refused to pick them up again and you said we were planning to take them to Mrs. Beynon, who had not been feeling well? That was when his smile turned reproachful."

"I left mine on the ground too and swore I would never tell another lie in my life," Harry said, and they both laughed.

Lieutenant Colonel Bennington, Abigail noticed, was swirling his wine and gazing into his glass. She thought about him going down to the village, getting acquainted with the people she and Harry had known all their lives. He had not answered her earlier when she had suggested that he must be eager to go home. When Grandmama Kingsley asked him a few days ago if he was one of the Somerset Benningtons, he had simply said no. Did he *have* a home? Or a family? He had been recruited as a private soldier when he was fourteen. Twenty years ago. He was thirty-four years old now, then, ten years older than she. Whom had he left behind all those years ago? Anyone? Had he ever gone back? Would he *go* back?

But she did not want to wonder about him. She still found his company uncomfortable and wished fervently he had not remained here—or that she had not.

She served the sweets and he poured more wine, though Harry set a hand over the top of his glass and shook his head.

"If I get drunk," he said, "I might start to sing."

"Oh goodness," Abigail said, "we must certainly not risk that."

He took a couple of bites of his custard tart and then set his plate aside and lay back on the blanket, one knee raised, one arm flung across his eyes, though he was in the shade of a tree.

"I know how a prisoner must feel when he is released from jail," he said. "Though I suppose it is unfair to all those people who kept me alive and did their best for me to compare either a hospital or a convalescent home to a prison."

And within minutes he was asleep, his breathing deep and even. Lieutenant Colonel Bennington looked up at Abigail after he had watched Harry for a while.

"He is being healed," he said softly.

It was the first time he had come outside twice in one day. And he was eating more than he had done even a week ago.

"Yes," she said, and looked to where Beauty, her bone having been stripped down to a bare whiteness, was sniffing her way along the tree line. "I am going to take a walk. Would you care to join me?"

It had seemed only polite to ask. She did not expect that he would accept. He could use the need to keep an eye on Harry as an excuse.

"Yes," he said, and picked up one of the apples before getting to his feet.

Well, she was stuck with his company now. She must get used to it, she supposed. He was staying here. So was she. She wondered if he was as disturbed about it as she was. But she knew he was. There had been a certain look on his face when he had realized this morning that she was not leaving with everyone else. She had assumed he must be aware of that fact as she had told everyone else, but apparently not. Just as she had not known that *he* was staying indefinitely.

Beauty lifted her head, looked back at them, realized they were going for a walk, and went galloping toward them. Abigail wondered how she could ever have been afraid of the dog.

He was disturbingly tall and broad shouldered. The lieutenant colonel, that was.

Seven

She was not small as women went. The top of her head reached above his chin. But she was delicate and slender. And beautiful. And what he had taken at first for a haughty coldness was actually more of a quiet, reserved sort of dignity, Gil had come to believe—with some reluctance. He did not want to find himself liking her. For if he liked her, he might start finding her attractive. She was entirely the wrong sort of female for him to be attracted to. He would by far rather stick to women of his own class. Yet here she was, staying after everyone else had left and intending to remain indefinitely. And making it altogether less comfortable for him to stay.

Miss Abigail Westcott, he had concluded during the past week, when he had watched her far more than he had wanted to and far more than was good for him, did most of her living inside herself. Like an iceberg, she showed the merest tip of her totality to the world, even her family. Perhaps especially to them. He wondered if they realized it.

It was probably not fair to compare her to an iceberg.

Why the devil had he accepted her invitation to walk with her?

She had no doubt asked out of her lady's notion of politeness and had not wanted or expected him to come.

Without saying a word or perhaps even *thinking* one, she nevertheless made him feel like a great ugly lump. He was almost tempted to slouch along beside her to bring himself closer to her height. Instead he squared his shoulders and raised himself to his full height. The scarred side of his face was toward her. He did not make an excuse to shuffle over to her other side.

He hated the way she made him feel self-conscious. It was not a feeling to which he was accustomed.

Beauty pranced from side to side before them, yipping and waving her tail. She assured herself that no, he had not been teasing but was indeed going for a walk, and turned about to dash off ahead of them.

"Why are you not married?" he asked abruptly.

Now why out of all the myriad questions with which he might have attempted to open a polite conversation had he chosen that particular one? Unsurprisingly she turned her head sharply to look up at him, and he could almost see her mind shaping the words *how dare you!*

"I suppose," he said before she could speak them aloud, "that was an ill-mannered question. But you must surely have had offers. You are not a very young woman, but you are beautiful."

He sorted through the gaucherie of his words while she continued to stare at him.

"Why are *you* not married?" she asked him. "You are not a very young man." She did not add *but you are handsome*, he noticed.

He bent to pick up a stick and hurled it as far as he could across the lawn for Beauty to fetch. It was one of the dog's favorite games. He took a bite of his apple. They had stopped walking, he noticed. "I am not married," he told her, "because my wife died."

Well, there. *That* took the wind out of her sails. She stared silently back at him for several moments.

"I am sorry," she said.

"Why should you be?" he asked. "You had no way of knowing."

Now he was adding churlishness to a lack of basic good manners. She waited as though expecting some further explanation. He took another bite of his apple and walked on. He was not in the habit of talking about himself, least of all about his marriage. She continued walking too after glancing back, presumably to see that Harry was still asleep on the blanket.

"Contrary to what you seem to believe," she said, "I have *not* had any offers even though I am twenty-four years old. I might, I believe, have had a couple during the past few years if I had given some encouragement to two gentlemen who indicated a possible interest. Perfectly worthy gentlemen."

"But you did not encourage them," he said.

"No."

He refrained from asking why. It was none of his business. And he did not need to know. He was curious, though. Was not marrying the single most important life goal for women of all classes? Did they not all consider anything above twenty a dangerous age still to be single? She was twenty-four.

"Worthiness alone is not enough," she went on to explain. "Neither is steadiness of character, nor the means with which to provide me with a home and the comforts of life to which I am accustomed. Or even good looks and amiability. I have remained single because I have found nothing and no one to tempt me to marry."

"Yet," he added.

"Yet," she conceded. "I am not afraid of being single. I *am* afraid of making a marriage I would regret."

Ah. He bent to pick up the stick, which Beauty had set at his feet before looking expectantly up at him, panting excitedly and dancing about with impatience to be gone again. He feinted once, twice, and then hurled the stick. The dog roared off in hot pursuit.

"And what," he asked, "*would* tempt you? Love?"

They were walking close to the tree line, moving in and out of the shade provided by branches that overhung the lawn. They would make an elliptical sort of circuit about the lawn, he supposed, so as not to allow Harry out of their sight.

"I believe it may be easy enough to fall in love," she said, "especially if the man is young and handsome and charming and vibrant of manner. I am not at all sure being in love would be a good basis for marriage, however. It would not last, I suspect, if there were not far more to sustain it."

"And of what would that *far more* consist?" he asked her. This was a strange conversation to be having.

It seemed for a while that she must agree with him. She did not answer. Instead she gazed off into the trees, away from him. Then she stooped for the stick before he could and threw it in a short arc for Beauty to chase with glee. She spoke at last after looking back once more to check on her brother.

"It is sometimes easier to define what one wants in the negative rather than the positive," she said. "I suppose at one time I expected to be married for who I was. Or rather for *what* I was. I was *Lady* Abigail Westcott, daughter of an earl. I was eighteen years old, passably pretty, educated, and accomplished in all the knowledge and skills expected of a lady. I was to have a large dowry. And I was about to be turned loose upon the *ton*. I was to make my curtsy to Queen Charlotte and then have a grand come-out ball followed by a full Season upon what is known as the great marriage mart. I expected to attract an eligible husband, and would of course have done so. That is the way it happens in the world that was still mine at the time. Perhaps I would have been happy. Perhaps I still would be."

"But then everything changed," he said, "and your life was ruined." He had thought about what had happened to their family as it had affected Harry's life. Now he considered it from her point of view. She had been a girl on the brink of womanhood with a bright, secure future assured her.

Which only went to prove that the future was never to be taken for granted.

"On the contrary." She was frowning, he saw. "It was almost as though I had dreamed through the first eighteen years of my life and would have continued to do so until my death if I had not been jolted awake."

That was an unexpected way to look at the disaster of what had happened to her. Had she not lost all her hopes and dreams?

"Let me tell you what happened to my sister Camille," she said. "She had already made her come-out. She was betrothed to a viscount. She was a very proper lady, a very strict follower of all the rules and conventions of society. She was straitlaced and rather humorless. She was my sister and I loved her, but I do not believe she was generally well liked. Her betrothed forced an abrupt end to their engagement when the truth of her birth was revealed. She had more to suffer than the rest of us, and suffer she did. But consider her now. You saw her during the past week. She is almost unrecognizable as the Camille I remember. She is happy. She is lovable. She and Joel will probably end up with a dozen children both their own and adopted, and she will welcome each one of them with an all-embracing love. She is beautiful, but in a far different way than she was six years ago. My family still talks of what happened as the Great Catastrophe, as though the words would have to be capitalized if written down. But it was not a catastrophe for Camille. It was the best thing that ever happened to her."

He did not take his eyes off her as she spoke with a warm sort of passion. Her cheeks had acquired a blush of color, and her eyes, large and blue, had gained depth. And he felt her perilous attraction.

"But Harry?" he said. "And you?"

They both glanced back toward the picnic site as they turned away from the trees to walk up in the direction of the stables before making their way back across the top of the lawn, just below the terrace.

"Harry," she said, "is alive."

"And that is enough?" he asked.

"It is always enough," she said. "Or at least it is the main ingredient for being enough."

"And you?" he asked again. "Is it enough that you too are alive?"

"Yes," she said, her voice suddenly curt. "To return to your original question, I do not want to be married because of what I am, Lieutenant Colonel Bennington. At present that is the illegitimate daughter of the late Earl of Riverdale, under the determined protection of the powerful and well-connected Westcott family as well as that of the Marquess of Dorchester, my stepfather. Neither do I want to be married *despite* what I am. I want to be married—*if* I am to be married at all, that is—for *who* I am."

"And who is that?" he asked. Beauty, he noticed, had tired of the stick-chasing game. She had abandoned the stick in the middle of the lawn and gone to stretch out at the foot of the blanket upon which Harry lay.

"Ah," she said, "that is the key question." She did not have the answer, it seemed, or if she did, she was not sharing it.

"You wish to be married for who you are," he said. "But whom do you wish to *marry*, Miss Westcott?"

She turned her head to dart an appreciative look at him. "Ah," she said, "you do understand. Most women are married. Very few, it seems to me, *marry*. It is always the man who begins the courtship and the man who discusses the marriage contract with another man of her family. It is the man who proposes marriage. It is the man who takes her to live with him and expects her to change not only her name but her very life to fit his. It is the woman's part to be married and to make the best of it."

"Should everything be reversed, then?" he asked.

"Oh, by no means." She actually smiled for a moment and lost her look of cool beauty to become simply pretty. "That would not redress the imbalance, would it, but merely tip it the other way. I believe Camille and Joel married *each other*. So did my mother and Marcel. And other members of my family. You did not meet Cousin Elizabeth this week—Lady Hodges, Alexander's sister. She is still recovering at home from a confinement. She is almost ten years older than her husband, but *they* married each other against all the odds. One only has to see them together for a few minutes to know that they belong together, that they are vibrantly happy."

It was love after all, then, for which Abigail Westcott searched— and waited. But not the sort of being-in-love infatuation he had felt for Caroline when he married her. Though, truth to tell, that was a grossly oversimplified explanation of how he had felt about her and why he had wed her. Ultimately they had married because she was with child.

Miss Westcott seemed to be reading his thoughts. "Did you love your wife?" she asked.

He felt himself closing up—not that he had ever opened up to her or anyone else. He looked away as his thoughts turned to his wife. There had been lust. There had been *being in love*. There had been dazzlement, an incredulous sort of wonder that she could be so powerfully attracted to him when she might have had her pick of any number of handsome, wealthy, well-connected officers, all of whom were gentlemen, all of whom were clamoring for her favors. And there had been the naïveté, of course—a humiliating, disastrous abundance of it. For it was only later, after they were married, after he had taken her to his home in England, that he understood what it was about him that had attracted her—and no longer did. They were the very things that ought to have repelled her, in fact. And half of them had been imaginary. Perhaps more than half. He was not at all the person she had mistaken him for. Except in one thing. He was as far from being a gentleman as it was possible to be.

Ancient history, all of it.

Except that there was Katy.

"I married her," he said, and he could hear the stiffness in his voice. "I cared for her in every way I knew how. She died."

It was no answer, of course, and her silence accused him. She had been open with him. He had been the opposite with her. But to hell with it. No man enjoyed talking about *feelings*, for God's sake, or about love and marriage and all the rest of it. Or about his own failed marriage, which had left pain like a raw thing ripping him apart. Or about humiliation that had torn at his very manhood. He felt suddenly irritated, perhaps the more so because he knew he was the one who had started it. She quite possibly would have been happy to discuss the weather or nothing at all during their walk.

Harry had raised himself on one elbow.

"One of these days," he called out cheerfully as they drew within earshot, "I am going to get out of this habit of having an afternoon nap." He laughed and pushed Beauty's head away as she went to stand beside him and tried to lick his face.

I MARRIED HER. I CARED FOR HER IN EVERY WAY I KNEW HOW. SHE DIED.

Lieutenant Colonel Bennington's words played and replayed themselves in Abigail's head far too often for her comfort during the following days. They had seemed totally devoid of emotion, a possibility that chilled her. Or perhaps they resonated with an emotion too deep to break through in words—and *that* was a possibility that wrenched her heart. It was impossible to know which of the two extremes had been in those words. Or perhaps neither. Perhaps he had merely been stating facts. But it seemed to Abigail that this man was unknowable and deliberately so. He was totally self-contained. Trying to know him was a bit like trying to know granite.

Not that she cared. She did not want to know him. He was Harry's friend, but she had not warmed to him. It was not just that she had been made to look foolish during that first meeting with him—though that had not helped, she had to admit. Actually he made her feel foolish all the time.

She had been taken completely by surprise to learn that he had been married. She could not imagine it. Neither could she imagine the woman who would want to marry him. Oh, but yes, she could. What a stupid thing to think. Although she cringed inwardly at the very sight of him and was distinctly uncomfortable when forced to be close to him, she was honest enough with herself to recognize the source of what she had at first taken for revulsion.

He was disturbingly attractive in a way she could not put into words. She suspected it was something physical, but did not want to explore that possibility. She tried not to think about him at all. She tried to ignore his presence at Hinsford. And it was not as difficult as it might have been. He stayed out of her way except during mealtimes and other times when the three of them were together.

She did admit, reluctantly, that his presence here was good for her brother. He did not fuss over Harry or try offering him any personal care, even an arm to lean upon. The day after everyone left, Harry sent for Mark Mitchell, the publican's son, who had briefly been his valet before the great disaster. Since then Mark had worked with his father at the village inn. Harry offered him his old job back, and he accepted it and moved in the same day.

Lieutenant Colonel Bennington confined his role to that of companion and friend. He conversed with Harry, played chess with him, moved chairs out onto the terrace and sat there with him on a particularly warm day. He walked with him, accompanied him to the stables to look over the horses and carriages, drove him in the gig one afternoon to the village tavern and to church on Sunday morning while Abigail chose to walk. Occasionally he sat quietly reading with Harry in the library. Abigail was surprised to discover them thus employed one rainy afternoon when she went in to ask if they were ready for tea. Harry was reading one of the London papers, which had come with the post that morning, while Lieutenant Colonel Bennington was reading a book.

"You actually *like* books, Gil?" Harry asked, lowering his paper.

"I sometimes wish I could read faster," the lieutenant colonel told him. "I suppose that comes with practice. But yes. Being able to read is a privilege. The vicar who taught me at a village school always said that, much to the eye-rolling disgust of all his pupils, including me. But he was right. I read now because I can."

He was reading *Tom Jones*, Abigail could see. He was returning his attention to it as she withdrew to give the order for tea to be brought up. Another little fact was added to the bank of her knowledge about him. He had learned to read at a village school. He did not often read but considered it a privilege to be able to do so. He was not a fast reader.

The neighbors, as Lieutenant Colonel Bennington had predicted, came during the days after the family left. The vicar and his wife were first, as promised, and they were soon followed by others, most of whom came to pay their respects to Harry, to see for themselves that he was recovering his health and to assure themselves that he intended to remain here, at least for the foreseeable future. They came to inform him that he—and Miss Abigail, of course—would be invited to tea and to dinner and to informal parties and assemblies as soon as he was well enough and strong enough to go about. A few of the men who had been his particular friends while he was growing up, most of them now established farmers with wives and even children, promised to come again and stay longer. They hinted at fishing and shooting parties as soon as Harry was feeling up to it.

Some of Abigail's old friends came specifically to call upon her, though most of them looked in upon Harry too, the unmarried ones perhaps to see if he was as handsome as he had given promise of being as a very young man. They were interested in the lieutenant colonel too, of course, having heard about him from the men who had met him at the tavern. But men never could remember the truly important details, they observed to Abigail. Men could never remember if a stranger was young or tall or handsome or charming or in possession of some sort of fortune.

"I was quite determined to discover that he is gorgeous," one friend said. She was sitting in the conservatory with Abigail and another mutual friend, looking out upon rain. "Especially after the Reverend Jenkins told Mama and Papa that he is a lieutenant colonel and assured Mama he must be a single gentleman since he is apparently staying here for some length of time. I would not exactly call him *gorgeous*, though, now that I have seen him for myself."

"What *would* you call him, then?" the other friend asked.

"He actually looks a bit frightening," the first said. "If I were an enemy soldier, I would not want to see him coming at me with a sword. Would you?"

"I would not want to see *anyone* coming at me with a sword," the other said with a deliberate shudder. "But to be perfectly frank I would not mind at all if I saw Lieutenant Colonel Bennington coming toward me to . . . ask me to dance, perhaps. What do *you* think of him, Abigail?"

"I think he is a good friend to Harry," Abigail said. "And that is really all that matters."

It irked her that she had somehow been drawn during their walk after the picnic into saying things she did not say to many people, or to *any* other people, in fact. She had never before openly discussed her reluctance to wed, her fear that she would never find that one special man who would want to marry her, not because of who she was or despite who she was, but because she was . . . well, *herself.*

And who is that? he had asked her.

She had been unable to answer. She still could not. It was a little disturbing not to know who one was deep down inside oneself. But perhaps it was not so much that she did not know as that she could find no words, even inside her head, with which to describe it.

She just *was*. That was all.

But how could one explain that to another person? How could she expect ever to find a man who would want to marry her just because she *was*? It was absurd. And she would have to return the compliment, would she not? She could not expect any man to love her that deeply if she did not also understand that *he* simply *was*, and that his *wasness* or *isness* made him forever the love of her heart. The love of her life.

Now her head was in a spin. She needed another language. The language of love, perhaps?

Her friends had looked at each other, at her, and back at each other.

"She likes him," they said in unison, and laughed so infectiously that Abigail joined them. Let them think what they would.

Lieutenant Colonel Bennington spoke at the breakfast table one morning about his need for a horse of his own. Yes, it was all very well for Harry to invite him to take any of the horses from the stable at any time, but . . .

"I understand, Gil," Harry said after raising one hand. "None of the horses here are really meant for riding. Besides, a man needs a horse of his own. You will not find anything suitable in the village, but it is a mere ten-mile drive to the closest market town. Why do we not go and have a look? I am itching for an outing that will take me farther than the church or the tavern. We can take the gig."

"Perhaps," his friend said, looking across the table at Abigail, "Miss Westcott would care for the outing too."

Oh, she would. When she had come from London, she had brought with her neither her embroidery nor her knitting, and she was desperately missing both.

They ended up taking the old carriage that had been used for years when they were living here. It had been kept in good repair during the more than three years since Abigail had lived here last.

There was not a great deal of conversation during the journey. They were all reasonably comfortable in one another's company, and there was always something to watch beyond the windows. But Abigail gave in to curiosity when her eyes inadvertently met those of the lieutenant colonel, who was sitting on the seat facing hers.

"What happened?" she asked, indicating her own right cheek

while she looked at his. It was an abrupt and impertinent question, and she fully expected that he would dismiss it with an answer along the lines of *war happened*.

"What happened," he said, "was that my officer, a young boy who ought still to have been in leading strings, took fright in his first battle when enemy cavalry decided to charge our part of the line. He ordered us to run for our lives and he put the spurs to his horse to lead the way. He was the only one with a horse."

Harry grimaced. "Some officers are an embarrassment to themselves and a danger to the rest of us," he said.

"Was it not good advice, then?" Abigail asked.

"A man on foot can never outrun a horse," the lieutenant colonel explained. "What a foot regiment in line must always do to counter a cavalry charge is form a hollow, outward-facing square of men two deep, the front row kneeling with their bayonets pointing outward, the back row firing their guns over their heads. It works every time. Horses will not charge a wall of bayonets, and men get killed by the volleys when they urge their mounts too close."

"Horse sense," Harry murmured.

"I bellowed at my men to form a square," Lieutenant Colonel Bennington said. "I was their sergeant. Eventually they did, but not before far too many of them had been killed or horribly wounded. Cavalry-men stab many fleeing soldiers in the back. But what they like best is to ride past them and slash back with their great cavalry swords, blinding and maiming and killing that way."

"That is what happened to you," Abigail said.

"I was fortunate," he told her. "The sword got neither my eyes nor my throat, except for one small slash. I was fortunate too not to be hated by my men. A couple of them grabbed me and dragged me into the center of the square, where I suppose they expected me to bleed out and die while they fought."

"It is a sort of unwritten rule among officers," Harry said, a hint of reproach in his voice, "that ladies are given no details of war."

The lieutenant colonel looked at him and then back at Abigail. "I beg your pardon," he said stiffly. "I memorized the written rules. I never did learn all the unwritten ones."

"I did ask," she said.

He fell silent, perhaps humiliated by Harry's quiet rebuke, and Abigail was left to wonder again who exactly he was. Not a gentleman, almost surely. There was that village school and that recruiting sergeant. So how had he ended up an officer? A lieutenant colonel, no less.

"I suppose, Harry," she said, "we know practically nothing of all the horrid things that happened to you during the wars. We knew only of the wounds you could not hide from us."

He had been sent home once during the war and had arrived unexpectedly at the house in London where Alexander now lived, in such a confused mental state brought on by fever that he had thought it was still his and that he would find Mama and her and Camille there.

"I suppose," she continued when he merely frowned at her, "that all the letters in which you told us what a jolly lark it all was, being with the armies, were so many lies."

"Oh, I say, Abby," he said, "I had to keep Mama's spirits up somehow. I knew how much she worried. And I was not exactly lying. It *was* a lark much of the time. Was it not, Gil?"

"There were good times," he said, looking at Abigail. "There was camaraderie. And we saw the best of humanity as well as the worst. There are good people with the armies, women as well as men, despite the fact that Wellington described his soldiers after Waterloo as the scum of the earth. I like to think there was at least some fondness in the description. As well as pride."

He turned his gaze upon Harry then, and Abigail saw that her brother had fallen asleep, his head against the side cushion next to the window. She frowned across at Lieutenant Colonel Bennington.

"These are healing sleeps," he said quietly, as he had said during the picnic a week or two ago. "You must not worry. He is vastly better than he was when I found him on my return from St. Helena. His will to live and thrive has strengthened. And he has your cook to feed him."

She swallowed against a lump in her throat and nodded.

They did not talk again before they arrived at their destination.

3 1308 00367 6624

Eight

They left the carriage and horses at an inn, where they also reserved a private parlor for the day. After partaking of coffee and glazed buns Harry went with Gil to look over some horses while Miss Westcott walked to a shop that sold needleworking supplies. She seemed to remember from a previous occasion that it was not far away and refused to allow the men to go out of their way to escort her there. She also scorned her brother's offer to hire a maid from the inn to accompany her.

"I am twenty-four years old," she reminded him.

Gil had never been much of a horseman, though as an officer he had been forced to ride more frequently than he had done as a boy or when he was in the noncommissioned ranks. He took his time about his choice of a horse now, though he was also aware of the need not to exhaust Harry. That was a needless worry, however, as he soon realized. His friend was every bit as exhilarated by the task at hand as he was.

There were several mounts that would do perfectly well, but Gil wanted to choose just the right one. It was true that his dog had chosen him on the battlefield at Waterloo rather than the other way around, but nevertheless Beauty had taught him the importance of the special bond that could exist between man and beast. Just any dog would no longer do for him. Only Beauty herself. In the same way he wanted the one horse that belonged to him, or to which he belonged.

It did occur to him that it was a good thing Harry and the other men hovering about could not read his thoughts. They would think him daft at the very least. Or else totally unknowledgeable about all he ought to look for when buying a horse—and they would not have been far wrong on that.

He picked a white mare with light brown markings—even his mental description of it demonstrated his ignorance. It was neither the biggest nor the sleekest nor the loveliest of the mounts paraded for his inspection, but when he rode it around the paddock into which it had been led, it snorted and whinnied softly to him and responded just as it ought to his somewhat inexpert handling. After he had put it through its paces, he smoothed a hand over its neck and it whinnied again.

"Yes, girl," he said. "I understand. You want to belong. It is what we all want."

"You are quite sure, Gil?" Harry asked after he had dismounted and announced his choice. He sounded a bit dubious. "I thought perhaps the black stallion . . ."

"An excellent pick," Gil said. "Just not mine. Why not buy it for yourself?"

"Ha," Harry said, but the single syllable sounded a bit wistful. "It feels like forever since I was last on a horse's back. But he *is* beautiful and almost certainly a prime goer."

"He would give you an increased incentive to get fit enough to ride," Gil said. He kept his eyes upon the white and brown mare, allowing Harry to think for himself, to make his own decision—about his recovery, about riding again. About the stallion.

They both purchased their horses, which were to be delivered to Hinsford within the week. By the time they arrived back at the inn, Miss Westcott was sitting in the private parlor, drinking a glass of lemonade.

"I have not ordered our luncheon," she told them, "even though it is rather late. I was not sure when you would be back. Were you successful, Lieutenant Colonel Bennington?"

"I was indeed," he told her. "So was Harry. The horses will be taken to Hinsford."

"Harry too?" She looked as if she was caught between pleased surprise and concern.

"I thought to see the parlor piled to the ceiling with all your purchases, Abby," he said, sinking into an armchair, resting his head against the back of it, and closing his eyes.

"Well, that was it, you see," she said, laughing. "There were too many to carry, and a few of them are quite bulky. I thought perhaps the carriage could stop outside the shop when we leave here and I can just run in and get them."

"I shall go and fetch them for you now if you will give me the direction," Gil offered.

"Oh, thank you," she said, flushing. "That is very good of you. But luncheon—"

"I for one could not eat a thing just yet," Harry said. "Give me a short time to rest while Gil goes for your things."

"Oh dear," she said. "I am afraid you would not have enough arms or hands, Lieutenant Colonel. You would need to be an octopus. In the coming weeks I expect to have some time on my hands for plying my needle, and I like some variety. I am afraid I got carried away somewhat and purchased enough to keep me occupied for a year. I was quite embarrassed when I saw the pile I had had the shopkeeper set aside for me. I shall come with you." She got to her feet and donned her bonnet and gloves.

Gil offered his arm when they stepped out of the inn. It was not something he would feel obliged to do in the country, but it seemed the gentlemanly thing to do on the streets of a market town. She hesitated a moment but then slipped her hand through his arm and he got a whiff of her scent. It was not a powerful perfume. Perhaps it was no more than the soap with which she had washed her face or her hair. It was delicate. And feminine—as was she.

"You did not try to discourage Harry from purchasing a horse of his own?" she asked him.

"It was not my place to do any such thing," he said. "Having a horse he wishes desperately to ride will spur him on—ah! Pun not intended. It will perhaps give him an extra incentive to regain his strength. Seeing me go out riding will make him even more determined."

"I constantly tell myself that I must not coddle him," she said, sounding a bit rueful. "Unfortunately my instinct urges me to do just that. But you are right, and I *will* curb the instinct. It is not easy, Lieutenant Colonel, to have a man one loves very dearly away at war, to have no news of him for weeks, sometimes months on end, and to await that news with trepidation, not knowing what it may be."

A man one loves very dearly. Caroline had not even awaited news of him after Waterloo. She had left for her house party, he had discovered afterward, at almost the exact time the battle was being fought.

It was as if Miss Westcott had read his thoughts again. "Who awaited news of you?" she asked. "Was your wife still alive when you were fighting? And who else?"

"No one," he said, speaking more harshly than he intended as he drew her to one side of the pavement to allow a woman with a laden basket over her arm to pass in the opposite direction. "My mother died when I was still in India. I suppose there are uncles and aunts and cousins galore not twenty miles from where I grew up. Perhaps even grandparents. I would not know. I never met them. They turned my mother off when it became obvious that she was expecting me. As for my father, I have never met him. I did not even know who he was until in a burst of paternal concern for my well-being he purchased my ensign's commission after he had learned of my mother's death and discovered my whereabouts. He also purchased my lieutenancy, after which I wrote to inform him that if he secured a captaincy for me it would be refused. I have not heard from him since. I doubt he sought news of me after the various battles and skirmishes of the wars."

Before he could fathom what the devil had prompted that outburst, she had stopped walking and so had he. Well, at least now she would know with whom she walked—and with whom she shared a house at Hinsford.

"I am sorry," she said, and she sounded as though she really was. Her head was tipped a little to one side, and her eyes were large and unblinking. "I can tell from your voice that you believe me to have been unpardonably inquisitive. You are right. I have been. Forgive me, if you please. This is the shop."

She signaled to the building beside them and turned to enter it. He followed her inside—and felt immediately like the proverbial bull in a china shop. There were several ladies fingering bolts of cloth or examining cards of lace or rummaging through bins of ribbons and buttons and other objects. The shopkeeper behind the counter was showing a length of velvet fabric to a buxom older lady and a thin young one. All of them abruptly stopped what they were doing—or so it seemed to Gil—to look at the new arrivals and then to gawk some more at him while he drew himself up to his full height, clasped his hands at his back, and tried to look at ease.

"Ah, Miss Westcott," the shopkeeper said. "You have come for your purchases, have you?"

"Yes, please," she said. "Lieutenant Colonel Bennington has kindly offered to help me carry them to the inn."

Everyone gawked a bit more and then returned to their former activities. The large lady at the counter shook her head in rejection of the velvet while her young companion looked relieved, and the shopkeeper abandoned them in order to titter and twitter her way to the back of the shop, where there was a mound of packages neatly wrapped and tied up with string.

Miss Westcott had not exaggerated. If all these were supplies for her needlework projects, she must be a prodigious needlewoman.

Caroline had despised embroidery—as well as watercolor painting and playing the pianoforte and letter writing and flower arranging and all the feminine accomplishments she complained her various governesses and finishing school teachers had tried to foist upon her, ruining her girlhood in the process. She did not intend to have her adulthood spoiled too, she had declared to him the very first time they met soon after she arrived in the Peninsula with her mother to spend some time with the general, her father. She intended to be *free*. She had plied a fan before her face as she said it and favored him with one of her brightest, most alluring smiles.

He ought to have known at that very moment that she was a woman to be avoided at all costs. That she was *trouble*, in other words. Instead he had been utterly dazzled, poor idiot that he had been, because the whole of her attention and the full force of that smile had been focused upon him. Gil Bennington, bastard son of a washerwoman.

"Right," he said now, looking at the bundles. "Which is the lightest of them?"

"Oh, that is easy," Miss Westcott said, pointing to a bulky, largish package. "That wool weighs almost nothing at all. It just takes up a lot of space."

"Perhaps you can carry that, then," he said. "I will manage the rest."

"Oh, I can take something else too," she said.

"I am sure you can," he said, turning his eyes upon her. "But you will not."

Their eyes tangled for a moment.

The shopkeeper tittered. "I can see it would be unwise to argue with an officer when he uses that tone of voice, dear Miss Westcott," she said.

What tone of voice?

For a moment he thought Miss Westcott was going to argue nonetheless, but she merely bent to pick up the wool. "Thank you," she said.

There was a large flat parcel, which apparently contained an embroidery frame, the sort that stood on the floor when unfolded. There was a smaller embroidery hoop, wrapped and stacked against the other. A long, heavier package, Gil was told, was full of sewing needles, crochet hooks, knitting needles, and scissors of various sizes and purposes. There was a heavyish bundle of linen cloth to be embroidered and another, softer package of embroidery silks and crochet thread. There was a second bundle of wool, wrapped separately from the larger one, which the shopkeeper had not wanted to make too unwieldy.

"Are you quite sure I cannot carry that too?" Miss Westcott asked as they stepped out of the shop.

"If I were to try releasing one thing," he told her, "I would probably drop the lot."

"I could not decide which embroidery frame I preferred," she explained as they walked. "So I purchased both."

"Yes," he said. "I had noticed."

She laughed suddenly and slowed her pace. "I doubt they have ever seen a man inside that shop before," she said.

"I believe it," he told her. "I can see why men do not take up knitting and such. They would never be able to pluck up the courage to go and get what they needed."

She laughed once more, and it occurred to him yet again that his first impression of her had been quite wrong. She was actually good-natured and not at all the pouty, wilting sort of female he had taken her for. He wished she were. Life would be easier.

"*Inquisitive* is sometimes a negative word," he said, referring back to what she had said before they entered the shop. "When coupled with *unpardonably* it very definitely is. Having told me how you waited in trepidation during the wars for news of Harry, it was perfectly natural and polite that you should then ask me who awaited word of me." She might as well know the whole of it. "I am the illegitimate son of a blacksmith's daughter, Miss Westcott. She kept her own body and soul together and mine after she had been banished from her home by taking in washing in a small village about twenty miles from her own.

I acquired what education I have in the village school and at the insistence of my mother. When my chance came to escape I took it without hesitation. By the time I was fourteen my mother had acquired a *friend* who did not appreciate me, just as I did not appreciate him. I took the king's shilling from a recruiting sergeant and left with him and a few other ragged recruits, and never looked back. Your family, I daresay, would have recoiled in horror if they had known all this while they were at Hinsford."

There was a longish pause. "I do not believe so," she said at last. "For one thing, you were a guest of Harry's. So were they. You were kind to him in Paris and in accompanying him home. You are his friend. For another thing, Harry too is illegitimate, thanks to a former head of the Westcott family—the son of my grandmother, the brother of my aunts as well as our father. Camille and I are illegitimate. And so, incidentally, is Joel Cunningham, Camille's husband, and their adopted children. I believe you misjudge my family. They are of high rank. Most of them are titled. And it may seem that they are high in the instep. In many ways they are. But their vision, never entirely narrow, has been broadened by the events of the past six years. And they love fiercely and well."

He was not sure she was right on all of that. There was a world of difference between his own birth and hers. She had a lady and a gentleman for parents. She had been brought up a lady, unaware of her illegitimacy. He had worn cast-off clothes and gone barefoot when he was not wearing ragged, ill-fitting shoes. She had enjoyed great privilege and the best education during her formative years, while he had been thin with semihunger and had learned his lessons from a vicar who was more well meaning than scholarly. She had enjoyed the respect of all who knew her. He had been despised by almost everyone and called names, the mildest of which was *bastard*. When Harry had joined the military, it had been as an officer, his commission having been purchased by his guardian. Gil had joined as cannon fodder.

But they were back at the inn, and he strode directly into the yard to deposit her packages in the carriage rather than carry them inside to the private parlor.

"I am not sure," he said, taking her bundle from her and loading it in with the rest, "whether the landlord will be prepared to serve us luncheon or if it must be tea. But whichever it is, I am ready for it."

"So am I," she said. "I am sorry for delaying you, Lieutenant Colonel."

"If you will recall," he said, "it was I who suggested going to fetch your packages."

"Then *you* should apologize for delaying *me*," she said, and smiled at him just a bit cheekily.

She had better not do too much of that, he thought as he indicated the side door into the inn and followed her toward it. It would not hurt to start finding her company tolerable, since they were stuck living in the same house for a while, but he certainly had no wish to start finding her attractive.

Only disaster lay along that road.

LIFE FELL INTO A NOT UNPLEASANT PATTERN DURING THE NEXT couple of weeks. Abigail went down to the kitchen each day to meet with the cook and plan the following day's meals. She joined Mrs. Sullivan in the latter's sitting room twice a week to discuss household matters. The table linens were growing thin with age and needed replacing. The upstairs chambermaid, married to one of the gardeners, had given her notice for a month hence since she was expecting her first child one month after that, and she would need to be replaced. The window curtains in the library were heavy and dark and made the room gloomy, a fact that had not escaped Harry's notice. Mrs. Sullivan was sure there was a lighter set in the attic, replaced during one of the brief extended periods the late earl had spent at Hinsford. He had disliked an excess of sunlight indoors. The two women went up to the attic to have a look.

Harry had dispensed with his morning sleep and was insisting that he should be woken during the afternoons after half an hour if he happened to nod off. More and more he did not sleep at all during the daytime, a fact that was helped along by the frequent arrival of visitors. He took a walk each day. Even on rainy days he went as far as the stables, especially after his horse was delivered. He even spent some time grooming it himself and promising it that he would ride soon.

It was going to be very soon, he told Abigail and Lieutenant Colonel Bennington at dinner one evening. He was sick of being a semi-invalid. He admitted he was irked to see his friend riding out without him—just as the lieutenant colonel had predicted.

Abigail entertained friends of her own at home and sometimes called upon them. She was soon knitting, embroidering, and crocheting to her heart's content. She was enjoying her newfound freedom to do whatever she wished without feeling obliged to do what would please her family. She felt contentedly at home at Hinsford. Even the presence here of Lieutenant Colonel Bennington was less annoying than she had expected it would be.

His story, briefly told, devoid of almost all detail, had nevertheless shocked her deeply. It was hard even to imagine the sort of poverty in which he had grown up and the humiliation he must have suffered as the bastard son of the village washerwoman. Yet his father was clearly a wealthy man.

She wondered if her family *would* have been a bit disapproving had they known more about him when they were here. There were surely limits to the open-mindedness they had learned in the past six years.

But how could Abigail resent his being here at Hinsford? He had no one. His mother, the only relative he had ever known, was dead. His wife was dead. It was no wonder he was such a self-contained, almost morose man. Abigail had suffered too, but in comparison with his, her own sufferings seemed trivial. From the first moment since the truth about her had come out she had been supported by a family's uncompromising love. She had a home to call her own. She had friends. And now she had a fortune far larger than her dowry would have been if she had married before her father died. It was a comfortable independence. More than comfortable, in fact.

Lieutenant Colonel Bennington spent time with Harry. He spent time alone too, out walking with his dog, riding his horse, grooming it in the stables. He spent time in the village, at the tavern, she suspected, though there was never the smell of liquor about him when he returned or any sign of inebriation. She guessed that he liked the company of other villagers and enjoyed listening to their stories. Perhaps he shared some of his own, though she somehow doubted it. Perhaps he just felt more comfortable with them than he did with her or even Harry.

He had not chopped wood since that first day. He did, however, help repair a leak in the roof above the tackle room. Abigail heard hammering coming from that direction when she was returning from the village one afternoon and was shocked to see him up on the roof. He had been bare to the waist again, hammering while one of the grooms was perched on the ladder propped against the gutter, presumably handing him the nails, and another stood on the ground below, his head tipped back to gaze upward. Abigail was thankful she was far enough away not to be noticed.

She noticed, though. How could she not? He looked as though he enjoyed physical exertion. There was an easy sort of grace about his body when it was hard at work.

Late on another morning she looked into the library to see if Harry wanted more coffee. She forgot her reason for being there, however, when she saw the lieutenant colonel up on a ladder by one of the tall windows.

"Whatever are you doing?" she asked, startled.

He looked down at her. "Taking down these curtains," he said. "They weigh a ton. Stand well back."

"But there are servants," she said.

"I had noticed," he told her. "There is also me."

"This was your idea, Abby?" Harry asked. He was standing at the foot of the ladder, supposedly to make sure it did not slip. "I must say it was an inspired one. These curtains are so heavy they will never pull back far enough to let in sufficient light. Besides which they are such a dark wine color they look black. When they are pulled across, it might as well be midnight even if it is actually noon on a sunny day."

"It was my idea," she admitted. "But I did not intend to give extra work to Lieutenant Colonel Bennington."

He was not bare chested this time. But he had removed both his coat and his waistcoat and had rolled up his shirtsleeves to the elbows. His grandfather had been a blacksmith, Abigail thought. He probably would have been one too if he had been born within wedlock. She could just picture him laboring at an anvil.

"This is not work if you listen to Gil," Harry said, chuckling. "It is just a little light morning exercise."

The curtains dropped to the floor a minute later, but the lieutenant colonel shooed Abigail away when she would have stepped forward to help fold them.

"They are far too bulky and heavy," he said as he came down the ladder, "not to mention dusty. I'll get the ones down from the other window and then fold them all and haul them up to the attic before putting the other set up."

Abigail would have gone away, but she wanted to watch. She went and fetched her crocheting—she was making a lacy shawl for her niece Winifred's fourteenth birthday, a garment she hoped would make the girl feel more grown up. And she watched the lieutenant colonel bring down the other set of curtains, fold them, and haul them all together out of the room. Shortly after, he climbed the ladder again and hung the beige brocaded curtains, which transformed the library into an attractive, light-filled room.

"Oh, thank you," she said when he was finished. "I am so sorry to have caused you so much trouble. But this room is far more pleasant now; I am grateful for your efforts."

His white shirt was streaked with dirt. So were his breeches. His hands looked grubby. A lock of dark hair had fallen across his forehead, as it often did. He was *not* a handsome man, she thought. Not in the way Alexander was, for example, or Marcel, even though her stepfather was in his forties. But Lieutenant Colonel Bennington was something just as appealing. Perhaps more so. He was *gorgeous*.

It was not something she conceded with any great delight. She was not looking for any sort of flirtation with him or anyone else. She was not interested in weaving any romantic or lascivious daydreams about him. She was prepared to accept him here; that was all. He was good for Harry, and really he did not interfere with her life in any way. He was quiet and courteous and absent much of the time. And he was always willing to make himself useful—to volunteer his services, in fact, since it would never occur to her to ask for his help.

She had learned on the way to the wool shop how alone he was in the world. Did that also mean he had no home of his own to go to? He had not told her where he had lived with his wife, if anywhere. Perhaps she had followed the drum with him. It was altogether possible—no, probable—that he had nowhere. It was also likely he had nothing apart from his officer's pay. Was that half pay now that he was not on active duty?

She tried not to think about him at all. Her pity was the very last thing he would want. And he seemed like the sort of man who could look after himself. But she knew what loneliness felt like even though she had never been physically alone. She knew what it felt like to be alone deep within herself. It could be frightening. Or it could lead one to make a friend of the aloneness and to be stronger and even happier as a result.

She sensed loneliness in Lieutenant Colonel Bennington. She did not know if it caused him pain. She really did not know him at all, in fact. He had allowed her a few brief, tantalizing glimpses into his life history, but otherwise he still presented the appearance of a shield, unknown and unknowable. She wondered how well Harry knew him but would not ask. It would seem somehow dishonorable to worm out of her brother what the lieutenant colonel chose not to tell her himself.

Later that week, she had a couple of letters in the morning's post, one from Marcel's great-aunt, and the other, a far fatter one, from Cousin Elizabeth, Lady Hodges. It was a beautiful day, far more like summer than late spring, and she had already had her meeting with the cook. She would take the letters with her out to the lake, she decided, and sit there basking in the sunshine for a while. The afternoon would be busy enough. The vicar's wife and a few other ladies were coming to tea. They wished to discuss with Abigail a church bazaar they were planning for later in the summer. Abigail suspected they were hoping to use the grounds of Hinsford for the event, as had happened a few times in the past when her mother was living here. She would be quite happy to agree if Harry had no objection.

She was sitting on her favorite flat slab of rock, conveniently positioned beneath a sheltering weeping willow, when she heard the telltale panting of an approaching dog. She was no longer even remotely afraid of Beauty and turned to greet her, but the presence of Beauty meant of course that Lieutenant Colonel Bennington was not far behind. Abigail pushed aside her feeling of annoyance, set her letters down on the rock, and looked up to smile politely at him.

He looked grim faced. More grim faced than usual, that was.

"I beg your pardon," he said abruptly. "If I had seen you before Beauty did, I would have stopped her from disturbing you. I see you have come here to read your letters."

He had had one too this morning.

"Did you see yours?" she asked him.

He stared back at her, his expression even grimmer, if that was possible.

"I saw it," he said.

Nine

He had seen it, seen that it was from his lawyer, grabbed it, and taken the stairs two at a time to read it in his room.

And then, having read the letter, he had come out walking, though at breakfast he had arranged to join Harry in a short while for a game of billiards. He would have gone riding if he could have been sure there would be no grooms in the stables. He did not want to have to encounter people. Besides, when he had left his room Beauty had come with him without waiting to be told she might. She had been whining almost soundlessly. He could not both ride *and* take Beauty. She was not fond of horses. She was especially not fond of *his* horse. There was a bit of jealousy at work, he suspected.

He had walked for what must have been an hour or more, striding along country lanes as though he were late for an appointment, trudging around the edges of cultivated fields and across open meadows, deliberately skirting about the edges of the village lest he be seen and hailed. Yet all that time he had been seeing nothing. He had forgotten to bring Beauty's leash, but today it did not matter. Today she did not dash off to make her own explorations or to try herding sheep that chose not to be herded. She stayed by his side, panting, occasionally glancing up at him, making that soft whining sound in her throat.

He had no consolation to offer her in exchange.

And then, back inside the park, while he strode past the lake, she left his side for the first time in order to go trotting off to some unknown destination. Unknown, that was, until, looking ahead to see if he could spot her, he saw Miss Westcott instead. He could see that she was seated on a flat rock under a weeping willow, where she had surely come for some privacy to read her own letters in peace. She no longer recoiled in terror at the sight of his dog. Indeed, she had already set aside the letter that was in her hand in order to pat Beauty's head and scratch behind her ear.

Beauty stood there accepting the petting, but without her usual silly look of bliss. Rather, she looked back at him with lolling tongue and pleading eyes. *Look whom I have found for you.* He had not wanted her to find anyone. He had wanted to be alone, and she had seemed to sense that ever since they left his room. Until now. It felt like betrayal. But it would have been impolite merely to whistle for her and walk on. It would have been equally discourteous to walk on without whistling. Miss Westcott had seen him, and she knew he had seen her.

Damnation!

He had not even begun to deal with the turmoil roiling about in his head. He had not even tried to quell the dizzying spin of emotions that were tumbling about in his mind and the rest of his body. He had not even known where he had gone or why he was making his way back to the house now. Habit, maybe? Because there was nowhere else to go? Because his room had a door that could be shut and locked, and perhaps mind and emotions could be marshaled into some sort of order in its small, private confines?

He approached Miss Westcott with reluctant feet and apologized for disturbing her. For he *had* disturbed her. Why else would she have brought her letters to such a secluded place if not to enjoy them uninterrupted? He had seen her when she picked them up from the tray in the hall. She had looked from one to the other of them, equally pleased to see both.

Then she asked her question—*Did you see yours?*

His letter, she meant.

"I saw it," he told her—and ought to have turned and walked away. It was probably what she expected him to do and what she *wanted* him to do. It was what *he* wanted to do, God help him. But Beauty, rigid in every limb, stood by the stone on which Miss Westcott sat and gave her opinion in that soft, distressed whine again. She was not ready to move on.

Look whom I have found for you.

And so, instead of murmuring some excuse or no excuse at all, calling his dog to heel, and moving on, he spoke again in a harsh voice he barely recognized as his own.

"All lawyers ought to be hanged, drawn, and quartered," he told Miss Westcott. A wonderful pleasantry to blurt out to a delicately nurtured female.

"Oh," she said, drawing her knees up before her on the stone and wrapping her arms about them. She was wearing one of her flimsy muslin dresses. She was not wearing a bonnet. She looked young and pretty and innocent, and he had avoided her as much as he decently could since he had inexplicably told her some facts about himself. He had assumed that was what she must want. He should leave her now to enjoy her letters.

"At the very least," he added. He turned to gaze out over the lake. There was not a ripple on its surface. He had not noticed that there was no wind today. He had not noticed how warm it was either, how blue the sky. How perfect the day if one was only in the right mood for it.

He heard her draw breath as though to say something. A few moments later he heard the indrawn breath again. And this time she did speak.

"Your letter was from a lawyer?" she asked.

"He came highly recommended," he told her, "with fees to match his reputation. He is also as slow as a lame tortoise. And he is useless."

"Oh," she said again. Perhaps she could not think of anything else to say. How could she? She did not know what the devil he was talking about.

He turned back to face her. The fronds of the willow did not entirely shade her. She sat in dancing, dappled sunlight. *Dancing?* There must be some small breeze, then. Beauty was still standing beside the rock, still tensely watching him. Finding herself observed, she whined again.

"He has failed in everything I set him to do," he said. "Even the most modest of those things. All he can report to me is that I am about to be charged with assault."

She did not even say *oh* this time. She gazed back at him, her teeth biting into her bottom lip.

"Assault?" she said at last.

He sighed and went to lean his back against a stout tree trunk, slightly behind her line of vision unless she turned her head. She did not turn it.

"I made a nuisance of myself after Waterloo," he told her. "I came home to find Caroline gone. My wife, that is. I did not know where to look for her. I tried her mother's house in Essex. I thought perhaps she had gone there. Her mother would not even receive me—Lady Pascoe, that is. She sent word down to me that Caroline was not there and that I was not welcome. It was only later, after I had talked to a few fellow drinkers at the inn where I had put up for the night, that I discovered a slightly different truth. Caroline was indeed not at her mother's house, but Katy was. I went storming—"

"Katy?" Miss Westcott turned her head to look at him. Beauty was seated beside the rock now, her back to the lake, her gaze steady upon him too.

"My daughter," he told her.

"Oh." The word made almost no sound. "You have a *daughter?*"

God, he was making a mess of this. He ought to have held his tongue. Why had he not?

"Caroline had taken her to her mother," he explained. "I went back to the house as soon as I could the following morning in a white fury. I was prepared to tear the house brick from brick. I demanded my child. I ordered that she be got ready to go home with me within the hour. I was her *father*, after all. She was my *baby*. I tried to force my way beyond the hallway, into which I had already stepped uninvited."

"But why," Miss Westcott asked, "was Lady Pascoe not delighted to see you? Why—"

"I thoroughly frightened all the servants," he said without answering her first question or allowing her to finish the second. "All the men came into the hall, presumably with the idea of chucking me out of there, but they kept their distance when they saw and heard me. I was ready to take them all on bare-handed, and I believe they concluded the odds were in my favor—as they were. But then Lady Pascoe came herself—she has courage, I will give her that—and told me that I would gain access to her granddaughter over her dead body. She stood at the bottom of the staircase as though daring me to do it. I could hear—" He paused for a long moment. "I could hear an infant crying upstairs. I left."

"But where was your wife?" Miss Westcott asked.

"Gone to a series of house parties," he said. "Soon to be dead. I was soon gone too. From there, from home, from England. I believe the general, Caroline's father, must have had something to do with my posting to St. Helena. Nobody else from my regiment was sent there. I wrote a letter from the island demanding that my daughter be returned to me the moment I came home. I wrote another after word reached me of Caroline's death, threatening dire consequences if they refused to give my daughter back to me when I returned. There was no reply to either letter. I wrote a third on the boat back and would have mailed it as soon as I set foot upon French soil. But— Well, someone in whom I confided during the voyage—he was a chaplain, though why I started talking to him I have no idea, just as I have no idea why I am telling you all this now. The chaplain advised me strongly not to send the letter but to hire a lawyer instead. He urged me to do the thing correctly and rationally and according to law. The law, after all, was—*is*—on my side. So I did. An agent of mine in London engaged a lawyer on my behalf. He is supposedly the best there is. My troubles were supposedly over. I knew they were not, of course. When he advised me to leave everything to him and to say nothing to anybody until he had the matter settled for me, I knew there was only trouble ahead."

"But surely," she said, "your mother- and father-in-law must realize that you were distraught when you came home after the Battle of Waterloo and discovered your wife and daughter missing. Surely they understand that you could have physically assaulted someone during that second visit—one of the servants or even Lady Pascoe herself—but chose not to. Surely they know that you could have forced your way upstairs and snatched your child away but did not do that because she was crying and you did not wish to frighten her further. What exactly is your lawyer trying to accomplish?"

"At the very least visitation rights," he said. "I need to see her. I *must* see her. At best full custody. She is my *daughter*, my *child*. I am her *father*. Indeed, mere visitation rights would be in no way adequate. It is *they* who need to negotiate visitation rights with *me*. And I would not be unreasonable. They are her grandparents, after all. I suppose they love her. I must believe that they do or go mad."

But he was not entirely ignorant on that score. Six months after he arrived on St. Helena he had received an unexpected letter that Katy's nurse, Mrs. Evans, had written him the day after he tried to force his way into the general's house to take back his child. She was the nurse he had hired after the baby's birth. Her letter had been sent to Rose Cottage and from there to his agent in London and from there to St. Helena. In the letter Mrs. Evans assured him that Katy was safe and well and that Lady Pascoe had an affection for her though she spent very little time in the nursery. Mrs. Evans knew very well that what her ladyship believed about the lieutenant colonel was untrue, but he must not despair. She, Katy's nurse, would lavish all the love of her heart upon his daughter until he could take her home to love himself. She hoped it would not be long. She had asked him please not to reply to her letter. He had not done so.

Caroline had not spent much time with their baby either. Apparently upper-class mothers did not. They had other, more important things to do with their time. And what were servants for? Yet—the Westcott family had spent a good deal of time with their children when they were here a few weeks ago.

Miss Westcott had turned her face away again. Her forehead was resting on her knees. Sunlight and shade danced over the delicate arch of her neck.

"I do beg your pardon," he said, pushing away from the tree. "I have not told these things to anyone before now except my lawyer—and that chaplain. Even Harry knows no more than that I was married and have a child who is staying with her grandparents until I feel ready to take her home. I suppose he believes I am still too battle weary to deal with the challenge of being a father on my own. You caught me at a raw moment, Miss Westcott. Or rather you were forced into encountering me at a raw moment. I had no business burdening you with my nightmare. I will not bother you again. In fact, I will not bother you at all for much longer. It is time I went home. Procrastination can be excused for only so long."

She lifted her head to look at him once more, a frown between her brows. Beauty was whining again.

"You have a home to go to, then?" Miss Westcott asked.

"Yes," he said. "I do."

She waited, perhaps for more detail, but he gave none. Rose Cottage was his private domain, his only real possession apart from Katy—and he never thought of her as a *possession*. Rose Cottage was his anchor, his own little piece of this earth. He was afraid to go there.

Afraid of finding a dead dream. He did not know what would be left to him if his dreams had died.

"Are you indeed being charged with assault?" she asked him. "Or are you merely being threatened?"

"Threatened," he said. "Just as we have threatened them with a charge of unlawful confinement of a minor child and the unlawful refusal to release her into her father's care."

Yes, it had become that ugly. And that ridiculous—a mouse squaring off against a lion. With him playing the part of mouse.

"But would you not be able to fight the charge against you?" she asked him. "Your behavior immediately after discovering that your wife had disappeared and your child was being withheld from you was probably unwise, but it was understandable. *I* understand it. You were distraught but not actually violent."

"I have spent the last twenty years killing more men than you can possibly imagine, Miss Westcott," he said, crossing his arms over his chest.

"That was in battle," she said. "Surely General Pascoe—is that the name of your father-in-law? Surely he more than anyone else understands the difference between a man's behavior in war and his behavior in his personal relationships."

"You forget, Miss Westcott," he said, "that I am a guttersnipe. And my looks are not exactly reassuring. I can only imagine what any judge looking at me and hearing about those visits I made and reading the letters I wrote would be prepared to believe."

"You were upset," she said, "because your child was being denied you. You did not actually do anything violent. Did you? Did you hit anyone? *Touch* anyone?"

"Not on that occasion," he said. "But I did slap Caroline and caused her to flee in terror when she believed I would be coming back home after Waterloo."

"Oh," she said, and turned her face sharply away again.

"Or so she told her mother," he added. "Whom would you believe in a court of law, Miss Westcott?"

He heard her sigh. She hid her face against her knees again.

"I really did not intend to spoil your quiet seclusion here," he said, taking a step away from the tree. "I trust your letters were happier ones than mine?"

"Yes," she said, her voice muffled against the fabric of her dress.

"Beauty," he called. But he did not have to order his dog to heel. She was already scrambling to her feet and coming toward him. She pushed her cold nose into his hand. Again there was that almost soundless whine. He let her lick his hand and turned to walk away.

"Lieutenant Colonel Bennington," Miss Westcott said.

He looked back at her. She had raised her head again.

"Stay at Hinsford," she said. "I daresay your lawyer is still negotiating with the general's lawyer. The threats from both sides were an opening gambit, I suppose?"

"It is what my lawyer assures me is happening," he said, "so that they can proceed to negotiate from a position of mutual strength. In my opinion he is an ass. Ah, the devil! Forgive me. For both words. I am more accustomed to conversing with men than with ladies."

She waved away his apology. "Give him time, then," she said, "unless he has informed you that there is nothing more he can do for you. But it does not sound as if he has said that. Stay here. Let the lawyers do their work and trust that yours really is the best."

Lieutenant Colonel Bennington must not despair, Grimes had assured him in this morning's letter, despite the assault charge that had been threatened. The lawyer had had his military record investigated and had found it impressive and impeccable. He advised patience. Such cases took time to resolve.

The eternal lawyerly answer.

And Miss Westcott's answer too. It was no answer at all.

But that was unfair. She had urged him to stay when she might just as easily have urged him to leave, knowing that trouble and scandal might be brewing and that her fragile reputation and Harry's might suffer as a result. She might have used this revelation of his as an excuse to be rid of a man she had learned recently was not a gentleman. Very far from it, in fact.

"I will leave you in peace," he said, having thoroughly disturbed her. "And I will think about staying longer."

But what he *did* think about on the way back to the house was the fact that he had unburdened himself to her. He had told her about Caroline's leaving him. He had told her about Katy, about his frantic, totally rash behavior when he had been refused admission to his mother-in-law's house even though his daughter was there. He had told her— Ah, he had told her about that worst of all moments in his life when he had heard his baby crying upstairs and had been unable to go to her without knocking Lady Pascoe out of his way. He had told Miss Westcott of his present predicament. Drop the claim, General and Lady Pascoe were warning him through that threatened criminal charge, or end up with a long jail term or a court-martial *and* a lengthy prison term, perhaps even a firing squad, for assaulting his wife and threatening his mother-in-law. The wife of a general, no less. That second charge was the more serious. A man, bizarrely, had the right to beat his own wife.

He had told Miss Westcott almost everything. A woman he scarcely knew and with whom he had never been comfortable. Yet, rather than shrink from him, she had urged him to stay. As though somehow she understood. *No one* could understand what it felt like . . . He had spent almost two years hearing a baby cry in his nightmares while he found it impossible to reach her.

His throat felt sore as well as his chest and he realized in some alarm—and no small embarrassment—that he was on the verge of tears. Beauty, trotting along at his side, was pushing her nose into his hand again.

Dogs, he had learned a number of times since Waterloo—*this* dog anyway—had an uncanny gift of empathy. It was as though they possessed more senses than people had. So much for the superiority of the human species.

Beauty was a gift given to him in the form of an ugly, scruffy, hungry puppy when the battle rage had scarcely seeped out of his blood and in England Caroline was fleeing after leaving their daughter and a false explanatory story about him with her mother.

He stepped out onto the lawn below the house and saw that Harry was on the terrace, walking from the direction of the stables.

"I have the best-groomed horse in England," he called out cheerfully.

"It is probably time you thought about riding him, then," Gil called back.

"I have been thinking of little else for the last two days," Harry said. "Were you afraid I would beat you at billiards, by the way?"

"Mortally," Gil told him.

IT WAS A LONG TIME BEFORE ABIGAIL LEFT HER REFUGE BENEATH the weeping willow. She rested her chin on her updrawn knees and gazed across the lake without really seeing anything. Her letters lay beside her, forgotten.

She never would have guessed after her first encounter with Lieutenant Colonel Bennington that he was a man of such complexities. A man so filled with pain. Her heart ached because he had entrusted her with the dark secrets he had kept from almost everyone else, even Harry. Why her? Just because she was here when he had needed to unburden himself? If he had not seen her, or rather if his dog had not led him to her, would he have gone home and told it all to Harry instead?

For some reason she could not explain to herself she doubted it.

Which meant—

What *did* it mean? Was there some sort of connection between them? But how could there be?

He had a daughter.

He was a father, denied access to his child. She had no children of her own, but even she could not imagine anything worse than being kept from one's own baby.

Her new knowledge added poignancy to the memories of him with the children of her own family. He had taken baby Sam from Camille one afternoon when she had needed two hands to retie the bow at the back of Alice's sash before the child tripped over it. Sam, half asleep after a recent feed, had gurgled up at him, and he had looked back at the baby with an expression that was not really a smile but . . . Well, it had seemed to Abigail that perhaps he was smiling inside.

Had his heart also been aching with the memory of holding his own baby and breaking at the knowledge that he might never do so again? It was a thought too hard to bear.

His daughter was in the care of her grandparents. And now there was an ugly legal custody battle looming. But surely a father had the right to custody of his child. There should be nothing to be settled. But he had behaved in a threatening manner when he was at the home of his parents-in-law. He had written threatening letters. Worst of all, perhaps, his wife had told her mother he had physically abused her. And he was a battle-hardened soldier of brutal looks and lowly origins. *Very* lowly. No, it was not going to be easy for him to win.

Katy.

He had called the child *Katy*.

She was a person. They were not fighting over an inanimate object. The lieutenant colonel had demonstrated his full awareness of that when he had left his mother-in-law's house without the child because he could hear her crying upstairs, perhaps with fright.

Perhaps his case was not utterly hopeless. His wife was dead, after all, and there was presumably no hard evidence beyond what she had told her mother that she had ever been slapped or otherwise violently used by her husband. Besides, he had had every right according to law to discipline his wife. The law sometimes needed a jolly good shaking in Abigail's opinion, but of course it had been written by *men*. What did she expect? That its decrees would be fair to women? But her thoughts were digressing. He had behaved badly to his mother-in-law and her servants when he went to fetch his daughter, but he had not actually struck or apparently even touched anyone. Yes, there seemed to be hope.

But none of any of that really mattered, she knew.

Power was what counted in this world. And money and influence, both of which were mere aspects of power. And the power in this situation was all on the side of the general and his wife. Powerlessness was Lieutenant Colonel Bennington's lot. And he clearly knew it. He had poured everything out to her this morning from a position of despair. He would not otherwise have confided in her of all people.

Where was his home? And *what* was his home? A hovel or a respectable house? It must surely be the latter if his wife and baby had lived there. But was it likely to be more than marginally respectable? How would he pay his lawyer? He had said the man was the best, and the best was expensive, especially when he worked—how had the lieutenant colonel phrased it?—at the speed of a lame tortoise. Would he have anything left with which to raise a child? An officer's pay was not very large, was it? And was he now living on half pay?

Oh, the odds were all against him even though he was Katy's father.

It was no wonder he was in despair.

And she was entirely helpless to offer any aid or solace. There was nothing she could do.

Except one thing, she thought as she got to her feet at last. As she shook out the skirt of her dress, picked up her letters, and began the walk back to the house, she knew what she could and had to do was make him more welcome here than she had done thus far. Not that she would be able to overdo the good cheer lest he feel uncomfortable rather than welcome. She must not make him feel that she pitied him—though she did. What she must do was make it easy for him to remain here as Harry's friend. She must see to the smooth running of the house in the meanwhile and remain in the background.

She must carry on as usual, in other words.

Oh, how helpless women were. All they could do was nurture those people within the small confines of their world. But who knew? Perhaps nurturing was ultimately as important as anything else. Look where the wars waged by men had got the world. Into ever more wars and conflicts—that was where.

The two lawyers, having flexed their muscles by making nasty threats against each other's respective clients, would now get down to some serious negotiating, the lieutenant colonel had said—*from a position of strength*. How utterly foolish. Where was the strength in threats that might have to be put into effect? Why not simply *talk*? There was a child involved, the whole of a child's future and happiness to be decided upon. Why were threats necessary?

All this was none of her business, she reminded herself as she made her way across the lawn toward the house.

Except that he had made it her business by talking to her. She wished he had not. She even felt a bit resentful . . . But no. That was not really true. She actually felt touched. Honored.

If only there were something she could *do*.

Ten

After the sunshine and heat of the morning it rained during the afternoon, typical of English weather. Gil had his game of billiards with Harry after all. Miss Westcott came to watch, bringing her knitting with her. She was making a coat, bonnet, booties, and blanket for her cousin Elizabeth's new baby, she explained when Harry asked.

It felt deceptively soothing to move about the table hitting balls, standing aside when it was Harry's turn, hearing the faint click of the knitting needles, the louder one of the cue hitting a ball, and the steady drumming of rain against the windows. There was almost no conversation as they all concentrated upon the task at hand.

Perhaps, Gil thought, he had overreacted to his letter. He had seen it as an announcement of utter failure and looming disaster. Perhaps indeed what he needed more than anything else was patience. After all, his legal case to take Katy back into his own care was a strong one. He was her father, and he had provided her with a home and financial support and had never deserted her.

He wished fervently that he had calmed down sufficiently during his walk this morning simply to nod pleasantly when he saw Miss Westcott at the lake and call his dog to heel.

Having poured out all or most of the sordid details to her, however, he now felt it necessary to recount them to Harry too—his host here at Hinsford and supposedly his closest friend. Unfortunately, he had always found sharing himself one of the most difficult things to do. After a friendless, solitary childhood, he had effectively shut the door between himself and everyone outside himself when he had lied about his age and gone off with a recruiting sergeant. He had locked and barred that door after he became a commissioned officer. Had he been afraid of being found? Or perhaps of being found *out*?

The best he could do now, he supposed, as before, was leave everything to his lawyer and do nothing to try to help his own case. But inaction was torture to him. To prove it, it seemed, he hit the ball much too hard, with disastrous results, and Harry laughed as he took his place at the table.

"We are not playing cricket, Gil," he said, and went on to take the game.

Gil won by three games to two. By then Harry was yawning and Miss Westcott, hearing him, put her knitting away in a brightly embroidered bag she had made since their visit to town. She got to her feet with the announcement that she would have tea fetched to the drawing room.

"I had better tell you, Harry," Gil said before she left, "what I told your sister this morning when Beauty discovered her refuge out at the lake. It is only fair you know too since there may be further developments while I am here. Indeed, you may decide that you wish me to leave, for it is remotely possible that I will be arrested and hauled away in chains."

"That is surely nonsense," Miss Westcott said. "But I do think it wise that you confide in Harry too, Lieutenant Colonel. I shall leave you."

"Well, this sounds intriguing," Harry said cheerfully as he put away his cue. "And I no longer feel like crawling off to bed."

And so Gil told him before they went together to the drawing room, where Miss Westcott was already pouring the tea. She gestured them toward the table upon which tea plates and napkins had been set out beside larger plates of scones and sliced seedcake. There were pots of strawberry preserves and clotted cream for the scones.

"I say," Harry said, taking a piece of cake, "I remember Lady Pascoe. A worse dragon you cannot imagine, Abby. Worse by far than General Pascoe, whose bark was always worse than his bite, I thought—though it was a pretty ferocious bark at that. It was clear to see who ruled that household. She ought to have been the general, by thunder. She would have had us all shaking in our boots in good earnest. She would have put the French to rout a few years before Wellington did it."

"Is she a kind grandmother, do you think?" Miss Westcott asked, and Gil, who had been about to help himself to a scone with cream changed his mind and merely accepted a cup of tea from her hand.

"She doted upon Caroline," he said. "She will surely see Katy as Caroline's child and will not punish her for also being mine." He did not mention the fact that she spent very little time with Katy—if what Mrs. Evans had written almost two years ago still held true.

"Lawyers can be the very devil," Harry said. "Mine used to bore me silly after my father died. He could prose on forever. And it was he who uncovered the truth about my father's two overlapping marriages. I daresay it needed uncovering, though. Poor Anna, living all those years in an orphanage, not even knowing her proper name. She went by the name of Anna Snow, when in reality she was Lady Anastasia Westcott. We were thunderstruck when we found out, were we not, Abby?"

"We were," she admitted. "And we behaved badly for a while, Harry, something I will always regret, for *none* of it was Anna's fault. But we have strayed from the topic of Lieutenant Colonel Bennington and his daughter. Is there any help we can offer beyond moral support? I keep thinking there must be something."

"I am really not asking for help," Gil said hastily. "This is my problem to deal with. I am only sorry you have to know anything at all about it. But Beauty discovered you under that willow tree this morning, Miss Westcott, just when I was feeling at my most frustrated after reading the letter from my lawyer. I must, of course, leave the matter in his hands, as I have been doing since my return from St. Helena, and trust that he knows what he is doing. It is not easy for a soldier to trust someone else to do what he yearns to do himself, preferably with his sword or his fists."

She was frowning, her own plate of food and cup of tea apparently forgotten on the table beside her. "You told me your lawyer claims to be negotiating from a position of strength," she said, "while the general's lawyer must be assuring his clients that he is doing exactly the same thing. There must be some way of tipping the scale in your favor, Lieutenant Colonel. There must be a way of making your case to take your daughter into your own care more convincing."

"Without the fists and the sword?" he asked.

"Forget fists and swords," she said. "They are not the answer to everything or even to very much. There has to be something else that does not involve violence."

Why was she so concerned? And why had Harry not ordered him to leave as soon as his story had been told? Perhaps he ought to take matters into his own hands, after all, and pack his bags.

"What you need, Gil," Harry said, frowning in thought, "is a wife. A mother for your daughter."

"Unfortunately," Gil said, "Caroline is dead."

"Well, of course she is," Harry said with a dismissive wave of one hand. "If she were not, we would not be having this discussion, would we? You would not even be here. You would be at home with her and your daughter. You need a *new* wife."

And somehow as he said it Gil found himself locking eyes with Miss Westcott. Her cheeks turned scarlet under his scrutiny as she looked sharply away and reached for her plate. What the devil? She did not think Harry was suggesting *her* for the role, did she? And she did not think he—

"Someone like Abby," Harry said, his voice cheerful again, totally unaware of the acute discomfort he had just caused his two companions. And he was not finished. "She would be ideal, in fact. She—"

"Harry!" she cried, her voice an agony of sound. "You are embarrassing Lieutenant Colonel Bennington horribly."

"Am I?" he said, and looked from one to the other of them. "But you look the more embarrassed of the two, Ab. My apologies to you both. That is what comes of thinking aloud. But you must confess a new marriage *would* be the ideal solution, though not necessarily with Abby. A judge would hardly withhold custody from both a father *and* a mother, would he? You need to meet someone, Gil. Soon. Is there anyone among our neighbors who has taken your fancy?"

Gil got to his feet though he had not touched his tea. "Absolutely no one, Harry," he said firmly. "And even if I had, how flattering would it be to the woman concerned if I asked her to marry me so that I could recover my daughter from the clutches of her evil grandparents? I am taking myself off to my room. I daresay Beauty is ready for another walk, rain or no rain."

He took the stairs two at a time again.

Beauty, who had been dozing on her pillow beside his bed, was indeed ready for a new adventure. She always was. She scrambled to her feet in her usual ungainly manner, shook herself, and trotted beside him down the stairs and out into the rain.

You need a new wife. Someone like Abby.

Good God!

Oh, devil take Harry and his unbridled tongue.

"DID I EMBARRASS YOU, AB?" HARRY ASKED AFTER THE DOOR closed behind his friend.

"Of course you did," Abigail said.

"I was thinking out loud," he told her.

"Sometimes," she said, "that is not a good habit to cultivate. Especially in the hearing of people likely to be horridly embarrassed." She sipped her tea, pulled a face when she discovered it to be cold, and set her cup back on its saucer.

"It seemed like a good idea at the time," he said. "Actually, Abby, it still does. Having a new wife would almost be bound to help Gil's cause."

"But *me?*" she said. "Are you out of your mind?"

"Possibly," he conceded. "I have spent a lot of time out of it during the past few years. Perhaps permanent damage has been done. But why *not* you?"

She stared at him, speechless.

"You are lonely," he continued. "I may not have spent a great deal of time with you in the past six years, Abby, but I still know you well enough to understand that. You were always far more quiet and reserved than Camille ever was when you were growing up, but at least you always knew your way forward. You would have made your come-out and you would have had dozens of suitors to choose among, and you would have chosen the one that best pleased you. By now you would be married and raising your children and living the life you had always expected and wanted."

"How do you know what I wanted?" she asked, frowning.

"You wanted what every girl wants," he said. "You are not going to deny it, are you? There is nothing wrong with wanting marriage and a family, Abby."

"I was blind," she said. "I was blinded by what was expected of me. So was Camille. She would have married Lord Uxbury. I probably would have ended up marrying someone similarly horrid."

"No, you would not," he said. "Cam was an idiot in those days. All that mattered to her was doing what society and her lady's upbringing expected of her in the hope that at last she would win our father's love. It never would have happened even if he had lived to be a hundred and even if she had wed one of the royal dukes. He cared for no one but himself. She is far better off now than she was then. She is *happy*, for God's sake. But you were always different. You would have chosen far more wisely than she did when she picked Uxbury. And you would have been contented forever after even if not wildly happy."

Abigail was surprised at how well Harry seemed to understand his sisters as they had been. She had not realized it at the time. He had been a careless young man, seemingly concerned only with sowing his own wild oats.

"Well, I am glad it did not happen," she said. "Glad for Camille and glad for myself. Glad for Mama too. I am not so sure about you. It must have been dreadful losing your title and your fortune as you did."

He shrugged. "I have managed. I have even managed to survive." He grinned.

"Harry," she said, frowning again, "I am not lonely. Or if I am, it is not a gnawing ache. Certainly not a raging pain. And I would rather be lonely than married to the wrong man. Or grabbing the first one that seems attainable. I might have done that twice over during the past couple of years at Redcliffe. I did not do it. I am not afraid to be single. There is some freedom in the single state."

"Not a great deal for a woman," he said bluntly. "What if I get married one of these days, eh? What will you do then? For my wife would be mistress of Hinsford, and I know you well enough to understand that you would feel more than a bit awkward about remaining here then even if both I and my wife urged you to stay. Where would you go?"

"I will decide that when the time comes," she told him. "*Are* you planning to marry?"

"Not in the foreseeable future," he said. "But I probably will one of these days. Could you not be happy with Gil, Abby? He is an excellent fellow. And I think he may be just the one for you."

"Oh," she said crossly. "When did you decide to become a matchmaker, Harry? I scarcely know Lieutenant Colonel Bennington. He scarcely knows me. And if you think we should suddenly decide to marry each other just so that he will have a better chance of recovering his daughter, then you must have windmills in your head."

"Not *just* because," he said. "Though it *would* surely give him a better chance. I had no idea until an hour or so ago, you know, that General Pascoe and his wife would not give the child up to him. I thought he just needed a bit of time first before he took on the responsibility. It is a monstrous thing."

"It is," she agreed. "But I am not going to marry him just *because* it is. And he is not going to marry me either just to give himself an advantage in a legal wrangle. As much as anything else, Harry, there are his birth and upbringing to consider. Can you just imagine how everyone would react if I announced my intention of marrying him? Even given the blot on *my* birth?"

"You mean Mama and the grandmothers and all the rest?" he said. "We have not discovered their breaking point yet, have we? They would not let us go even though we are bastards. They accepted Joel when Cam took it into her head to marry him. They have accepted her adopted children. They did not go into a collective swoon—at least, I did not hear that they did—when Cousin Elizabeth decided to marry a man almost ten years her junior. Maybe they do not have a breaking point. But even if they do, do you care, Abby?"

Did she? *Would* she? If she made a marriage so outrageously inappropriate that her family turned their backs on her? It would—

"It is a nonsense question," she said crossly. "I am not going to marry Lieutenant Colonel Bennington. He is not going to offer for me. But you have put us in a ghastly predicament, I would have you know. I am going to find it difficult to look him in the eye the next time I see him, and I daresay he will find it just as hard to look me in mine. You are a horrid man, Harry, just as you were a horrid boy."

He grinned at her and then yawned hugely.

"I am sorry to have upset you," he said. "I really am, Abby. But I still think—"

"Oh stop," she said irritably, getting to her feet and grabbing her knitting bag from beside her chair. "Go and have a sleep. Perhaps you will wake up with some sense restored to your brain."

All she got for a reply as she left the room was a chuckle followed by another yawn.

She hurried up to her room rather than go to one of the other day rooms and risk being walked in upon. The thing was that Harry's outrageous suggestion had made some sense. Having a wife probably *would* increase the lieutenant colonel's chances of getting his daughter back. But why oh why oh why had he decided to suggest her as a possible candidate? It was ghastly beyond belief. She *was* lonely, though she rarely admitted it to herself in such stark terms. But the idea of trying to alleviate it by marrying *him* rather than any other man she knew—either of the two who had hinted an interest in her during the last couple of years, for example—was . . . Well, it was preposterous. She felt quite uncomfortably breathless, and her knees felt weak.

She had a sudden and vivid memory of walking beside him to the needlework shop, her hand through his arm, every cell of her body aware of his tallness and overall largeness, of the hardness of the muscles in his arm, of the shaving soap or eau de cologne that he wore. Something distinctly masculine, whatever it was. The very idea of being *married* to him, of touches far more intimate than a hand through his arm, kisses, for example . . . Oh, it was a lowering admission to make even in the privacy of her own mind when she was twenty-four years old, but Abigail had never been kissed. She had never particularly wanted to be, not by any specific man anyway. What would it be like to be kissed by Lieutenant Colonel Bennington?

Oh, blast Harry and his bright ideas.

She closed the door of her room firmly behind her, set her workbag neatly in its place, and went into her dressing room to splash her face with cool water. Why could the mind not simply be shut down when one was mortified by the thoughts and images that were racing through it without a request for permission? How she hated Harry.

Sometimes he just blurted out whatever came into his head, without any consideration of the impact his words might be having upon his listeners.

However was she going to face Lieutenant Colonel Bennington again?

Well, there was only one answer to that question, she thought as she dried her face and hands with a towel. She must face him as soon as possible so that she would not give in to the temptation to hide forever.

She grabbed a shawl and drew it about her shoulders, leaving a fold to be drawn over her head, before going back downstairs and stepping outdoors. She stood on the top step and looked around. The rain seemed to have stopped, at least temporarily, though the clouds still hung ominously low. She was fortunate—though she did not *feel* fortunate. He was coming diagonally across the lawn toward the house, the shoulders of his coat and the brim of his hat looking damp, his boots liberally strewn with wet grass. A bedraggled-looking Beauty loped along at his side though she increased her pace when she spotted Abigail. He looked up, saw her, stopped a moment, his face looking a bit like granite, and then kept coming. It was too late now for either one of them to turn away.

"Beauty, sit," he called as soon as his dog reached the terrace, thus saving Abigail from being effusively greeted by a wet dog. He himself stopped a few feet farther back.

"I would disabuse you of any notion that I put Harry up to that," he said stiffly. "And I apologize for any embarrassment you may have suffered. The embarrassment I *know* you suffered, in fact. And for the insult. You must have been outraged and justifiably so."

"It must be wet among the trees," she said. "And there is no real shelter in that direction. The rain is going to come down again at any moment, I believe. There is a summerhouse the other way." She pointed to the east. "Have you seen it? It is lovely in midsummer, for it is shaded by trees on three sides and affords a lovely view over the village and the countryside beyond on the fourth side. It is also dry inside on a rainy day. There is a good path leading to it."

"I have seen it," he said. "I have even sat inside it a time or two. Are you wanting a word with me, Miss Westcott? I would have expected it to be the last thing you would desire."

"I thought perhaps we ought to talk," she said, "rather than tiptoe about each other for the next few days, either pretending that the other does not exist or else pretending that Harry did not say what he said. I could wring his neck."

"You would have to stand in line," he said grimly. "I was prepared to do the tiptoeing. But you are probably right. Let us go and talk, then. Good God!"

The exclamation was occasioned by Beauty's decision at the very moment when Abigail had started down the steps to shake herself dry. There was a considerable amount of her to shake.

"I was beyond range," she assured him not quite truthfully, laughing just a bit, when the dog had finished.

She led the way east along the terrace and around to the back of the house, where a graveled path had been made across the east lawn and through a grove of trees to the clearing beyond where the round wood and glass summerhouse stood. It was at the top of a gradual slope so that there was indeed a panoramic view to the south.

A low-backed, leather-cushioned bench was built around the inside wall. It was a private place to come with a book—or a companion with whom one wished to have an uninterrupted conversation. Although perhaps they would say no more to each other here than they could have said on the steps outside the house.

"It was unpardonable of Harry to say what he did," Abigail began when they had seated themselves, some distance between them. Beauty had settled on the floor for a nap in a shaft of what was bound to be very temporary sunshine. "But *have* you considered marrying again as a way of convincing a court to return your daughter to you?"

There was a lengthy silence. What he had or had not considered was, of course, none of her business. But he *had* confided in her this morning, quite unbidden, and he had repeated that confidence to Harry this afternoon. He could not expect them to remain mute and unconcerned.

"I did not have a happy marriage," he said curtly at last. "I am not likely to wish to repeat the experience."

Frankly, she was not surprised. He was a hard and dour man. And a very silent man most of the time. She did not envy any woman who chose to marry him. She knew nothing about his late wife, but .., Well, just that. She knew nothing.

"Is that perhaps an unreasonable attitude?" she asked. "My mother had a long and unhappy marriage—or supposed marriage—to my father, but she is extremely happy now with Marcel. My cousin Elizabeth had a miserable first marriage but is very happy in her second. Why would you assume that if you married again you would be as unhappy as you were the first time?"

Perhaps because it had been his fault. Perhaps because . . . *Had* he been rough or violent with his wife? Such men surely did not change.

"Why even talk of happiness or unhappiness," he asked her, "when, if I followed Harry's suggestion, my sole purpose in marrying a second time would be to get my daughter back? It would be insulting to the woman."

"Why?" she asked. "You would be choosing a mother for your daughter as well as a wife for yourself. Presumably just anyone would not do. You would choose with care. Where is the insult in that?"

"You are wrong in one assumption," he said. "I would be choosing *only* a mother for Katy. Or, rather, a woman upon whom a judge might look favorably as a mother. And what would happen if it did not work and I still lost custody of my child? I would be stuck with the wife and she would be stuck with me with no reason for being together except a nuptial service and a signature in a register that would bind us for life."

"That is a very despairing attitude," she told him.

"Or a realistic one," he said. "I have little to recommend me to a judge, Miss Westcott. I am fully aware of that."

He was right, she thought. However had he come to marry the daughter of a general, who also apparently had a title if his wife was *Lady* Pascoe? If it came to a matter of power and influence, as it well might, his position would be very weak indeed.

"What is your home like?" she asked.

He turned his head and looked narrow eyed at her. "It is called a cottage," he said. "Actually it is larger than the sort of home that description calls to mind. Yet it is not quite a manor, I suppose."

She was surprised. However had he acquired it? Had it come with his marriage? A wedding gift, perhaps, from her parents? It seemed unlikely. How did he maintain it? She waded all the way into impolite inquisitiveness.

"Do you have money?" she asked him.

The narrow-eyed look lasted longer this time, and she was very aware of his size, of his facial scar, of his masculinity. She was close to being suffocated by it, in fact. She ought to have opened a few of the windows before sitting down. She fully expected that he would rip up at her.

"I have money," he said softly. "Did you imagine I was still a penniless urchin?"

"I did not *imagine* anything," she said, feeling the heat in her cheeks. "I did not know. It is why I asked."

And then the ripping up came after all—in a quiet voice that was somehow worse than a bellow would have been.

"You did not explain," he said, "that you were inviting me here to interrogate me, Miss Westcott. I thought it was to clear the air after Harry invited us to marry each other. I feel as though I am being interviewed for employment. As your husband, perhaps."

She closed her eyes and swallowed. If her cheeks did not burst into flames, it would be very surprising.

"No," she said.

"What, then?" he asked her.

She opened her eyes and forced herself to look at him. As she expected, he was hard-jawed, cold-eyed, and very clearly angry despite the softness of his voice. Well, she was a bit angry too. How dare he accuse her of . . . *interviewing* him?

"I do not know," she said. "I wanted to clear the air. And perhaps help a bit. I seem to have made matters worse."

He got to his feet abruptly and went to stand close to the windows at the other side of the summerhouse, gazing out over the fields beyond the village. Beauty scrambled to a sitting position, her tail thumping the floor. The break in the clouds that had allowed that shaft of sunshine through had closed up again. It was raining lightly. Abigail could hear it drumming against the roof.

"I do not need help," he said, "though I must thank you for listening to my ravings this morning. And apologize for them. I do not need your well-meant offer of help, Miss Westcott. I will deal with this myself."

How? But she stopped herself from asking the question aloud.

There was a lengthy silence that Abigail did not know how to break. Nor could she think of a way of decently ending this tête-à-tête. He was standing tall, his hands clasped behind him, his booted feet slightly apart, and it seemed to her as though some of the air had been sucked from the summerhouse. She felt as though it were filled instead with his very masculine presence.

Whyever had she invited him here?

"Do you wonder why she married me?" he asked, as though he had heard her thoughts of a few minutes ago. "Me, a scarred and ugly gutter rat, when she was the lovely, pampered daughter of General Sir Edward Pascoe and could have had her pick of several dozen sons of lords?"

Ah, he was a baronet, then, the general. Abigail said nothing. She did not believe he expected an answer.

"She liked to be treated roughly—at certain times," he said. "It was why she married me, though I did not understand that at the time. She knew who I was and where I had come from. It excited her when it ought to have repelled her. My appearance excited her—big and rough and tough. The same for my reputation as an officer—and the fact that I had once been a sergeant. She did not want to be a lady, she told me. She was fresh out of school and bored with being genteel. She wanted to wallow in the muck and the gutter. With me."

Abigail sat very still, appalled. There was such a contrast between the softness of his voice and the viciousness of the words he was speaking.

He half turned and looked at her over his shoulder. His face was hard and harsh and a bit frightening. He did not look away. And she could not. She shook her head slightly.

"Do you tell me this," she asked him, "because you believe it is the way I see you? Rough and tough? Belonging in the muck and the gutter?"

He did not answer. He continued to look at her.

"If it is," she said, "I am insulted."

Still he said nothing, and she got to her feet, intending to leave. But she stood still instead, frowning at him. It was not a large summerhouse. There was no great distance between them. Beauty had moved away to lie down again beneath the bench.

"I am not . . . *titillated* by your humble roots, Lieutenant Colonel Bennington," she said. "Nor do I see you as defined by them. I am not excited by your size or the . . . harshness of your face or your scar. I am not your first wife."

His expression had changed only enough to accommodate a frown.

"Neither," she said, "am I applying for the position of second wife."

"I am sorry," he said, turning more fully to face her. And when she did not immediately reply, he said it again. "I am sorry."

"So am I," she said.

She took a step forward. She had intended to move toward the door, but the step had also taken her closer to him. And she stopped and looked up at him. She drew breath to say something but could not remember what it was, if she had ever known. She bit her lip instead, and when his hands cupped the tops of her arms and her shoulders, she took another step forward and he kissed her.

The shock of it robbed her of both breath and thought for a few moments. She had never been kissed before. She had never known quite what to expect. But not this, surely. Not from *him*, at least. He kissed softly, with slightly parted lips that moved over her own, enveloping them, warming them, tasting them while his hands held her shoulders, but not in a viselike grip. She might have moved away at any moment. But his hands held her firmly enough to keep her a little away from him. She felt his kiss with the whole of herself anyway. She felt it in every part of her being, a warmth, an aliveness, a yearning, a something else to which it was impossible to put a name.

By the time he released her she felt very close to tears.

His face still looked like granite.

She turned to the door and opened it.

"Beauty," she heard him say, "sit."

She made her way out of the summerhouse and back along the path toward the house in the drizzling rain.

It was not rain she felt on her cheeks, however. The moisture was too warm.

Eleven

Beauty, on her feet, tail waving, looked from the door to Gil. She whined once.

"Tell me," he said, addressing her, "that what just happened did not really happen."

She could offer him no such assurance.

"Could you not lie for once in your life?" he added.

Apparently not.

He sat down on the bench, set his elbows on his spread knees, and pushed his fingers into his hair. He rested his forehead against the heels of his hands. His dog sat at his feet and looked up at him, her head cocked slightly to one side.

What the devil . . . *What the devil* had that been about?

Had he just doubled the complications in his already complicated life?

"What *is* it about Abigail Westcott?" he asked aloud.

Beauty thumped her tail.

The first time, and the second time too, he had set eyes upon the woman he had disliked her intensely. She had symbolized for him all that he most detested about ladies—*ladies*, as opposed to *women*—dainty and delicate and vaporish, yet cold and haughty with a distinct air of entitlement. And despite the irregularities of her birth she was a lady. With a capital *L*. He had avoided her all he could during the week when her family was here and had been horribly dismayed when he discovered she was staying on after they left. Since then he had avoided her when he could and treated her with cool courtesy when he could not.

Yet he had told her more about himself than he had told anyone else in his life, even Caroline. Even his lawyer and that chaplain on the boat back to France. *She liked to be treated roughly—at certain times. She wanted to wallow in the muck and the gutter. With me.*

Good God! Had he really told her those things?

Abigail Westcott showed no sign of wanting any rough play. She had not even touched him when he had touched her. Even her lips had not pushed back against his, though they had softened and trembled slightly. He would wager a bundle that had been her first kiss.

She had not pulled away from him either. Or shown any sign of horror or revulsion. She had looked briefly into his face afterward and then left. She had even closed the door quietly behind her.

He raised his head and let his hands hang down between his knees. The clouds were breaking up again. The fields and hedges that stretched into the distance in a patchwork of greens and browns were dappled with sunshine and shade.

Damn Harry!

He had sat down earlier at the table in his room and written out a two-column list of all the points that would be in his favor and all those that would be in General and Lady Pascoe's favor if there were a court case to decide Katy's fate. He had omitted the possible criminal charges each might bring against the other, assuming they were just so much posturing on the part of the lawyers, a ploy to convince their respective clients that they were tough negotiators and worth every penny of their exorbitant fees. The only points he could think of for his column were the facts that he was her father, that he had a home to which to take her, and that he had the wherewithal to support her. Three points, reasonably solid. He did add after thinking about it that he had never deserted her or consented to have her taken to the home of her grandparents, but that sounded a bit whiny and he had crossed it through.

There were ten points in the general's column, all of them perfectly sound. But really the list was pointless. For everything boiled down to the fact that the general and his wife had birth and power and influence on their side while he had none of the three. Most telling of all, they had Katy. The power of possession.

He desperately needed something to help redress the imbalance. Would a wife do it? If he had the fatherhood, the home, the money, *and* the mother to offer in his effort to sway a judge—assuming that the matter went to court, that was—would he be granted custody? Or, even better, would Katy's grandparents cede the custody to him without out a battle if he married a wife of whom they must approve?

Someone like Abigail Westcott, who was the perfect lady? But no, she was not quite perfect, was she? Her birth was illegitimate. Besides, they were unlikely to approve of anyone who would be supplanting Caroline, their only child, upon whom they had doted.

It was hopeless. The whole damnable situation was hopeless.

Beauty scrambled to her feet and nudged at his hands with her cold, wet nose. He patted her head and straightened out her ears with his thumbs, even the one tip that would never stay straight.

"I am not *really* considering it, anyway, Beaut," he said. "And even if I were, *she* most certainly is not."

Beauty woofed.

What he should do now, Gil thought as he got to his feet to return to the house, and what he *must* do—no more procrastinating—was leave here. Go home. See what the house looked like after all this time. See what it *felt* like to be back there.

He would leave tomorrow or the next day at the latest.

At dinner that evening, however, Harry announced that he was ready to go riding.

"Do not say a word, Ab," he said, addressing his sister. "I will not be deterred."

"I had no intention of saying a word," she replied. "Or ten words. Or even a hundred. I know how pointless it would be. Besides, I did not stay here to fuss you, Harry."

"But I will need you to ride with me, Gil," Harry said with a rueful grin at his friend. "*Not* to hold my hand, but to stop any of the grooms from insisting upon doing so. I could not bear to have one of them riding along beside me like a dashed nursemaid, waiting for me to topple off. You can scrape up the pieces if I should do that."

"You would never be able to hold your head up again," Gil said. "Assuming you had a head left to hold up, that is. I will do my best to keep you in one piece *and* up in the saddle. No jumping of hedges or gates, though."

"Good Lord, no," Harry agreed. "Not for the first hour, anyway."

So, Gil thought, he was stuck here for at least a few more days, perhaps a week. Harry needed him.

IT WAS TWO DAYS LATER BEFORE HARRY ACTUALLY WENT FOR HIS first ride. It rained steadily for much of those two days, clearing up only late in the afternoon of the second day. On the third morning, however, the sun was beaming down from a clear blue sky with not a cloud in sight.

Abigail worried, of course. She worried that Harry was not strong enough to ride yet. She worried that the horse he had purchased was too powerful for him in his weakened state, though she knew that one of the grooms had been riding it, breaking it in so to speak, making sure the horse had no unexpected quirks that might be a danger to Harry, who had not ridden for almost two years. She worried that he would overtax his strength and ride too far.

She held her tongue, however.

She walked out to the stables with him and Lieutenant Colonel Bennington. She had not avoided the latter during the past two days. There would be too much awkwardness in the maneuvering doing that would have involved. But she *had* thought of going back to London. Except that she did not want to go. And why should she allow herself to be driven from her own home by a few impulsive words from Harry and a brief kiss from his friend?

She would *not* allow herself.

The horses were saddled and ready in the stable yard. Even so, both men checked everything for themselves. Lieutenant Colonel Bennington mounted and rode to the gateway where Abigail stood watching. He gazed down at her, and she raised her eyes unwillingly to his. He looked extremely powerful on horseback. Also grim. Always grim.

"He is ready for this," he told her quietly so that Harry would not hear.

"Yes," she said. "I am sure he is."

He was telling her, she realized, that he would look after Harry and make sure no harm came to him. He knew she was worrying though she had said nothing. These two men had ridden across Spain and Portugal together, she reminded herself, and across the Pyrenees into France. They had fought together in fierce and bloody battles and skirmishes she had known nothing about until months later. They had fought together at Waterloo. Of course he would watch out for Harry, just as Harry would watch out for him if the situation were reversed.

"Thank you," she added.

Harry rode up at that moment, looking slender and boyish and eager. Almost—ah, *almost* like his old self.

"You ought to come too, Abby," he said.

She had thought about it. "Not today," she said, smiling at him. "I have other things to do."

They both tipped their hats to her with their riding whips and rode off in the direction of the drive.

She spent the next hour in the morning room, writing letters to Camille and her mother, raising her head at the slightest sound to look through the window to see if they were returning. She looked up sharply when she heard at last the sound of horses' hooves clopping up the drive. They were back. She blotted her letter to her mother, cleaned her pen hastily, and hurried out to the stables to be there when they dismounted.

"Here we are, Abby," Harry called cheerfully. "Both of us in one piece. You need not have worried."

"Who said I was worried?" she retorted. "I had better things to do than worry about you. I have written to Camille and Mama."

"And that is why you are out here almost before us, I suppose?" he said as he dismounted.

He did not insist upon unsaddling his horse as Lieutenant Colonel Bennington was doing, she noticed. A groom was doing it for him.

"It felt good to ride again?" she asked.

"It is the best feeling in the world, Abby," he said. "You really ought to have come with us. Send my love to Mama, will you? You have not sealed the letter yet?"

"No," she said.

"Then if you mentioned that I had gone riding," he said, "add a postscript to assure her that Gil brought me home safely, not a scratch upon my person."

"I will," she said. "I am not spying upon you on Mama's behalf, you know, Harry. Or spying at all, in fact. But you cannot stop us from being *concerned*."

"I know." He grinned. "And I appreciate that you are. I am going to put my feet up for a while before luncheon. You do not need to walk me back to the house. Stay and have a word with Gil. I am sure you are itching to ask him how I *really* fared."

She was not itching for any such thing. But Lieutenant Colonel Bennington had heard, so she waited politely for him to be finished with what he was doing while Harry set out alone for the house.

"I steered him clear of all six-foot hedges," he told her when he joined her in the stable yard doorway a few minutes later. "It was a very sedate ride, Miss Westcott, and he was a bit frustrated by that very fact. He has always been a neck-or-nothing rider, as I daresay you know. But he has surmounted another hurdle in his recovery."

"I really did not need a full report," she said, flushing. "I do try not to fuss over him." He smelled of leather and horse, as Harry had. It was not an unpleasant smell. "It is just that . . . Well, we spent years worrying, as thousands of mothers and sisters and wives did, and then months on end preparing ourselves for what seemed his certain death. He is precious to us."

"He will do," he said. "He will do very well indeed. I have never known a tougher soldier than Harry Westcott."

She nodded and turned to make her way back to the house. She had never thought of Harry as tough when he was a boy or very young man. In many ways he seemed the same now as he had ever been. But he was not, was he? He had lived through six years that might have broken him or toughened him. Just as she had lived through the same years, grappling with them in her own way.

She hoped that Lieutenant Colonel Bennington would stay in the stables for a while after having a word with her. He had not been avoiding her during the last few days any more than she had avoided him, but he had not sought her company either. But he fell into step beside her now, a silent presence on her right side. She kept her hands clasped firmly at her waist while he held his behind his back. He was the one who broke the silence.

"I believe, Miss Westcott," he said, "I owe you an apology."

"Oh? For what?" she asked foolishly, turning her head to look up at him.

"For kissing you," he said. "It was unpardonable."

"Yet you ask my pardon?" she said.

"I do."

She wondered, as she had done surely a hundred times since it had happened, why he had done it. And why she had allowed it. *It was nothing*, she was on the verge of saying now. But it had been something. Of course it had. She had slept badly since. She had found herself reliving the kiss and feeling guilty about doing so. As though she sought some thrill in what had not been thrilling. Or ought not to have been.

"Then you have my forgiveness," she said.

"Thank you."

Had this not happened before? Ah yes, out in the woods when he had apologized for misleading her into thinking him a servant. And in the process of speaking to each other now, they had somehow stopped walking—in the gap between the stables and the house, the very place where she had stopped walking on that day she had watched him chopping wood. There was another pile of wood there now, she could see.

"When do you expect to hear from your lawyer again?" she asked. Silly question. It was only three days since he had received the last letter.

"I have no idea," he said. "This is an eternal waiting game, Miss Westcott. The sort of thing I am least suited for. But I will not wait him out here for much longer. I can promise you that. I will stay long enough to be sure that Harry feels perfectly comfortable in the saddle, perhaps another week, and then I will be off."

"To your home?" she asked.

"Yes," he said.

"Would you be thinking of leaving," she asked him, "if I were not here?" She could have bitten out her tongue, but the question had been asked.

There was a lengthy silence, during which time they stood where they were.

"The thing is," he said at last, "that procrastination can become a way of life. Waiting can become total inaction. I came here because I was needed—and because I could not bear the thought of going home alone. I have been here several weeks and will be needed for perhaps another one. Harry is growing stronger by the day. He will have you for company after I am gone and numerous friends and friendly neighbors close by. I would be deluding myself if I stayed here after next week because I thought my presence indispensable."

"Yes." She sighed. "Sometimes one does wonder if one lives quietly from choice or if in reality one is merely waiting for something that may never come."

She could almost read his thoughts. It was a woman's place to wait and a man's place to do. And why were they standing here? She had a letter to finish and a postscript to add. And what had made her suddenly fear that she was wasting her life? *Was* she at peace here? Or was she merely waiting endlessly?

"You could come with me," he said.

She whipped her head about to look up at him, her eyes wide. *"What?"*

"The devil!" he said. "What *is* it about you, Miss Westcott? We have already quite firmly agreed that Harry's suggestion was outrageous. Shall we—" He was gesturing ahead along the terrace.

"To your *home*?" she said. "As your *wife*?"

"At the risk of repeating myself rather too often," he said, "I beg to apologize."

"*Did* we agree?" she asked. They probably had. She could not remember. "It was not an *outrageous* suggestion."

"I am a guttersnipe," he said, and he turned his head to look about them. "Oh, for God's sake. We cannot stand here forever. Take a turn about the lawn with me."

But they went only partly across it before Abigail stopped again. "I cannot keep up with your pace," she said.

He stopped and took a step closer to her.

"*Guttersnipe* is merely a word," she said. "An ugly one I suppose you have decided to attach to yourself so that no one can hurt you by insulting your origins. You already accept the worst anyone can say about you. But what does it *mean*? That you grew up very poor in a household with only your mother? That you were rejected by all her family members you never knew and despised by all the so-called respectable folk among whom you lived? You learned to read and write, thanks, I daresay, to your mother and a vicar who did not turn you away from his school. You enlisted with a recruiting sergeant and made your way up through the ranks to become a sergeant yourself. After your father purchased a commission for you and then a promotion, you rose through your own efforts to the rank of captain, then major, and eventually lieutenant colonel. You must have worked hard to speak and behave like a gentleman in a gentlemen's army. You have a home that is larger than a cottage. You have money. Is it time, Lieutenant Colonel Bennington, to stop calling yourself a guttersnipe?"

"It is what I would be called—among other things—if I tried to marry a lady," he said.

"Is that what happened when you married the general's daughter?" she asked. "Was she of age? Why did he not stop you if he despised your origins so much?"

"She was increasing," he said.

"Oh." She could feel her cheeks grow hot.

"Forget I suggested you come with me when I leave here," he said. "I rescind the offer."

"*Was* it an offer?" she asked him. "Or merely a suggestion?"

"Forget it," he said, "whatever it was."

And they walked on, though she noticed that he shortened his stride to accommodate hers. She did not know where they were going. They were headed toward the trees, but he turned before they were among them, to walk along the bottom of the lawn in the direction of the place where they had had a picnic the day her family left.

It seemed he had no more to say.

"Who is your father?" she asked him.

She did not expect him to answer. He did not for a long while.

"Viscount Dirkson," he said curtly.

A *viscount*. She had not expected that. She had thought perhaps some wealthy farmer or businessman. The name sounded vaguely familiar, though she was sure she did not know the man. How could she? She had never mingled with the *ton*. He had been one of her father's crowd, perhaps? That would not be a strong recommendation.

"I know nothing more about him than his name," he said. "I did not know even that before he purchased my commission. My mother never spoke of him, even when I was at the stage of boyhood when I pestered her for information. I merely got cuffed about the ears for my pains. Later I did not want to know. And after I *did* know, I was neither interested in learning more nor desirous of taking advantage of his sudden wish to be my benefactor."

It was understandable, she supposed. Even commendable.

"Have you decided," he asked her as they turned just before reaching the drive to make their way up the lawn toward the house, "who you are?"

"Who . . . ?" She looked at him blankly.

"You told me once that if you ever married," he said, "it must be because of who you are rather than what. By *what* I took you to mean the illegitimate daughter of a former Earl of Riverdale. But when I asked what you meant by *who*, you said something like that being the key question. You also said that if you ever wed, you wanted both to marry and to be married. Meaning, I believe, that you wanted it to be a mutual choice and decision of both partners. You did not want to be the passive recipient of a wooing and a marriage proposal."

"Did I indeed say all that?" she asked him. "How embarrassing. It sounds as though I was barely coherent. At the picnic, was it, after everyone had left? But I believe you must have rightly interpreted what I was trying to say. I am not the illegitimate daughter of an earl. Or, rather, I am. But I am not defined by that identity. Or by the fact that I am a Westcott on my father's side and a Kingsley on my mother's. I am not defined by my education and upbringing. I would never be defined by the fact that I was someone's wife or someone's mother. Or by any other label."

"Who, then, are you?" he asked.

"The bottom fell out of my world six years ago, Lieutenant Colonel Bennington," she said. "That is a phrase often used carelessly to describe some minor upset. For me it felt frighteningly real. For a while I was careful to behave with quiet decorum as though by doing so I could hold my world together. In reality there was a yawning black hole inside me that stretched to infinity. I did not know who I was. I did not even know if I could lay claim to my last name—Westcott. My mother changed hers to Kingsley, but it had been her name before she married. It had never been my name. I survived by learning to embrace that black emptiness, and I discovered that actually it was an infinity of light and possibility. I learned that my real self is inner and infinite and indestructible and quite independent of circumstances or labels."

They stepped in silence onto the terrace a short distance from the front doors.

"I also learned," she added, "never to try to describe all that to anyone else lest they think me mad. I suppose *you* think me mad."

"I do not," he said. "I believe I even almost understand."

"Almost?"

He stopped walking and tapped his right temple with his forefinger. "Not here," he said. "It makes no sense at all here. But . . . yes, I understand. One is not defined by the circumstances of one's life even though they shape one's destiny and character and give one a place in the world. They shape how other people see one. Other people never see the real person."

"Ah," she said, smiling warmly at him and forgetting entirely for the moment that he was someone she found both unapproachable and strangely attractive. "I have always *longed* to meet someone who understands. And someone I can understand."

He gazed back at her with dark, inscrutable eyes and a bearing so military that he might almost have been on parade. And she wished the terrace could open up and swallow her. He could not possibly understand. She barely understood herself.

"I believe," she said, "that *if* your suggestion that I go with you was a firm invitation, and *if* I wanted to go, I would defy the whole world in order to do it. The world—the world of people and society, I mean—really means nothing to me any longer. But they are two very hypothetical *if*s, Lieutenant Colonel. Now, if Harry knows we are still out here, he will be thinking you are telling terrible tales about his physical weakness and his poor horsemanship."

They walked the short distance to the door without speaking.

"Damn Harry and his bright ideas," he said as they made their way up the steps.

Abigail blinked at his choice of language.

Twelve

Over the next week Miss Westcott was invited a few times to take tea with friends and neighbors. Once she was asked out to dine and was escorted home late in the evening by the husband of the friend who had invited her. Gil too went visiting a few times with Harry. It was clear to him that the family had been well liked when they lived here years ago. Their change in status appeared to have made little or no difference to the respect and affection in which they were held. The late Earl of Riverdale, on the other hand, had *not* been well liked, Gil understood. Neither had he spent much time at Hinsford.

Harry was getting noticeably stronger, and he seemed happy enough at least for now to be here at his old home. He was comfortable being waited upon by servants, most of whom were old retainers, with his personal needs served by an excellent valet, whom he had known all his life. He was surrounded by neighbors and old friends. He was beginning to take an active interest in the running of the home farm and in the life of the neighborhood.

Gil could see clearly that Harry no longer needed him. It was time to go. Especially as he had almost invited Abigail Westcott to go with him and she had almost accepted and it would be a disaster for both of them if that happened. How could he even be *thinking* of it—except that Harry had put the idea into his head, and hers too, and he could not seem to dislodge it. It was utter insanity and must be put to rout in the only truly decisive way. He must leave.

Then came another letter from his lawyer, a little more than a week after the first. Nothing more had been said about charging Lieutenant Colonel Bennington with assault, Grimes reported, and he had made no further threat about charging General Sir Edward and Lady Pascoe with unlawful confinement of Miss Katherine Bennington. The general's lawyer, on behalf of his clients, seemed rather to be pushing for an early court date in which a judge would decide the child's fate. Since they seemed determined to keep her and raise her themselves, it would appear they were confident of winning such a case without going the ugly length of charging the child's father with a crime.

In the final paragraph his lawyer had suggested that Lieutenant Colonel Bennington seriously consider making a bold move to improve his chances of winning the case. Had he thought of retiring from the military in order to demonstrate that he was ready to settle down and personally take on the raising of his child? And had he considered remarrying so that the child would have a mother to return home to as well as a father? Grimes respectfully recommended that he make both moves without delay.

Rather than going up to his room to read the letter as he had done the last time, Gil had chosen to read it at the breakfast table. Miss Westcott was there reading a letter of her own and Harry was glancing through a London paper that had been delivered with the mail.

"From your lawyer again?" Harry asked. He had closed the paper without Gil noticing him do it.

"Yes." He folded the letter and set it down beside his plate while Miss Westcott looked up. "It seems you have a lawyerly mind, Harry. Grimes suggests exactly what you recommended to me last week."

"That you marry Abby?" Harry said. "Intelligent man."

"Not Miss Westcott specifically," Gil said. "But he does advise me to retire from my military career and remarry if I am to hope that a judge will look favorably upon my bid to reclaim my daughter. God damn it, I—Oh, the devil. Pardon me, Miss Westcott. But it boils my blood to discover that I have to fight for my own child when I never consented to giving her into her grandparents' care. She had a perfectly decent nurse in my own home as well as several competent servants. She would have been safe and well cared for there even with Caroline gone. Does a father have no rights in this country? Must he—"

"There is no point in ripping up at Abby and me," Harry said, cutting him off. "We are already in your corner, Gil. The thing is, are you going to follow your lawyer's advice? Are you going to give up your commission?"

"I think I might," Gil said cautiously. "In fact, I most certainly will. I had been intending to go home within the next few days in any case. I need to be there, to settle, to have my own place of belonging again. I need to see that it is ready for Katy. I have already missed more than two years of her life. And it has been clear to me that I cannot pursue a military career *and* be a good father."

"There is no better feeling than that of being in your own home to stay," Harry said. "And are you going to marry Abby?"

"God damn it—"

"*Harry!*" They spoke simultaneously.

"Well?" Harry looked from one to the other of them. "*Are* you? Or let me put it another way. Abby, are you going to marry Gil?"

Instead of snapping out an angry denial, she drew a deep breath and released it on an audible sigh. Instead of speaking, she closed her eyes.

"I think, Harry," Gil said, scraping his chair along the floor with the backs of his knees as he got to his feet, "indeed, I *know*, there is much truth in that old saying that three is a crowd. This may not be my house, but I have been severely provoked. So has your sister." He pointed at the door of the breakfast parlor. "Out. As fast as your legs will take you."

Harry looked toward the sideboard as he stood. "I daresay that order includes servants too."

The butler made his stately way across the room and held the door open while Harry winked at Gil and waggled his eyebrows at his sister before stepping out of the room. The butler followed him out and shut the door firmly behind them.

"When he chooses to be," Miss Westcott said, "Harry is every bit as obnoxious as he used to be when he was a boy. More so. Oh, a hundred times more. I am so mortified I could . . . scream."

Fortunately she did not do so.

"Miss Westcott," Gil said, still on his feet, "*will* you marry me?"

"Oh." She set her letter down beside her plate, paused to line it up parallel with the edge of the table, and leaned back in her chair as though to put more distance between herself and him. "Has it really come to this, then?"

"I do not for the life of me know," he said. "*Has* it?"

"It would be madness," she said.

"It would," he agreed. He gripped the back of his chair and looked down at his own letter. "*Will* you?"

She did not answer for so long that he thought she might remain forever silent. And who could blame her? He stole a glance at her and saw that she was staring into space, a slight frown between her brows. It really would be madness. He took his cup and crossed to the sideboard to pour himself more coffee. Then he stood with his back against the sideboard, his cup cradled in hands turned suddenly cold. He heard the echo of her words—*Has it really come to this, then? It would be madness.* And "this," he realized, was one of those pivotal moments in life that would forever change it regardless of what they decided.

They were damned either way.

There was a bone-deep, well nigh debilitating fear just before a battle, something bordering upon panic. He would defy any military man, of whatever rank, to claim that he had never, not even once, considered running. Deserting. Some poor sods actually did it and found themselves tied to a whipping triangle for a lashing or even facing a hanging as a result. It was a fear that disappeared once the action started, to be replaced by the mad bloodlust that was sometimes called courage.

He felt a similar sort of fear now and could not understand why he had just poured himself more coffee. Just to warm his hands maybe? Or to enable him to put more distance between them? Would the fear disappear if she said yes? But to be replaced by what?

She was looking directly at him, he realized, and they locked eyes.

"I think we had better do it," she said.

"Why?" he asked, gripping his cup more tightly.

Unexpectedly she laughed. And good God she was pretty. He did not believe she was really amused, though.

"What would be in it for you?" he asked her. "It is perfectly obvious what would be in it for me."

She broke eye contact with him in order to look down at her plate. "I have been thinking since we spoke several days ago," she said. "I have been waiting for six years. Not entirely passively, it is true. I have spent the time . . . exploring who I am, deciding what I want of life and what I do not want. I have found myself glad that circumstances prevented me from moving blindly forward with the life I had been brought up from birth to expect. It was so mindless, that life, so devoid of any real understanding, of any real *choice*. But those expectations need to be replaced with something else, or I will live the rest of my life waiting for I know not what and trying to persuade myself that I am contented with the way things are."

"Is marriage to me that something else, then?" he asked.

Her eyes came back to his. "I do not know," she said. "But I do not suppose it is ever possible to be absolutely, perfectly sure of anything that is in the future, is it? One can only do what feels right."

He considered taking a drink of his coffee. But he could not be certain his hands would be steady.

"And the idea of marrying me feels right?" he asked.

"Nothing has before now, you see," she said. "And it is not just because I want to help you retrieve your daughter. That would feel— oh, like a good reason in a way, perhaps, but not the *right* reason. It is also because I want you."

Her cheeks flushed and her eyes returned to her letter while he froze.

I want you.

Just what Caroline had said every time they met, until they lay together against all his better instincts. But Miss Westcott was not Caroline. Not even close.

"Why?" he asked her.

"I do not know," she said again. "I mean, with my head I do not know. I cannot give a rational explanation. Even with my heart I do not know, for I do not believe I am in love with you. It is just that . . . I think you are worth knowing, though I cannot be sure. And I think I want to live with you, to *be* with you. I am sorry. This sounds like utter nonsense. Only I have never even been tempted to marry before, you see, and now I am, and I think I would be sorry if I convinced myself that marrying you would be madness and let you go. I think I would miss you after you were gone. I know I would. I think I would be unhappy."

Good God. He wanted to run a million miles. Desert the field.

"What if," he said, "when you get to know me, you discover that I am not at all what you want?" As Caroline had.

She laughed unexpectedly again and looked back at him. "I do not *know* what I want," she said. "I have no preconceived notion of what being married to you would be like. I am certainly not being blinded by romance. I can only feel that this is what I ought to do and what I want to do if I am given the opportunity. And it would seem that I am being given it."

I think I would miss you after you were gone. I think I would be unhappy. But she *had* also said her heart was not involved.

"I have killed many men, Miss Westcott," he said.

"Yes." She sighed. "I know. But you also saved an ugly puppy from starvation and allowed Robbie to spend hours with the dog in your room, your own private space, because you felt his need. You have been kind to Harry. I will not allow you always to see yourself in the darkest possible light."

"As a guttersnipe?" he said.

"Yes, that too," she said. "You did *not* grow up in the gutter. Your mother housed you and fed and clothed you. But even if you had, your basic human dignity would not be the less. Why should a king be of more value as a human being than a vagabond?"

"Those are revolutionary words," he said, "for a lady who grew up among the aristocracy."

"They are truths I have learned, or, rather, worked out for myself, during the past six years," she said.

He turned and set his cup, the coffee untouched, on the sideboard behind him. He folded his arms over his chest.

"Would you wish me to ride to London to speak with your mother and stepfather, then?" he asked.

"Oh no," she said sharply, her eyes widening. "No. You would find yourself surrounded by the whole Westcott family in no time at all, Lieutenant Colonel Bennington. They thrive upon crises."

"Gil," he said. "It is my name. Short for Gilbert, which I have never liked." Their marrying would be a family crisis, then, would it? But of course it would. For whether she liked the word or not, he would always be a guttersnipe.

"Gil," she said.

"Do you prefer Abigail or Abby?" he asked.

"Those close to me call me Abby," she told him.

"And am I to be close to you?" he asked.

"Yes." She frowned.

"Abby, then," he said. "You do not wish me to speak to anyone at all?"

"It is Harry rather than Marcel who is head of my particular family," she said. "Marcel has been very kind to me, but I never think of him as my stepfather and he has never called himself that or tried to exert any sort of fatherly authority over me. I do not need anyone's consent, of course. I am three years past my majority."

"I will, nevertheless, speak formally with Harry," he said.

"Is it real, then?" she asked meeting his eyes.

"I believe it is," he said, holding her gaze. "Abby, will you marry me?"

"Yes," she said, and without her looking away, her teeth sank into her lower lip.

He wondered what the devil he was doing—or, rather, what he had done. Was this all about Katy? It felt like more than that.

"How do you wish to proceed, then?" he asked. "With a planned wedding—with guests? Or with a quiet one by special license?"

"The wedding guests would all be my family and neighbors," she said. "It would not seem right. Besides, such a wedding would take time to plan. You do not have time to spare, do you? You need to be married as soon as possible."

Was it all about Katy, then? She had said that for her it was not. But for him? Did he have any feelings for Abby Westcott? Any expectation of being able to make her happy? He would be presenting her—he hoped—with a ready-made child. That was not necessarily a good thing for her. Was it? Another woman's child? But clearly she knew what she was getting into on that score.

"I shall go up to London for a license, then," he said. "Today. I ought to be back by tomorrow night or the day after tomorrow at the latest. I will have a word with the vicar before I go."

"Oh," she said. "It *is* real, then."

"Abby." He strode across to her side of the table and set one hand on the back of her chair, the other on the table beside her empty plate. "It is not too late now to change your mind. It will not be too late when I return. It will be too late only after the nuptial service and the signing of the register."

"Ah, but I do not want it to be unreal," she said, looking up at him.

She wanted him. She had said that. In a few days' time she would be his wife. He suddenly wondered how sweet making love to her would be. He would find out soon enough, he supposed.

He bent his head and kissed her, and she turned on her chair and raised her hands to his shoulders. Her mouth was soft and warm and sweet as it had been in the summerhouse, but this time she kissed him back, pushing her lips tentatively against his own and slightly parting her lips. A novice's kiss. He felt instant desire. He wondered how *passionate* coupling with her would be. Ladies were said not to favor passion. Caroline had been the exception to that rule, though he was not sure *passion* was quite the word to describe her preferences.

But he must not think of his first wife when he was about to wed a second.

She kept her hands on his shoulders after he had lifted his head from hers, and gazed into his eyes. He had not noticed fully before just how blue hers were.

"Take the carriage," she said. "It is too far to ride. You have not done a great deal of riding in your life, have you? You were not born in the saddle."

As gentlemen were? "It is that obvious, is it?" he said.

"No," she told him. "It was an educated guess. But your answer was a full confession." She smiled.

Not many people had smiled at him in the course of his life, he thought. It was rather a startling realization.

"I will take the carriage," he promised, "if Harry has no objection. Shall we go and find him?"

"Yes." She slid her hands from his shoulders and got to her feet, a little slip of a thing. Well, not so little, perhaps. She was of medium height, even a bit above it. But she was slender and delicate and . . .

And he wanted her too.

* * *

ABIGAIL DID NOT CHANGE HER MIND. SHE DID NOT PANIC OR FALL into the trap of questioning herself. She went quietly about her business, which consisted mainly of going through the linen cupboards with Mrs. Sullivan, a tedious but necessary job of sorting out which sheets were in perfectly good condition, which needed some mending, and which were fit for nothing more than to be cut up into cleaning rags. It was the perfect time to do it—rain fell outside almost from the moment she watched the carriage make its way down the drive, bearing Lieutenant Colonel Bennington—Gil—off to London. She hoped the roads were not so muddy that they would make travel hazardous.

She spent some time too at her needlework, more often than not her embroidery, which required the most concentration and artistry since she did not use a pattern but devised her own design as she went along. Beauty was usually at her feet, a disconsolate lump despite the fuss both Abigail and Harry made of her.

"She misses Gil," Harry said on the second evening, tickling the dog with the tip of his shoe.

"Yes, poor thing," his sister agreed.

"Do *you*, Ab?" Harry asked. "Miss him, I mean? I have been feeling a bit guilty, I must admit. Did I push you into something you would not have done unless I had? Did I rush you, since there does seem to be a bit of a hurry for him to get married? Did I do the wrong thing? I wish actually I had kept my mouth shut."

"Well, it is too late now," she said, reaching out to turn the candelabra on the table beside her so that the candlelight would shine more directly onto her embroidery. "But when have you known me to do anything, Harry, just because you told me to do it? Or because you tried to goad me into doing it?"

He thought for a few moments. "Never?" he suggested.

"Right first time," she said.

"You have no regrets, then?" he asked.

She sighed. "If I did," she said, "I would call the whole thing off, you know. No one is attempting to coerce me, least of all Gil."

"Well, that is a relief to know," he said. "I had a hard time sleeping last night. And you need not say it served me right. I know it."

"If I regret anything," she told him, "it is that there will be no one at our wedding except you. No family, I mean. They will not even *know*. Not even Mama and Camille. I suppose I could have written to them both and sworn them to secrecy. But then we would have had to wait for them to come, and there would be no one to come for Gil. And we would have to tell them the full truth about him and about my reason for marrying him in such a hurry. And they would try to talk me out of it."

"Do you think they would?" he asked.

"He grew up as the poorest of the poor, Harry," she said. "His mother raised him alone. She took in other people's washing in order to scrape together a living. He was reviled and bullied by other children and, I daresay, by adults too. He lied about his age in order to enlist with a recruiting sergeant. He became an officer only because his father, who had had *nothing* to do with Gil all his life, decided at last to do something magnanimous for his son. And now Gil's daughter has been taken by her grandparents, who argue that he is unfit to have her because he physically abused his wife and threatened violence to the grandmother and her servants. How do *you* think Mama and Camille would react? Not to mention Grandmama—*both* grandmamas—and Aunt Matilda and Alexander and Avery and all the rest of them?"

"I suppose if I did not know him already," Harry said, "I would be wanting to plant him a facer for so much as *looking* at you, Ab. And I would have you locked up in your room and fed bread and water for looking back."

"So," she said, "it is altogether wiser to wait and present them with a fait accompli."

He grimaced. "I do not envy you."

"No, I do not envy me either," she said, leaning back to notice in some surprise that she had just embroidered a large, cheerful daisy and that it was perfect as the centerpiece for the silken garden she was creating with her needle. "But will it work anyway, Harry? Will he get his child back once he can produce me as his wife? I am not necessarily the best choice, am I? I would expect General Sir Edward Pascoe and his wife *and* their lawyer to pounce with eager triumph upon the irregularity of my birth."

"You will just have to find a way of arguing back," he said. "You are, after all, Abby, the daughter of an aristocratic marriage everyone thought was regular for more than twenty years. Who was—or is—Gil's father?"

"Viscount Dirkson," she said. "Do you know him?"

"Oh hell," he said. "Pardon me for the language. Dirkson was one of Papa's set. He is notorious for every excess and debauchery you could name—or at least he used to be. I am six years out of date with *ton* goings-on. What do—"

But his next few words were drowned out and the rest of his sentence abandoned as Beauty scrambled to her feet, barking loudly. The dog dashed first to the window and then to the drawing room door, at which she pawed frantically as she continued to bark.

Above the noise she was making, Abigail could hear the unmistakable approach of horses and a carriage. At half past ten o'clock at night.

Beauty made another dash to the window and her head briefly disappeared beneath the curtains. They came billowing out into the room as she pulled her head free and galloped back to the door.

Abigail's stomach performed a great flip-flop as she threaded her needle through the cloth stretched over the embroidery frame, moved it aside, and got to her feet.

"Is he back home?" she asked as the dog turned to her, prancing excitedly and still barking her head off. "Let us go and meet him, then."

The dog bounded out as soon as she had opened the door. Almost before Abigail had got through it herself, she could hear Beauty in the hall below, barking at the front door. The butler was drawing back the bolts and opening the door as she came downstairs.

And there he was, looking large and commanding in a greatcoat and tall beaver hat, striding into the hall. Beauty, barking and whining and panting, planted her great front paws against his chest just below his shoulders and, instead of reprimanding her or pushing her down, he wrapped his arms around her and hugged her.

"Missed me, did you, girl?" he said. "I suppose you have been locked up the whole time in a small kennel in a dark room with one bare bone and half a bowl of water?"

Beauty woofed in ecstasy.

"It was one piece of dry bread actually," Abigail said, and his eyes came to her. "I was not expecting you until tomorrow."

He set Beauty's paws back on the floor and closed the distance between them, his right hand outstretched. He shook hands with her quite formally, his grip firm.

"But I want to get married tomorrow," he said. "Unless you have changed your mind, that is. If you have, please say so without apology. You are under no obligation to me."

"I have not changed my mind," she said. And the realization struck her rather like a thunderbolt that this time tomorrow she would be his wife. They would be embarking upon their wedding night. For the first time she felt a touch of panic. He was so very large and *dour*. She did not believe she had ever seen him smile.

"Very well," he said, and he looked beyond her toward the staircase, her hand still enclosed in his. "Are you up, Harry? Is it not long past your bedtime?"

"It is just as well I was not asleep," Harry said. "I would have had a rude awakening. Can you not train your dog to bark quietly, Gil?"

"I will leave that to Abby," Gil said, and released her hand as he returned his gaze to her. He patted his greatcoat close to his heart. "I have them here. The license and the ring. And I spoke to the Reverend

Jenkins just after I left here yesterday. He is free tomorrow morning and the day after. But I prefer tomorrow. Can you be ready?"

"Yes," she said. "Of course."

She remembered Camille and Joel's wedding in Bath Abbey and her mother and Marcel's in the church at Brambledean on Christmas Eve just as the first snow started to fall, the whole family in attendance. She remembered Alexander and Wren's wedding at St. George's on Hanover Square in London and Elizabeth and Colin's at the same venue. But she also remembered that when the family was busy planning a grand wedding for Anna and Avery, Avery had called upon Anna one morning and borne her off to a quiet church on a quiet street in London and married her with only his secretary and Cousin Elizabeth for witnesses. Elizabeth was fond of saying that it was one of the most romantic weddings she had ever attended. And there was probably no happier marriage than Anna and Avery's. At least it appeared happy to Abigail.

Anyway, it did not matter what sort of wedding anyone else had had.

Tomorrow was *her* wedding day. Hers and Gil's.

Thirteen

H arry, looking almost too exhausted to stand on his feet, had nevertheless turned into the authoritative head of the household and brother of the bride before he went to bed.

"It might not be a family wedding with a full complement of guests the two of you are having tomorrow," he had pronounced from the bottom stair, "but by thunder it is going to be done properly. It is going to be an occasion to remember."

One thing *being done properly* entailed for two military men, apparently, was wearing full regimentals. Gil hauled out his uniform, which he had not worn since leaving St. Helena, and discovered that his green coat was sadly soiled and badly creased—not to mention the rest of his gear. He took the coat downstairs before going to bed and stood outside the kitchen door in the darkness brushing it vigorously before sponging off those stubborn stains that refused to yield to the brush. He was caught in the act by the cook, who had not been in bed, she was quick to explain to him, but rather in conference with Mrs. Sullivan and the butler in the housekeeper's room.

"There are to be only two outside guests for luncheon tomorrow, according to Mr. Harry—*Major* Harry, that is," she said, "those two being the Reverend and Mrs. Jenkins. But the meal is to be a wedding breakfast, we have been informed, since Miss Abigail is to marry you in the morning and who am I to call it a havey-cavey business when her ladyship, Miss Abigail's mama, has not long returned to London with his lordship, the marquess, her husband, and all the rest of the family except Mr. and Mrs. Cunningham, who returned to Bath with *their* family and Mrs. Kingsley?"

Fortunately her monologue did not turn into an all-out scold, for she had spotted the coat Gil held in one hand and the brush in the other. What she noticed, with sharpened eyes and thinned lips, was the creases.

"That coat is in such a state I would be ashamed to let you be seen wearing it, Lieutenant Colonel," she informed him, "when you would be coming from this house, where we have maids who know how to use an iron and turn people out right and proper with not a crease or a wrinkle in sight. Give that here."

In vain did he protest that he would do it himself, as he was perfectly capable of doing, if she would just point him in the direction of an iron. He was asked, rhetorically, he guessed, if he supposed the irons would heat themselves, a question that was followed by a not particularly complimentary remark about men. While she spoke, the cook was kindling the fire in the stove from the embers and banging down upon it two hefty irons and dragging out the board from some inner sanctum. She clucked her tongue over a few faint stains that were quite indelible and had been on the coat for as long as Gil could remember. She went in search of cloths and cleaning potions and the Lord knew what else.

"You are not going to do it all yourself, are you, ma'am?" he asked her, seriously embarrassed. By now it must be perilously close to midnight.

"I am not dragging one of the maids out of her bed just because a *man* does not know how to treat his property with the proper respect," she said. "And what, Lieutenant Colonel? Do you think I am capable only of *cooking*?"

He wisely refrained from answering and watched meekly while those few faint indelible stains became delible, if there was such a word. The army wives who had used to clean his uniform very creditably would have been put to shame. He continued to watch while she ironed the coat. He dared not bring his boots down to brush and polish while she was busy or she would probably have insisted upon doing that job too. And he dared not prepare to polish the buttons on his coat . . .

"I'll get them buttons and them other taradiddles on the shoulders and cuffs shined up proper too," Cook said as she replaced one iron on the stove top and picked up the other. "It's a disgrace you would have been to this house and yourself and Miss Abigail, Lieutenant Colonel, if I had not happened to be up late on account of your wedding breakfast. All spots and creases."

"Yes, ma'am," he said, standing in the middle of her kitchen, his feet apart, his hands clasped behind his back. She could not see his grin. She reminded him a great deal of those camp followers, who had bossed and sassed and coddled the men—husbands, lovers, officers, grizzled old veterans, new recruits, and all the rest of them alike.

"And you needn't just stand there pretending like you are doing something," she said without looking around at him. "You can get yourself out of my way and off to your bed for your sleep. And if you don't look after Miss Abigail proper, you will have me to answer to next time you come here, lieutenant colonel or no lieutenant colonel."

"Yes, ma'am," he said. "Good night, ma'am, and thank you."

His coat and the shirt—fortunately clean—and other items of his uniform that he had set out ready in his dressing room before lying down were all hanging up when he went in there early the next morning to get his boots, which he planned to take out to the stables to clean. All—not just the coat—were freshly cleaned and ironed. Even his shako, set neatly on a side table, had been brushed and cleaned and its metalwork polished to a high gleam. And—the devil!—his boots, placed neatly side by side beneath the hanging clothes, were spotless and defied their advanced age by being so shiny he could almost see his image in them.

Good God, he must have been deeply asleep not to have heard all the nighttime traffic.

Only his sword had escaped attention, for which fact he was profoundly grateful. It had been generally known within the regiment that no one—and that meant *no one*—touched Lieutenant Colonel Bennington's sword unless he wanted his ears blistered. He bore it off now to the stables to put a fresh edge on the blade and to oil it and shine both it and the scabbard until they met his exacting standard. More exacting than usual this morning. It was his wedding day.

He had not allowed himself to think too deeply about that fact. It was a mental discipline he had acquired during the war years and had stood him in good stead. Never borrow trouble from the future and never lament the past unless there was something one could do to fix its effects. The present offered quite enough with which to occupy oneself. It was not a simple system, of course. One could not, by a mere effort of will, eliminate the past and ignore the future. There was that prebattle terror, for example, which he had never been able to avoid.

And now, suddenly, there were prenuptial nerves. And second and seventeenth thoughts. And the terrible clutch of fear at his stomach that he was possibly putting himself through all this for nothing. He might never see Katy again. And if he was putting himself through it for nothing, what did that say of what he was doing to Abby?

And *this* was the very reason one needed to stop letting one's thoughts roam where they would. Roaming thoughts were a menace. They were forever trying to destroy or at the least annoy their host.

When he was dressed, unaided, despite Harry's offer to send his valet to him, he looked at himself in the full-length pier glass in the dressing room and was satisfied that he would be making an appearance that would be respectful to both his bride and the occasion. Women, he believed, set great store by weddings. For a moment his mind touched upon the farce of his first wedding, which Lady Pascoe had insisted upon making into a grand regimental affair so that no one would suspect that it was a *forced* wedding, but he pushed the memory aside.

Of course, he still looked like a savage beast, which he had been called on more than one occasion, not always as an insult. But Abby had not been blindfolded when she agreed to marry him.

Good God, he could still not understand why she had done it.

Harry had insisted that his breakfast be sent up to him since it was imperative that he not see the bride until she joined him in church. So, after he was dressed, far too early, he had nothing to do but pace his room like a caged animal. He was to ride to church in the carriage. He had protested that it would look a bit ridiculous when the walk to the village and the church was not a long one and the day was fine after the rain of the last few days, but Harry had been adamant. Gil was *not* going to arrive at the church in mud-spattered boots and frightening the villagers by looking as though he were marching to battle.

So he rode to the village in the ancient carriage, which had been ruthlessly cleaned and polished after its muddy return from London last evening, and stepped inside the church, which had been starting to look familiar to him. It did not look so familiar this morning, however. The altar and the wall sconces were overflowing with flowers, and fresh candles burned everywhere except on the altar, where new tapers were nevertheless ready. It looked also as if the pews had been polished and the floors swept and mopped. The old church smell, which he rather liked, had been overlaid by the mingled perfumes of flowers and polish and wax candles.

The vicar's wife—she was to be the second witness to the wedding, with Harry—dressed surely in her Sunday best, was moving one of the vases on the altar to a position half an inch to the right of where it had been. She turned to smile at Gil and scurry to her seat in the second row of pews, as though the service were about to begin.

The vicar came bustling out of the vestry, his face wreathed in smiles, his hand outstretched for Gil's.

"This is a joyous occasion, Lieutenant Colonel Bennington," he said. "A wedding is always joyous even when the couple chooses to celebrate it quietly, without any noise or fuss."

"It looks as if *someone* has certainly been fussing," Gil said, looking about the church.

"Well," the vicar said, "Mrs. Jenkins has always been particularly fond of Miss Abigail. And of Miss Camille too—now Mrs. Cunningham—and Mr. Harry. *Major* Harry, that is. And since their dear mother is not here to fuss over Miss Abigail herself, then Mrs. Jenkins insisted upon doing it in her place, at least in her own little domain here at the church."

"Everything looks and smells wonderfully festive," Gil said, raising his voice so that Mrs. Jenkins would hear him too. "Thank you, ma'am."

Everything also felt suddenly very real indeed.

And so he awaited his bride. And his future—which he tried not to think of. Today, this moment was what mattered now.

He was about to deprive Abigail Westcott of her freedom, he thought as he studied, without really seeing it, the stained-glass window that pictured Jesus surrounded by little children. She had waited patiently for six years to use that freedom in the pursuit of a life that would bring her fulfillment and happiness. And now she had chosen to gift him with it.

He contemplated the vast responsibility he was about to take on.

After a few minutes he glanced down at his boots to make sure they had not acquired even a speck of mud in his progress along the church path. He checked the positioning of his sword at his side, adjusted his red sash, and glanced at the church door. He thought fancifully that perhaps it would never open again. But then he heard the approach of a carriage and was aware of it stopping at the church gate. He took his place before the front pew while the vicar, now in his full vestments, lit the candles on the altar and made his way along the short aisle to the church door to greet the bride.

Gil was suddenly glad that Harry had played the autocratic family head and insisted upon formality even in so small a wedding. Gil had pictured the three of them walking to church and making their way together to the altar rail, where he would present his license and he and Abby would be married, sign the register, and walk back to the house, all within half an hour or so. It was the sort of wedding Abby had chosen and he had wanted. But every bride, he believed, and yes, perhaps every bridegroom too, needed some sort of ceremony, something to set their wedding day apart from all other days. Some sense that a momentous milestone had been reached and then passed.

His bride stepped inside the church with her brother and Gil felt his mouth turn dry.

AFTER HARRY HAD DECIDED LAST NIGHT THAT HIS SISTER WAS not just going to wander off to church in the morning to be married, but that she was, by thunder—*his* words—going to have a *wedding*, guests or no guests, Abigail had abandoned her plan to wear her favorite blue day dress for the occasion. Instead she had hauled out from the back of her wardrobe the sprigged muslin dress that hung there a little separate from all the other garments so that it would not crease though it was seldom worn. She was not sure why she had even brought it with her from London. She had had it forever and a day, but she had worn it no more than half a dozen times. She had worn it first to Camille and Joel's wedding in Bath—oh, goodness, five years ago. She had worn it last a few months ago to the large neighborhood party her mother had organized for the eightieth birthday of the Dowager Marchioness of Dorchester. It was delicate and pretty and always semifashionable because it had never been ultrafashionable. It was not quite formal enough to be an evening dress, but it was more than just a day dress. She had always loved it.

Now it would be her wedding dress.

It would have been far too fancy for a stroll into the village, but she would not be strolling anywhere on her wedding day, it seemed. Harry had insisted that she would travel to church in the carriage with him. *Not* with Gil too. He would go ahead of them, because a bridegroom was not supposed to set eyes upon his bride on their wedding day until they met in church. But, absurdity upon absurdity, he had insisted that Gil go to church in the carriage too lest he muddy his boots, which was altogether possible after the rain of the last few days.

Now, early in the morning, Abigail had discovered that her straw bonnet, the one she most wanted to wear, was far too plain for this particular dress and for the occasion. After a few moments of near panic—what *would* she wear on her head?—she had the idea of decorating the brim with live flowers instead of the modest cluster of silk ones that adorned it now. She donned her dressing gown over her nightgown and ran down the back stairs in order to take a shortcut through the kitchen to the garden at the back where the flowers for the house were grown in neat, colorful rows alongside the vegetables.

She did not escape notice as she had hoped to do, however. Even before she reached the back door the cook had hailed her, and the two kitchen maids with her gawked. She should have gone around the outside of the house, Abigail thought, but then she would have felt obliged to get dressed first, and she might have risked being seen by her bridegroom and forever dooming her marriage to whatever ghastly fate lay in store for such unfortunate couples.

"I just need to cut a few flowers to trim my bonnet," she explained, holding it up, though why she had brought it down with her she did not know, since she would need both hands to cut and carry the flowers. "I thought it would look prettier. For a wedding, that is."

The cook was standing over a large earthenware bowl, almost up to her elbows in dough, but she clucked her tongue and gestured quite eloquently with her elbows.

"Are your hands clean, girl?" she asked one of the maids. "They are? Take that there bonnet from Miss Abigail, then, and bring it into Mrs. Sullivan's room. Then go out and cut a nice lot of flowers. Take the basket with you." She turned her attention to the other maid as the bonnet was whisked from Abigail's hand without a request for permission. "Carry Miss Abigail's breakfast tray up to her room and then come right back down to take over from me here. I will join Mrs. Sullivan as soon as I have scrubbed up. Between us we will have the best wedding bonnet ever seen on a bride's head. Miss Abigail, you go back up to your room right now, and I do not want to see hide nor hair of you again until you come down to go to church with Mr. Harry— *Major* Harry. Your bonnet will be brought up to you when it is ready."

Abigail felt like a little girl having her hand slapped for trying to take a newly baked biscuit off the cooling tray and then finding herself seated at the table, swaddled in a napkin tucked beneath her chin, and two already-cooled biscuits on a plate before her.

"Oh dear," she said. "I have made a nuisance of myself when I can see you are busy. I could very easily—"

"Are you planning to send roots down into the floor, girl?" the cook said to the maid who held the breakfast tray. "Off with you now. And, Miss Abigail, out of my kitchen. I have a wedding breakfast to prepare and a wedding bonnet to trim."

And the thing was that Abigail went, as meekly as that child she used to be would have done.

Long before Harry came for her she was wearing her dress and the pearl necklace Marcel had given her for her twenty-first birthday. *Real* pearls, he had assured her with a grin, referring to the large, vulgar and very fake ones Mama had worn to their wedding. Apparently he had bought them for her as a sort of joke at a village fair the day they met. Abigail added her pearl earbobs after styling her hair in a simple knot and coaxing a few tendrils to wave over her ears and neck.

And then her bonnet arrived in the hands of one of the maids, who carried it rather as though it were a bowl full of some precious liquid in danger of spilling over. She was smiling broadly.

"It is that pretty, Miss Abigail," she said. "Cook says it is her masterpiece, and Mrs. Sullivan says no one will mistake you for anything but a bride. She says I am to put it on for you so that none of the flowers get squashed and so that it sits just so. Oh, Miss Abigail, you look pretty, if you don't mind me saying so."

Abigail had planned a discreet border of small flowers about the seam where the crown met the brim. Something delicately pretty and just a bit festive. This looked more like a lavish bowl of flowers—mostly varicolored sweet peas—in glorious bloom. The straw hat itself was almost invisible, except the top of the crown and the edge of the brim. The ribbons had been changed from pale blue to bright pink, and where they were attached to the bonnet they had been formed into elaborate rosettes.

"Well," she said, swallowing her dismay, "let us see what it looks like on my head, shall we?"

Was it possible to postpone her wedding? *Cancel* it?

But after she had sat down on the bench in her dressing room, her back to the mirror, and the maid, anxious and frowning, had placed the bonnet on her head and repositioned it three separate times and then tied the ribbons close to her left ear and fluffed out the bow before standing back and smiling again—after all that Abigail turned half fearfully to look at her image in the mirror and . . .

"Oh," she said, "it *is* pretty."

"I should dashed well say it is," Harry said from the doorway. "Stand up and let me have a good look at you, Abby. I say, you look as fine as fivepence."

The maid curtsied and disappeared, and Abigail took a good look at her brother. He had definitely put on some weight. Not a great deal, but enough that he had lost that gray, gaunt look he had had when he came home. He was tall and lean and handsome in his green regimentals, which were a bit shabby, perhaps, but perfectly clean and well pressed. He looked like a warrior who had seen battle, and that was exactly what he was.

"Do I?" she asked him. "I do not look a bit . . . ridiculous, considering the fact that there will be no guests?"

Not even Mama.

Or Camille.

For a moment her stomach threatened to turn bilious.

His eyes searched hers. "I would think, Abby," he said, "that on a person's wedding day there is only one other person who matters. At least, that is what I would expect of *my* wedding day. Gil will be there, will he not?"

"Oh goodness," she said, and laughed. "I hope so."

"Well," he said, "he went off in the carriage twenty minutes ago, and it has returned empty and is ready at the door for us. So I assume he is waiting for you in church and has not run off on foot."

"Oh, Harry," she said, "you look very handsome."

"No. Do I?" he asked her, grinning. "Not the pale cadaver you ran from the day you arrived here?"

"And when I ran," she said, "the first person I saw was Gil, stripped to the waist and chopping wood. I mistook him for a servant, scolded him for his state of undress, and threatened to report him to you."

"Good God," he said. "I'll wager you were mortified when you discovered the truth. You have no second thoughts, Abby? You are sure this is what you want to do?"

"I am sure," she said. "And I do not appreciate your trying to put last-minute doubts in my head. Shall we go?"

He stood back from the door so that she could precede him from the room. "You look awfully beautiful, Ab," he said.

"Awfully?" she said, taking his arm to descend the stairs.

"I am full of awe," he explained.

The carriage, Abigail saw when the butler opened the door and they stepped outside, was gleaming even though it had returned from London little more than twelve hours ago. And the sun was shining from a clear blue sky. The grass, still wet from the rain, was twinkling in the sunlight.

Oh goodness, this was her *wedding day.*

The carriage had attracted some attention, she saw as it drew to a halt before the churchyard gates several minutes later, perhaps because it was making its second journey there in less than an hour. Some people stood still a little farther along the street, looking back. A few were drawing closer. And others began to join them when first Harry descended, all splendidly turned out in his uniform, complete with shako and sword, and then Abigail, holding his outstretched hand, followed him out in her sprigged muslin dress and her flower-bedecked bonnet. She spotted one of her closest friends among those who were drawing nearer.

But Harry was leading her along the churchyard path and opening the door. The familiar smells of the church met her—some combination of old hymn books and candles and polish—before they were overtaken by the scents of all the flowers with which the church was decorated.

Just like a garden.

Oh my! Her bonnet would be quite eclipsed. But who—?

She had no time for further thought about her surroundings, however. Harry had closed the church door and she had turned to look beyond the vicar toward the altar.

Her bridegroom was awaiting her there.

Looking tall and broad shouldered and splendid in his regimentals. Looking also unsmiling and grim faced, his facial scar somehow accentuated by the dim lighting and the shadows cast by the tapers burning on the altar.

She drew a slow breath and slipped her hand through Harry's arm, and together they proceeded down the aisle.

Fourteen

G il felt as though someone had robbed him of breath. He had always considered Abby pretty and dainty in her unadorned day dresses, her hair styled simply. Today she was nothing short of beautiful. Her dress looked as though it had been embroidered all over with tiny flowers, and it fell in straight, soft folds from just below the bosom. It was low cut with short puffed sleeves over tight gauzy sleeves reaching to her wrists. Her bonnet had been trimmed lavishly with fresh flowers of a glorious mix of bright pastel shades. And as soon as her eyes alit upon him they held his, large and steady.

He felt again the full weight of what he had done and what he was about to do. There should be a churchful of family, friends, and neighbors gathered here to witness her wedding day. Instead the church was empty except for the vicar's wife in the second pew. He should be gazing at her with love overflowing from his heart after a courtship of a decent length during which he had wooed an answering love from her. Instead, her brother had put the germ of an idea into his head, his lawyer had reaffirmed it, and he had rushed ahead with the idea that having a wife might make him seem more eligible as a father to the judge who would hold Katy's fate in his hands.

This was somehow all wrong, and part of him wanted to take a step toward her, both hands raised to stop her from approaching any closer. *Go back,* that one part of him wanted to say. *Go back home. Let us start again and do this the right way.*

If there *was* a right way. How could they possibly make a match of it when their backgrounds and upbringing were as different as they could possibly be and they had nothing in common except the basic illegitimacy of their birth? When they scarcely knew each other and did not even pretend to love each other? When their reason for marrying was not what it ought to be?

But the wave of guilt and near panic was momentary. He had thought the whole thing through on his journey to London and again on the way back. There was no deceit on either side. And no self-deceit either. Neither of them was going blindly into this marriage. They were wedding mainly for a reason that had nothing to do with each other, it was true, but it was nevertheless a noble reason. It was one that would surely bring them closer together—*if,* that was, they succeeded in getting custody of Katy. Moreover, they were not averse to each other. He wanted her. And she wanted him. Some of her words had echoed in his head throughout his journey and came to him now again.

It is not just because I want to help you retrieve your daughter . . . It is also because I want you . . .

I think I want to live with you, to be with you . . .

I think I would be sorry if I convinced myself that marrying you would be madness and let you go. I think I would miss you after you were gone . . . I think I would be unhappy.

And then she slipped her hand through Harry's arm, and . . . smiled.

Wayward thoughts fell away, and his whole focus was upon her. Upon Abby. His bride. And nothing else really mattered. It did not matter that the pews were virtually empty. He was marrying her, and this time he would get it right. He *must,* for her sake, for the sake of his daughter and their future children. And yes, for his sake too.

Please, God, let him get it right this time.

It did not occur to him to smile. Solemnity did not call for levity, and it was a solemn occasion like none other he had ever experienced. The church fairly pulsed with holiness.

When Harry gave her hand into his, he held it enclosed tightly in his own and then loosened his grip while her brother moved to his other side to perform the second half of his duty, as his best man this time. The vicar stood before them, looking with a kindly smile from one to the other of them.

"Dearly beloved," he said in a tone that matched the smile and somehow filled the church.

Gil fixed his eyes upon Abby's face. And she gazed back with flushed cheeks and slightly parted lips and a fragrant garden of beauty like a halo about her head. Her voice was soft, slightly trembling when she spoke her vows to him. His own seemed rough and curt in contrast. When Harry handed him the ring Gil had purchased in London to the measure of one she had given him to take for that purpose, he slid it onto her finger and saw it there, the gold, eternal band of his commitment to her.

And this time, with this woman, it will be eternal, he vowed silently. He wanted desperately to love her, to be able to make her happy, to be a family with her and their children. He wanted the dream—home, wife, children, love, happiness. Not fleetingly—gone almost before he could grasp it, darkness at its heart—but forever. For the rest of their lives and beyond. A foolish, silly dream that no one looking at him at any time during his thirty-four years would ever have suspected. He wanted it.

The vicar was pronouncing them man and wife, and he had a vise-like grip on her hand and was gazing down at her with a look of granite. Not that he knew it. It was just not his habit willingly to show a chink of vulnerability in his armor. The only time he had done it fully and consciously was with his newborn baby.

The vicar led the way to the vestry, where they signed the register and Harry and Mrs. Jenkins signed as witnesses. Harry hugged Abby and held her tightly for several moments while Mrs. Jenkins shook Gil by the hand and informed him that Miss Abigail—Mrs. Bennington—was very precious to them all in the village and was very certainly precious to him too. He wondered if she was convinced of that latter statement.

"I intend to cherish my wife quite as dearly as you could wish, ma'am," he said, and she beamed comfortably at him, not apparently offended by the stiffness of his tone.

Then Harry was wringing his hand while the vicar's wife hugged Abby and the vicar smiled benignly upon them all.

"There *is* something to be said after all for a quiet wedding," Harry said. "It is no less touching than a big one, is it? And I was no less conscious that it was *my sister* I was giving into your care." He was looking steadily into Gil's face.

"Did I ever let you down on the battlefield?" Gil asked.

"You never did," Harry said. "But this is not a battlefield."

"I give you my word," Gil told him, "that I am to be trusted in this too, Harry."

He led his bride slowly along the aisle of the church even though there was no one in the pews to watch them go. He and Harry donned their shakoes, and Harry slipped out ahead of them.

Ah. But there were people outside. Indeed, there was a sizable cluster of them beyond the church gate where the carriage awaited them, and they all burst into applause and whistles and even cheers when Gil appeared with Abby, no doubt having learned from the coachman the nature of what had been going on inside the church. If they had had any doubt, it would certainly have fled when Harry turned back toward them, a drawstring bag in one hand, dipped the other hand inside, and showered them with flower petals.

"Oh." Abby laughed. "How very foolish."

It was a bright, girlish laugh. *But how very wonderful,* she seemed to be saying. And if he had thought her beautiful before their nuptials, then now she was . . . Was there a more accurate word to describe her? But yes, there was. She was *radiant*.

Because this was her wedding day and she had married *him*.

She laughed again as another shower of petals fluttered over their heads.

And then Harry was opening the church gate for them and standing at attention in order to salute a superior officer. Gil returned the salute and experienced an alarming urge to weep.

He resisted it.

Outside the gate he lost his bride for a few moments while two young ladies he had seen before rushed at her, asking a dozen questions apiece even as they hugged her, and other villagers crowded around and called greetings and a few questions of their own. The landlord of the inn caught Gil's eye and winked at him. A few other men with whom he had shared a glass of ale at the tavern grinned sheepishly at him.

At last he handed Abby into the carriage, about the roof of which a garland of flowers had appeared since he came to church in it earlier, though as far as he could see from a single glance there were no old boots or old hardware attached to the back of it to create an unholy din when the conveyance moved. It was no wonder, though, that the villagers had known there was a wedding in progress inside the church.

Harry, rather than join them inside, climbed to the box to sit beside the coachman. It was something he would have been incapable of doing without some help a mere few weeks ago.

The door was shut upon them, Abby waved to the villagers still gathered outside, and the carriage rocked into motion just as the church bells pealed. And yes, there was something underneath after all that rattled and grated and scraped and otherwise announced to the world that a bride and groom rode within.

He turned his head to look at his wife. She was gazing back and reaching for his hand. He closed his own about hers and remembered not to grip too tightly.

"Well, Mrs. Bennington," he said.

"Ah. I like it," she told him. "I am glad you are not a Jones or a Brown or a Smith."

"You would not have married me if I had been any one of those?" he asked, his eyebrows raised.

"Absolutely not," she said. "I have been waiting, you see, not for a good man, but for a good name."

Her cheeks were flushed, her eyes were sparkling, and . . .

"You have a petal on the side of your nose," he told her.

She brushed at the wrong side and he removed the petal himself with the thumb and forefinger of his free hand.

"But did it come from Harry's hoard," he said, examining it, "or from the garden upon your head?"

"I almost canceled the wedding," she told him. "Our cook caught me sneaking out of the house this morning to gather a few small blooms with which to decorate my straw bonnet. She shooed me back upstairs to eat breakfast and hide from you while she did the job herself in Mrs. Sullivan's room. This is the result."

"She ironed my coat so ferociously last night when I went to do it myself," he told her, "that it could almost stand alone. And when I got up early this morning to polish my boots, I discovered that I could almost see my face in them. If any Frenchmen had seen them like that in battle, they would have stopped their charge to hold their sides while they doubled up in laughter. The wars might have been over far sooner than they were."

She lifted her free hand to tap the button closest to his heart. "And someone polished your buttons and all the other metalwork too?" she said.

"It was certainly not my handiwork," he assured her.

"She is a tyrant," she said. "She is also a very good cook."

"Yes," he agreed.

She was looking into his face, her finger still lightly circling his button. "Do you ever smile, Gil?" she asked.

"Of course," he said, frowning.

"But not today?"

"It is a solemn occasion," he said. "Today we were wed."

"Yes," she said, and *she* smiled at *him*.

He dipped his head and kissed her.

Smiles did not come naturally to him. He must learn how to let out the ones that were sometimes there deep inside him. When he first saw her in church this morning, for example. When the vicar pronounced them man and wife. When they stepped out of church to cheers and applause and a shower of flower petals. Now, this moment.

"Tonight," he said as he raised his head, but the carriage was drawing to a halt outside the house, and it remained an unexplained promise.

Tonight.

ABIGAIL MIGHT HAVE BEEN ALERTED TO WHAT WAS TO COME BY the fact that the butler opened both front doors of the house with a stately flourish even before the carriage had come to a complete halt and stood to one side of the doorway, clad in a different uniform from the one he had been wearing when she left the house with Harry. This was a smarter, newer uniform, presumably one he reserved for special occasions.

But she was not alerted. She was too caught up in the euphoria of a wedding that had been far more . . . oh, *splendid* than she had expected it to be. And that one word Gil had spoken before the carriage halted was ringing in her head.

Tonight.

The coachman opened the door of the carriage and put down the steps. Gil descended to the terrace and turned to hand her out. She smiled at Harry, who was standing at attention and had just saluted

Gil again. Sometimes she forgot they were both military men, officers, Gil holding the superior rank. He kept hold of her hand as they went up the steps and past the butler into the hall—where they were met by two lines of servants, one on either side of the doorway, all smartly uniformed, all solemn and silently at attention. Even the grooms and gardeners were among them, as well as the steward and the foreman from the home farm and Harry's valet.

They were silent until the butler stepped inside and nodded a signal that had them all suddenly smiling and applauding.

It was an extraordinary and touching moment in what even last night she had expected to be a very quiet, ordinary day in which she and Gil would slip down to the church to be married.

The butler gave a brief, stilted speech and Mrs. Sullivan an even shorter one. Then the steward called for three cheers, which were delivered self-consciously before everyone dissolved into laughter and covered it with another round of applause.

"Thank you," Gil said when there was quiet again. "I give you all my word of honor as an officer in the Ninety-fifth Foot Regiment that I will care for your Miss Abigail, now Mrs. Bennington, every day of my life."

Abigail turned her head to look up at him in some astonishment and realized that he was addressing *his own people.* These were not aristocrats or even gentry folk. They were his own sort and he respected and honored them. He would even, on occasion, chop wood for them and hang curtains for them and mend roofs for them. Or *with* them. It was an insight into his character that she would not forget.

"Thank you," she said, smiling at each of the servants in turn. "You have all helped make this day very special."

"It won't be so special if my breakfast gets ruined," the cook said, and the butler dismissed the servants even as she was rounding up her helpers and shooing them in the direction of the kitchen.

"I say," Harry said, "that was a surprise. I did not think of suggesting it, but clearly I did not need to. It is a wonderful thing to be at home, Abby, is it not?"

"It is," she agreed, turning to him. But it was not to be her home any longer, was it? Her home was to be wherever Gil took her. He had a house called Rose Cottage in Gloucestershire. For a moment she felt panic claw at her stomach. During the past hour her life had changed in every way possible and forever. But it was too late to panic. Hinsford had been her childhood home, and it had been a good place to grow up, thanks to her mother. She was going to have to make Rose Cottage a good place for her own children to grow up.

Foolishly, she was thinking for the first time of her own children as well as Gil's daughter. *Their* children.

"Sherry in the drawing room?" Harry suggested. "The vicar and Mrs. Jenkins ought to be here soon."

"I need to go and remove my bonnet and comb my hair," Abigail said, and was glad when Gil did not offer to escort her upstairs. She needed to be alone—just for a few minutes to catch her breath. She took the stairs at a run and stood with her back against the door of her bedchamber, her eyes closed.

And she wondered what her mother was doing at this precise moment, and what Camille was doing, and Anna and Jessica. And Grandmama Westcott and Grandmama Kingsley and . . . Oh, and *all* of them. Going about their business and their pleasure, quite unaware that this was her wedding day, that she had just married Lieutenant Colonel Bennington.

She swallowed a lump in her throat and willed herself not to cry. It would not do to go back downstairs with red eyes and blotchy cheeks. For she was not unhappy. She was very far from being that. It was just that she . . .

Oh, she *missed* her family.

She drew a few steadying breaths and took a step into the room, her hands going to the ribbons of her bonnet just as there was a light tap on the door. She considered not opening it. She was not ready to meet the world yet.

"Abby?" It was Gil's voice, and she opened the door.

He stepped inside and closed the door behind his back—and it struck her that he now had a perfect right to be in her room behind a closed door when she was unchaperoned. He was frowning. His eyes were searching her face.

"What is it?" he asked her. "Regrets?"

She shook her head and swallowed. The swallow sounded horribly audible. "No," she said. "No regrets."

"What, then?" he asked. "Your mother? And your sisters?"

"I cannot help thinking," she said, "that they will be disappointed."

His expression turned even more stony. "That you married in such haste?" he asked. "Without their being here?"

She nodded.

"And that you married *me*?" he asked more softly.

She shook her head and bit her lip for a moment. "I cannot predict how they will feel about that, Gil," she said. "I do not know how *any* of my family will feel. Except Harry. But if they are disappointed in whom I have married, then that is something they must deal with—or not. *I* am not disappointed."

"We will leave for London tomorrow," he told her.

She nodded. They had not made plans beyond today, but it was the obvious next step, for more than one reason. And there was no point in delay. Indeed there was every point in *not* delaying.

"We will call first upon your mother," he said, "and upon other members of your family if you wish. I will take you to meet my lawyer. And I will set in motion what needs to be done to effect my retirement from the military."

"So much to do," she said. It seemed almost overwhelming.

"There is nothing to do today," he told her, "except enjoy what is apparently being billed as a wedding breakfast. And then the rest of our wedding day. And our wedding night. Tomorrow will take care of itself."

She nodded.

"We had better get that bonnet off your head before it wilts and get your hair combed without further delay," he said. "I have a strong conviction that your cook would not take kindly to our being late for our wedding feast."

We?

"I suppose it will wilt," she said. "But—"

"But the bonnet still looks very splendid," he said. And before she could remove it herself, he reached out to undo the ribbons beneath her chin and lift the hat carefully from her head before striding over to the table beside her bed and setting it down.

"Ah," she said, "it has not wilted yet."

She glanced into a mirror, saw that her hairstyle was too squashed to be revived with a mere bit of finger work, and removed the pins from the knot at the back of her neck. She went through to her dressing room as she did so, embarrassed at his seeing her hair cascade untidily about her shoulders. But even as she seated herself on the bench before her dressing table, he followed her in and leaned past her to pick up her brush. And he proceeded to remove all the snarls and knots from her hair without once causing her to wince.

"May I hire you as my personal maid?" she asked as she twisted her hair into a knot again.

"How much do you pay?" he asked her. "I do not come cheap."

Ah. Humor. There had been some of it in the carriage too. How lovely. She smiled at his image in the mirror and got to her feet.

He offered his arm and led her downstairs to the drawing room, where the vicar and his wife were sitting with Harry. And over the following two hours they drank sherry, moved into the dining room, which rivaled the church for its floral splendor, and partook of a lavish feast, followed by toasts from both Harry and the vicar, and speeches from Harry and Gil. They ended the breakfast with wedding cake, which had somehow been elaborately iced and decorated despite such short notice, and champagne, which had been produced from somewhere in the bowels of the cellar.

Later, after the Reverend and Mrs. Jenkins had taken their leave, they took Beauty for a walk—or rather *she* took *them*, running ahead or in a wide circle about them before stopping in front of them, front legs flat on the ground, wide rump elevated, tail wagging, as though inviting them to a race, and then dashing off again.

After they had returned to the house Abigail wrote letters to Camille and Winifred and her grandmother Kingsley in Bath, and Gil surprised her by writing to Robbie with stories about what Beauty had been up to since the boy went home. He even, Abigail saw with delight, drew a few pen sketches of the dog, one of her looking exactly as she had looked when she stopped in front of them earlier, complete with wavy lines on either side of her tail to suggest movement.

Harry, after an hour's rest in his room, took his horse and rode to the home of one of his boyhood friends. He sent back a note a mere hour later to inform them that he had been invited to stay the night. He would be home first thing in the morning, however, he had added, since he knew they intended to make an early start for London.

"Your brother has tact," Gil said.

Abigail felt herself blushing.

Tonight . . .

Fifteen

The drawing room seemed unnaturally large with just the two of them in it, sitting on either side of the fireplace when they might surely have sat side by side on one of the sofas. His fault, Gil freely admitted. There was no fire burning, as it had been a warm day and had not cooled off significantly during the evening. Beauty was stretched out before the hearth anyway, snoring softly.

Abby was not embroidering or knitting or busy with any of her other customary needlework activities. Instead, she clasped her hands loosely in her lap. Yet she did not look relaxed. His fault again, surely. She had made a few attempts to begin conversation, all of which he had thwarted by answering briefly. He had never quite mastered the art of conversation at which polite society was so adept. It was his turn to choose a topic, one he must keep going this time. But she spoke again before he could think of something.

"I am rather wealthy," she said abruptly. "I thought you ought to know."

"Wealthy?" He raised his eyebrows. He had assumed she had nothing after being dispossessed several years ago.

"When it was discovered that Anna was our father's only legitimate child," she explained, "and that according to his will everything except the title and entailed property went to her, she was not at all happy about it. She wanted to share everything with the three of us in equal parts. To our shame, we spurned her offer. We were not even willing to recognize her as our sister. I do not know quite why. Perhaps it was because she was so *happy* to discover that after all she had family, most notably us, half siblings. We, on the other hand, hated her. Or perhaps we felt we were being condescended to by a nobody of an orphan from an orphanage. I hope it was not that. It would be horribly—and inappropriately—snobbish. But it may well have been."

"It would have been perfectly understandable," he said, though he felt a certain indignation on behalf of the woman who had always thought herself a penniless orphan. But that penniless orphan was now the Duchess of Netherby. Cinderella, he had called her, a comparison she had rejected. "It all happened very suddenly, did it not, and came as an utter shock to your whole family?"

"If it *was* the reason," she said, "it has not been the reason for a long time. We are better than that, I believe. We have tried to love her, and we have largely succeeded. Indeed, it would be hard *not* to love Anna. She has been unrelentingly kind and affectionate toward us. When she learned a few weeks ago that I was planning to remain here instead of returning to London, she took me aside and begged me to accept my share, which she had set aside for me from the start and willed to me. Apparently Camille accepted her share several years ago, before she married Joel, though I did not know that until Anna told me. I accepted. My father was an extremely wealthy man. My quarter of everything he left to Anna is a fortune in its own right. I thought you ought to know."

"So that I can live on your money?" he said.

Her cheeks flushed and her hands clenched in her lap. "You told me you had your own," she said. "But I do not know how much. I do not imagine it can be a great deal. I just wanted you to know that . . . there is no reason in the world, Gil, why we cannot live on my fortune."

"Except for my male pride," he said.

"You do not need—" she began, but he held up a hand.

"When I fought in India, as a private soldier, as a corporal, and then as a sergeant," he told her, "there were sometimes rich prizes to be won in the form of gold and precious jewels. It was neither strictly lawful nor particularly ethical, I suppose, but it happened. Not to everyone. Not even to very many. One had to be in the right place at the right time. But it happened to me and I managed to keep possession of what I had won until I came home as a newly commissioned officer. I bought my house with some of the proceeds. I invested the rest with an agent in London who was recommended to me. He has proved to be an honest and knowledgeable man. As well as managing my fortune, he manages the staffing and financing of my home and the farm that came with it."

"Fortune?" she said, frowning.

"To me it is a fortune," he said. "I can live comfortably if not lavishly on the income from it for the rest of my life. You have not married a fabulously wealthy man, Abby, but you have not married a poor man either. And I *did* give an accounting of my worth to Harry when he interrogated me before I went to London. He was satisfied. I do not need or even want your fortune. You may spend it on yourself and our children."

She looked down at Beauty, who was trembling and yipping in the throes of a dream.

"Will there be children?" she asked. "I thought that perhaps your daughter—"

"She will need brothers and sisters," he said. "I once thought, you know, that I would like a dozen children so that I could give them the sort of life children should have. But— Well, perhaps three or four?"

"I would like that." Her eyes had come back to his. There was a flush of color in her cheeks.

And he dared to dream again. Tomorrow they would go to London and call upon his lawyer. Soon they would have Katy and take her home. And he would make Abby happy, and they would have more children and . . .

His thoughts were interrupted by the arrival of a footman, still in his best uniform, with the tea tray, and neither of them spoke even after he left. Abby poured and he went to take his cup and saucer from her hands and the piece of their wedding cake she had put on a plate for him.

"Thank you," he said.

"Tell me about your childhood, Gil," she said, sitting back in her chair, her own plate in her hand.

"I survived it." But that answer, besides being another conversation killer, was not good enough. She was his wife now. Good God, *his wife.* "Thousands had it much worse. At least I always had a roof over my head and some food in my stomach and clothes to wear, even if they were often ill fitting and bore patches upon patches. I had a mother who cared for my basic needs and insisted I attend school and instilled basic good manners in me. She was not demonstrative by nature—at least, not during the years I knew her. She never showed me open love in the form of hugs and kisses and smiles and words of approval and encouragement. But love, I have learned in all the years since my boyhood, comes in many forms. She never abandoned me. And sometimes, I suspect, she went hungry so that I could eat. She was always pale and thin with red, chapped hands and forearms from all the work she did at her washtub."

His heart ached for her in retrospect. She was probably eighteen or nineteen when she gave birth to him, though he never knew her age.

He had had no friends, and the children who occasionally played with him would do so only until their parents found out. Friends were something he had always yearned for. But children were resilient. On the whole he had not missed what he never had. The vicar had been

strict with him at school but good to him too. He had taken Gil fishing with him once—ah, what a vast and memorable treat that had
been—with the purpose, it seemed, of explaining to him why he
needed to learn to read and write, though both skills appeared useless
and boring to him at the time. Those abilities would be his escape
route into a life that would raise him from abject poverty and perhaps
bring him happiness and fulfillment. Gil had enjoyed the fishing, ignored the lecture, and taken two fish home for his mother to cook for
their supper.

"It was the proudest moment of my life," he told Abby. "But perhaps the advice he gave me, at which I silently scoffed at the time, bore
fruit after all. It would not have been possible for me to be promoted
in the army as I was if I had been unable to read and write. I have been
happy in the army, especially when I was a sergeant."

"You were not happy to be an officer?" she asked.

He thought about it. "I suppose I welcomed the new challenges,"
he said. "And if I had not been an officer, there would not be Katy."
There would not have been the disaster of Caroline and his marriage
to her either. "And if I had not been an officer, I would not have come
here with Harry. I would not have met you."

She set her empty plate aside. "Is that not a strange fact of life?"
she said. "If *that* had not happened, then *this* would not have happened, and then *that* would not. And so on. I am glad we met. I am
glad you learned to read and write."

"Against all the odds," he said. "I was a morose, rebellious pupil.
I skipped school a few times, but my mother had a stout wooden stick
she used for dunking the wash in the tub. She also used it on my back-
side when I skipped school. And washing clothes had given my mother
strong hands and arms."

"She wanted a better future for you," Abby said.

"I suppose so," he said. "I often wish my adult self could go back
and sit down for a good talk with her. She had a hard life. I do not
even know if I was born of a consensual encounter between her and

the man who begot me or something worse. I am sorry. I ought not to have said that aloud."

"My father went through a grand *ton* wedding with my mother," she told him, "knowing full well that he was already married to someone else—Anna's mother, who was dying of consumption but was still alive then. My father was desperately poor, and my mother's dowry was large. We are not responsible for the ugliness surrounding our own births, Gil."

"I like to think," he said, "that my mother was proud of me before she died. I was a sergeant. I wrote to her a few times, though she would have had to have the vicar read the letters to her. I like to think she would have been proud of the man I have become. She always fed stray cats and dogs, you know. It used to make me furious. We had no spare food to give away."

"I think," she said, "you loved her."

He found himself blinking against a stinging sensation behind his eyes. Good God, he was not about to weep, was he? What the devil would she think of him?

"I suppose," he said, "I ruined her life the moment she conceived me. But she never, ever said so or even implied that it was so."

"I am sure she *was* proud," Abby said softly, though there was no way she could know any such thing.

"Come to bed?" he said.

She gazed at him for several long moments.

"Yes," she said, getting up to stack their dishes on the tray before pulling on the bell rope to summon the footman to remove it.

Beauty scrambled up, shook herself all over, and yawned hugely.

Gil got to his feet too and, after the tray had been removed, offered his arm for his wife's hand.

Beauty trotted after them as they climbed the stairs.

Gil stopped outside Abby's room, took her hand from inside his arm, and held it in both his own. "You would like me to come here?" he asked. "Rather than you come to me?"

"Yes," she said.

"I'll return in a short while, then," he told her. "I had better take Beauty outside for a few minutes first."

He leaned past her and opened the door. He shut it after she had passed through.

"Well," he said, looking down at his dog, "you are going to have to sleep alone tonight, Beaut. But a walk first? A very short walk?"

Beauty wagged her tail.

SHE OUGHT TO BE FEELING NERVOUS, ABIGAIL SUPPOSED. BUT SHE was twenty-four years old and of course she knew a thing or two, though no one had ever spelled out the lesson for her. Knowing what happened was somewhat different, of course, from knowing how it would feel. But she was far more eager than apprehensive.

Being a twenty-four-year-old virgin was not altogether a comfortable thing. For there were longings and needs that one felt from really quite an early age, and they did not lessen with time. Quite the contrary, in fact. But as a lady—even an illegitimate lady—one could not express those longings in any way except through marriage. Hence the husband search as soon as a girl left the schoolroom—or the unexpressed reason, anyway.

Even as recently as a month ago she had been seriously fearful that she might never marry. Not because no one would ever offer, but because she would never feel . . . *right* about any man who did. She would not marry in order to gain a foothold back in the world of the *ton* that had once been hers. Neither would she marry a man of slightly lesser rank who was prepared to overlook the blot on her birth. Yet she had always believed she could not possibly marry quite outside the world in which she had been raised. It was not snobbery but practicality. It was a matter of compatibility.

But was that what she had done today? The answer was undoubtedly yes. The worlds in which she and Gil had grown up were more like different universes.

Why, then, did marrying him *feel* right?

Her small trunk and portmanteaux were packed and stacked neatly in her dressing room with her new, brightly embroidered needlework bag, she saw. Mrs. Sullivan had told her she would send up a maid to do it. The same maid had set out the prettiest and fanciest of her nightgowns and brought up a pitcher of hot water, which was now lukewarm.

They would be leaving in the morning, quite early, and she did not know if they would be coming back anytime soon, and even when they did it would be only to visit. Hence the fact that she was to take all the belongings she had brought from London. It had not lasted long, her homecoming. But during it she had found the one man who felt right to her as a lifelong mate. She could be wrong, of course, but one could not live one's whole life avoiding everything that might prove to be a mistake. One might thus pave the way to an old age that would be full of regrets for things one might have done but did not. That would be even worse.

She undressed and washed and drew on the nightgown. She brushed out her hair, considered braiding it so that it would not get hopelessly tangled during the night, and decided against it. She went into her bedchamber and pulled the curtains back from the window. She could see only the reflection of the candles burning on the mantel behind her, but it was a cozy sight. She half opened one of the windows and listened to the sound of silence. Strangely, it *did* have a sound, different from the indoors. It was the sound of vastness and peace. It was like an assurance that all was well and always would be.

An owl hooted in the distance.

He must have come back inside with his dog. She could not hear them. But even as she thought it, there was a light tap on her door and it opened.

"Ah," he said after stepping inside and closing the door behind him. "Beautiful."

"Thank you." She smiled at him.

She would not say he looked handsome, exactly. He was wearing a silk dressing gown of a dark gold color and tan slippers. But both garments, rather than diminishing his size and the power of his physique, somehow enhanced them instead. For the silk was a fine fabric and clung to him above the belt. She had seen him naked to the waist. She had seen him wearing only hip-hugging breeches and boots that molded his calves. Now he seemed somehow less clothed, and she felt a stabbing of what she recognized as raw desire in her womb.

His dark hair had been freshly brushed. Even so, that one errant lock had fallen over his forehead. His dark eyes looked very directly at her. He must have shaved before coming here. But he could not shave away the brutal scar. He looked stern and dour, with not even a gleam of an answering smile. But she realized something about him suddenly.

His stern expression was a mask, a defense. It was something all his life experiences from childhood on had imposed on him. The world might reject and isolate and ridicule and even hate him, but it would never see him vulnerable. That he had suffered had come through in some of the things he had told her during the past few weeks and in what he had said earlier about his childhood. But it would never show on his face.

Well, we will see about that, Lieutenant Colonel Gil Bennington, she thought.

She was not the love of his heart. Probably no one ever had been, even his first wife. And perhaps no one ever would be. He was a man of unusual reserve. But he was also an honorable man. And there was kindness in him, even gentleness, despite the outer appearance of granitelike toughness he liked to project. Oh, and love too. And love did indeed come in many forms, as he had said earlier when speaking of his mother.

He came across the room to her, set his hands on either side of her waist, and looked at her, rather the way he had done on that very first day but from closer—from her head to her bare toes and back up. His eyes on hers, he drew her against him, one arm sliding about her waist, the other hand coming to cup the back of her head beneath her hair, his fingers pushing through it. And he kissed her.

She might have swooned if he had not been holding her firmly. For it was not an embrace just of lips and mouths this time. She was touching him all along the front of her body, and he was all warmth and hard muscle and a hand that moved lower down her back to nestle her against him where he was hardest. And he smelled of something—eau de cologne? shaving soap?—unmistakably male. She could do nothing but yield to the pressure of his hands and press herself to him and open her mouth to him and wonder if anything they did on the bed could possibly be more shocking or more wonderful.

"No maidenly nerves?" he asked, his lips still almost touching hers, his eyes gazing into her own. And though he did not smile, nevertheless she thought there was a thread of humor in his voice.

"No," she said. "But you must forgive me for not knowing what to do."

"You were doing well enough a moment ago," he said.

"Was I?" She had not known it.

"Come to bed," he said.

"Yes."

She lay down and he came to the side of the bed and leaned over her. "Do you want darkness or candlelight?" he asked.

Oh. Would it not be a bit embarrassing . . . But she could not bear not to see him. "Candlelight," she said.

He drew back the covers she had pulled up to her waist and she realized his intent when he took hold of the hem of her nightgown. A moment later the garment was on the floor at his feet and she wished she had opted for darkness. But only briefly. His eyes moved over her, and it seemed to Abigail that he liked what he saw. And as he looked, he undid the knot in his belt and shrugged out of his dressing gown. He was not wearing a nightshirt beneath it.

Oh my!

He came around the bed and lay down beside her. He did not draw the covers over them. And she began to find out what it felt like, this nameless experience for which she had yearned in secret through all the years since she had grown past childhood and into womanhood.

His hands, slightly rough, even calloused, and dark against the paleness of her body, moved over her in what might have seemed a leisurely exploration except they left in their wake a longing that became as physical as it was emotional and a raw need for something more. He leaned over her and kissed her as his hand moved between her thighs and his fingers explored secret places that surely ought to remain secret—except that the rawness of her need became almost a pain. And then, quite shockingly, the feeling moved beyond pain into something unutterably pleasurable as his thumb pressed upon part of her and she said something incoherent and he murmured something equally unintelligible into her mouth.

Yet there was still the leftover ache of longing, and he came over her and pressed his knees between hers and brought her legs up to twine about his own. His hands came beneath her, and she felt him there where she throbbed with need again, and he came into her. She expected shock. She expected pain. And there were both. But there was wonder too and the desire to feel it all, even the pain, and to enjoy every single moment of it.

When he was deeper in her than she had ever known was possible, he held still and she sighed. He lifted some of his weight off her onto his forearms and looked into her eyes, mere inches from his own.

"I am sorry," he murmured. "I am heavy."

"But every pound feels good," she said.

He began to move then, out to the brink of her and in deep. And again and again while she closed her eyes. Hot, wet, hard. With steady, firm rhythm. She matched it after a while by flexing and relaxing inner muscles and then rotating her hips the better to feel him. And she opened her eyes again and looked at him in the flickering candlelight, at his muscled shoulders and chest slick with sweat, at his closed eyes, a frown of concentration between his brows, at the terrible scar left behind by a cavalry blade.

He dipped his head, and his weight came down on her again as his hands slid beneath her to hold her still and steady while the rhythm of his loving increased. And then he held deep and she felt the hot flow of his release inside her.

There was no great moment of release for her, but she did not believe she had ever been happier in her life. Which was how anyone would wish to feel on her wedding night at the moment of consummation.

He sighed, his breath warm against her ear, and lifted his weight away from her and off her. He moved to her side and lay there, his shoulder heavy against her own.

"Did I hurt you?" he asked. The back of his hand was over his eyes, she could see.

She knew she would be sore tomorrow. She already was. But how was she to explain that some pains were also pleasure, that even her soreness was something to savor?

"Silence is my answer," he said softly. "I am sorry, Abby."

"I am not," she said. "And I was silent because I could not find the words with which to say that pleasure and pain can sometimes be the same thing. A strange paradox. There was pain, Gil. There was also pleasure. More pleasure than pain."

"Do you want me to return to my room?" he asked.

The candles were still burning. His shoulder was warm against her own. Actually it was slightly above the level of hers. She could tip her head sideways and rest it against his shoulder.

"If you wish," she said. She had not thought about it as a possibility. It would be horribly bleak if—

"What do *you* wish?" he asked.

She laughed suddenly and he removed the hand from his eyes and turned his head to look at her. "We could go on this way all night," she said. "What do *you* wish? No, what do *you*?"

"Hmm," he said.

"Stay," she told him. She laughed softly. "If you wish."

"Oh, I wish," he said. "Mrs. Bennington."

She closed her eyes and swallowed and felt the bedcovers come up over them. She nestled her head against his shoulder when he lay down again. And he reached for her hand and laced their fingers together.

Tonight . . .

It had not disappointed.

Mrs. Bennington.

Sixteen

Harry was home in time the following morning to sit down for an early breakfast with them. Their leaving together this morning felt a bit like abandonment, and they both told him so in their own way. But he would have none of it.

"Abby," he said when she teared up after being told that the carriage was already before the doors, being loaded with their bags, "you stayed here because you wanted to be at home, not because I needed you. I have loved having you. I always will love it. But you must rid yourself of the notion that I might fade away without your being here. I am sorry if that sounds a bit brutal."

Then he turned to his friend. "As for you, Gil, to be honest with you I do not know if I actually would have come to Hinsford and stayed if you had not said you would come with me. I suppose I would have gone to London and hated it. I did need you during that journey even though I also had Avery and Alexander. And I needed you for a few weeks afterward—I know that. But no longer. I would have been happy to have you here indefinitely as a friend, but I do not *need* you. I still sometimes feel as weak as a kitten, but a *large* kitten growing larger every day, not the runt of the litter. I have everything I need here—people to cater to my every need, things with which to occupy myself, friends, neighbors."

There were more tears out on the terrace half an hour or so later. Abby clung to Harry, both laughing and crying.

"Goose," he said. "Go and be happy, Ab, and I will *stay* and be happy. No, really. I do not envy you going to London. And facing everything that is awaiting you there. I'll think about you from the peace of my own home. Let me know what happens."

"I will," she promised. "Take care of yourself, Harry. At least I know you are safe. Oh, I cannot tell you how happy I am to know that."

"Goose," he said again as she turned away and Gil handed her into the carriage.

"I am a bit of a careless fellow," Harry said, "but my family is precious to me, Gil."

"I will look after her," Gil promised, keeping his voice low. "I am not using her *just* as a means of getting my daughter back." He hoped he was telling the truth.

"I have had a couple of sleepless nights, I am telling you," Harry said, "remembering that I was the one who suggested it."

"Then you may sleep well tonight," Gil said. "I am very glad you did suggest it. I shall return the carriage tomorrow. And your groom." The groom was going to ride his horse during the journey. Gil would purchase a carriage of his own and more horses in London.

A few minutes later Gil was handing a large handkerchief to Abby to replace the ridiculously small thing with which she was dabbing at her eyes as the carriage moved from her childhood home.

"Thank you," she said, her voice tearful as she spread it over her face. "He is right. I *am* a goose."

Beauty woofed from the seat opposite.

Just a very few weeks ago she had chosen to stay at Hinsford so that she could enjoy its quiet familiarity. Now already she was leaving behind both those things. She had married Gil, someone she scarcely knew, and was heading into a vast uncertainty. All she knew about their immediate future was that it was bound to be unpleasant. She had her family to face, for one thing. And then all the nasty business with his lawyer and his former in-laws. She blew her nose, tucked his handkerchief away in a pocket of her cloak, and turned a smiling, rather red-blotched face toward him.

"I am sorry," she said. "I hate goodbyes."

He thought perhaps it was more than the goodbye she was hating. He guessed that reality was hitting her this morning. As it was him. He took her hand in his and held it on the seat between them. Conversation, he thought. *Conversation.*

Beauty was offering no help. She had laid her chin on her paws and closed her eyes.

"Rose Cottage," he told her, "seems to have come honestly by half its name at least. It is a house of mellow yellowish stone with big windows and a great deal of natural light within. There are twelve bedchambers upstairs and . . . but I have not counted the number of rooms downstairs. I would have to think about it. They are large and spacious, though. It is not really a cottage of course. Far from it. The garden is not really big enough to be called a park, but it is large, and it is filled with flower beds, unlike Hinsford's, as well as lawns and trees. There is no lake. But there is a rose arbor on one side of the house, or, rather, a rose *garden*, all arches and trellises and secluded seating areas. I wish I could describe the colors and the smells, but I lived there only during the winter months and very early spring. I saw snowdrops and primroses in the grass to the east of the house and a few daffodils. I employ gardeners known for their skill with flowers. I imagine it is all very beautiful now and will be for several more months."

He had set out to distract her and seemed to have succeeded. Her face was turned toward him and she was still smiling, but no longer just bravely. There was warmth in the expression.

"It sounds lovely," she said.

"It is," he assured her. "It is on the outer edge of a village with farmland behind it. Not as big as the farm at Hinsford, but it is busy and prosperous. I have a good manager."

"I look forward to going there," she said.

"Some people look forward to going to heaven after they die," he said. "For years after I purchased it, Rose Cottage was the earthly heaven to which I aspired."

"It was your dream," she said. "But you have actually lived there for only a few winter months?"

"I took Caroline there in 1814, after Toulouse," he said. "Katy was born there. I took her to see the roses. But of course they were not nearly in bloom and she was but a tiny baby anyway. And then, before they *did* bloom, I was called away for what culminated in the Battle of Waterloo. I made the biggest mistake of my life in going, one for which I am even now being punished."

Their clasped hands were on her lap, he realized suddenly. She must have moved them there. She was holding his hand with both her own.

"What was mistaken about it?" she asked.

"I ought to have resigned my commission and stayed," he said. "I was married. I had a child. I thought my main responsibility was to my regiment and the cause of right, whatever that means. I was wrong. My main responsibility was to my family. Caroline did not want to be left. She hated it at Rose Cottage and she hated . . . motherhood. Katy was helpless to make any sort of decision. I made the wrong choice and I lost her as a result. Perhaps permanently."

"Would you have saved your marriage by staying?" she asked.

He thought about it. But he had done that many times before and knew the answer. "No, I do not think my marriage could have been a happy one," he said. "But I would have had my daughter."

"How did your wife die?" she asked.

Conversations were damnable things, he thought. They involved baring one's soul and exposing all one's guilt and all one's pain. Or perhaps it was just marriage that was the damnable thing.

"She fell," he said curtly. For a few moments he did not want to say anything more, but he could hardly leave it there. "She was somewhere in Cornwall and descending a steep cliff path she had been warned was dangerous. That very warning would have impelled her to do it, of course. She was like that. She fell. The people who were with her could not save her. They *had* heeded the warning." Actually, the official report he had read had mentioned just one person, a man. Probably a lover. But what did it matter now?

"I am sorry," she said softly.

"The devil of it is," he said, "that I am not."

And she sat back in the seat, still cradling his hand in her lap, and turned her head toward the window on her side.

"I hated her," he said. "I did not wish her harm, and I did not *do* her harm, but I have been unable to grieve her death."

She drew breath as though to say something but did not do so.

"You have married a hard man, Abby," he said.

"I do not believe so," she said softly. "I hate her too. She never intended to return, did she? She had abandoned both her child and you. And she lied about you to save face with her mother."

They traveled a long way in silence, his hand in both of hers. He wondered if he would ever forgive himself for leaving his family when he had known Caroline to be desperately unhappy and when he had had *a child* who needed her father at home with her. And he wondered if he would ever forgive Caroline for loving no one but herself and craving adventure, the rougher the better, and for lying about him as an excuse for dumping their child upon her mother before she ran away in pursuit of her own pleasure. The only thing he *could* forgive her for was dying.

Bitterness and hatred were like an ulcer bleeding into the innards. Especially, perhaps, when there was self-hatred too. He had never used violence upon Caroline, not even when she had begged for it during sex. But he had abandoned both her and their baby for the greater glory of war, and so he was equally to blame for the troubles he now faced. Oh, he could argue, as he sometimes did, that he had left his wife and child well provided for, even if he had died in battle, but it was not an argument that convinced him.

"Abby," he said, "I will do better. Even if, God help me, I never get Katy back, I will do better."

She turned her face back toward him. "I did not know," she said, "that you blamed yourself."

"I will do better by you," he told her, "and our children. Some lessons are bitter ones, but I have learned mine."

"We will get her back, Gil," she said. "She has a father and a mother and a home to go to. And though you blame yourself for abandoning her, the world will not see it that way. You obeyed when you were called back to duty because this country and the whole of Europe were at a moment of peril. Almost no one would blame you for going except you."

"You are too kind," he said.

She took him by surprise then. She raised his hand with both of hers, kissed the back of it, and held it briefly against her cheek.

"We will get her back," she said again.

"Abby," he said a few moments later, "I am sorry I hurt you."

"Last night?" She looked startled, and she blushed.

"I am sorry," he said.

"I am not." She lowered her head so that he could not see her face fully. "I am twenty-four years old. Perhaps you do not understand what it is like to be a woman who does not marry young. She cannot indulge in casual amours, as I believe most men do. I have wanted . . . what happened last night for a long time. Pain and all. I am glad it has happened at last." She drew breath, hesitated, and then continued. "And I am glad it was with you."

There had been no one since Caroline—until last night. He had been tempted a few times, but the days of his lusty youth were behind him and rutting with a whore or even with a willing camp follower had lost its appeal.

"You must not drag around *that* guilt with you on top of everything else," she said, turning a blushing, laughing face his way and swaying against his shoulder. "I am very glad it happened."

"Thank you," he said, and turned his head to kiss her. Her hands tightened about his, and he prolonged the kiss.

She was sweet—sweet to look upon, sweet tasting, sweet to bed. Only he guarded his emotions. The turmoil of his first marriage had drained them and bewildered him and sent him scurrying deep inside himself, where he had spent most of his life. He did not want to get too emotionally attached to Abigail, and he hoped she would not get too attached to him. Let them have a rational marriage, with respect and loyalty and decent lovemaking and some affection. And children.

Let them not—oh, please, let them not fall in love.

She was gazing into his eyes from a few inches away. "What?" she asked.

"Nothing." He released his hand from hers and turned his head toward the window on his side. "We are coming to a posting inn. There are people. I do not want to embarrass you."

But instead of looking mortified or embarrassed and moving smartly away to sit decorously at his side, he discovered when he turned back toward her that she smiled slowly at him, giving him the full effect of those blue eyes.

"Will we stop to eat?" she asked. "I would love a cup of tea if nothing else."

Beauty sat up, her tongue flopping, and looked hopefully in the direction of the window.

WHEN THEY ARRIVED IN LONDON, THEY STOPPED FIRST AT THE Pulteney Hotel, at which Gil had reserved a suite of rooms a few days ago when he was in London. Abigail had voiced a token protest, since Marcel's town house was large and he and her mother would surely expect them to stay there. Privately, though, she was glad. She did not know quite what reaction to expect to their news.

It was late afternoon when they finally arrived at the house and were admitted by Marcel's butler, who took Abigail's appearance upon the doorstep quite in his stride.

"Good afternoon, Miss Westcott," he said. "You will find the family in the drawing room. Whom shall I announce?" He looked with polite inquiry at Gil.

"Lieutenant Colonel Bennington," she said. "But there is no need to announce us."

"Very well, miss," he said, turning to lead the way upstairs and open the drawing room doors for them.

The family was there, the butler had said. Of whom did that consist apart from her mother and Marcel and probably Estelle? But at least there *was* someone at home. She had feared there might not be and they would have to do this all again this evening or even tomorrow.

Inside the drawing room, Abigail took in the scene in one glance. Yes, they were there, the three of them. So was Bertrand, who kept bachelor rooms of his own but was often here. And so were Cousin Althea Westcott, Alexander's mother, and her daughter, Cousin Elizabeth, with Colin, Lord Hodges, her husband. Two-year-old George was on Colin's lap. The bundle in Elizabeth's arms was presumably Eve, the new baby.

The next moment the men were on their feet and her mother was hurrying toward her, both hands outstretched, her face lighting up with delight.

"Abby!" she exclaimed. "But what a wonderful surprise. You did not breathe a word about coming up to town. Is Harry with you?" As she took Abigail's hands in a strong clasp, she looked eagerly beyond her only to see that it was not Harry standing in the doorway. Her hold on Abigail's hands loosened. "Lieutenant Colonel Bennington. You have come too? Then Harry must be with you. Where—"

"Mama," Abigail said as Marcel smiled at her and squeezed her shoulder in welcome before offering his hand to Gil. "Harry is at Hinsford. We came alone."

"Alone?" her mother said, her smiles turning to alarm. "Is it Harry? Is there something wrong with—"

"Harry is perfectly fine, Mama," Abigail assured her, cutting her off as she released her hands and stepped to one side of the doorway so that she was not standing directly in front of Gil. "We would not have left him if he had been indisposed. We have come here to tell you we are married. Gil and I. Yesterday. At the village church. Harry gave me away. The Reverend and Mrs. Jenkins came to breakfast afterward."

Oh dear. She had not meant to make the announcement so bluntly and in such disjointed fashion, her voice breathless, before they were even properly in the room. She had visualized . . . Oh, but it was too late now.

"What?" Her mother's face had turned pale, and one hand crept to her throat. She had almost whispered the word

"What?" Estelle's voice was closer to a squeal. *"Abby?* You are *married?* To Lieutenant Colonel Bennington? Without *telling* anyone? You absolute wretch, you!" She came hurtling across the room to catch Abigail up in a hug before blushing and holding out a hand to Gil.

"But *why?*" Abigail's mother asked, looking from her daughter to Gil and back. "What—"

"I think, my love," Marcel said, patting her arm, "we had better invite Abigail and her new husband to come and be seated while Bertrand sends down for some wine. Maybe champagne, Bertrand? I am sure they fully intend to explain why they have dashed so madly into marriage. We will hope for a story of high romance. In the meanwhile, Althea, Elizabeth, and Colin, allow me to present Lieutenant Colonel Bennington, the friend who brought Harry home from Paris and stayed with him. Mrs. Westcott, Bennington, and Lord and Lady Hodges. Elizabeth and Alexander are Cousin Althea's children, and Colin is Wren's brother. This is a complicated family. I would have thought twice about marrying into it if I had been sufficiently warned."

Cousin Althea smiled and nodded. Colin stepped forward to shake Gil by the hand. George, up on Colin's arm, stretched out his hand too, and Gil took it entirely within his own.

"You are probably wishing us at Jericho, Abigail," Elizabeth said, her eyes twinkling, "and you too, Lieutenant Colonel. But here we are to welcome you to the family and to hear your story firsthand. Forgive me for not getting to my feet. If this little one's sleep is disturbed, she becomes very cross."

Abigail bent over her to peer at the slumbering baby—she had round, fat cheeks—before sitting down on a love seat and making room for Gil beside her. He did not sit down, however. He went to stand behind her. And the room fell silent while everyone's attention turned to the two of them. Her mother, Abigail saw, was still standing close to the door, her face pale. Abigail drew breath to speak, but it was Gil who spoke first.

"I had a child with my first wife, who died a few months after Waterloo," he said. "She was the daughter of General and Lady Pascoe. My daughter was taken, without my knowledge or consent, to live with her grandmother while I was in Belgium. By the time I came home after the battle, my wife was . . . gone and Katy's grandparents were unwilling to allow me to take my daughter home. Lady Pascoe would not even allow me to see her. I—"

"But whyever not?" Cousin Althea asked.

"My marriage was not a happy one, ma'am," he explained. "My wife told her mother that I had mistreated her, that I had been violent. And when I went to fetch my daughter from her grandmother's home, I am afraid I did nothing to help my case. I behaved badly. I raged and threatened and—"

"And did you use violence upon your wife?" Marcel asked while Abigail's mother, standing close to him, raised a hand to her mouth and closed her eyes.

"No, sir," Gil said.

"If you raged and threatened," Marcel asked, "why did you not end up with your child? I assume the general was still from home?"

"He was," Gil said. "I had got myself inside the house despite the effort of several servants to keep me out, but then Lady Pascoe came downstairs and stood blocking the staircase. And I could hear Katy crying upstairs. She was less than a year old. But she sounded frightened."

"So you went away," Elizabeth said.

"Yes," Gil said. "Very soon after that, out of the blue, I was posted to St. Helena. General Pascoe's doing, without a doubt. My wife died while I was there. By now they have dug in their heels. They have threatened through their lawyer to have me charged with assault if I do not go away quietly. Through *my* lawyer I have threatened to charge them with kidnapping. However, negotiations are ongoing and seem to be leading to a hearing before a judge, who will decide my daughter's fate. I believe I have right and the law on my side, but General and Lady Pascoe have rank and power and influence on theirs."

"And so," Colin said, "it occurred to you and your lawyer that your chances would improve considerably if you married again and had a mother to offer the child as well as a father."

"Yes," Gil said.

He was, Abigail thought as she sat stiffly on the edge of the love seat, making a mess of this.

"But that is *outrageous*," her mother cried while Marcel set a hand on her shoulder. "You have *used* Abby. You have—"

"It is not so, Mama," Abigail said. "When I agreed to marry Gil, I was in full possession of all the facts. We did not marry *just* to improve his chances of regaining custody of his daughter. We married each other also because we wanted to." She was not at all sure that was true of Gil, but she did not believe it was not true either. "I am happy with what I have done. I hope you can be happy for me. I hope you all can."

There was the briefest of silences.

"*I* am happy," Estelle cried, and rushed from her own chair to sit beside Abigail and squeeze her hand. "Though I may never forgive you for not inviting me to your wedding. And just wait until *Jessica* hears the news."

"I am happy for the two of you as well," Cousin Althea said. "And I wish you every success with your court case, Lieutenant Colonel."

"Thank you, ma'am." He inclined his head to her.

"Small, private weddings can be the loveliest things," Elizabeth said. "I am sure yours was, Abigail and Lieutenant Colonel Bennington. I hope we will hear details. If not, I shall have to write and pester Harry." Her eyes were twinkling again.

Bertrand came to offer his hand to Abigail. He was grinning. "I would say you have done well for yourself considering the fact that you were an aging spinster, stepsister," he said. "You have married a high-ranking officer and gentleman." He took her hand in his and leaned over her to kiss her cheek.

"I am not a gentleman," Gil said from behind her. Abigail did not have to look to know that he was wearing his granite expression.

Everyone looked inquiringly at him. Elizabeth was smiling as though awaiting the other half of the joke. Abigail felt her teeth sink into her bottom lip as she turned her head to look back at him. He was standing in a familiar pose—military bearing, booted feet slightly apart, hands at his back.

"I was recruited by a sergeant when he passed through the village where I lived with my mother," he said. "I lied about my age—I was fourteen at the time. I was a sergeant in India several years later when . . . someone who appeared to feel he owed me something purchased an ensign's commission for me and later a lieutenant's. I progressed from there on my own. It is not an impossibly difficult thing to do during wartime. But my military rank notwithstanding, I am not a gentleman. My mother was unmarried. She scraped together a living by taking in other people's washing."

The tension that was in the brief silence that followed his words could surely be cut with a knife, Abigail thought.

"One might call me a guttersnipe," Gil added, "though my wife does not like the word."

Two servants chose that precise moment to bring in a tray of glasses and two bottles of champagne. They set everything down on the sideboard and left with downcast eyes, no doubt unnerved by the silence.

Her mother meanwhile had crossed quietly to the window. Marcel had followed her there, but while she stood looking out, he faced into the room, his hand on her forearm.

"And, in case anyone has forgotten," Abigail said, "I am not a lady."

She heard her mother moan softly.

"If any of you are thinking that I married beneath myself," Abigail continued, "you are mistaken. I married the man I wished to marry. No one has ever understood, but I will tell you now. What happened six years ago set me free. I did not realize it at the time, of course. It took me a long while. But I have never wanted to be restored to my former social position, all patched up and almost as good as new. I have wanted to be who I am. That too I did not understand for some time. But when I did, then I knew also that I was free, that what happened on that terrible day that sent Harry into the military and Mama and Camille and me fleeing to Bath was actually the greatest blessing of my life. I did not marry Gil *because* he is no more a gentleman than I am a lady. Nor did I marry him *despite* the fact that we had vastly different upbringings. I was free to marry him because I wanted to."

"Oh, Abigail," Elizabeth said, while Estelle squeezed her hand so tightly it hurt. "Yes, do take her, Mama." She handed the baby to Cousin Althea, while George on Colin's lap played with his watch fob. Elizabeth came to sit on the arm of the love seat before patting Abigail's hand. "Camille married the man of her heart. So did Viola— your mother. Now it is your turn to do the same thing. Bertrand, at the risk of sounding ill-mannered because I am a mere guest here, are you never going to pour that champagne and make the first toast to your stepsister and your new stepbrother-in-law?"

Bertrand hurried over to the sideboard. But what a travesty of a celebration, Abigail thought.

"I hope Harry had a proper talk with you, Bennington," Marcel said, sounding more austere than Abigail had ever heard him before. "I hope he did not consent purely out of friendship. I hope—"

"I did not need his consent," Abigail said sharply, "or anyone else's. I am twenty-four years of age."

"We did have a talk," Gil said. "I was able to satisfy Major West-cott that I am capable of keeping his sister in the manner of life to which she is accustomed. I was also able to satisfy him that I will hold her in respect and affection for the rest of my life."

"Then we have something to celebrate and you may distribute the glasses, Bertrand," Marcel said. "Are you satisfied, Viola?"

"If my son gave his approval," Abigail's mother said without turning, "and if Abby is happy with her choice, then I must be satisfied."

The weight upon her shoulder, Abigail realized as Bertrand handed her a glass bubbling with champagne, was Gil's hand.

Seventeen

T hey had their first quarrel after returning to their hotel in an
uneasy silence.

"It was extremely kind of Elizabeth and Colin to have the sudden
idea of hosting a wedding celebration for us, was it not?" Abigail said,
her face flushed, her voice determinedly cheerful, or so it seemed to
Gil as he closed the door of their suite behind them. "They have not
spent much time in their own home here since their marriage, partly
because of their children being born and their preference for the country, and partly because they have been having it completely refur-
bished. Colin's mother lived there for years, and her tastes are as
different from theirs as it is possible to be. It was, apparently, a mon-
strosity. Did you like them? And Cousin Althea? Elizabeth is everyone's favorite within the family. She is always calm and cheerful. Her
eyes are always smiling."

"They seem like pleasant people," he said.

"The event is to be a *family* celebration," she continued, "though it
was thoughtful of Colin, was it not, to ask if there was anyone you
would like them to invite too. It will not be a large event, and it will
not be at all intimidating. You know everyone. Camille and Joel will

not be there, of course, more is the pity, or Grandmama Kingsley, or my uncle and aunt from Dorsetshire. He is Mama's brother, a clergyman. And Harry will not be there."

"Neither will I, Abby," he said.

She whirled about to look at him, dismay on her face for a moment. He had not moved away from the door. Then she laughed.

"What?" she said. "A wedding celebration without the bridegroom? It is unheard of. It cannot be done."

"I will not go," he said. "I did not say I would. Perhaps you did not notice."

He had rarely been more uncomfortable in his life than he had been during that visit to Dorchester's house—in a grand, even opulent drawing room inside which his mother's hovel would have fit four or five times. After the great reveal and the shock and the hearty congratulations of the first fifteen minutes or so, all had become brittle gaiety as champagne had been passed around and impromptu toasts had been made with the grand pretense that everyone was perfectly happy to discover that Abby, one of their own, had married a guttersnipe. And yes, he would continue to use that word in his own mind. It was the reality.

He ought not to have married her.

It was too late for that thought now, though.

One thing about the aristocracy and the upper classes in general was that they were almost invariably polite. They had good manners instilled in them from birth. He had been both the beneficiary and the victim of that fact as a military officer. He had been both again this afternoon. For there was no doubt in his mind that they had all been horrified by the news and had remained horrified to the end. Yet they had all covered over their true sentiments, perhaps for Abby's sake since she was already married to him and could not be persuaded to change her mind, perhaps because he was Harry's friend and they all adored Harry. Or perhaps simply because they all had *manners*.

It had been a particular struggle for the Marchioness of Dorchester. Understandably so. She was Abby's mother. She had been gracious but almost silent. Gil would wager her mouth had not even touched her champagne.

And then, before he and Abby could escape to return here, Elizabeth, Lady Hodges, had had her bright idea, immediately seconded by her husband and backed up by her mother. Since the whole Westcott family except for Harry had missed the wedding, they must now celebrate it belatedly with a party at the Hodgeses' town house. Soon. The day after tomorrow. How exciting it was going to be!

Public executions could be exciting too. Gil did not doubt that every last one of the Westcotts would prefer to give him one of those except that good manners—and perhaps the law—stood in their way.

He could hardly blame them. He ought, of course, to have taken more time to think through the whole business of marrying Abigail Westcott. For he had known full well deep down that it was the worst idea in the world. But it was too late to go back and do things differently. Approximately thirty hours too late.

But he was, by God, not going to a Westcott family wedding party to have the whole farce of this afternoon's visit reenacted with a larger cast. The very thought of it . . .

"We cannot just not go," Abby said.

"Watch me," he said curtly. "You may go. I shall not try to persuade you out of going. I am certainly not going to command you not to attend. You are free to do as you wish."

He was being petty.

"But I could not possibly go without you," she said. "It would be absurd."

"Then do not go," he said. "Write and explain to Lady Hodges that we are too busy to attend any party. It would not be a complete lie. Or tell her the truth if you will. That I refuse to go."

"Gil," she said, "it would be *very* bad mannered."

Very. She had emphasized the word.

"And good manners matter to you more than anything else," he said.

She frowned. "No. But they do matter," she told him.

"I beg your pardon," he said, still petty and unable or unwilling to do anything about it, it seemed. "I was raised to believe good manners consisted of saying *please* and *thank you* in the appropriate places. I did not understand that they also involve attending functions one has no wish to attend and ones that no one else wants to attend either."

"My family will enjoy getting together to wish us well," she said. "It is what we do. We celebrate together and we commiserate together."

"And which will it be this time?" he asked. Nasty. Worse than petty now. Mean.

"Gil." She tipped her head to one side, still frowning. She had not yet removed her bonnet. Neither of them had sat down. "It was a surprise to everyone. But they all accepted it after they had got over their shock. And they all understand that you are the same person they met and liked at Hinsford. Your background does not matter to them."

"If you believe that, Abby," he said, "you have windmills in your head."

"That is not very kind," she said.

"One can only imagine," he said, "how the Earl of Riverdale, the head of your family, will react to learning how I duped him when I came from Paris with him and then mingled with his family for a whole week. One can only imagine how the Duke of Netherby will feel. And the dowager duchess. And the Dowager Countess of Riverdale. I could continue."

"They will receive you kindly," she said. "You are my husband."

"So the respect in which I will be held by the Westcott family will depend upon that slender thread, will it?" he said.

"Am I nothing more to you than a *slender thread*?" she asked.

He opened his mouth to retaliate and snapped it shut again. He broke eye contact with her and looked beyond her to the clock on the mantel.

"Abby," he said, "I have no wish to come between you and your family. None whatsoever. I know they are precious to you, and I know they love you. But I cannot be drawn into that particular fold. I will not try. Please do not ask it of me. And please do not ask it of your family. The kindest thing I can do for you is to stay away from them. Perhaps in time they will at least be reassured on your behalf when they know that I treat you well."

"Gil—" she began, but he held up a staying hand.

"I am going to go down to the stables to assure Beauty that I have not run away," he said. "I'll take her for a walk. I'll check on my horse too while I am down there. By the time I return it will be dinnertime."

And he turned and opened the door and half stepped through the doorway before stopping. He drew breath and released it on a sigh. He stepped back inside, closed the door without latching it, and strode across the distance between them. He wrapped one arm about her waist, the other about her shoulders, and pulled her hard against him before kissing her. Her spine arched inward and her hands splayed over his chest while she kissed him back.

A few moments later he was making his way downstairs. Beauty had a small stall of her own in the stables, with fresh straw and her pillow and a large bowl of water. He had made arrangements for her to be fed regularly and walked by a groom. But she always hated being in places where she must be separated from him. And he, dash it all, hated it too.

Their first quarrel—his and Abby's, that was. And a pretty serious one too. He wondered if they would recover from it.

He ought to go to that party, he supposed. It would be just a few hours out of his life. He ought to go through the motions of being welcomed into the family and feted. He ought to *be polite*. He had spent years, after all, learning to be a gentleman so that he could be a good officer. He should be willing to do this for Abby's sake.

But he could not.

He *would* not.

*   *   *

THEIR FIRST QUARREL. NOT MANY MORE THAN TWENTY-FOUR hours after their wedding. And a nasty one. One that might continue to divide them for the rest of their lives.

After Gil left, Abigail stood where she was for a full minute before turning to go into her bedchamber to change for dinner. She felt quite trembly, perhaps because she knew he had a point. The hour of that visit had been one of the most awkward of her life, with everyone pretending to be happy about her marriage once they had recovered from the initial shock—and Gil standing in almost the exact same spot all the time they were there.

Her mother had not even made much of an effort to pretend. But why would she? How would *she* feel, Abigail asked herself, if *her* daughter did something similar? She remembered how she had felt a few years ago when Mama had seemingly disappeared off the face of the earth on her way to Hinsford from Bath. Abigail, together with Joel and Alexander and Elizabeth, had tracked her all the way to a remote cottage in Devonshire and found her there, deep in an affair with Marcel—who had a reputation as a dreadful rake. Abigail had been horrified, among other things, even though Marcel had tried to cover up the impropriety by announcing that they were betrothed.

She heard Gil come in and go to his room about half an hour after he had left. She was seated in their private sitting room, pretending to read a book, when he came out, dressed for dinner.

"Gil," she said before he could say anything or before a silence could settle between them and be too awkward to break, "I understand. I *do*. I shall let Elizabeth know that if she wishes to invite the family to tea at her house, I will be delighted to join them, but that it must not be announced as a wedding celebration. I shall tell her how busy you are."

"Is that the polite way of saying I simply will not go?" he asked her.

She hesitated. "Yes," she said.

"And so you put me in the wrong," he told her. "I force you to lie for me."

"Can we just leave it at that?" she asked him. "Not quarrel anymore?"

"Is that what we have been doing?" he said. But he held up a hand before she could answer. "Yes, it is, and I am entirely to blame. I am sorry, Abby. I should have realized . . . I ought to have understood."

"Understood what it would mean suddenly to find yourself married into an aristocratic family?" she asked. "Even though I am only an illegitimate member?"

"It did not strike me quite so forcefully with my first marriage," he said. "I was not made to feel welcome from the start, and there was never any question of my meeting any member of the general's family or of Lady Pascoe's. Give me time. And yes, we will leave it at that for now. Let us go down to the dining room and think of some other topic of conversation to pursue during dinner."

"Agreed." She smiled at him and took his arm.

They talked about India. At least, *he* did while she listened with great interest and asked questions. And she talked about growing up at Hinsford, amusing him with stories about some of the people he had met during the weeks he had spent there.

They sat for a long while over their tea after they had finished eating and were the last of all the hotel guests to leave the dining room. Even so they went to bed early, exhausted after a day of travel and the emotional stress of the visit to her mother and the quarrel that had followed.

Not too exhausted, however, to make love before they slept. And how wonderful it was, Abigail thought as she drifted off to sleep, cradled in one of his arms, her head half on his shoulder, half on his bare chest, to be married at long last. And to be married to Gil. He was very different as a lover from anything she had expected. Not that her expectations had been very detailed, since she had no experience whatsoever by which to set them. But she had expected something far more . . . brisk. And forceful.

He was a gentle lover. And he took his time about making her feel somehow cherished, both before he entered her and after. He loved slowly and thoroughly and, she supposed, expertly. She was still a little sore from last night, but when he had asked about it as he was coming into her tonight, she had denied it. For the soreness had felt almost lovely. Ah, it was a good thing she did not have to put her feelings into words. They would make no sense. Her *feelings* made all the sense in the world.

She did not want to be in love with him. Theirs had never been billed as a love match. It was a practical arrangement between two people who had come to like and respect each other and who had both admitted an attraction to each other.

It would be foolish to fall in love.

GIL TIPPED HIS HEAD TO THE SIDE TO REST HIS DAMAGED CHEEK against the top of Abigail's head. Her hair was warm. Her naked body, like his own, was still damp from lovemaking. She was lovely to make love with. It felt so very good to have a woman of his own, a wife, a friend. A lover.

She was also one of *them*. To reason that they were equals because both were the by-blows of aristocratic fathers would have been an absurdity. Her mother was not a blacksmith's daughter. Neither had she been turned off by her family to raise her children in desperate poverty in a hovel, despised by everyone and his dog.

But a sense of victimhood was an ugly thing to nurture. He had shared it with a thousand other recruits in the ranks but had shaken it off, to be replaced by a determined self-respect when he rose first to the rank of corporal, then to that of sergeant. It had come sneaking back on him after he had been commissioned as an ensign, and then thrust off again during the years following as he doggedly taught himself to speak and behave as a gentleman even if he could never be one or be quite treated as one. His hard-won pride in himself had been severely shaken throughout the whole Caroline saga. He supposed now it had never fully recovered since. And today it had been very nearly shattered.

Both Dorchester and his wife, Abigail's mother, had invited them to stay there—for dinner, for the night, for as long as they intended to remain in London. Fortunately for him, Abby had been adamant about coming back to the hotel instead. He still did not know what he would have done if she had been eager to stay.

He would have suffocated. At the very least. Even though he had shared their company and that of other Westcotts for a whole week not long ago.

Abby's head had shifted. She had tipped it back so that she could see into his face. In the flickering light of the candles they had left burning on the dressing table she looked flushed and tousled and lovely. He kissed her softly on the mouth and felt a renewed stirring in his loins.

"You cannot sleep?" she asked him.

"Perhaps I am simply lying here enjoying the aftermath of a bedding with my wife," he said.

She smiled slowly, but she was clearly not convinced. "You are not relaxed," she said.

He had thought he was. Lovemaking did that to a man. But perhaps only in body. His mind had been churning with thoughts and emotions that had somehow got trapped up there with them. Negative, self-pitying emotions. Her family had been the model of good manners—and would continue to be, he would guess, provided he did well by Abby, as he fully intended to.

He *hated* his victim persona. Like an addiction, it could never seem to be conquered once and for all. It always found a way back in.

"Perhaps," he said, "that is because I am not yet finished. You have married a greedy man, Abby."

But she was still unconvinced.

"Gil," she said, "my family is important to me, and I will always want to be close to them. But if ever I had to choose between them and you, I would choose you without any hesitation. When I married you in the village church, I meant every word I spoke. I married you body, mind, and spirit."

"I would never, ever ask you to choose," he told her. "And I am of the firm belief that no one in your family would ask it of you either."

She smiled her slow, lovely smile again. It was starting to do strange things to his stomach.

"Tell me about your mother," she said.

Ah, it was starting again, was it? The probing at each other, the unmasking, the getting to know each other at ever-increasing depths. It was something that he and Caroline had not done. He was not sure he wanted to do it with Abby. Except that she wasn't giving him much choice. And he seemed unable to resist. And it must continue if theirs was to be a real marriage with a chance of lasting contentment.

He felt a lurching of sudden longing for his mother, who had died far too young, exhausted no doubt by the hardness of a cruel life. He sighed.

"If I had to describe her with one adjective," he said, "it would be *proud*. We lived in a house unworthy of the name. It was really fit for nothing but to be pulled down. She kept it spotlessly clean and tidy. She kept *me* clean and dressed me in clean clothes every day even when they were so patched that there were patches upon patches. She forced me to sit silent and idle in a corner for a whole hour at a time whenever I retaliated against those children who called me names by calling *them* names with language that belonged in the gutter. She insisted whenever I showed signs of slouching along the street, hoping not to be noticed, that I straighten my shoulders and hold my chin high. She always did the same herself. No one walked with a more regal posture than my mother, even when she was carrying a heavy basket of laundry."

"What did she look like?" she asked.

"It seems strange," he said, "but I do not believe children really notice how their parents *look*. Children do not see their parents as *people*, but only as mother and father. At least, I suppose that applies to fathers too. She was thin rather than slim. She was pale with faded fair hair. But when I bring her face to mind, I can see that she must once have been pretty. Perhaps *very* pretty."

She smiled and raised one hand to run her fingers lightly along his facial scar.

"I was incensed when she acquired a *friend* just before I left," he said. "I had looked forward to the day when I could be the man of the house and enable her to take in less washing and have a few brief spells each day simply to put her feet up. One of my most enduring dreams was that I would come home one day having spent some of my earnings on a new dress and new shoes for her and see the look of surprise and delight on her face when she saw them." He sighed, then continued. "He was a groom at the big house a few miles away, that friend, and he bought her a dress and a bonnet one day while I was at the village tavern trying for at least the dozenth time to persuade the publican to hire me to muck out the stables. I wanted to kill that groom. I wanted to rage at the pleased look on my mother's face. I hope he continued to look after her when I was gone. I hope she had a few happy years before she died. I wrote to her a few times from India. I even sent her money. But she could not write back. She could neither read nor write."

"You loved her," Abby said.

"We did not deal in such emotions," he said. "The poor do not, you know. They cannot afford love."

"Oh, Gil," she said, "you cannot possibly believe that. Even with the few details you have given me, I can tell that your mother loved you. And it is perfectly obvious you loved her."

"I do not know anything about love," he said. He could not imagine his mother ever using the word. He was quite sure she never had while he lived with her.

"Of course you do," she told him. "You love Katy."

He closed his eyes and did not say anything for a while. Truth to tell, he was fighting a soreness in his throat and up behind his nose. It would be shameful indeed if he allowed it to reach his eyes.

"I have not seen her since she was a baby," he said at last. "I do not even know what she looks like now or what her voice sounds like. I do not even know how much she can talk. When *does* an infant learn to speak? She would not know me. It is possible she does not even know of my existence. She would probably be frightened of me if she saw me, especially if I tried to take her from the only home she knows."

"Love will not always cause you pain," she said. "And even when it does, it is better than the alternative. Being without love would be only one remove from despair. I cannot imagine anything worse."

Was she asking him to love *her*? Was she hinting that she might love *him*? But it was only a word, was it not? He would not be able to define it if his life depended upon it.

"You love Beauty," she said. "And she loves you."

"Old softie of a dog," he said, and she laughed. He loved her laughter. There. He had used the word in his head. He *loved* her laughter.

But he wanted their relationship to stay like this. Pleasant—except when they quarreled. At this moment it was very pleasant, without any of the wild passions, almost all of them dark, that had swirled through and about his first marriage.

He found her mouth and kissed her, and then prolonged the kiss because she was warm and soft and inviting. He pressed his tongue inside, and she sucked on it before he curled the tip and stroked the roof of her mouth until she made a low sound deep in her throat.

"Come across me," he said. When she looked inquiringly at him, he moved his hands to grasp her by the hips and lift her over him until she was straddling his body. Her knees were on either side of his hips, her hands spread over his chest, and her hair was falling forward in a tangled cascade over her shoulders.

She had a body that delighted him—flat stomach and ribs, breasts just large enough to fit into his hands, rose-tipped nipples that hardened easily against the light stroking of his thumbs. Her hips were shapely though not large. Large enough, though, he thought, to allow for the easy passage of a child. Her legs were slim and long. And her skin in the candlelight was the color of alabaster and as smooth as the finest silk.

He guided her over him and drew her down onto his erection. Her eyes closed and she clenched inner muscles about him, and it was exquisite pleasure-pain.

"Ride," he said.

Her eyes flew open and came to his. Then they drifted closed again and she rode. He lay still for a long time, reveling in the feel and sight of her, his hands and forearms along the outsides of her bent legs. His body urged him to grasp her hips, to drive up into her, to force a climax and release and relaxation. His mind, that hornet's nest of churning emotions for the past several hours, commanded him to be still, to allow himself to be . . . loved. Or *enjoyed*. That would be a better word. For there was no doubt that she was enjoying what she did.

And then her eyes came open again, looking very blue in the guttering light of the almost-spent candles, and her hands slid up to his shoulders, and her head bent closer to his.

"Gil," she whispered, and he obeyed instinct and grasped her hips and took them swiftly and together to the place for which they strove.

The breath shuddered audibly out of her when finally they were still and the tension had gone, and he brought her down to lie full on him, her legs relaxed on either side of his own, her head turned face in against his shoulder. With one foot he nudged up the bedcovers until he could grasp them with one hand and pull them higher.

"Gil," she murmured again.

Now at last he would sleep. Thoughts had been routed by sexual satisfaction and the warm, relaxed weight of his wife's body on his own. He did not try to find words.

He was still inside her.

Eighteen

They spent a large portion of the following morning in the gloomy, wood-paneled chambers of the law firm of Grimes, Hanson, and Digby. Mr. Grimes was a thin man of medium height and silver hair, a pair of spectacles resting halfway down a sharp nose so that he could peer downward through them when reading and over the top of them, with a slight dip of the head, when he was talking to his client. He appeared unassuming and unimpressive, but his eyes, which looked alternately upward and downward, were keen, and his questions proved thorough, his opinions and pronouncements blunt.

He looked Gil over from head to foot as he shook hands with him, his eyes resting rather longer upon his facial scar than on any other part of him.

"I do not know, Lieutenant Colonel," he said, "if you intend to take my advice and resign your commission or retire from the army. But I would strongly recommend that you wear your dress uniform when you appear before the judge who will decide your case. Your formidable appearance will be less daunting perhaps when seen in the context of your military background."

Gil had taken great care over his appearance, since this was his first face-to-face meeting with his lawyer. But apparently he looked sinister nonetheless. It did not help that he towered over the man by a good six inches, and that he probably weighed twice as much.

"I shall think about it," he said, nodding curtly. "Allow me to present Mrs. Bennington, my wife."

She had dressed in a rather severely styled moss green walking dress, which nevertheless looked smart and expensive and accentuated the slimness of her figure. She had styled her hair smoothly over the crown of her head and twisted it into a knot at the back of her neck beneath her brown bonnet. There was not a stray curl in sight. There was a certain regality about the way she reached out her right hand toward Grimes and slightly inclined her head. She looked every inch the Lady Abigail Westcott she had once been.

"How do you do?" she said.

"Ma'am?" The lawyer took her hand and bowed over it before returning his gaze to Gil. "I am delighted that you followed this particular piece of advice of mine," he said. "Will you come into my chambers and be seated, Mrs. Bennington? Lieutenant Colonel?"

A clerk followed them in, bearing three cups of coffee on a tray with a silver jug of milk and bowl of sugar.

"I will also be putting an end to my military career," Gil said when the clerk had withdrawn and closed the door quietly behind him. "I intend to be a full-time husband and father."

Grimes nodded his approval and turned his attention back to Abby. "And who, ma'am, might you be?" he asked, his eyes peering very directly at her over his eyeglasses.

Gil bristled. "I hardly think—" he began, but he was stopped by an imperious hand, which was raised palm out.

"I am sure you do not, Lieutenant Colonel," he said. "But it is the first thing Sir Edward Pascoe's lawyer will want to know. And *only* the first. He will want to know—and he *will* discover—everything there is to know about your wife in the hope of finding something or several things that would disqualify her from being a suitable mother for Miss Katherine Bennington."

"If anyone has anything to say in criticism of my wife," Gil said, on the verge of getting to his feet and taking Abby away from there, "he may say it to me, sir. You can be sure I—"

But again he was interrupted, this time by Abby's hand coming to rest lightly upon his sleeve.

"Mr. Grimes is not offering me an insult, Gil," she said. "He is merely doing his job, which is to gather as much information relevant to your case as he possibly can so that he can make a convincing argument in your favor and be ready to counter any argument the other lawyer will make."

"Thank you, ma'am," Grimes said. "That is exactly correct."

Gil clenched his hands in his lap.

"I was Abigail Westcott," Abby told him. "I am the daughter of the late Earl of Riverdale and the present Marchioness of Dorchester. The one negative fact about me that you will need to be prepared to deal with is that, unknown to my mother until after my father's death six years ago, her marriage to him was not valid. He had a wife still living when he married her."

"Bigamy?" The lawyer frowned.

Abby inclined her head. "And illegitimacy for my brother and sister and myself," she said.

"I fail to see—" Gil said, but her hand tightened about his arm and he fell silent again.

There followed seemingly endless and very personal, intrusive questions of his wife. Gil sat through it all in stony, suffering silence as he began to realize just what he had exposed her to by marrying her. Not only this interrogation by a lawyer who was supposedly on his side, but the future indignity of full exposure by a less friendly lawyer in the presence of a judge and surely of General Sir Edward and Lady Pascoe too. He closed his eyes at one point and wondered how he could possibly have slept so comfortably last night and again after waking early and making love to his wife for the third time. He must be a prize idiot. He had had no inkling of the ordeal that was ahead for her this morning.

"I believe your husband's chances of persuading a judge to award him custody of his daughter are somewhat improved, Mrs. Bennington," Grimes told her by way of summary when he had seemed to run out of questions. "My learned colleague, the general's lawyer, will of course make much of the irregularity of your birth, and indeed it is a great pity there is that. However, your mother has since married the Marquess of Dorchester, your brother is a major in an infantry regiment, your sister has made a respectable marriage to a portrait painter of some means and growing renown, and your maternal uncle is a clergyman with a living in Dorsetshire. Your father's family, which includes the present Earl of Riverdale, your cousin, has not disowned you. Neither has the dowager countess, your grandmother. Or, according to your account, any other member of the Westcott family. You were raised and educated as a lady. You have a tidy fortune of your own. I think all this may do nicely."

"But my chances are only *somewhat* improved?" Gil asked testily.

"There is your appearance," Grimes told him bluntly. "Unfortunately, Lieutenant Colonel, when one hears the accusation, which you claim to be false, that you were physically abusive to your wife, one is inclined to believe it. And when one hears the story, which you do not contest, of your storming the general's house when he was not at home to protect his wife and granddaughter, terrifying the servants as well as the lady and the child, then one is even more inclined to give credence to your late wife's accusations."

"I am to wear a mask, then, am I?" Gil asked him, frowning. "That of a curly-haired, round-cheeked cherub, perhaps?"

"Unfortunately," Grimes said, apparently unperturbed by his clearly irritated client, "people are prejudged upon their appearance, even when the one who does the judging does not realize it. And your inclination to become angry does not help your case."

"Well, what do you expect?" Gil asked him.

"I expect that you will learn to follow my instructions when it comes to the hearing," Grimes said. "If, that is, you are serious about recovering your daughter. I expect, sir, that you will learn to curb your temper no matter what my learned colleague may be saying that outrages you. You must trust me. I cannot promise beyond all doubt that I will win a favorable verdict for you, but I *am* your best hope."

"I am to smile and grin, as though I have not a care in the world or a sensible thought in my head, then, am I?" Gil asked, his frown deepening.

Grimes did not answer. Abby's hand slid along Gil's forearm until it was tucked within his own.

"We will both trust you, Mr. Grimes," she said. "And by the day of the hearing we will both *look* as though we do." She smiled at Gil, and he wanted to punch someone. Not her. Not Grimes either. But *someone.*

"What *may* help," Grimes said, "is an explanation of how you got that unfortunate scar across your face, Lieutenant Colonel. Can we make something heroic of it? I do know about your leading a forlorn hope while you were in the Peninsula, and I shall certainly work that into my defense of your character. The facial wound was not acquired on that occasion, by any chance?"

"No, but I know the story," Abby said. "He was slashed by the sword of a cavalryman in India while saving the lives of hundreds of his men by ordering them to form square instead of fleeing in panic."

"Form square?" The lawyer raised his eyebrows.

Gil explained.

"It is a pity," the lawyer said, "that you were merely a sergeant at the time. However, I believe the story must be worked into what I say. It will encourage the judge to see you differently. And at least the uniform in which you will appear will be that of a lieutenant colonel. It displays a few medals, I hope?"

"Yes, a few," Gil admitted reluctantly. He hated all this. *Hated* it. And all because Caroline had taken Katy to her mother instead of leaving her safe and well cared for at Rose Cottage with her nurse and other servants whom Gil had trusted.

But there was no point in crying over spilled milk. Wherever had that saying originated? he wondered idly.

The wearying questioning continued. Many of the questions Gil had surely answered before in letters. But he answered them again. Grimes wanted details about the house in Gloucestershire, the servants who worked there, and the neighbors who lived close by. He wanted a list of persons who would be willing to give Lieutenant Colonel Bennington a good character and was clearly unhappy that Gil could give him the names only of fellow officers, none of whom, including Harry, lived close enough to make a personal appearance at the hearing. His mind touched upon the Westcotts, most notably the Duke of Netherby and the Earl of Riverdale, but knowing what they did of him now they must not be feeling kindly toward him. Grimes wanted to know about Gil's relationship with his first wife, especially while they were living at Rose Cottage. Were there any servants or neighbors who might be drawn into testifying to loud arguments or verbal or physical abuse? Or their absence?

"Not that the law does not allow a man to discipline his wife in any way he sees fit short of killing her," he added. "But we must hope the judge does not decide you are too violent a man, Lieutenant Colonel Bennington, to be granted charge of a child."

"*My* child," Gil said curtly. "But anyway, yes, there were arguments. Are there not always disagreements and arguments in any relationship? There was no abuse, physical or otherwise, unless insisting that my wife stay safe at home with our baby while I went to war without them counts as abuse."

"Hardly," the lawyer said, and Gil regarded him with narrowed eyes.

Do not lose your temper, he told himself. *Practice what Abby has promised you will both do by the time of the hearing before a judge.*

The questions continued.

Grimes expected the case to come to a quick resolution. It would not drag on indefinitely. General Sir Edward Pascoe's lawyer was pressing for an early appearance before a judge. The general and his wife were already in London in anticipation of it.

"I am also eager for an early resolution," Gil said as his lawyer got to his feet in a clear indication that their meeting was over. "I wish to return to the country with my wife and daughter."

Abby extended her hand to Grimes, thanked him for his time, and assured him that they trusted him.

"He is not confident," Gil told her as they walked away from the chambers. "I ought to have chosen someone different. Perhaps it is still not too late."

"I believe," she said, "I would feel more worried about Mr. Grimes if he *were* confident. He is amassing facts in great detail, Gil, so that he may make the very best case possible for you. He is neglecting nothing, including the effect your scar and my birth might have upon the judge. He will explain the scar, I am sure, in a way that shows you as the hero you were on that occasion. I am sorry about the other. If only I were still *Lady Abigail,* I would undoubtedly be more of an asset to you."

"If you were still Lady Abigail," he said, "you would not be married to me at all, Abby. You would have married some grand lord years ago and presented him with half a dozen children by now."

"Oh. One each year since I was eighteen?" she said. "That does not sound pleasant at all. I am glad, then, that I am not still Lady Abigail."

"So am I," he said. "I want those six children—or maybe not quite as many—to be mine."

She turned her head to smile at him, her cheeks flushed, her eyes shining, and devil take it, he wanted her. Right here in the middle of a busy London street. And he wondered if perhaps he had already impregnated her. Two nights. Four times. It was a bit of a dizzying thought. But for the moment it had at least distracted his mind from the growing worry of what would happen about his daughter.

"Gil," she said, "I believe Mr. Grimes is a competent lawyer. He asked questions I would not have thought of myself. I do not believe that anything General Pascoe's lawyer says can possibly take him by surprise. He will have his answers and arguments ready. You must trust him."

"That is easier said than done," he said.

"Yes." She squeezed his arm.

AFTER LUNCHEON AT THE HOTEL AND A BRIEF WALK WITH BEAUTY, they went their separate ways. Abigail went to call upon her mother in a hackney carriage the hotel receptionist had summoned at Gil's bidding. Gil himself was going to the Horse Guards to begin proceedings to end his military career.

"Are you quite sure it is what you wish to do?" she asked with one foot on the step of the carriage, her hand in his.

"Yes," he said. "It has been a good career, but I do not think I would make a good peacetime officer, Abby. I thought I would go insane with boredom on St. Helena. And I would not want to take you to follow the drum in the event I was posted to another country. I would like even less leaving you behind to wait for my return. Besides, I have a hankering to go home, to settle down at last. Regardless."

He looked like granite again when he said that final word.

She had a hankering to go home too, Abigail thought as the carriage moved away from the hotel and she raised a hand in farewell. To Rose Cottage, even though she had not yet seen it. She liked the sound of it. It was set in gardens that were alive with color in the summertime, Gil had told her, though he had not seen it for himself. And it would be full of the fragrance of roses and the beauty of their blooms. The house was large but not quite a mansion. A smallish manor, perhaps. And it would be hers by virtue of the fact that she was

Mrs. Bennington, a name she hugged to herself. She wanted so badly the sense of belonging that her own home would bring. Even Hinsford had not quite brought it, and Harry had reminded her of the fact when he had asked her what she would do if and when he brought a bride to live there.

Did she love Gil? She was not sure. But it seemed somehow irrelevant. She did not need to be in love, to be walking on air, to have stars in her eyes. For of one thing she *was* sure: She had married the man of her own choosing—the one and only. Hurried as the whole business had been, she had not felt a moment's regret since.

Not even, she thought, taking a deep breath as the carriage stopped outside Marcel's house, over the trouble she had caused with her family. It was something they must grapple with—or not. It was not really her problem.

Nevertheless she was relieved to find that her mother was alone in the private sitting room that adjoined her bedchamber. Marcel was at the House of Lords, and Bertrand had escorted Estelle to a garden party even though Abigail's aunt Louise had offered to take her with Jessica.

"He is a steady young man," her mother explained, drawing Abigail down to sit beside her on a couch, "and keeps an eagle eye upon his sister even though she is quick to remind him that she is twenty-one years old and his elder by twenty minutes. He knew I wanted to remain at home this afternoon and that I would prefer to do so alone. You said you might come."

"I believe I said I *would*," Abigail said. "I suppose the whole family knows by now."

"It would be surprising if anyone did not," her mother said. "Elizabeth was busy organizing a second wedding breakfast for you until she received your note to inform her that Lieutenant Colonel Bennington has business that will keep him occupied for every waking moment during the next week or two—or words to that effect. But she still wants the family to go there for tea tomorrow, and she very much hopes you will go too, Abby. I am sure there is a letter on the way to you at the Pulteney."

Abigail sighed. "I will go," she said. "There is no point in hiding, is there? And actually I have no desire to do so. There is nothing to hide *from*. Is everyone very upset?"

"Matilda and Mildred and Louise called here this morning," her mother said. "Your father's three sisters. The triumvirate. The eternal fixers. I suppose they spoke for everyone. They are *concerned*, Abby, especially when for six years you have shown such marked reluctance to marry *anyone*. Of course they are concerned. But if you believe anyone is going to cast you off, then you have not been paying much attention since your father died. What their brother did to me and to you and Camille and Harry, and what he did to Anna's mother and to Anna herself, shook his three sisters to their roots, you know. What he did to us he did to *them*. And to your poor grandmother, Humphrey's *mother*. You would have to do a lot worse than marry a man who is not a gentleman born, Abby, to alienate them."

"I had never thought of matters quite that way," Abigail admitted. "I suppose I have assumed that only the five of us—you, Camille, Harry, Anna, and I—were directly affected by what happened. But of course we *all* were—Alexander, Grandmama, the aunts. Everyone."

"Abby." Her mother leaned across the space between them and patted her hand. "I have only one real question for you today now that I have recovered from yesterday's shock, and we are alone. Can you be happy with Lieutenant Colonel Bennington? It is a pointless question, I know, since you have married him and nothing can change that. But . . . *can* you?"

"I can, Mama," Abigail said. "I'm as sure as I can possibly be that I can."

Her mother sighed with what might have been relief and closed her eyes briefly. She drew breath, and it seemed for a moment that she was about to say more. But she did not do so. She opened her eyes, smiled, and pulled on the bell rope beside the couch to summon the tea tray.

"Who could possibly have dreamed just a little more than six years ago," she said, "that life would turn so topsy-turvy for us all?"

"Happily so," Abigail said.

"Anna, after growing up in an orphanage, married a duke," her mother said. "Camille married a schoolteacher from the orphanage where he grew up when she was once betrothed to a viscount. Harry barely survived the wars as a military officer when he was once Earl of Riverdale. You have married a man who could not possibly be lower on the social scale than he is, when once upon a time the world of wealth and privilege was about to open to you in all its splendor. And I married a rake."

She laughed, and they were silent for a while as the tea tray was brought in and she poured them each a cup.

"I believe we are all the happier for the turmoil we have been through, Mama," Abigail said. "Even Harry is safe and recovering well now he is at home. He is even riding again."

"And you?" Her mother frowned at her, her cup halfway to her mouth.

"I would rather be married to Gil than to any aristocrat you would care to name," Abigail said.

"But you do not *know* any aristocrats outside the family," her mother pointed out, and they both laughed.

"But . . ." her mother said. "There is this nasty business looming with Lieutenant Colonel Bennington's daughter and General Pascoe. Marcel says that both he and his wife are powerful and influential people. And you are going to be drawn into the nastiness. They are in London. Did you know that?"

"I did," Abigail said. "We spent the morning at the chambers of Gil's lawyer. He is very thorough. Gil is afraid to trust him fully, but I do. I believe the hearing with a judge will be soon."

"That poor little girl, being pulled this way and that," her mother said with a sigh. "Though I suppose she knows nothing about it, does she? I just *wish* you were not involved, Abby. But I will say no more on the matter. You *are* involved. You went into this marriage with your eyes wide open, and you are of age. You would be quite within your rights to tell me to mind my own business. Now. How are we going to persuade this husband of yours to take his place in the family? I do at least partly understand his reluctance, you know. I tried to distance myself from the Westcott family after I learned that I had no claim whatsoever to call myself a Westcott. Will he come to Elizabeth's for tea tomorrow if I send a personal note? I fear I behaved badly yesterday."

"I think not, Mama," Abigail said. "I will tell him what you have said, but he is deeply aware of the inferiority of his social rank, and he also feels that he was somehow deceiving you all about himself when you were at Hinsford. I suppose he decided then that it did not matter too much since he did not expect to meet any of you ever again."

"Well," her mother said, "we will have to see what happens tomorrow at Elizabeth and Colin's. I daresay the whole matter will be discussed to death, and all sorts of plots and plans and schemes will be hatched. I almost feel sorry for the poor lieutenant colonel. The Westcott family can be as fearful to face as swords and guns."

"Perhaps," Abigail said, "everyone will be secretly glad of his absence, Mama. You cannot be sure the family will rally in its usual manner."

"You and I are ladies, not gentlemen, alas, Abby," her mother said, smiling at her, "but how much would you care to wager upon that?"

Nineteen

It had been a busy day, not just physically, but emotionally too. Meeting his lawyer face-to-face at last, being interrogated by him—yes, it was the right word—and having Abby interrogated, and learning that General Pascoe and his wife were in London and the hearing before a judge was imminent had all raised Gil's anxiety level considerably. With his head he might persuade himself that his case was a strong one and that within a few weeks at the longest he would be on his way home to Gloucestershire with his wife and daughter. But with his gut he was fearful and not convinced of anything. For what General Sir Edward and Lady Pascoe wanted, they invariably got. Except, a little voice in his head said, the sort of husband they had wanted for their daughter. And that very fact would make them even more determined not to be thwarted again by the same man.

The afternoon had not improved his mood. He had seen Abby on her way to visit her mother alone, knowing that she would make excuses for him. He knew he had hurt her by refusing to participate in the Westcott family wedding breakfast Lord Hodges and his wife had wanted to put on for them. It had perhaps been selfish of him. On top of the guilt of that thought, he had spent much of the afternoon putting an end to all that had given him identity and focus and self-esteem for twenty years. He had begun the process of retiring from his regiment and the army. And though he had much for which to retire—home, family, fortune, the peaceful, settled life he had always dreamed of—nevertheless it was a wrench to cut himself off from all that was familiar to him. And the future was never assured.

Abby returned to the hotel soon after him, looking as tired as he felt, though she smiled at him and asked about his afternoon. She told him of her mother's fear that it was her reaction to yesterday's news that had determined Gil to stay away from the celebration planned in their honor.

"She hopes that if that is so, you will reconsider," Abby said.

Perhaps it was foolish of him not to do so, especially since it would not involve the ordeal of meeting any of them for the first time. He had spent a week at Hinsford with most of them and had felt relatively at ease with them. He had liked them and felt liked in return. But he knew that his reluctance to meet them again was for that very reason. He had deceived them during that week, allowing them to assume that because he was a high-ranking military officer he must also be a gentleman. And then he had married one of their own, without asking any of them except Harry.

He could not do it. He could not face them again. But by refusing he was hurting Abby.

"I told her you would not," she said. "But I promised to pass along the message."

"The plans will go ahead regardless?" he asked her.

"Well, not as a wedding breakfast," she said. "But yes. Cousin Elizabeth and Colin have invited the whole family to tea tomorrow, and I will go. They will want me there. I suppose I will be the guest of honor."

"I have a million and one things to do," he told her. "We need a carriage and horses. I have an appointment to see my agent. He oversees the management of my home and farm—of *our* home—and he looks after my investments. I rarely get to meet him in person. He is a busy man. I do not suppose it would be easy to change—"

"It is all right, Gil," she said. She stepped closer to him and set a hand on his arm. She was smiling, an expression that went all the way back into her eyes to fill her whole person. Or so it seemed to him. He felt humbled. He must be a great disappointment to her. "I understand."

She ought to be raging at him. He stood staring mutely at her, ready, it seemed, to rage at *her* for not raging at *him*. But then . . .

"*I cannot think of anyone or anything else but my baby, Abby,*" he blurted, and for a moment he was terrified that he was about to break down. He gulped for air and hid his eyes with the thumb and forefinger of one hand grasping his temples.

"I know," she said softly. And she stepped right against him and wrapped her arms about him while his own grabbed for her and held her close. Too close. He must be hurting her. He swallowed and almost lost the battle to start bawling. "I know."

But she did *not* know. How it had felt to hold that baby in his arms, knowing she was *his* to love and cherish and nurture and keep safe and secure in the unconditional love of a parent. How it had felt to leave her when Napoleon Bonaparte had been gathering an army again and another colossal battle seemed likely and he might die and never see her again. How it had felt to arrive home, alarmed by Caroline's letters, to find the house empty of all but a few servants, none of whom knew where his wife and daughter had gone. How it had felt to be denied admittance to his mother-in-law's home even after he had learned that Katy was there. How it had felt to hear her cry, perhaps with fright at all the shouting that was going on downstairs. How it had felt to leave there alone. And then to be sent to St. Helena, as much an exile as Bonaparte himself. How it felt now to know that his fate lay in the hands of a judge, who did not know him or the depths of his feelings. No, she did not know. How could she?

But she held him and endured the way he was clutching her to himself in such a way that she was probably having difficulty breathing. No, she did not know. But she understood. Good God, he did not have the exclusive rights to pain. She had suffered too. She had been a young girl, about to make her debut into society. How eager and excited and full of hope and expectation she must have been. Only to have it all taken from her along with the very roots of her identity. No, she was not immune to suffering.

He loosened his hold and regarded her wearily. "You look tired," he said. She was still wearing her bonnet, a small-brimmed, high-crowned frivolity that made her look purely pretty. Not that she really needed a bonnet to do that. He pulled loose the ribbons beneath her chin.

"So do you." She moved back a half step and spread her hands over his chest. "It will soon be over, Gil."

"That is what I am afraid of," he said.

"I know." She swayed against him again as he removed her bonnet, and set her forehead against his shoulder. "It is the waiting that kills, and you have been doing it for close to two years. Let me order up some tea. It is too early to go down for dinner."

"I would rather go to bed," he told her.

"If you would prefer," she said, raising her head and smiling again. He saw the moment at which she realized what he meant. "Oh." Her smile faded and she blushed rosily.

"It can be done during the daytime, you know," he said. "It is physically possible. It is not *just* for the nighttime."

She laughed and something caught at his stomach. Or perhaps it was his heart.

"Oh," she said again.

"We might even sleep," he said. "Afterward."

ABIGAIL ARRIVED AT LORD HODGES'S HOUSE ON CURZON STREET the following afternoon with her mother, Marcel, and Estelle, who had come to the Pulteney Hotel for her. Gil had taken Beauty for a walk in Hyde Park. After that he had an appointment with his agent.

Everyone else had arrived before them, perhaps by design, Abigail thought, since she surely was the guest of honor. They had gathered to see *her*. It was not long since she had waved them all on their way back to town from Hinsford. But of course everything had changed since then.

She felt ridiculously nervous as Colin and Elizabeth's butler escorted them upstairs and announced them after opening the drawing room doors. "The Marquess and Marchioness of Dorchester, Lady Estelle Lamarr, and Mrs. Bennington." Just as though they were stepping into someone's ballroom for a grand *ton* event. Not that Abigail had ever experienced one of those in person.

Mrs. Bennington. It still sounded strange.

Alexander was standing with his back to the fireplace. Abigail's grandmother, the Dowager Countess of Riverdale, was seated in a large chair to one side of it, Aunt Matilda standing beside her chair, vinaigrette in hand on the chance that her mother might need to be revived in the excitement of the moment. Aunt Mildred and Uncle Thomas, Lord and Lady Molenor, were seated side by side on a love seat. Aunt Louise, the Dowager Duchess of Netherby, was sitting with Jessica and Wren on a sofa. Cousin Althea Westcott, Elizabeth's mother, was sitting on another chair, Anna perched on the arm. Avery, Duke of Netherby, was seated somewhat apart from everyone else, as though he considered himself more an observer than a participant. Bertrand was standing beside him. Colin and Elizabeth, both on their feet, both smiling warmly, were coming toward them, hands outstretched to greet them.

Abigail drew a deep breath and smiled. She understood perfectly why Gil could not face this.

"Well, Abigail," her grandmother said. "Explain yourself."

"You must not excite yourself, Mama," Aunt Matilda said.

"I am not excited," the dowager told her. "And put that thing in your hand away unless you intend on using it yourself. Abigail?"

Colin, having smiled at Estelle, shaken Marcel by the hand, and kissed Viola's cheek, had just turned to Abigail to take her hand in both his own. He laughed. "Allow the poor lady to catch her breath and be seated first, if you will, ma'am," he said, offering his arm. "We have kept the chair by the fireplace for you, Abigail. We are delighted you have come."

She was not to escape so easily to the relative safety of the chair, however.

"But a hug before you sit down, Abby," Anna said, hurrying toward them and pulling Abigail into her arms. "I liked Lieutenant Colonel Bennington extremely well while we were at Hinsford, and I wish you both all the happiness in the world."

"Thank you," Abigail said.

"So did I, and so *do* I," Wren said, hugging Abigail after Anna had let her go.

"Abby." Jessica caught hold of her next. "I did not know what to think when I heard. I still do not. You might have knocked me over with a feather. I was quite convinced that you would *never* marry, and the thought made me miserable. I do know you would never have married where your heart was not engaged, so I must be happy for you. But I am not sure I will *ever* forgive you for not inviting me to your wedding. I have not even decided yet if I will even talk to you again." All the while she was squeezing Abigail tightly.

"I feel the same way," Estelle said.

"Well, I hope you both decide in my favor," Abigail said, "or I will have to be content with delivering monologues whenever I am in company with you."

Aunt Louise claimed a hug next. "Goodness me, you took us all by surprise, Abigail," she said. "I did not see it coming while we were at Hinsford. And even looking back I cannot see any signs of what was in the wind."

"I do not believe anything *was* in the wind while we were there, Louise," Uncle Thomas said. He had come to shake Abigail heartily by the hand and kiss her cheek. "I wish you well, my dear. Lieutenant Colonel Bennington seems like a fine young man."

"Oh, Abigail," Aunt Mildred said when she hugged her. "It really is quite romantic. Just as Avery's dashing off with Anna to marry quietly while we were all planning a grand wedding for them was."

"I just wish," Cousin Althea said, "that Lieutenant Colonel Bennington had come with you, Abigail. He looked very uncomfortable yesterday afternoon when I met him for the first time. But he will get used to us."

"We all know why he has not come," Abigail's grandmother said when Abigail sat down at last and everyone else had resumed their places. The hubbub of sound stopped with her words. "And why he will not allow a wedding breakfast. We know everything except why you did it, Abigail. Why you married a man you knew to be ineligible, a man with problems that may well drag you and your family down into the dust. Why you married him in such a havey-cavey manner, without letting even your mother know. Do you have such little respect for yourself?"

"Mama!"

"No, Mother, I will not have Abigail harassed."

"Perhaps we ought—"

Aunt Matilda, Abigail's mother, and Elizabeth spoke simultaneously. Aunt Matilda even forgot to try pressing the vinaigrette upon Grandmama.

Alexander stopped them with a raised hand. "No," he said. "The concern is one we all feel. Perhaps we needed Cousin Eugenia to express it so bluntly. And perhaps we ought to give Abigail a chance to answer for herself."

An uneasy silence settled on the room.

"Or not," Avery said quietly from his corner. "It seems to me that Abigail was invited here for tea."

"Oh, she *was*, Alexander," Elizabeth said. "We want to rejoice with her."

"*Rejoice*," Grandmama said scornfully. "In the absence of the bridegroom. He will not come here to face us himself."

"Because he agrees with you, Grandmama," Abigail said, and felt all attention swing her way. "He believes he does not belong here. But he does belong with *me*. I married him, knowing full well who he was and why he needed to marry without delay. Harry knew everything, and he has known Gil for years. They are close friends. Harry approved of our marriage. The Reverend Jenkins married us in the village church and came to the house afterward with Mrs. Jenkins for a wedding breakfast. Mrs. Jenkins decorated the church with flowers, and the staff at Hinsford decorated the house. They greeted us formally when we returned from church. It was a sudden wedding because Gil needs a wife to give him a better chance of recovering his daughter from his first wife's parents, to whom she was taken without his permission while he was in Belgium just prior to the Battle of Waterloo. It was a sudden wedding, but it was not clandestine."

"His reason for marrying you and for doing it in a hurry is obvious," her grandmother said. "Your reason is less clear, Abigail. Were you so desperate for a husband? Yet for six years you have resisted all the attempts of your family to introduce you to eligible gentlemen."

"Marcel," Abigail's mother said, getting to her feet, "take us home, please. It was not for this that we—"

"It is all right, Mama," Abigail said. "I was aware of the tension in this room even before we entered it, and it is as well that Grandmama had the courage to confront it."

Her mother subsided back into her seat while Abigail returned her attention to her grandmother.

"I was not desperate," she said. "I was quite prepared to go through life unmarried if I did not meet the man who would be perfect for me. I found him in Gil, though I do not believe I will ever be able to explain to anyone what I mean by that. I married him because I wanted to, and I married him in a hurry because that was what he needed. I am sorry that I have upset you all. But I am not sorry for what I have done. I expect to be happy."

"Brava, Abigail," Avery said from his corner. Everyone turned his way.

"That is all very well to say, Avery," Aunt Louise said. "But Lieutenant Colonel Bennington refuses to face Abigail's family, he is embroiled in what might well be an ugly fight over custody of his daughter, and he is the illegitimate son of a washerwoman."

"None of which matters," Elizabeth said, "if Abigail is happy with him. He is a man who has achieved a very high military rank. Avery has told us that he has won several commendations for bravery, most notably for leading a successful forlorn hope when he was in the Peninsula. He is Harry's friend and was kind enough to accompany him home and stay with him while he recovered his health and strength. He obviously cares very deeply for his daughter if he is fighting to get her back when he could very easily leave her with her grandparents and not have to worry about the raising of her."

"I do not care what anyone says," Estelle cried. "If Abby has married him, I am prepared to like him. I *do* like him. Who can forget how he allowed Robbie to take over his dog while we were all at Hinsford?"

"Well done, Stel," Bertrand said. "Our stepsister is old enough and mature enough to know her own mind. If she is happy, I am happy for her."

"Well said, young man," Cousin Althea said.

"What we need," Aunt Matilda said, her cheeks flushed with color, "is a *plan*. Whether we like it or not, Abigail is married to Lieutenant Colonel Bennington. I am not even sure I do *not* like it. Clearly she cares for him, and perhaps that matters almost more than anything. We need a plan for drawing him into the family, for making him feel welcome. Not just on sufferance, but *welcome*."

"And how are we to do that, Matilda?" Aunt Louise asked.

"And we need a plan," Aunt Matilda continued, ignoring her

sister's question, "to make sure that he and Abigail succeed in getting custody of his child. It is quite unthinkable that a father not be allowed to take his own child home with him when he clearly loves her and did not consent to her being taken to her grandparents in the first place. He does love the child, Abigail? I cannot imagine you would have married him if he did not."

"He adores her," Abigail said.

"Matilda is right," Aunt Mildred said with a sigh. "We do need a plan. But what?"

"Abigail," Alexander asked, "who is Lieutenant Colonel Bennington's father? Does he know?"

She hesitated. Gil did not like to talk about his paternity. He had not even told his lawyer. When asked yesterday morning, he had evaded the question.

"Viscount Dirkson," she said.

There was a brief silence.

"Viscount *Dirkson*?" her mother said.

"Gil does not make it generally known," Abigail said. "He did not even know who his father was until after his mother died when he was a sergeant in India. The viscount purchased his ensign's commission and then his promotion to lieutenant. Gil stopped him purchasing any further promotions and even regretted the ones he had been surprised into accepting. He wanted nothing to do with his father. He still does not. As far as he is concerned he had only one parent."

"Viscount Dirkson," her mother said again. "He was a member of the set with whom Humphrey consorted."

"And that is not a strong recommendation," Grandmama said. "Most of my son's friends were unsavory characters. Just like him. So Dirkson abandoned his by-blow, did he?"

"Even so," Uncle Thomas said, "something might be made of the fact that Bennington is well born, at least on his father's side."

"I am acquainted with his son," Bertrand said. "I mean reasonably well acquainted. We were at Oxford together. He was a year ahead of me."

Aunt Matilda was still clutching the vinaigrette, but she was not pressing it upon her mother. Rather, she was pressing it to her bosom. "There is a likeness," she said. "I ought to have seen it. Without the scar surely I would have. He was a strikingly handsome man."

"And a rake, Matilda," Aunt Mildred said. "He was not the sort of friend one would have wished Humphrey to have. He was not the sort of friend one would have wished upon *anyone*. But then, our brother was not either."

"We definitely need a plan," Aunt Louise said. "We need to put our heads together. That young man may not want our acquaintance or our help, but he is married to Abigail and he must be given no choice."

Uncle Thomas groaned and Colin grinned.

"Perhaps," Elizabeth said, smiling and clapping her hands together as she got to her feet, "the campaign can be postponed until another time. We invited everyone here to celebrate Abigail's marriage even though her husband cannot be with us. Let us celebrate from this moment on. Tea will be awaiting us in the dining room. Colin, will you escort Abigail there while the rest of us follow?"

"It will be my pleasure," he said, smiling kindly upon Abigail as he approached and offered her his arm again. "Camille mentioned in a letter to Elizabeth that Joel has bought young Robbie a new dog and he is a far happier child for it. And the idea came from your husband. You must tell me more."

"Oh yes," Abigail said as they led the way to the dining room. "Apparently Robbie chose a collie and they are inseparable. But do let me tell you about Beauty—Gil's dog—and my first encounter with her."

There was a banquet spread upon the table.

FORTUNATELY THE DOWAGER COUNTESS OF RIVERDALE WAS ALready lying down for her nap when young Bertrand arrived at the house the following afternoon. Lady Matilda Westcott had been ready with an explanation should one be needed, but she was very glad it was not. She had been unable to invent anything that would sound convincing.

Matilda was ready to leave the house—she had chosen her very best outfit, a dark green dress and pelisse and bonnet she usually reserved for the occasional garden party she attended with her mother—and hurried downstairs to the hall before the butler could bring her a message.

"Good afternoon, Bertrand," she said briskly, pulling on her gloves before extending her right hand for a firm handshake. "You are very prompt. I like that in a young man."

He was twenty-one years old and tall and lean and dark and handsome and must already have a whole army of young ladies in a flutter. And he would only improve with age, just as his father had done. The Marquess of Dorchester must be approaching his middle forties by now, but he and Viola still made an extraordinarily handsome couple.

Bertrand was bowing and wishing her a good afternoon and flushing and looking as mystified as he had yesterday when she had taken him briefly aside after tea at Elizabeth's and asked if he would be so kind as to offer her his escort this afternoon. He must have thought she had taken leave of her senses, fallen off the cliff into senility. But the poor boy was a gentleman through and through and had assured her that it would be his pleasure. He was also a smooth liar. He had looked even more mystified and perhaps slightly alarmed when she had asked him not to tell anyone. He had assured her he would not. But why would he? A young gentleman surely did not boast of escorting his aging stepaunt about London.

But if that was so, he was not at least going to hide her inside a closed carriage with all the curtains drawn. From the step outside the house Matilda looked down upon a smart curricle and pair.

"Oh my!" she said.

"I hope you do not mind, ma'am," he said. "I would have had to hire a chaise or ask my father—"

"Mind?" Matilda said. "My dear young man, I have not ridden in a curricle since I do not know when. But I am not in my dotage yet. Not even a twinge of the rheumatics."

After he had assisted her into the curricle and taken his place beside her and gathered the ribbons into his hands, he looked at her inquiringly. "And where may I have the pleasure of taking you, ma'am?" he asked.

"I thought," she said, "you might enjoy calling upon your Oxford friend Mr. Sawyer. I do not know his first name."

He looked blankly at her. "Sawyer?" he said. *"Adrian* Sawyer?"

"If that is his name, yes," Matilda said. "Son of Viscount Dirkson. *Legitimate* son, that is."

The blank look continued for a moment, to be replaced by a hint of a smile. "Lady Matilda," he asked, "what are you up to?"

"Oh dear," she said. "Do you not know him well?"

"Actually," he said, "I knew him quite well before he came down, a year ahead of me. I have not seen him since, though someone did mention seeing him in town a few weeks ago."

"Then perhaps," she said, "it is time you became reacquainted. I knew his father, Bertrand. A long time ago, when he was a friend of Humphrey's. My brother," she added by way of explanation. "I cannot call upon him alone. It is not done, you know. Even a maid would not lend me sufficient respectability."

One of his horses snorted, apparently impatient to be moving.

"So I am to call upon an old university friend I have not seen in a year, bringing my stepsister's aunt along with me for company, am I?" he asked.

"I suppose," she said, "I will be a great embarrassment to you."

He regarded her in silence for a moment while the other horse snorted and the first tossed its head.

"I would guess," he said, "that this has to do with Lieutenant Colonel Bennington."

"Well," she said. "It does. And I suppose you are wondering why

I have not sent Thomas to make the call. Or Alexander or Avery. Or even your papa."

"What if neither Adrian nor Viscount Dirkson is at home?" he asked.

It was, of course, a distinct possibility. Indeed, it would be nothing short of a miracle if neither one was out. This was madness, but—

"I do not even know where he lives," Bertrand said.

"I do," Matilda told him.

Twenty

T he miracle happened. By the time it did, however, and Viscount Dirkson's butler had admitted Lady Matilda Westcott and Viscount Watley to a handsome visitors' parlor leading off the hall while he went to see if his lordship and his son were at home—a euphemism for discovering whether they wished to see their visitors—Matilda was heartily wishing it had *not* happened. And from the look on his face, she guessed that Bertrand was wishing it too.

Perhaps this had *not* been a good idea after all.

In all of thirty-six years, Matilda had caught only the occasional glimpse of Viscount Dirkson. She had not come face-to-face with him in all that time. By design, of course. On both their parts, no doubt. She had never, *ever* been such a bold hussy as to come to his house. It really was quite inexcusable even if she *had* brought Bertrand with her and made it seem that he was the caller in chief while she was just the inadvertent hanger-on.

Whoever was just a hanger-on with her twenty-one-year-old step-nephew? Was there even such a relationship?

If she could have crept out through a side door or dropped out of a window, she would cheerfully have done it. But the damage had already been done. The butler had borne her name upstairs and it was too much to hope that if she disappeared, Viscount Dirkson would believe his butler must have been having hallucinations.

Bertrand was looking rather as though he had tied his neckcloth too tightly. She could not abandon him now even if there were a window conveniently open.

Oh dear.

And then the door opened and they came in together—one older gentleman, one younger. They looked nothing alike, Matilda thought while there was still a coherent thought in her head. The older one was tall, a fine figure of a man, with a full head of hair, silvered at the temples, pepper and salt elsewhere. Mostly pepper, she decided. He did not look his age, which she knew was in the mid-fifties. Men were so fortunate. They aged far more slowly and gracefully than women did. The two of them had discovered once upon a time that he was precisely one month to the day older than she. The younger man was shorter, fair haired and fresh faced, and slightly on the stocky side. Like his late mother. He was looking pleased. His father was looking neither pleased nor displeased. He was looking directly at Matilda.

Oh dear.

"Bertrand!" the younger man exclaimed, striding forward, his right hand outstretched. "It *is* you. I wondered. You used not to use the *Viscount Watley* part of your name. How do you do? This *is* a pleasure."

"How do *you* do?" Bertrand said. "It is just a courtesy title, you know. May I have the honor of presenting Lady Matilda Westcott? She is my stepmother's sister-in-law."

"How do you do, ma'am?" Mr. Adrian Sawyer said, making an elegant bow. "Are you acquainted with my father? Are *you*, Bertrand?"

And the moment had arrived. Actually, it had done that several moments ago. Matilda dipped into a curtsy and then wished she had merely inclined her head with grave dignity.

"Matilda," Viscount Dirkson said, making her a bow but not proceeding farther into the room. He was looking at her, narrow eyed, as well he might. What *on earth* had put it into her head to come here? For now he was ignoring Bertrand.

"Charles," she said, and then could have bitten out her tongue. Oh dear, she was too old for this. Far too old. She had been poised and firm minded for years and years. This was no time to revert to girlhood dithers and blushes.

He had switched his attention to Bertrand and his son. "I believe we met once in Oxford, Watley," he said. "I am sure my son is quite delighted by your call. The two of you must have much to say to each other and much reminiscing to do. You will doubtless feel more comfortable if Lady Matilda and I are not present to hear you, and no doubt *we* will feel more comfortable too not to have to listen. Ma'am, may I show you the garden? There is a pretty display of flowers at present."

Oh dear.

"Thank you," she said, and was surprised and relieved to discover that her legs took her across the room toward him without tottering or folding under her.

He said nothing as he walked beside her through the hall and along a corridor that circled behind the staircase, his boot heels clicking on the tiled floor. He led her out through a back door into a garden filled with the color and perfume of myriad flowers. There was a well-scythed lawn out there too and a wrought iron seat beneath a chestnut tree.

"Well, Matilda," he said as he closed the door behind him.

"Charles," she said, turning to look at him and clasping her hands firmly at her waist. His face was leaner than it had been when he was a young man. His cheekbones and features were more pronounced.

But he still looked handsome and remarkably like his son—his *other* son—but without the scar. "I have come about your son."

Gone already, then, was the pretense that she had come because Bertrand, who had happened to be escorting her—where?—had suddenly conceived a burning hankering to call upon an old university chum of his he had not seen in more than a year.

He gazed at her, his hands clasped behind his back. He had made no attempt to show her the garden or to lead her toward the seat. "I assume," he said, "you are not talking about the son who is currently in conversation with your . . . stepnephew?"

"I am talking about Lieutenant Colonel Bennington," she told him. "Perhaps you did not know he was back in England. That he came from Paris with my nephew, Major Harry Westcott, and stayed with him for a while at Hinsford Manor in Hampshire. You almost certainly would not know that he married my niece, Abigail Westcott, less than a week ago and is in London to try to regain possession of his daughter. Your granddaughter." Goodness, she had not even thought of that relationship until this moment.

"I confess," he said, "I did not know of his marriage. You used the word *try* when you spoke of his taking his daughter home from her grandparents' house."

He was not going to deny that the lieutenant colonel was his son, then. And he clearly knew some things about him. Some fairly recent things. He knew the child was with her grandparents.

"General Sir Edward Pascoe and Lady Pascoe are determined to keep her," Matilda told him. "They are determined to blacken his name and convince a judge that he is an unfit father. And they are powerful people."

"More powerful than . . . my son?" he asked her.

"I very much fear so," she said.

"But what is it you wish me to do, Matilda?" he asked, leaning slightly toward her, his dark eyes boring into hers.

She kept her feet planted where they were and did not take the step back she desperately wanted to take.

THE FOLLOWING WEEK WAS NOT A HAPPY ONE.

A letter from Mr. Grimes arrived while they were at breakfast the morning after the tea at Elizabeth and Colin's. In it he informed Lieutenant Colonel Bennington that there would be a hearing one week hence before Judge Burroughs to decide the issue of the custody of Miss Katherine Bennington. The lawyer was confident of success for his client but would appreciate another meeting with him the following day. There was no need to trouble his wife to accompany him. In the meantime Grimes strongly advised that his client gather as many testimonials to his character as he was able. Personal appearances would be better, but, failing that, letters would be desirable.

"With one week to go," Gil said. "And I know no one, Abby. I would not know where to write to former commanding officers, and even if I did, there would be no time both to send a letter and to receive a reply."

"There is Harry," she said.

"Yes," he said. "There is Harry." And he set his linen napkin down beside his half-empty plate and got abruptly to his feet. He left the hotel dining room without even asking Abigail if she was ready to accompany him.

From that moment on he almost completely retired into himself. He sent her on her way each morning to one member or another of her family, summoning a hackney carriage for her since their own would not be ready for delivery for several more days. She visited relatives, went shopping with them or to the library or a gallery, and smiled cheerfully, pretending to a happiness that was fast faltering.

She did not know how Gil spent the days. When she asked him each day on her return to the hotel, he gave vague answers. When she arrived back early one afternoon and went down to the stables with the idea of taking Beauty for a walk, she found the dog gone. But Gil did not mention later the walk he had presumably taken with her. He did not talk about anything else he did during those days either.

During dinner each evening she always told him about her own activities in exhaustive detail so that there would not be total silence. He made brief comments to indicate that he had been listening, but there were no reciprocal stories. They spent the rest of their evenings reading in the sitting room that was part of their suite. Or, rather, they held books open in their hands and directed their eyes at a page. Abigail even remembered to turn one now and then.

Worst of all, he stopped sleeping with her—and making love to her. He slept in the second bedchamber, which he had used merely as a dressing room for the first few nights.

"I am feeling restless," he said by way of explanation the first night it happened. "I would not wish to keep you awake, Abby."

She said nothing and made no protest. For she knew it was nothing personal. She understood that every moment of this week was like a nightmare to him. And she knew him well enough to realize that his first reaction to adversity was always to lock himself up inside himself so that he would not break apart. He had come close to breaking down and weeping, she knew, that one afternoon. She did not know if it would have been good if he had or if it would have spelled disaster. From childhood on he had learned to hide from the world in the only really safe place and the one that was always available to him. He had learned thus to cope alone with all that was bad and threatening.

But oh, she wished he would pull her in there with him. She was his *wife*. Moreover, she loved him. Yes, she did. Of course she did. It was purely silliness to pretend that she did not. It was why she had married him. Not because she was mindlessly *in love*, but because she loved the person he was. And she did know him even though he had confided so little. She knew the goodness and steadiness and kindness that were fairly bursting from the granite exterior he showed the world. She knew the dream of love and family and home that had sustained him through most of his life.

She yearned to be trusted. To be loved. But she would bear with him for this week. She did not doubt he would far prefer to be facing a thousand battles than the one that actually awaited him in the form of Judge Burroughs within the next few days.

And she wondered what would happen if he lost the battle. What would his life become? What would hers become? What would happen to *them*?

Oh, it was a very unhappy week. It seemed to crawl by and gallop by. And yes, it did both simultaneously even though the hands of the clock probably ticked by at exactly the same pace as they had done last month and last year and would do next month and next year. And there was no comfort—not from her family, in whom she would not confide, not from Gil, who was locked in his own tortured world, and not from herself.

She did not know what would happen. And she hardly dared hope even though there *was* hope. Of course there was. She had married him to give him more of it.

She awoke from a broken sleep very early on the morning of the hearing. Dawn was graying the window, and she could see it because the curtains had been drawn back. Gil was standing there silently, gazing out.

"Gil?" she said.

He turned toward her, a silhouette against the early light. "I am sorry, Abby," he said. "I have woken you."

The window was open. The room was chilly, though the bedcovers were warm about her.

"No, no," she said, moving over to one side of the bed. "You must be cold, standing there. Come and warm yourself."

He continued to stand there for a few moments, but then he came toward the bed, shedding his dressing gown as he came. He was indeed cold. She drew the covers about him, wriggled closer, and held him against her. He was naked.

"You could not sleep?" she asked.

"It occurred to me," he said, "that I might be able to get to sleep here. But then I was afraid of waking you. It seemed selfish. It *seems* selfish. I am sorry."

"Oh, Gil," she said. "I have missed you."

"I am making you cold," he said, his teeth chattering slightly.

But she would not let him pull away. "I have missed you," she said again.

He sighed and she felt some of the tension go from his body. "Abby," he said, "no matter what happens . . . today I promise to spend the rest of my life making you happy. I have been neglecting you, have I not? No, do not answer. I have been neglecting you. Because my head has been all abuzz and I have not wanted to infect you. A poor excuse. But it will not happen any longer. I will not give up the treasure I have because I may not be able to get the one I want. The *other* one. I—" His teeth chattered again even though his body had begun to warm.

"Gil," she said, "I am your wife. I understand. We will do this together—this living, no matter what the future holds in store for us. The future is the one thing we can never plan for even though we are always trying. Are we not foolish? We will deal with it."

"Together," he said.

"Yes." The most beautiful word in the English language. "Together."

He repositioned himself so that he could set one arm about her shoulders and beneath her neck, and he held her close to him. They lay together, relaxed and comfortable, and he kissed her, his mouth soft and warm and lovely. And they did not even need to make love for the pleasure to be felt. He slid into sleep, his breathing becoming slower and deeper. Abigail smoothed a finger over the seam of the scar across his shoulder and followed him within minutes.

*   *   *

THEY WOULD GO TOGETHER THE SHORT DISTANCE TO JUDGE BUR-roughs's chambers, Grimes had told Gil during a brief meeting they had had the day before. It was a pity there would be no one there to speak personally to the lieutenant colonel's character, and it was re-grettable that there had not been time enough for an answer to have come in reply to the letter that had been sent Major Westcott. It was a shame too that there had been insufficient time to write to any of the servants at Rose Cottage. But it was to be hoped they had a strong enough case to contrive without.

Grimes had written to the Horse Guards awhile ago and then sent a clerk there to bring the dispatches from both India and the Penin-sula in which the lieutenant colonel had been singled out for special commendation. Those would surely help. The financial papers Grimes had received from his client's agent here in London demonstrated that he had carefully husbanded his resources for a number of years and was well able to keep his child in a manner worthy of the granddaugh-ter of General and Lady Pascoe. And Lieutenant Colonel Bennington was in the process of retiring from active service and had a new wife, a mother for his daughter, and she was a sensible and eminently gen-teel young lady even if it *was* a pity about her birth.

All the while Gil was listening to him he had wondered why the man had not arranged for character witnesses either in person or by written statement a great deal sooner than he had. He had been Gil's lawyer for several months. Had he been taken by surprise at the speed with which the case had come before a judge? The twinge of doubt he had been feeling ever since he hired the man had become a raging flood of suspicion that he was incompetent. Yet the whole of Gil's life and Katy's depended upon his being *competent*.

It was too late now, however, to do anything differently.

He asked Abby at a breakfast neither of them ate whether she thought he ought to wear his uniform as Grimes had urged him to do or regular clothes. He was very nearly a retired officer rather than an active one, after all, and the whole point of retiring was that he would be living permanently at home, to be a father to his daughter throughout her growing years. Nevertheless, the uniform might make him look more impressive. In what way, though? Did he want to impress as a soldier? Or as a man?

She tipped her head to one side, the crease of a slight frown between her brows. "Not the uniform, I think," she said. "If General Pascoe wears his, then you will appear more . . . paternal in contrast."

Did it really matter, though? Would Judge Burroughs make his decision based upon *looks*? How *would* he decide?

"It was my thought too," he said. "Though I do not believe I could look paternal if I tried from now until eternity."

He wore a dark green coat tailored by Weston over a gray waistcoat and paler gray pantaloons with Hessian boots and white linen— all of which items he had purchased since his arrival in London. He tied his neckcloth without any fancy folds or frills. He wore no jewels, adding only his pocket watch and chain. He brushed his hair, willing that one errant lock to stay back, and looked critically at his image in the glass, something he was not in the habit of doing.

He did not look even remotely paternal. He looked like a soldier in disguise. Perhaps if he slouched his shoulders a little . . . And wore a mask over one half of his face . . . Perhaps if he had bought gold rings and a diamond cravat pin and fobs and other taradiddles for his waist. And a quizzing glass with a jewel-encrusted handle. If he had had his hair cut à la Brutus. Bought a smart cane. Bought those Hessians with the gold tassels instead of these plain ones. Arranged for shirt points so high and stiffly starched they would almost have pierced his eyeballs and made it impossible to turn his head.

He shared a rueful smile with his image and turned away from the glass.

Abby, he saw when he stepped into the sitting room of their suite, was dressed smartly and soberly in a walking dress of silver gray trimmed with black. The silk ribbons that trimmed the crown of the matching bonnet and were tied in a bow to one side of her chin saved her from looking as though she were in half mourning, however. They were boldly striped in black and white and sunshine yellow. The shoes that peeped from beneath the hem of her dress were also yellow. Her hair was brushed smooth beneath the bonnet.

So this is it, he thought as he watched her draw on a pair of black gloves and then offered her his arm. And he wondered in what direction his life would have turned by the time they came back here.

Less than an hour later they entered the hearing room that was part of the chambers of the judge, a little less formal than a public courtroom but not by much. It was a big square room with a door in each side, a long desk upon a slightly raised dais at one end, two oblong tables below it with three chairs set behind each, facing the dais. Behind the tables, there were rows of chairs, presumably for witnesses or spectators important enough to be allowed in to observe the proceedings. The chairs behind one of the tables were empty, Gil saw with a single glance as he followed Grimes into the room with Abby. The chairs behind the other table, three rows of them, were filled.

In that first moment and at that first glance his heart sank. The Pascoes clearly *had* been able to amass numerous character witnesses.

But then Abby's hand tightened convulsively about his arm and Gil's eyes focused upon General and Lady Pascoe, already seated at one of the tables with the man who was presumably their lawyer. The chairs behind their table were the empty ones. He looked more closely at the people filling the rows of chairs behind the still-empty table. They were not strangers. They were the *Westcotts*.

"Oh dear God," Abby murmured.

Including Joel Cunningham, who was supposedly in Bath with Abby's sister, his wife, and their family.

Gil had no time to react. His lawyer led them behind the empty table and seated himself with them before leaning toward Gil. "Is that blond gentleman with all the jewels the *Duke of Netherby*?" he asked in a hoarse whisper, his eyes fairly popping from his head.

"He is married to a Westcott," Gil whispered back. "And his step-mother is a Westcott."

"Dear me," Grimes said. "Yes, I knew that. Dear me."

A door beside the dais opened at that moment and a bailiff stepped through. "All rise for His Honor, Judge Burroughs," he said.

And Gil, Westcotts or no Westcotts, rose to his feet while the imposingly robed and wigged figure of the judge swept into the room and ascended the dais. Gil felt the bottom fall out of his stomach. Abby's hand was in his, he realized. He clutched it tightly enough to break bones.

Twenty-one

No one had breathed a word about this during the past week. The aunts had, of course, talked at Elizabeth's tea about putting their heads together to form a plan. They always did that whenever they perceived a need within the family. Rarely did their plans come to fruition.

But today the family had come in force. To offer moral support. To—

Abigail's thoughts paused for a moment while she turned her head sharply as the judge settled behind his desk and everyone else sat down. Her mind had just caught up to her eyes. *Joel* was here. When had he come up from Bath? And for what purpose? Just for this? But *why*?

Fleetingly, before she turned her head back to face the judge, she noted that there was a stranger seated on a chair behind the back row. Perhaps he had sat in the wrong place. Perhaps he had come for the Pascoes.

General Pascoe, seated at the other table—at least Abigail supposed it must be he—was resplendent in his dress uniform. Perhaps after all it would have been better if Gil—

But the proceedings were beginning, and the judge announced that this was an informal hearing in which he sincerely hoped an amicable arrangement could be made for the future care of Miss Katherine Mary Bennington. But what was informal about it?

He then called upon General Sir Edward and Lady Pascoe's lawyer to make his case for the child's remaining with her grandparents and for excluding Lieutenant Colonel Bennington from having any and all access to her.

The general, his medals clinking against one another as he moved in his chair, looked formidable as well as resplendent. Lady Pascoe looked no less forbidding. She was younger than Abigail had expected. She looked elegant and haughty and had a commanding presence. It seemed doubtful that she allowed her will to be thwarted very often.

And then, just as their lawyer was getting to his feet and clearing his throat while thrusting his hands beneath his robe to clasp them behind his back, a door opened abruptly. Abigail turned to look behind her and there was a panting and a woofing and a scrabbling of nails upon uncarpeted floor and a joyful bark—and Beauty came galloping into sight, to stop beside their table, waving her tail and trailing a leather leash.

"Oh, I say. I am most dreadfully sorry." It was Harry's voice. "She was no trouble at all until she spotted Gil. Lieutenant Colonel Bennington, that is."

"Sit, Beauty," Gil commanded before she could jump up on him or decide to do an exuberant dash about the judge's dais.

Beauty sat and looked adoringly up at her master before transferring her attention to the judge as though granting him permission to proceed.

Harry?

And in full military uniform, Abigail saw when she darted a glance over her shoulder. There was a buzz of sound from her family before the judge banged his gavel on his desk. He looked far from pleased.

And surely, Abigail thought—oh, please, please God—she was going to awaken from this bizarre dream now. Gil beside her was looking like granite. And surely, since this was clearly *not* a dream, everything was ruined.

Disaster had struck.

"And who," the judge asked, glaring ferociously back toward the rows of chairs, presumably at Harry, "might you be, young man? And who in thunder gave you leave to bring a—that *is* a dog, I presume?— into my courtroom?"

Gil, Abigail was aware as she set a hand on his arm, was taking slow, deep breaths. His eyes were closed. Beauty was panting happily.

"Major Harry Westcott, Your Honor," Harry said. "Mrs. Bennington's brother and Lieutenant Colonel Bennington's friend and fellow officer. I sincerely apologize for the interruption. There was a spot of bother with one of the carriage wheels just five miles outside of London, and by the time I got to the Pulteney Hotel Gil and Abby were no longer in their rooms and Beauty was not in her stall. One of the grooms was walking her. Then there was a bit of a delay getting her in here. I had to explain that she is to be a character witness for my brother-in-law."

The judge gazed steadily at him for a few silent moments. "I am almost sorry I asked," he said at last, and Abigail felt the first faint glimmering of hope. Judge Burroughs had a sense of humor, did he? "Be seated, Major, and let me not hear another word from you until or unless you are called upon to testify. And keep that canine seated and quiet and that leash in your hand, Lieutenant Colonel Bennington, if you do not wish to have it ejected."

Gil bent over to pick up the leash. "Stay!" he commanded when it seemed Beauty was about to scramble to her feet on the assumption there was a walk in the offing.

She stayed.

"Your Honor," General Pascoe's lawyer said, outrage in his voice. "I must—"

"If you are about to lodge an objection," His Honor said, "it is overruled. For now. Proceed, if you will. I am rather hoping to be out of here before dark. My hopes for an early luncheon have already faded. Or, indeed, for any luncheon at all. I do not intend to stop until this thing is settled. It is my fondest wish that no one plans to be long-winded."

The general's lawyer proceeded with an eloquent recounting of facts and opinions, none of which came as any great surprise to Abigail. Mrs. Bennington—the first Mrs. Bennington, that was—had been snared by the innocence of youth into marrying a man of low birth and no connections to speak of during the Peninsular Wars and found herself settled in a cottage in the remote English countryside that was far inferior to what her birth had accustomed her to. There she was abused by an autocratic and bad-tempered husband and abandoned with her newborn child when he went off to join the Duke of Wellington's forces gathering in Belgium. Fearing his return for both herself and her daughter, Mrs. Bennington placed the child in the safekeeping of her mother, Lady Pascoe, before fleeing to take refuge with dear friends. Not long after, she met her unfortunate demise, a tragedy that would never have occurred if she had not felt compelled to run from her own home.

And so it continued with an account of Gil's behavior when he had arrived unannounced at the general's home while Lady Pascoe was there alone and undefended. The lawyer made much of Gil's second visit there and of Lady Pascoe's courage in keeping him from her granddaughter, who was shrieking with terror. Parts of the two letters Gil had written not long after from St. Helena were read aloud and both missives were offered into evidence.

A final plea was made to leave the child with her grandparents, who could raise her in a manner appropriate to her mother's birth and in a place where she would be safe and well cared for. And loved. The lawyer wound up his argument with an affecting description of the maternal love her ladyship lavished upon her granddaughter now that her only daughter had been snatched from her as a result of the abuse she had suffered at Lieutenant Colonel Bennington's hands. His behavior from the outset had, in fact, shown him to be a man of brutish upbringing and unbridled passions. Not only was he unfit to have the care of a child, even with the acquisition of a new wife—whose own birth was not without blemish—but he was also unfit to visit his daughter at her grandparents' home or to have any dealings with her whatsoever. And on the subject of the new Mrs. Bennington's birth—

"Thank you for keeping your case brief," the judge said, interrupting, though it was not clear if he spoke ironically. "There are no character witnesses to support General Sir Edward and Lady Pascoe's claim to be suitable guardians for their daughter's child, who is not yet even three years old?"

"Your Honor." Their lawyer sounded shocked. "General Pascoe's military reputation is well known and above reproach, and Lady Pascoe, as the whole of the fashionable world is well aware, is the sister of—"

"Yes, yes." The judge waved a dismissive hand. "Foolish of me to ask. It is the turn of Lieutenant Colonel Bennington's side to persuade me of his claim to assume his daughter's care. It is to be hoped the persuasion will be brief. It is also to be hoped that not *all* of these illustrious persons now adorning my courtroom are intending to testify. I can look with some resignation upon the loss of my luncheon. I am not sure I can do the same for my dinner. Or for tomorrow morning's breakfast."

He definitely had a sense of humor, Abigail thought, but a strange one. It was impossible to decide which side it would favor. But a judge was not meant to favor either side. That was the whole point of his position. Besides, he had not heard their side yet. She set her hand over Gil's on the table and felt it jump slightly beneath the pressure. She did not believe she had ever felt more terrified in her life. She could actually feel the blood pounding at her temples.

"Lieutenant Colonel Bennington's military career has been a

model of extraordinary service and courage and achievement, Your Honor," Mr. Grimes began after he had got to his feet, cleared his throat, and grasped the edges of his robe just below the shoulders. "He has been singled out for commendation in no fewer than six official dispatches, one from India when he was a sergeant, four from the Peninsula after he became a commissioned officer—including one that followed his successful leadership of a forlorn hope—and one from the Battle of Waterloo. I have here, Your Honor, copies of those dispatches that I obtained from—"

"Yes, yes," the judge said with another wave of his hand. "Leave them where they are. In the unlikely event I should feel the need to read either them or the letters sent from St. Helena, I will know where to find them. We will grant your client's prowess on the battlefield, as we will grant General Pascoe's. Get to the child, Mr. Grimes."

Mr. Grimes got to her. He described—briefly—the size of the deceptively named Rose Cottage in Gloucestershire, the number of servants who saw to its smooth running, Gil's financial ability to finance it and to raise his daughter in some comfort there. The documents he had received from Gil's agent were waved away with the dispatches from the Horse Guards and the letters from St. Helena. He described the arrangements Gil had made to ensure the safety and care of his first wife and his daughter before he answered the call of duty to hurry off to Belgium, where he distinguished himself—

"Yes, yes." The judge was getting a mite impatient, Abigail thought. Or a mite *more* impatient.

"Before he left for Belgium," Mr. Grimes said, "there was no question, Your Honor, of his child's being taken to her grandparents' home in Essex and left there. No permission was either asked or granted. If there was abandonment, it was not on Lieutenant Colonel Bennington's part but upon that of the late Mrs. Bennington, who did not even remain at her mother's house to care for the child herself. My client, upon his return from Belgium, was beside himself with worry when he arrived home to find his wife and child missing and the servants without any knowledge of *where* they had gone. His agitation upon learning when he first called upon his mother-in-law that his wife was not there was perfectly understandable, especially as he was not permitted to enter the house. His anguish when he discovered through conversation he overheard, at the inn where he was putting up, that though his wife was indeed not at her mother's house, his daughter most certainly was can only be imagined. What fond father would *not* have returned to that house to demand that he see his child and take her home with him, where she belonged? And may it be noted, Your Honor, that when Lady Pascoe and her servants refused him access and barred his way from going upstairs to the child's nursery, he heard his baby crying with fright—and went away rather than terrify her further by forcing his way to her. There, Your Honor, is the action of a loving parent."

"Yes, yes," the judge said. "Spare us more of your soaring rhetoric, Mr. Grimes. You are doubtless about to inform us that the same understanding of a parent's anguish must be extended to the letters your client wrote from his island posting."

"Yes, Your Honor," the lawyer said, sounding somewhat disconcerted.

"Then we will pronounce it so extended," the judge said. "Proceed."

Mr. Grimes proceeded, and ended by explaining how his client had prepared to take back his child and ensure her future care and happiness by taking a new wife, who was unquestionably genteel. She was the daughter of the late Earl of Riverdale and the present Marchioness of Dorchester.

"Yes, yes," the judge said. "I am not so out of touch with polite society, Mr. Grimes, as to have failed to notice that I have almost the whole of the Westcott family before me, plus a few spouses, including His Grace of Netherby. I assume you have dragged them into court this morning—or is it already this afternoon?—to impress me into incoherence with their testimonials to the good character of your client and his wife."

He glared at Abigail's gathered family as though they were a pack of felons, while Mr. Grimes looked unhappy and Beauty woofed and looked hopefully up at Gil as though to say that Judge Burroughs was not the only one forfeiting his luncheon.

"Stay," Gil said quietly.

"These illustrious persons, Your Honor," Mr. Grimes said, "have chosen to come here with no urging on either my part or my client's."

"It is my sincere hope," the judge said, "that they are not all going to insist upon addressing this court. I will hear from one representative, if, that is, they have not all come here merely to be spectators and remain mute. Meanwhile, however, I will hear from the one character witness I have been informed of. Assuming that the . . . dog does not have a human voice, I will allow one human to speak on his behalf. I must confess myself more than a little curious to hear what he has to say. Or she. With a name like Beauty, one can only hope, I suppose, that he is in fact a she. Major Westcott, will you provide that human voice?"

"I will, Your Honor," Harry said, while Mr. Grimes first hovered beside the table and then sat down.

Abigail found herself gripping Gil's hand. Were these proceedings about to descend into farce when so much rode upon the outcome?

"Lieutenant Colonel Bennington discovered the dog on the battlefield of Waterloo after the fighting was over," Harry explained. "She was a puppy at the time, starving, frightened, and apparently a stray. He fed her and took her into his care and has kept her ever since. She is, as you can see, Your Honor, both obedient and devoted to him. As he is to her."

"Alas," Judge Burroughs said. "The story is not nearly as colorful as I had hoped. The dog has not saved his life upon any occasion, I suppose, or, better yet, the life of a child?"

General Pascoe's lawyer tittered, and the judge fixed him with a severe eye.

"Not literally, Your Honor," Harry said. "But my brother-in-law has come from Bath specifically because Gil's dog has in a very real way saved his son's life."

"Ah," the judge said. "This is better. Identify yourself, brother-in-law from Bath, and tell your story."

Abigail turned her head to see Joel first half raise a hand and then get to his feet. He looked considerably embarrassed.

"Joel Cunningham, Your Honor," he said. "My wife is a former Westcott, Mrs. Bennington's sister. We have a seven-year-old son, an adopted child who came to us from an undesirable, even abusive, background. For three years we have been trying with limited success to induce him to trust us and to trust that life itself is not his enemy. During a recent week we spent at Hinsford Manor with the rest of my wife's family and with Lieutenant Colonel Bennington, my son discovered Beauty—the dog, that is—and became inseparable from her. The lieutenant colonel allowed Robbie to spend all his daytime hours with her, even when that meant allowing the child into the privacy of his own room. He showed endless patience and kindness to a troubled boy, who now has a dog of his own and is at last showing distinct signs of improvement. My wife and I will be forever grateful to our new brother-in-law."

"And his dog," the judge added.

"And his dog," Joel agreed. "And might it be added, Your Honor, that Lieutenant Colonel Bennington showed himself to be patient and gentle and good-natured with all the young children who were at Hinsford during that week."

"It has been added," the judge said, "whether I wished it to be or not."

"Yes, Your Honor," Joel said, and sat down abruptly.

"Now," the judge said, "I will hear from one representative of the Westcott family, unless by some miracle no one wants to speak at all."

Abigail glanced behind her again. Alexander was getting to his feet.

"I am the Earl of Riverdale, Your Honor," he said, "and head of the family. I have not known Lieutenant Colonel Bennington for long, but what I have seen has convinced me that he is an honorable man of steady character and mild-mannered disposition. I met him in Paris earlier this spring when I went there with the Duke of Netherby to bring home Major Westcott, who was still recovering from wounds sustained at Waterloo. The lieutenant colonel, having just completed a year of duty on St. Helena, was eager to return to England to see to his own pressing affairs. But he nevertheless delayed his journey after discovering his friend Major Westcott in a convalescent hospital for officers. He made arrangements to bring Harry home and remain with him while Harry recovered sufficient strength to be left alone. He continued steadfast in that commitment even after His Grace and I arrived in Paris. His behavior was exemplary throughout the journey and during the following week, while Netherby and I remained at Hinsford and were joined by the rest of the family. He left Hinsford only a week ago after marrying Miss Westcott, my cousin and Harry's sister—and after assuring himself that Harry was fit to be left alone."

"Hmph," the judge said, but it appeared he had nothing to add.

"And may it be said, Your Honor," Alexander continued, "that the lieutenant colonel's choice of a bride and mother for his child cannot be faulted. Mrs. Bennington is a perfect lady in every way. She is modest and sensible and good-natured. And she is a Westcott. We are a close-knit family and invariably stand by our own in both triumph and adversity. When Lieutenant Colonel Bennington made his choice of wife, he also—perhaps without fully realizing it—chose us to be his family. And when he chose her as a mother for his daughter, he was choosing us to be her cousins and aunts and uncles—and grandmother and great-grandmother. Miss Katherine Bennington will never be without the security of family as long as there is one of us alive."

"We have a courtroom full of orators," the judge said. "Thank you, Lord Riverdale. It is only a shame we do not also have members of the lieutenant colonel's family present. We might all leave here in tears."

"There is one such member here, Your Honor," a voice said from the back of the room. Abigail turned her head sharply to see that the stranger was on his feet and it was he who had spoken. "I am Charles Sawyer, Viscount Dirkson. Lieutenant Colonel Gilbert Bennington's father."

"Ah," the judge said, "what more could I ask?" He banged his gavel on his desk to hush the swell of sound that had followed the stranger's words.

But he was a stranger no more. Abigail gazed at him in shock, and Gil, she could see, without turning his head, had stiffened in every limb. His head had snapped back rather as though someone had punched him on the chin. His hands were in fists on the table before him, the leash clutched in one of them. Beauty looked up at him and very softly whimpered.

"Let us hear from you, Lord Dirkson, by all means," the judge said. "The surprise witness. I shall be the envy of my peers when word spreads."

Abigail laid a hand on Gil's arm but she doubted he noticed. His eyes were closed again, his face angled up slightly toward the ceiling.

"Miss Bennington, the lieutenant colonel's mother, was a proud woman," Viscount Dirkson said. "She was the daughter of a prosperous blacksmith when I met her and . . . indulged in a brief liaison with her. She was turned out by her father and her whole family when it became known that she was with child, and she lived in desperate poverty as a washerwoman in a village nearby for the rest of her life. She would accept no support from me for either herself or her son— our son. Any gifts I sent were refused. But I never lost sight of either of them. I had my ways of knowing.

"Gilbert was a good child. He minded his mother and learned his lessons and endured the inevitable bullying of other, more fortunate children with a pride she had taught him. At the age of fourteen he went off with a recruiting sergeant and was soon sent to India, where he was obedient to his superiors and did his duty and demonstrated courage. He was never once written up for disciplinary action. He rose rapidly to the rank of corporal and then sergeant and distinguished himself in each role. I was proud of him."

He stopped briefly when Gil suddenly brought down the side of one fist on the table. Everyone in the room jumped and looked his way, including the judge, who was frowning. He did not say anything, however—Gil was still sitting as before, his head tilted back, his eyes closed. Viscount Dirkson continued.

"Miss Bennington died," he said, "and at last I felt free to offer some support to my son. I purchased an ensign's commission and then a lieutenant's for him. But he had more than his share of his mother's stubborn pride. He wrote to inform me that any further attempt of mine to interfere in his career or his life would be rejected. So I returned to viewing his career from afar.

"There has been nothing, Your Honor, in all the details I have learned that has shaken my pride in the upbringing his mother gave him and the way he has conducted himself since leaving his home. He honored his mother after leaving by writing to her and sending her money. I know him to be an honorable, dependable man of loyal, steadfast character. It is my opinion that Miss Abigail Westcott would not have married him if it were not so. The Westcotts have a reputation for marrying only when their hearts are fully engaged with someone they deem worthy of their love." He sat down.

"We may need handkerchiefs after all," the judge said, drumming his fingertips on his desk before sitting back in his chair, frowning and pursing his lips.

Gil sat staring downward, absolutely immobile. Abigail set her hand in his and he gripped it tightly without turning to look at her.

"In an ideal world," the judge said after a full two minutes of silence, during which all attention was focused upon him, "this case would have the simplest of solutions. In a *sensible* world, that is. General Pascoe, you and your lady are Katherine Bennington's grandparents. I daresay you love her as the only child of *your* only child, sadly now deceased. Grandparents are *supposed* to love their grandchildren.

It is unnatural if they do not. They are supposed to spoil them and then gleefully restore them to their parents so that they may deal with the consequences. Only under extraordinary circumstances do they take and *keep* their grandchildren and refuse to allow the parents even to see them. In this case those circumstances hinge upon the unsubstantiated account your daughter gave her mother of abuse at her husband's hands and presumably fear for the child's safety. Yet it would seem to me that any mother fearing for her child's safety would be unwilling to let that child out of her sight, especially when her husband could be expected to return at any moment. Yet your daughter went off to visit friends.

"And you, Lieutenant Colonel Bennington, are the child's father. You would seem to live in a comfortable home under comfortable circumstances. You left your wife and child well provided for there when you were called away to distinguish yourself at Waterloo. You can hardly be accused of abandoning them when your duty was clear. I assume General Pascoe responded similarly and was himself in Belgium when your wife took your daughter to her mother. You behaved badly afterward when you raged at a lady who was both your mother-in-law and the grandmother of your daughter. You continued your bad behavior when you wrote angry, threatening letters from St. Helena. However, I cannot for the life of me think how else you could have been expected to behave. Any father under such circumstances would have raged similarly. Many would have dashed their mother-in-law to the ground in order to get to their child crying piteously in an upstairs room. And who would blame them?"

"Your Honor!" General Pascoe's lawyer protested, jumping to his feet.

Judge Burroughs's gavel banging against his desk made everyone jump again. "You are out of order!" he thundered. "Sit down, sir. Any more such outbursts and I will have you dragged from my courtroom in chains."

The lawyer resumed his seat as fast as he had left it.

"Mrs. Bennington," the judge said, frowning ferociously upon Abigail, "was the innocent victim of a father who behaved outrageously and criminally by contracting a bigamous marriage with her mother. I have never understood why the sins of the fathers should be visited upon their sons—or daughters in this case. It would seem to me that Mrs. Bennington has shown good judgment in marrying a man who is devoted enough to his child to put himself through *this*. And she married him on the full understanding that she would be taking upon herself the role of stepmother to his daughter. I believe that what Viscount Dirkson said of the Westcott family must be true."

Gil pressed Abigail's hand hard against his thigh.

"I suppose," the judge said, his eyes coming to rest upon Gil, "the scar that makes you look so like a disreputable pirate, Lieutenant Colonel Bennington, was honorably acquired in battle?"

Their lawyer had intended to talk about that, but the judge had cut him off.

Gil looked up at him. "Yes, Your Honor," he said. "In India when I was a sergeant."

"You were fortunate," the judge said, "not to have been decapitated. Though I daresay you did not feel fortunate at the time."

"No, Your Honor," Gil said.

"My *suggestion*," Judge Burroughs said, looking from one table to the other, "is that you get together in a private room, the four of you— the father, the stepmother, and the grandparents—and lock the door upon your lawyers while you come to a sensible, workable arrangement for the future of the minor child you all want. Consider what is best for her, if you will. And consider the accepted and traditional roles of parents and grandparents and be *sensible*.

"People cannot always be sensible, however, when passions run high, and I daresay that if locked together in a room the two men at least might come to fisticuffs. I would still suggest the meeting, but I will make a judgment in the event it should not happen or will not yield results satisfactory to all. I certainly do not wish to see you all back in my courtroom anytime soon. I find for Lieutenant Colonel and Mrs. Bennington as the parents of the child and therefore her natural guardians. And I do believe I will arrive home before my dinner grows cold and thereby avoid a scold from my wife."

"All rise," the bailiff said as the judge got abruptly to his feet.

And they rose while Abigail felt pins and needles dance painfully in her hands and her feet and Gil stood almost at military attention beside her, every part of his body, including his jaw and his face, looking as though they were sculpted of granite.

Beauty, also on her feet, woofed hopefully.

Twenty-two

G il's mind was no longer functioning. It had been so overloaded with information and emotion and hopes he dared not hope and fears he dared not deny that it had simply shut down. Yet as the door closed behind the judge, he knew it was all over, that arguments had been made on both sides, and judgment had been passed. And he heard the echo of something that had been said—

I find for Lieutenant Colonel and Mrs. Bennington as the parents of the child and therefore her natural guardians.

Other things had been said too, all of them lodged somewhere in his mind waiting to come forward to be heard and digested. But—

I find for Lieutenant Colonel and Mrs. Bennington as the parents of the child and therefore her natural guardians.

He turned toward Abby to find her gazing back at him, her eyes wide and suspiciously bright. "She is coming back to me?" he asked, afraid to believe.

"Yes."

And he grabbed her and held her tightly against him as though to save them both from falling off the world. He would have folded her right inside him if it had been possible. Something in his brain told him this was not the way a gentleman behaved in public, and they *were* in public, were they not? He could hear a buzz of sound around them. But to the devil with behaving like a gentleman. He rocked his wife in his arms, his eyes tightly closed.

Abby, Abby.

I find for Lieutenant Colonel and Mrs. Bennington as the parents of the child and therefore her natural guardians.

And Katy! He was going to get her back. He was going to be able to take her home to Rose Cottage. He and Abby. They were going to be a family. Perhaps after all dreams *did* come true.

Her arms were wrapped as tightly about him as his were about her, he realized. Obviously it did not bother her to behave in unladylike fashion with a roomful of people looking on. Or else his obvious need to hold and be held had taken precedence with her over keeping a proper distance between them, as a lady ought.

And other snippets of what had been said began to make themselves heard in his head.

She would accept no support from me for either herself or her son—our son. Any gifts I sent were refused.

I was proud of him.

So I returned to viewing his career from afar.

In an ideal world this case would have the simplest of solutions. General Pascoe, you and your lady are Katherine Bennington's grandparents. I daresay you love her . . .

Grandparents are supposed to love their grandchildren.

I daresay you love her . . .

My suggestion is that you get together in a private room, the four of you . . . while you come to a sensible, workable arrangement for the future of the minor child you all want.

Consider what is best for her.

. . . the minor child you all want.

I daresay you love her.

I find for Lieutenant Colonel and Mrs. Bennington as the parents of the child and therefore her natural guardians.

Perhaps only seconds passed before Gil loosened his hold on Abigail and became fully aware again of his surroundings. The Pascoes were still behind their table. The general was saying something to their lawyer, but they were all beginning to turn away. Beauty still sat beside their own table, her tongue lolling, her tail thumping on the floor. The Westcotts were turning to one another, shaking hands, hugging. The Marchioness of Dorchester was making her way toward Harry. And . . .

At the back of the room stood a stranger, tall, dark, though his hair was silvering, probably in his mid- to late fifties. A stranger Gil was seeing for the first time. A stranger whose voice he had heard for the first time a short while ago.

He stared at his father for the span of a few seconds before movement caught the corner of his eye and he turned his attention back to the Pascoes, who were following their lawyer from the room. Gil grasped Abigail's hand just as Grimes began to address some remark to them, and they moved away from the table together, stepping around Beauty.

"General," Gil called in the voice that had always made itself heard on a parade ground.

"Lady Pascoe," Abby called at the same moment.

They turned back, their faces masks of hauteur.

"Sir. Ma'am," Gil said, not even noticing that silence had fallen upon the rest of the room. "I believe we should hold that private meeting Judge Burroughs suggested."

"For what purpose, Bennington?" the general asked. "You have got what you want. What more is there to be said? You wish to gloat?"

Abby answered before Gil could. "You are Katy's grandparents," she said. "You have loved her and cared for her for two years. She knows you and loves you. She must continue to do so. Family is . . . oh, it is more important than anything else in this world. A child's affections should not be torn between her parents and her grandparents. She ought not to be made to choose, and no one should choose for her. Please let us sit down and talk, remembering that this is all about Katy far more than it is about any of us. Come to the Pulteney Hotel, where we are staying. Come for tea this evening or tomorrow morning or afternoon if you would prefer."

Lady Pascoe glared back at them, her chin high, her eyes cold, her mouth a thin line—an expression that was all too familiar to her son-in-law. General Pascoe looked long and hard at Abby and then in the same way at Gil.

"Tomorrow morning," he said curtly, holding Gil's gaze. "At ten o'clock."

"At our home," his wife added.

Both of them turned away again and left the room without looking back.

Gil released Abby's hand and swung about to look at the other people in the room. All Westcotts. No one else.

His father was gone.

He held up a staying hand when it looked as though Abby's mother was about to come hurrying toward them.

"I believed," he said, "indeed I still believe, that I did you all a wrong by allowing you to befriend me during that week at Hinsford when I did not explain to you who I was or where or how I grew up. It did not seem a very terrible wrong, however, as I expected never to see any of you again. But then I compounded it infinitely by marrying Abby. When I came here to London and refused to attend the family celebration Lord and Lady Hodges wished to arrange for us, I did so not out of any fear that I would be rejected and made to feel my social inferiority, but out of a concern that I would be stretching your good nature beyond a limit. It seemed to me that Abby could remain on good terms with her family while I kept my proper distance. It would appear I have been wrong about everything and that Abby has been right about her family all along. You are not going to let me go, are you?"

"I believe, Lieutenant Colonel Bennington," Lady Matilda Westcott said. "No, enough of that cumbersome title when you are family. I believe, *Gilbert*, that we might all have been here today even if you had *not* married Abigail. You were extraordinarily kind to Harry, and you were every bit the courteous gentleman when we all went to visit him. You were patient and good with the children. We all noticed it. Mama, do sit down and allow me to wrap your shawl more closely about your shoulders. There was a draft when—when someone opened the door behind us a short while ago."

Anna came toward Abby then to hug her, and the Marquess of Dorchester came to shake Gil by the hand and inform him that he and his wife were delighted that they were soon going to be able to welcome yet another grandchild into their family in the form of young Katy. The marchioness was demanding of Harry why on earth he had risked his health by coming all the way to London in person when a letter would surely have done just as well. Beauty, released at last from the command to both sit and stay, did a couple of exuberant dashes about the room before accepting the invitation to become acquainted with Lady Hodges and better acquainted with Lady Jessica Archer.

And reality struck Gil again with the force of a bolt of lightning.

I find for Lieutenant Colonel and Mrs. Bennington as the parents of the child and therefore her natural guardians.

He was going to see *Katy* again. Soon. He and Abby were going to take her *home* with them. He was going to *see* her. And hear her voice.

His *daughter*.

But—

"Who invited Viscount Dirkson here?" he asked of no one in particular. "How did he even *know* about this?"

Quiet prevailed again while everyone waited for someone else to answer.

"I believe perhaps it was I," young Bertrand said. "I happened to hear that his son—I mean Adrian, *another* son—was in town and I thought I would go and see him. We were quite close friends at Oxford, though he finished there the year before I did. I called on him and we talked. His father was there too. I suppose I happened to mention your name, Lieutenant Colonel. In connection with Abby, perhaps. And I daresay I mentioned *this*." He gestured vaguely at the room about them.

Gil looked hard at him. Why did he have the feeling there was more to the story? Some of the famous Westcott meddling, perhaps?

So he had a half brother, did he? Adrian. But he did not want to know. He did not want to know anything about his father's life.

He nodded at Bertrand before Lady Molenor, one of the Westcott sisters, hugged him and congratulated him.

"Once you marry a Westcott, Bennington," Lord Molenor said, "you become one forever after, even if you do retain your own name. You might as well get accustomed to it."

"Katy is now officially my granddaughter," the Marchioness of Dorchester said, extending a hand for Gil's. She was beaming at him. There might even have been tears in her eyes. "I am very happy for you . . . Gil."

And, taking her hand and glancing at Abby, who had tears on her cheeks as well as swimming in her eyes, he fought not to break down in front of the lot of them.

It was true. It was *true*.

"It is a blessing," the Duke of Netherby said with a languid sigh, "that the judge is no longer present. He would surely be handing out handkerchiefs and complaining about his dinner."

LADY PASCOE HAD NOT SAID WHERE THEIR HOME IN LONDON WAS, but it was not hard to discover. Alexander had volunteered the information even before they left the courtroom, and Colin had confirmed it. General Sir Edward Pascoe had a house on Portman Square.

Abigail and Gil arrived there promptly at ten the following morning, though neither had been looking forward to it.

"I think," Gil had said the previous evening, "we should just leave for Essex in the morning, Abby. It will be easier going there to fetch Katy when they are not there. And they will probably be relieved not to see us again."

But there had been no real conviction in his voice.

"You cannot just go there and snatch her away, Gil," Abigail had said. "She has not seen you since she was a baby. She will not even remember you."

He had grimaced and frowned.

"Besides," she had said, "we are the ones who offered the meeting, albeit here rather than at their home. It would be . . . dishonorable not to go." And besides again, the general and his wife were Katy's *grandparents*.

He had not argued the point. He had not been really serious anyway.

And so here they were, being admitted to the house on Portman Square by the general's butler and then to a small but elegant salon on the ground floor. Abigail smiled and was filled with dread as their hosts welcomed them with stiff courtesy—which did not involve handshakes—and directed them to two chairs before sitting down themselves. They were the child's *grandparents*, and they were soon to be deprived of the granddaughter who had lived with them for the past two years.

Winning the case had been the easy part, Abigail thought during an uneasy silence while the coffee tray was brought in and Lady Pascoe poured and offered a plate of macaroons.

"Judge Burroughs was wise to suggest that we meet, just the four of us together," Abigail said as a conversational opener, cup and saucer in hand.

It was the wrong thing to say. But was there a right thing?

General Pascoe sat like a block of granite—was it a military thing, that posture and look? But Harry had never had it. Lady Pascoe's mouth was set thin in a face that was cold and haughty.

"Judge Burroughs," she said, "ought to be removed from the bench in disgrace. The comments he inserted constantly into the proceedings were frivolous and inappropriate. We would have had a fairer judgment if there had been a jury. Your *husband*, Mrs. Bennington, is a cruel and abusive man. I daresay you have not discovered the truth of that yet. You will."

"What I *have* discovered, ma'am," Abigail said, "is quite the opposite. But I do understand that you are hurt and fearful for the granddaughter you have cared for throughout the past two years. You need not be afraid. I am to be her mama. My family, as my cousin the Earl of Riverdale said yesterday on behalf of them all, will take her under their collective wing as they have done with all the children of the family. We will bring her to Essex to visit you and the general, and we invite you to come to Gloucestershire to see her whenever you wish. I will even send you specific invitations. Any child who is surrounded by a large and loving family is fortunate indeed. I was such a child, and I am still surrounded by them despite the unsettling discovery that was made several years ago about my parents' marriage."

"You have a glib tongue, Mrs. Bennington," Lady Pascoe said.

"Ma'am," Gil said, "allow me to tell you, if you will, about the day Katy was born. Caroline had had a hard time and was exhausted. After holding my daughter for a minute or two, I was expected to relinquish her into a maid's care and go away to celebrate. I held her for a number of hours instead. My heart almost hurt with the love I felt for her. And I made the vow to myself that I would love her with every breath I drew for the rest of my life. And care for her. And allow her to grow into the sort of woman she was—*is*—meant to be. I have never broken that vow and never will. If there has been cruelty in my life—and there has been on the battlefield—it could never, ever spill over into my domestic relationships. Either with my wife or my daughter or any other children with whom I may be gifted. I have dreamed all my life of home and of family and of love."

His tone was clipped, his voice apparently without feeling. Abigail felt her heart break a little bit. He was thirty-four years old. He had had a desperately hard and lonely childhood, and life had been harsh for him in the army. But he had had a dream and had never relinquished it.

"An affecting speech," Lady Pascoe said.

"An olive branch," the general said, speaking for the first time. "It is easier to be magnanimous as the winner of an altercation than it is as the loser. My wife and I are the losers, Bennington, thanks to a judge I would dearly like to see strung up by his thumbs. But we have nothing to gain by calling you a liar or refusing the offer your wife has made. Caroline was our only child. Katherine is our only grandchild. My wife would not wish to cut herself off from all contact with her merely to spite you. Now . . . you will be wishing to see the child. Perhaps even to take her, though I am not sure the Pulteney Hotel is the best—"

"What?" Gil had shot to his feet. "Katy is *here*? *In this house?*"

"I see," Lady Pascoe said coldly, "that you are as uncontrolled as you ever were. I cannot have my granddaughter—"

"Ma'am," Abigail said, "*is* she here? Not in Essex?"

"She is upstairs in the nursery," General Pascoe said. "Her nurse is awaiting your visit."

"Oh." Abigail got to her feet and took Gil's hand. It closed about hers like a vise.

Lady Pascoe sat like a statue.

"I would ask," the general said, "though I cannot command, that you give her a little time, that you not take her away this morning. Give her a day or two. My butler will be waiting outside the door to escort you upstairs."

Abigail hesitated when they were at the door, and looked back.

The general was on his feet, his hands at his back. Lady Pascoe was still seated, her gaze directed straight ahead. Abigail hurried across the room toward her.

"Ma'am," she said. "Oh, ma'am, I understand your pain. We will deal with this gently, I promise you. We will take her home when she is ready to go. And we will see to it that her grandparents remain central to her life. I will not let a day go by without reminding her of you, and I will make sure she sees you regularly, either here or in Essex or at Rose Cottage. And I do commend you from my heart for the care you have given her all the time Gil has been away at his military duties."

Lady Pascoe's eyes had focused upon hers. "You do indeed have a glib tongue," she said. "I will hold you accountable, Mrs. Bennington, for any harm that comes to that child. Go, now. She is waiting for you."

THE BUTLER OPENED THE DOOR INTO A LARGE, COMFORTABLE room, brightly furnished, filled with sunlight. Gil stepped inside with Abby—and his heart stopped.

She was over by the window with Mrs. Evans—a tiny, dainty child in a frilly white dress with white shoes. Her very dark hair had been combed back from her face and tied high on the back of her head with a large white ribbon. The rest of her hair hung loose to her shoulders. She had a narrow face with a pointed chin and large, dark eyes.

Wary eyes.

She ducked half behind Mrs. Evans's apron as the woman smiled and clasped her hands at her waist. One dark eye and the white bow were still visible as well as half the white dress and one white shoe.

Katy.

Oh good God.

His heart remembered to beat again—with painful thumps that robbed him of breath.

The door closed behind him.

"Good morning, sir, ma'am," Mrs. Evans said, and Gil remembered her lilting Welsh accent. "We have been waiting impatiently, but now we are shy. Here is your papa at last, *cariad*. And your new mama."

Cariad. A Welsh endearment, Gil could remember her explaining when his daughter was a baby. The word for *love*.

Katy did not emerge from behind the apron. Neither did Gil emerge from wherever it was he had taken refuge. Somewhere inside himself. He stood rooted to the spot, his hands crossed behind him while Abigail proceeded farther into the room.

"Mrs. Evans," she said, extending her hand and smiling warmly. "Gil has told me about you. How pleased I am to meet you. And Katy. Did you dress up in your best clothes to see Papa?"

One little hand went up to touch the ribbon and she ducked an inch or two farther behind the apron.

"New shoes," she said.

And oh, God, her voice! High pitched and tiny, just like her.

"Oh. Let me see," Abigail said, and one little foot was pushed into full view and her skirt hoisted almost to her knee. "Very pretty. Do they pinch? Sometimes new shoes do."

A shake of the half-hidden head. And then for a moment both eyes came into view as she darted a glance at Gil. She pointed at him and then hid again.

"Not a day has passed," Mrs. Evans said, "when I have not told her about her papa and how he loves her and will come as soon as he is able to take her back home."

"And now he has come," Abby said.

"I have a dolly," the child told her.

"Oh?" Abby said. "May I see her?"

"Sleeping," Katy said.

"Ah, then I will speak very softly," Abby said. "May I see?"

And his daughter stepped right out of her hiding place and reached up a hand for Abby's before taking her to a doll's cradle nearby. "Sleeping," she said, pointing and turning her head for a swift peep at Gil.

"Ah, yes, so she is," Abby said softly. "She is warmly tucked up beneath her blanket. We must not wake her."

Katy peeped again and pointed. "Papa," she said.

"Yes," Abby said. "He has come to see you and now he is shy. Just like you were a little while ago. Should he go and hide behind your nurse, do you suppose?"

"No-o!" And Gil's heart stopped again as his daughter laughed, a child's delighted giggle. She pointed again. "Papa has an ow?"

"On his face?" Abby said.

"An ow," Katy said again.

"It was a big ow," Gil said. "But it is better now."

"Papa cry?" Katy asked Abby.

"A whole pailful of tears," he told her. "Then the ow went away. But this stayed." He pointed to his facial scar.

"Kiss better?" Katy asked.

"Do you want to try it?" Abby asked, but the child shook her head vigorously and half hid behind her.

"Give her time, sir," Mrs. Evans said.

"I have a dog," Gil said.

"Puppy?" An eye peeped at him again, and then the whole of her came into sight as Abby moved beside her and smoothed a hand over her hair.

"A *big* puppy," Gil said, showing Beauty's height with his hand. "A great, big softie. She likes children. She likes to shake hands and she likes to stand still to have her head patted."

Again the delighted giggle. "Big softie," Katy said, and went off into peals of giggles again. "Big softie."

"She would *love* to meet you," Gil said.

Katy shook her head, serious again. "Grandmama will not let puppies," she said. "Or kitties. Only in the kitchen. For the mice."

"Do you like kittens?" Gil asked.

"I *love* kitties," his daughter assured him.

"Perhaps," Gil said, "when you come home with me and your new mama, we will have a kitten that will be all your own."

He glanced at Abby, and she did not look dismayed. Was that a bribe he had offered? But he meant it. If a kitten would make his daughter happy, then she would have one. Beauty would probably love it too once she had recovered from a touch of jealousy.

"Would you like to meet Beauty?" he asked. "That is the puppy's name. Not here if Grandmama does not wish it. Perhaps—Mrs. Evans, does Katy get taken out for walks in the park?"

"Not often, sir," the nurse said, frowning, by which Gil understood that it never happened. "Just sometimes in the garden."

"Would you like to see the park and meet Beauty, Katy?" Gil asked.

His child, all big eyed, nodded, and then went darting across the room to tug at Mrs. Evans's apron. "May I, Nanny?" she asked. "Please, please, please? See the puppy?"

"If your mama and papa can arrange it, of course, *cariad*," Mrs. Evans said, smiling down at her and then at Gil. "It will be such a treat for her, sir."

"This afternoon while the sun still shines," he said. "I will have a word with General Pascoe on my way out. I shall send a chaise to fetch you and meet you by the Serpentine."

Mrs. Evans smiled.

Katy turned an eager face toward him before becoming suddenly shy again and pulling her nurse's apron over her head.

"Big softie," she said, and giggled again.

Gil looked at Abby and smiled.

Twenty-three

✿

Gil had *smiled*.

For the rest of the day Abigail felt rather as though she walked on air.

He had *smiled*.

Oh, it was largely because he had seen his child again and had heard her voice and her laughter and had begun, very tentatively, to establish a relationship with her. But it was at *her*, Abigail, that he had smiled with dazzling warmth. Including her in his happiness.

She did not believe she had ever been happier in her life.

Well, perhaps on her wedding day. And during her wedding night.

They arrived early at the park in order to allow Beauty a good run about an empty expanse of grass, endlessly chasing a large stick and bringing it back. But she wagged her tail, panting loudly, when it was time to reattach her leash, and trotted happily beside them as they made their way to the Serpentine, whose waters were sparkling in the sunshine.

Abigail took Gil's arm, but he shrugged it off and grasped her hand instead.

"Have I been silent and morose again?" he asked her.

If he had, she had not noticed. For this morning he had smiled, and that had made all the difference.

"No." She shook her head. "I think I should hate it if you felt obliged to chatter all the time. I think perhaps you would hate it if I did."

"Can companionship flourish in silence, then?" he asked her.

She thought about it and shook her head. "Probably not," she said. "Neither, I suspect, could it flourish in endless chatter. I think really close friends ought not to think about whether they are talking enough or too much or even just the right amount. As soon as conversation or its lack becomes self-conscious, companionship slips."

"Hmm. I will have to think about that," he said. "You have done much of your living inside yourself, have you not, Abby? I noticed that about you almost from the start. And the same has always been true of me. Do you suppose it will always remain that way?"

"Yes," she said, frowning in thought for a moment. "Marriage ought not to change two people. That, I think, would lead to unhappiness for one or both. It should only . . . enrich who they already are."

"So we will no longer do all our living within and hoard all our secrets to ourselves," he said.

"I hope not." She smiled at him. "How did this start?"

"I think it started," he said, "when you stepped past the corner of the house and saw me half naked, an axe in my hands, and I saw you horribly indignant and haughty because I had witnessed your terror."

"I was not terrified," she protested.

"Oh yes, you were," he said.

"Yes, I was." She laughed. "Big softie. That description amused Katy, did it not?"

"She is smaller than I expected," he said. "How could I possibly have created—cocreated—such a dainty little thing, Abby? And all decked out in white for our visit."

She had no chance to answer. They were walking along the path beside the Serpentine, Beauty on a short leash because there were other people around now, several of them eyeing the dog warily or giving her a wide berth as they passed. But then there was a shriek, and a little figure in pink detached herself from her nurse's hand and came hurtling toward them, arms outstretched, her eyes upon Beauty.

Katy.

She stopped abruptly, however, when she was still a safe distance away and pointed. "Puppy," she said.

"Stay at my heel, Beauty," Gil said quietly as he stepped off the path so as not to impede traffic. And he did what he had done at Hinsford with Wren's and Anna's children. He released Abigail's hand, went down on one knee, and held out a hand toward his daughter. "Come. Put your hand in mine. She wants to meet you."

Katy was not at all sure she wanted to meet Beauty. She might not have been sure she wanted to meet her papa this close either if her attention had not been wholly focused upon the dog, who woofed gently. Katy sidled off the path and reached out one hand until it was enclosed in Gil's. He drew her to the side away from Beauty and then sat her upon his thigh.

"Puppy," she said, pointing. *"Big* puppy."

"Bigger than you," he said. "Big softie. She is happy to meet you. See her tail waving?"

Abigail turned her head to smile at Mrs. Evans.

"Let me show you how to make friends," Gil said, taking Katy's hand palm-down in his. "You let her sniff the back of your hand like this, you see, so that she will get to know you. It tickles?"

"Ye-es," Katy agreed.

"And then," he said, "you turn your hand over like this so that she can sniff your palm too."

Katy shrieked with laughter suddenly and snatched back her hand. "Puppy lick. Nanny, look at me. Puppy has a cold nose. Again, Papa."

Beauty lowered her head obligingly and Gil patted her head, his daughter's hand enclosed in his own. But Katy pushed it away after a couple of pats. "Let me, Papa," she said. "Let me." And she patted

Beauty's head with growing enthusiasm until the dog lifted her head and licked the child's wrist.

"Big softie," Katy said, laughing.

"Her real name is Beauty," Gil said.

"Beauty," Katy said, patting the dog's head again and pointing to herself with her other hand. "My name is Katy. Grandmama calls me Katherine, but I am Katy."

Beauty woofed.

"Down, Papa," Katy commanded, and slid off his knee to get closer to the dog, which was indeed larger than she. She patted Beauty's side, stretched her arms along her, and laid one cheek against her. Beauty panted and stood still.

And Gil, still kneeling beside them, had tears swimming in his eyes. Abigail turned her head to converse with Mrs. Evans as some of them spilled over and trickled down his cheeks. He would be mortified if he knew she had noticed.

THEY CAME NEAR TO QUARRELING AGAIN DURING THE EVENING while they were seated side by side on a sofa in their sitting room. It had started out well enough. They had been reminiscing about the pleasures of the day—the visit to the Pascoes they had so dreaded turning suddenly and unexpectedly into that first meeting with Katy; the walk in Hyde Park during the afternoon. Katy had eventually insisted for a few minutes upon holding Beauty's leash in her own hand, and they had allowed it while Gil gave quiet instructions to the dog.

Abigail used the moment to have an earnest conversation with Mrs. Evans, who had told her that the general and his lady had always given their granddaughter the best of care but very little of their time.

"Make that virtually nothing in the general's case," she had added. "Lady Pascoe is affectionate when she *does* visit the nursery, and Katy likes her grandmama. But the tie is not a deep one, Mrs. Bennington. I would not say this to anyone but you or the lieutenant colonel, but you are her parents and I know you will worry about what taking Katy away from the general and his wife may do to her—and them. Provided you take me with you, ma'am—and I earnestly hope you will—Katy will have the continuity to smooth her way from one home to another."

The best moment of all during the afternoon had come half an hour or so after they had begun strolling along by the water. By that time Katy's energy was flagging. She had spent it not only holding Beauty's leash, but then tripping along between Abby and Mrs. Evans, a hand in each of theirs while she chattered away. She told Abby about her doll waking up after Mama and Papa left this morning and about the kitten she was going to have when she went to Papa's house—black with one big white patch over its eye—and about one of her new shoes that hurt after Mama left and Nanny took them both off and put some ointment on her heel to stop a blister and let her go without shoes until they came out. But at last she had been walking with lagging footsteps, and yawning.

"No," Katy had protested when Mrs. Evans had suggested it was time to go home for a nap. "Not tired."

A few moments later she had slipped her hands free and darted forward to where Gil was walking with Beauty. She had stopped in front of him and raised her arms.

"Up," she had said.

And that most wonderful of moments had happened. He had picked up his child—she weighed nothing at all—and she had wrapped her arms about his neck and burrowed her head between his shoulder and neck and promptly fallen asleep.

They had reminisced, he and Abby. But now they had almost quarreled, for with nothing left to say about this morning or this afternoon she had introduced another topic entirely.

"No," he said. He had been saying nothing but no for the last few minutes, and finally she had fallen silent. It was not the silence of easy companionship of which they had spoken earlier in the park, however.

And so he had been left with the last word, but it did not feel final. The echo of it accused him and made him want to rip up at her and stalk into his bedchamber and shut the door behind him like a petulant schoolboy.

She tipped her head sideways and rested her cheek against his shoulder. She did not play fair. How could one rip up at someone who had just made such a trusting, affectionate gesture?

"I really do not want to have anything to do with him," he said unnecessarily, since she had not protested his latest no. "And I do not suppose for one moment that he wants anything more to do with me. I do not know who on earth persuaded him to put in that appearance in court."

He had been severely shaken at seeing his father for the first time ever. It had struck him too that his father had been seeing *him* for the first time. He was uneasily aware that they looked a bit alike. How could one look like a total stranger, who happened also to be one's father?

Abby had suggested that they invite Viscount Dirkson to join them for coffee tomorrow morning. In vain had he reminded her that he was to take Katy riding on his horse in the morning—she had been wildly excited when he had suggested it even though it had been made clear to her that Mama and Nanny would not be accompanying them, or even Beauty. And he had already capitulated on the matter of a Westcott family tea tomorrow afternoon at the home of the Earl of Riverdale—a sort of welcome to the family for him as well as a farewell to them before they left for Gloucestershire within the next few days. Katy was even to be brought there to meet and play with her cousins in the nursery.

Now this. It was too much. It was the last straw.

"He was a friend of my father's," Abby said. "I daresay someone in the family informed him and he decided to attend."

"Interfering busybodies," he said.

"Yes." Instead of bristling with indignation and giving him the quarrel for which he was itching, she laughed.

There was a lengthy silence, during which she kept her head where it was and slid one hand down his arm to cover the back of his hand. He did not turn his hand over to grasp hers. The wiles of women. They did not play fair at all.

"It would have to be early in the morning," he said irritably. "I promised Mrs. Evans I would come for Katy at half past ten."

"I shall write now, then," she said, "and have the letter delivered tonight. I will invite him to join us here for breakfast at half past eight."

"He will not come," he said.

"That will be his choice," she said. "But you will have asked."

"*You* will have asked," he said.

"Yes." She rubbed her fingers over the back of his hand before getting to her feet and crossing to the desk, where there were paper and pens and ink.

He walked over there a little later, when he was aware that she was folding and sealing the letter she had written.

"Abby." He leaned over her and set his lips against the back of her neck. "This is *not* a good idea."

"Then you will be able to blame me forever after," she said, getting to her feet and turning toward him.

He took her in his arms and held her head against his shoulder.

"You care," he said.

"Yes."

"Why?" he asked.

"Because you are my husband," she said.

ABIGAIL ANSWERED THE KNOCK ON THE DOOR AT PRECISELY HALF past eight the following morning. Gil had left word at the desk downstairs last night that they were expecting a visitor and he might be allowed to come up unannounced.

He had hoped with all his being through a night of disturbed sleep, during which he ought to have been delighting in memories of the two meetings with his daughter, that the man would not come. He could not even think of him by name. Certainly not as his father. He hated the fact that now he could put a face to that nameless someone. And that he had been weak enough to give in to his wife's persuasions. Though he must not be unfair. She had not nagged at him after she had made the suggestion and he had said no.

Surely the man would not come, he had thought earlier this morning and again a few minutes ago when waiters had arrived in their sitting room with breakfast for three on covered warming dishes and a large pot of steaming coffee and had set the table for three.

But he had come. Abby was opening the door and smiling.

"Lord Dirkson," she said, extending her right hand. "It is so good of you to have come."

And he stepped into the room and took her hand and bowed over it. Gil hated the fact—*hated* it!—that even he could see the resemblance between himself and this man, who was tall and trim of figure with silvering hair and sharp, angular features set in lines that suggested cynicism and hard living.

"Mrs. Bennington," he said. "You will not remember this, but I met you when you were Lady Abigail Westcott and all of two or three years old. You had escaped from the nursery at the house on South Audley Street and had come to greet your papa's visitor. There was no sign of your brother or your elder sister, and soon enough you were whisked away back to the safe confines of the nursery. In the meanwhile you had made me the prettiest of curtsies, and I had responded with my courtliest bow."

Ah. The accomplished lothario. Not that he was flirting with Abby, but his words had the desired effect upon her. Her cheeks flushed, seemingly with pleasure, and she laughed.

"I wish I could remember," she said, and Gil wondered if the incident had really happened. She could hardly dispute it, could she, when she had been a mere infant?

The man turned toward Gil, and they looked measuringly at each other for a few moments while Abby closed the door quietly. He was taller than his father, Gil noticed. And the man looked his age.

"I have little right to be happy for you," Dirkson said. "I am happy nevertheless."

"Perhaps that ought to be *no* right," Gil said.

"Perhaps," Dirkson agreed. "She did a fine job with you, your mother."

"With no thanks to you," Gil said. "And I would prefer that you not sully her memory by mentioning her."

Dirkson inclined his head and Abby sat down on a chair beside the door and clutched a cushion to her bosom with both hands.

"This," Gil said, "was not my idea."

"I understand it was your wife's," Dirkson said. "I understood that when I found her note awaiting me when I returned home last night. I came out of deference to her, so that her feelings would not be hurt. I did not expect your forgiveness or come to ask for it."

His father spoke with soft courtesy. And he had put Gil firmly in the wrong without uttering any words of accusation—*I came out of deference to her, so that her feelings would not be hurt.* He had made it clear that his son, on the contrary, was showing discourtesy to his wife and was hurting her feelings. Which was exactly right, damn his eyes.

"Why would my mother not accept support from you?" The question was asked before he could stop himself.

"I was staying with a friend at a house not far from her father's smithy," Dirkson told him. "She was a comely young woman, the pride of her father and brothers, much admired by the young men of the neighborhood. I . . . seduced her with promises I do not remember making. She swore afterward that I had promised to marry her. Whatever I did promise, I am sure it was not that. But when I learned, a few months after I had left there, that she was with child, I offered to set her up in a decent house of her own and support her and the child she was expecting. She threw what she called my breach of promise in my

teeth and refused all support. She never relented. When I tried sending you gifts, she returned them if she was confronted with a mes-
senger, and threw them on a rubbish heap if there was no way for her
to send them back. I was . . . unhappy for your sake, but I honored her
pride and resilience. She proved that she could raise you alone."

Gil stared stonily at him.

"I make no excuses," Dirkson said. "I do not ask for forgiveness. I
do not deserve it. I beg your pardon for saying during the hearing a
couple of days ago that I was proud of you. I have no right to pride. I
had no hand in the shaping of you. Only in the begetting of you."

"Were you married," Gil asked, "when you were with my mother?"
He really did not want to know.

"No," Dirkson said. "My marriage came later."

"And you have a son," Gil said. Good God, he *really* did not want
to know.

"And two daughters," Dirkson told him. "I am fond of all of them
and proud of them as well."

"Who told you," Gil asked, "about the hearing?"

Dirkson seemed to consider a moment. "Young Watley—Bertrand
Lamarr—was at Oxford with my son," he said. "He is Mrs. Bennington's stepbrother."

"And he told you?" Gil asked.

"My son," Dirkson said. "But I was there too."

Gil looked steadily at the man who was his father. "Perhaps I have
one thing for which to thank you," he said. "The bleakness of my
childhood caused me to grow up with an unshakable dream. Of home
and wife and family. Of honesty and loyalty and steadiness of character. And of honor. And of love. That dream, sir, has come true."

He was aware over the man's shoulder of Abby lifting her hands
to cover her face.

"And it will be cherished for a lifetime," he added.

"Then I did well in that begetting," Viscount Dirkson said, turning
toward Abby, who lowered her hands and got to her feet. "I will not

trouble you further, Mrs. Bennington. But I thank you for the invitation. I have long wished to meet my firstborn son face-to-face. I hope that in retrospect he will not be sorry that he has met me and had a chance to say some of the things he has wanted all his life to say."

"Thank you," she said.

"You had better stay," Gil said at the same moment. "My wife wished for you to have breakfast with us, and her wishes are important to me. Sit down. Let us tell you about your granddaughter. If you are interested, that is."

It was grudgingly said. But how could he say it any other way? Besides, he wanted to know exactly what those gifts had been so that he could imagine the enormous pleasure his childhood self, absent all pride, would have drawn from them. Or even just one of them.

His father hesitated before nodding slowly.

"I am interested," he said, moving toward the table and the place Abby was indicating.

Epilogue

They arrived home in Gloucestershire a little more than a week after regaining custody of Katy, having spent a few days letting her get to know and become comfortable with them.

They had taken her for a boat ride on the river Thames and for ices at Gunter's. They had taken her to a family tea at Alexander's, where she had spent a couple of hours playing excitedly with her new cousins in the nursery. They had taken her on a separate visit to her new grandmama and grandpapa, Abigail's mother and stepfather, and her aunt Estelle and uncle Bertrand, who played a game of spillikin with her and pretended not to notice when she disturbed at least a dozen spills every time she pulled one free, shrieking with laughter as she did so. Harry had not been there. He had returned home to Hinsford two days after the hearing. Gil had taken Katy riding in Richmond Park with her uncle Avery and cousin Josephine, while several other members of the family had followed in a cavalcade of carriages for a picnic on the grass, preceded by a noisy game of hide-and-seek among the trees.

General and Lady Pascoe had declined invitations to the visits and the picnic, but they had received the Marquess and Marchioness of

Dorchester when they called one afternoon, and the Dowager Countess of Riverdale when she called the day after with Lady Matilda. When they said goodbye to Katy, the general had instructed her to be a good girl and mind her mama and papa, and Lady Pascoe had presented her cheek for Katy's kiss when Gil lifted her up.

Neither one had shown any strong emotion—which did not mean they felt none, Abigail realized. Katy had not seemed upset to be taken from them, perhaps because she did not understand what leaving meant. Though she *had* made very sure when Gil explained to her that they were going on a long journey to Papa's house that her nanny was going too.

Mrs. Evans had traveled in a separate carriage they had hired to convey her and all their baggage. For one short stretch of the journey Katy had sat in with her, but most of the time she wanted to be with Mama and Papa and, most of all, the puppy, with whom she cuddled when she was not wedged between Gil and Abigail in their new, very comfortable, though not opulent, carriage. A groom had been hired to bring Gil's horse by easy stages.

Abigail had promised to write frequently to Lady Pascoe to tell her how Katy did. She had promised also to keep on inviting them to Rose Cottage.

"You must come, please," she had said when shaking hands upon their departure. "We would not wish Katy to forget you—or her mother."

Lady Pascoe had merely looked steadily back at her, her face haughty and ever so slightly disdainful. But Abigail would persist. The woman had lost her only daughter less than two years ago. Now she was in a sense losing her granddaughter too.

Something else Abigail hoped for—though she kept it strictly to herself—was another meeting with Viscount Dirkson. She was not sure where or when, but she would not give up hope.

But now they were home. Or almost. Gil had said that Rose Cottage was on the outskirts of the village through which they were driving—a picturesque place with a village green and a church with a tall spire and an inn and a smithy and a cluster of shops and a few rows of pretty houses, several of them thatched. It looked more like an idealized painting of rural England than reality, but it was, in fact, very real. Katy was just waking up from a nap on Abigail's lap and was yawning and looking out the window.

"Duckies," she cried, pointing. "Look, Papa. Look, Mama."

And indeed there were a few of them bobbing on the surface of the pond at the center of the green.

"We will come back and see them one day," Gil told her.

"Tomorrow?" she asked.

"Perhaps," he said. "We will bring Beauty for a walk."

It seemed for a moment that they were driving right out of the village. But then there was a rustic wooden fence to their left with trees and bushes inside it, and then a wide wooden gate, beyond which was a paved path that wended out of sight behind the trees. Gil leaned forward and knocked on the front panel and the carriage drew to a halt.

"The carriage house and stables are at the back," he said. "But we will get out here and approach the house from the front."

He had been quiet for the last little while so as not to disturb Katy while she slept. But it had seemed to Abigail that he was full of suppressed excitement. She had felt it in him throughout the long, sometimes tedious journey from London.

His lifelong dream, he had told his father that morning at the Pulteney Hotel, had come true. But it had not really. Or not fully. *This* was his dream: Rose Cottage, the home he had purchased when he came home from India—and bringing his wife and child here. And spending the rest of his life here with his family.

It had happened once before, of course. He had brought a pregnant Caroline here in the wintertime, and there had been a brief blossoming of happiness with the birth of his daughter. The dream had turned sour and had threatened to die. But he had not let it go. He had fought to get his daughter back. He had married her, Abigail, to make that more possible. Though that, she knew, had not been his only reason. Or, if it had, it was no longer so. She knew he cared. She knew this homecoming was the more precious, the more perfect for him, because she was here too. They were husband and wife. They were family.

And this time it was summer.

Beauty leapt to the ground with loud huffs and puffs as soon as the coachman opened the door. Gil descended first after the steps had been lowered and swung Katy down before handing Abigail out. There was something different about his face. It was not quite smiling, but the disciplined austerity had somehow gone from it. It was as though he had allowed some of himself to come out from that place deep within where he had hidden most of his life.

He turned to open the gate, and Katy went skipping through it and along the path, Beauty loping along at her side. Gil offered Abigail his arm.

"I have never seen it in the summertime," he said. "I have not seen the flowers. Or the roses."

She smiled as she took his arm.

It was not a long garden path. It was not a huge garden. The house was not quite a mansion. But as they turned the bend in the path and it all came into view, they both stopped walking and merely gazed. Freshly scythed grass, almost emerald in color. Flowers in profusion in neat beds everywhere and hanging in baskets from the house eaves. Roses in abundance climbing trellises and spilling over low walls. Their scent filling the air. Curtains fluttering at open windows. And Mrs. Evans, who had come ahead of them from the last stage, standing in the doorway with the woman who must be the housekeeper, and opening her arms to Katy, who went dashing toward her, prattling something that was inaudible from where Abigail and Gil stood, Beauty at her side.

"Home!" Gil said, and he turned his head to look at Abigail, and his eyes filled with tears as they had on the bank of the Serpentine a week ago.

"Home," she said softly, lifting a hand to wipe away a tear that had spilled onto his cheek. "I do love you, Gil."

He blinked away his tears, released his arm from hers, and wrapped it about her shoulders to draw her against his side. They both looked ahead to the house and the little group gathered about the door.

"Abby," he said, "I am not sure how good I am at showing emotion. Not very good, I suspect. I might never say this again, but I will always, always mean it: I love you with all my heart. I am not even quite sure what that means. I could not define it in words if my life depended on it. But I know it is true."

"Let's not bother with words," she said, resting the side of her head against his shoulder. "They are not important. I understand. And *you* understand. That is all that really matters, is it not?"

"Yes." He hugged her against his side, looked down into her upturned face, and . . . *smiled*.

She would never, ever get over the wonder of that smile. And as she looked around the garden again and ahead to the house and the two women and the child and the dog gathered outside the door, she knew with a sudden rush of certainty that she had arrived at last. At that unknown destination toward which she had striven for six long, often lonely years. Not that *destination* was quite the right word, for she had learned during those years that one never quite arrives anywhere. Life was too full of unexpected twists and turns and challenges for that.

But she had arrived at a new starting point, one she knew to be *right*. She was with the man she loved and honored and the child she loved, and there was all the prospect of a happy future even though she would never make the mistake of calling it a happily-ever-after.

She was in a place she knew to be home, though she had not yet even seen the inside of the house. It was where she belonged. It was hers. And Gil's. And the home of their family, however small or large it turned out to be.

It was their own piece of heaven.

Gil was still holding her close and still smiling down into her face.

"Let's go home," he said.